CHAINS OF GOLD

Based on the true story of
slavery during the
California Gold Rush

KEN ROBB

ACKNOWLEDGEMENTS

Over the years, many have inspired me to tap into my imagination and the freedom it offers. Helping someone discover themselves is a wonderful gift. Many friends, family, and teachers supported me along the way, but most importantly, my mom.

We are on a journey to become who we are meant to be. There are rocky roads and dead ends. I was encouraged to persevere. I often reflect on Jimmy Stewart's line in the movie "Shenandoah": "If we don't try, we don't do. And if we don't do? Why are we here?"

Many writers inspire me. Some are famous, some are obscure. Many are overlooked and underpaid, particularly those in film and television. Writing is challenging and often unrewarding, but writers are dedicated to sharing their perspectives and telling compelling stories. William Faulkner said, "To understand the world, you must first understand a place like Mississippi."

I was intrigued by stories about Black miners during the California Gold Rush and wanted to learn more about their experiences. This led me to discover the story of Carter Perkins, who was enslaved in Mississippi and brought to California. His story became "Chains of Gold." I would like to thank all the individuals who keep history alive, including writers, museums, and archives. These stories should never die.

The most important person I want to thank is my wonderful wife, Julie. Aside from being my best friend and partner, she has stood by me throughout this journey. She's encouraged me, read my awkward drafts, edited them, and kept me away from the dark side of writing. Without her, I would never have written a single word. She has always helped me discover who I am.

CONTENTS

CHAPTER 1
CALIFORNIA
1852

Two burly deputies strain as they drag twenty-five-year-old Carter Perkins down a dimly lit, musty hallway lined with iron-barred jail cells. Despite his wiry frame, Carter fights with every ounce of strength he can summon, but his handcuffs and leg irons keep him restrained. Scratches and gashes mar his dark face, streaked with crimson blood. The hallway echoes with the clanking of his chains as he struggles.

The deputies overpower him, shoving him into a small jail cell. He collapses onto a cot as they slam the door shut. Carter scrambles to his feet and rushes to the bars, shouting, "You can't do this! I'm free!"

The deputies stride down the hallway toward the sheriff, a towering, dark figure lurking in the shadows at the end of the corridor.

The sheriff calls out with a Southern drawl, "You ain't free no more. You're going back to Mississippi, where y'all belong."

Desperate, Carter cries out, "I'm free! You can't cage me! I'll fight you in the courts."

"The courts have already decided. You're going back to Mississippi. You're a slave, you ain't nothing else," the sheriff says as he slams the outer door, plunging Carter into complete darkness.

"I am free! I'll fight!" Carter yells. His voice shatters the silence, echoing through the jail. He sighs as tears stream down his cheeks. The chains around his legs clank as he stumbles back to his cot.

CHAPTER 2
PERKINS PLANTATION
1849

Charles Perkins rides his beautiful steed, Star, whom he'd bought from relatives in Tennessee while returning home after graduating from Princeton in New Jersey. He wears a wide-brimmed white straw hat and his finest clothes. His long brown hair whips in the wind as he takes in the sounds and smells of Mississippi in the spring.

His anxiety grows with every mile as he nears home. As the eldest son, he is expected to manage and inherit the family plantation, but he has other plans for securing his fortune now that gold has been discovered in California. He has devoured every newspaper article and taken geology classes to gain an advantage.

Going to California will be expensive, but he has saved money from the profits of the cotton grown on land gifted to him on his sixteenth birthday. He used part of the inheritance from his maternal grandfather, Duncan Stewart, a descendant of the King of England, to pay for college, but he still has more left to seek his fortune.

He wonders how he will break the news. Surely his father will understand, but he knows his mother will resist. He plans to take several of the slaves he owns, perhaps two or three. He knows he must take Carter. Of all the people in Mississippi, Carter is the one he wants to see. The only one he trusts.

Charles reminisces about the day he received Carter as a gift from his father when they were nine. They grew up like brothers, but both the Perkins family and society forced them to conform to their roles as slave and master. Charles remembers their great adventures growing up, but the journey to California will be the greatest of all.

His memories of the past and dreams for the future consume him.

A mournful cry brings Charles back to the present. He urges Star into a swift gallop toward a clearing behind the Perkins slave quarters.

Carter and his uncle Robert are tied to posts. Their bare backs exposed. Robert's dark, muscular back is raw, marred with bloody lash marks.

Charles watches a small, wiry man he has never seen before swing his whip. It cracks and leaves a bloody lash mark across Carter's back from shoulder to waist.

Rage boils in Charles' chest as he takes in the brutal scene. The harsh reality grips him. The cruelty he had hoped to leave behind when he went to college slaps him in the face. Nothing has changed.

Charles spurs Star forward. He grabs the tip of the whip mid-stroke, yanking hard and sending the man sprawling backward. Charles rips the whip from his grasp.

The man scrambles to his feet, his eyes narrow in defiance. His hand drifts to the pistol at his hip.

"What's the meaning of this? How dare you whip my men?" Charles demands. "Who do you think you are?"

"Who the hell are you?" The man snarls.

"I'm Charles Perkins. Who the hell are you?" Charles yells, snapping the whip and holding it menacingly, poised to strike. Once purely Southern, his accent now carries a hint of Yankee twang.

"Oh, the college boy. I heard you were coming home. I'm Nick. I'm the overseer. They were late for work and off the plantation. They needed some learning."

Charles turns to Carter. "What happened, Carter? What's going on?"

Carter gasps, "Robert went to see his wife and children. He broke his leg on the way back. When he didn't show up, I went to find him."

"What do you mean, he went to see them? Where are they?" Charles asks.

With his hands bound above him, Carter struggles to face Charles. "They were sold to the neighbors down the road," he moans, his voice heavy with anger and grief.

Charles freezes at the weight of the words. How could this happen? How could his slaves have been sold without his consent?

Fury surges through Charles. Robert, his family, and Carter belong to him. While at college, he depended on Carter, Robert, and Sandy Jones, Carter's grandfather, to work the patch of land his parents had given him. Discovering a harsh overseer and learning that his slaves had been sold without his knowledge is a gut-wrenching betrayal.

He fixes a fierce, blue-eyed glare at Nick and orders, "Cut them down and free them."

Charles flips the whip at his side, daring Nick to defy him, half-hoping for an excuse to strike. He knows the consequences, the inevitable conflict with his father and family.

Nick reluctantly cuts Carter free.

Carter rushes to Robert and unties him. Robert grimaces, his face contorted in pain.

"My leg's broke for sure," Robert says, his voice trembling.

Carter drapes Robert's arm over his shoulder to bear his weight. Robert turns to Nick, fire blazing in his eyes.

Charles crouches beside Robert and examines his swollen leg. "It's broken," he says. "Where are Sandy and Patience?"

"Grandpa and Gram, I mean, Sandy and Patience, are planting cotton by the river," Carter tells him.

"Get to your cabin. Put ointment on the wounds and keep that leg elevated. Patience will know what to do. I'll bring her as soon as I can." Charles points toward a horse tied to a post. "Take Robert on that horse."

Nick scowls. "That's my horse."

Charles barely spares him a glance. "I know that horse. That's a Perkins horse. I decide who rides it and who doesn't." He makes a motion for Carter to help Robert onto the horse.

Nick storms toward the horse and scorns, "You can't do that!"

Charles swings the whip, cracking it sharply in front of Nick. "The hell I can't. Don't you have a plantation to oversee? Cotton needs planting."

Nick hesitates. He clenches his fists, wanting to strike at the arrogant, privileged college boy. But instead, he bites his tongue and mutters under his breath as he turns away.

Carter helps Robert onto the horse, then turns to Charles. "It's good to have you back."

"I wish I had gotten here sooner, but it's good to see you. I'm going to buy back your wife and kids, Robert. I promise. I'll get Patience. She can take care of your wounds and leg." He looks at Carter. "Can you get Robert to the cabins, or do you want me to help?"

"I'll get him there," Carter assures him.

Charles rides away in a cloud of dust.

Charles gallops down a worn field road toward Choctaw Bend at the edge of their sprawling plantation along the Mississippi. The road is packed hard from years of wagon traffic hauling cotton to a dock called Mound Landing, where it's shipped two hundred miles south to New Orleans.

As he rides, he admires the dark, fertile soil, freshly planted with cotton. A few fields are green with grain and corn for their livestock, which includes pigs, cattle, oxen, chickens, mules, and horses.

In the distance, more than a hundred slaves hoe a vast field. Their voices rise in song, filling the air with a rhythmic chant:

"I looked over Jordan, and what did I see?

Coming for to carry me home.

A band of angels coming after me."

Adults carve furrows into the earth while the older women drop seeds from canvas sacks. Small children follow, crawling on hands and knees to cover the seeds. Their clothes are tattered, but the Perkins family treats their slaves better than most. After all, they are their most valuable assets, without them, the plantation would fail.

Charles rides to Sandy Jones, who is hoeing beside his wife, Patience. The singing stops as Charles and Star halt in a cloud of dust.

Sandy removes his tattered hat, revealing short-cropped white hair. He wipes his sweaty brow. "Master Charles! Welcome home. It's good to see you. They said you'd return soon, but we didn't know when."

"It's good to see you, too, but there's a problem. Robert and Carter have been whipped, and Robert has a broken leg." Charles turns to Patience and points to a wagon loaded with sacks full of cottonseed. "I need you to help them. Take the wagon."

Sandy and several strong men quickly unload the sacks from the wagon. Patience climbs onto the wagon; despite her age, she remains strong and agile. She cracks a whip above the two mules and speeds down the field road. Charles watches her pass by his father and younger brother, who ride on horseback toward the field.

Sandy looks at Charles and says, "We'd better get to work." He walks to the field and sings loudly, "Swing low, sweet chariot..."

The others join in, their voices rising as they fall back into rhythm, hoeing and planting to the slow, steady beat of the song.

William Perkins, the respected patriarch of the plantation, rides alongside Charles' younger brother, Daniel. At sixteen, Daniel is shorter and stockier than Charles, with dark hair. William bears a resemblance to an older version of Charles, his face marked by wrinkles, and his hair streaked with gray.

William and Daniel pull their horses to a stop beside Charles.

"Welcome home, son," William greets and announces, though his proud expression tightens when he notices Charles' anger. His eyes settle on Nick's whip curled around the horn of Star's saddle. "I see you met Nick."

"It's good to be home, but things have changed," Charles replies, his voice cold, still reeling from the shock of seeing Robert and Carter being whipped. "When did we start whipping slaves? Why were my slaves sold without my knowledge?"

Before William can answer, Daniel cuts in, "Welcome back, brother. We sold women and children because we needed strong men for the field. Nick makes sure the work gets done."

Charles glares at him. "Are you running the plantation now?"

William intervenes. "Daniel has been a great help since you've been gone. The work is getting done better than ever."

Charles bristles. The thought of his little brother earning their father's trust is something he had never anticipated. He decides to let it go for now. A private conversation with his father will come later.

Even so, he knows he's leaving for California with or without his father's blessing. And if Daniel is to take his place, then so be it. The gold in California is a far greater opportunity.

William reads Charles' anger and says, "We'll talk about this later. I'm sure you are tired from the long journey.

Charles takes a deep breath and nods.

Daniel turns to the field hands and shouts, "Enough singing! Finish planting, then you can sing."

They pause, consumed by the harsh command. A heavy silence falls over them before they resume working.

Charles counters, "They work faster when they're motivated. I traveled a long way to be here for Easter. If the cotton's planted by sundown, they should get a feast tomorrow."

Daniel scoffs, "You didn't learn anything in college. You forgot how to manage Darkies. I'm not sure you ever knew how."

Charles remains unfazed. "Want to bet on it?"

Daniel smirks. "Two gold pieces."

Charles turns to their father. "If they finish by sunset, will you allow them an Easter celebration?"

William's expression remains stern. "They have a lot of work to finish, and they need to be ready for our Easter gathering in the afternoon. We have many guests. They can celebrate early tomorrow morning if they are done by sunset."

Charles grins at Daniel before riding to Sandy and telling him, "If the cotton's planted by sunset, you can slaughter hogs and have a big Easter feast. Sing as loud as you want."

Sandy nods. "Got it. We'll get it done."

"I'm sure you will. I'll meet you at the hog pens this evening," Charles says with a smile as he rides back to his father and brother.

Sandy turns to the field workers.

"Big Easter celebration if we finish by sunset. Let's get to it! Put your backs into it," he says as he launches into an up-tempo song. "Hoe, Emmy, hoe. You turn around and dig a hole in the ground. How Emmy hoe…" They all begin to sing along, and the pace quickens as the field hands match their movements to the beat.

Charles rides back to Daniel. "You're going to owe me two gold pieces. I need to check on Carter and Robert."

Daniel scoffs as Charles spurs Star forward, kicking up dust as he rides away.

Moments later, Charles pulls to a stop outside a slave cabin and rushes in to find Robert lying face down on a cot while Patience dabs the bloody lash marks on his back. His leg is bandaged with wooden braces up to his knee.

Carter sits on a stool next to Patience, holding a jar of tincture while she dips bloody cotton swabs. His slash wound is smeared with greasy ointment.

"I'm so sorry. I had no idea things changed so much," Charles says, frustration thick in his voice. "I'll get your family back, Robert."

Patience turns to him, her expression wary. "Getting Robert's wife and children back might not be easy. Things have changed more than you might think."

"I'll get them back!" Charles insists. He turns to Carter. "We need to talk."

Carter sets the jar of tincture on the stool for Patience and follows Charles outside. They walk a short distance to a vegetable garden behind the cabin. They call it their Sunday Garden, where the Perkins allow them to grow food. The Perkins try to give them Sundays off when the planting and harvesting allow.

"Long time no see, Carter," Charles declares as they shake, and then Charles pulls him into a hug, careful not to touch his wounded back. "I'm sorry I didn't get here sooner. I could've spared you the lash."

Carter shrugs. "I'm glad you're back. You spared me some lashes. I knew you'd come back and change things."

Charles hesitates, gathering his thoughts. "The thing is… You can't tell anybody. I haven't even told my father." He lowers his voice. "I'm going to California to strike it rich. You're coming with me. I plan to take a few others too, hopefully Robert, if his leg heals in time."

Carter steps back, his face twisting in shock. "California?"

"There's gold, and I'm going to strike it rich."

Carter shakes his head. "You're already rich." The words slip out before he can catch them.

"No, not for my family," Charles corrects. "For me. I want to travel the world and buy what I want, whenever I want. You'll be with me all the way." His voice brims with excitement. "We'll find gold. It'll be a grand adventure. We can always come back to the plantation, too. It will always be here."

Carter's brow furrows. "I've read about California. It sounds dangerous."

Charles grins. "I'm glad you're still reading. You have to take risks to get ahead in life." He claps Carter on his good shoulder. "Meet me at sunset at the hog pens. We're having an Easter celebration. I want you to serve."

Carter glances at his muddy boots and tattered clothes. "What will I wear?"

"You can wear my old clothes. I should still have a closet full of them. I'll bring them to the hog pen."

CHAPTER 3
CARTER'S LIFE IN MISSISSIPPI

Carter walks down a worn path toward the hog pens as Peg, a seventeen-year-old with braided black hair neatly wrapped in a bun, rushes to him. She wears a bright white cotton dress, though her apron is soiled from a long day's work in the plantation kitchen. Despite the long hours, she radiates youthful energy.

She stops before him, expecting a hug, but he only smiles.

Peg's dark brown eyes sparkle as she asks, "Everybody's buzzing about what happened. Are you okay?"

"I'm okay. What did you hear?"

"They say ole Nick whipped you, and Master Charles rode up and saved you." She gasps. "Let me see your back. Is it true?"

"It's mostly true. Uncle Robert got the worst of it," Carter says, turning and lifting his shirt.

Peg leans in, her face tightening. "That must hurt bad."

"It doesn't hurt anymore. Gram fixed it." Carter pulls his shirt down and takes a deep breath. "I smell chicken."

"I saved you some from the Perkins' dinner. Figured you'd be hungry." Peg reaches into her apron, pulls out a napkin, and unfolds it to reveal golden, crispy fried chicken.

"You aren't supposed to take food from the house," Carter blurts as he looks around to ensure no one's watching, before snatching a piece and devouring a bite.

Peg giggles. "I knew you'd be hungry."

Carter swallows as he wipes his mouth. "I've got to help get the hogs ready for tomorrow. There's going to be a big Easter celebration."

He tries to sound excited, but exhaustion creeps into his voice with the thought of all the work ahead. He's overwhelmed with the idea of going to California, but he can't tell her.

"I'm making chicken soup. Stop by my cabin after you're done with the hogs," Peg says, flashing a broad smile.

Carter smirks. "I doubt you'll be up that late."

Still chewing, he grabs another piece of chicken and walks off.

Moments later, Carter is ankle-deep in a pen, tapping a giant hog with a long stick. Sandy stands outside the pen, leaning against the fence beside Charles.

"That's a big one. It could feed a lot of people," Charles says, looking at the size.

Sandy shakes his head. "That's a sow, she's pregnant. She can have lots of piglets. We can't slaughter her. We need more pigs." He eyes Charles. "How many are coming?"

"Family from Tennessee and Virginia," Charles replies. "Plus, friends and neighbors. We need to plan for eighty. Father may invite more from the church."

Sandy does the math in his head. "With us included, that's over two hundred and fifty. We'll need at least two more big hogs."

"Is there bacon in the smokehouse?" Charles questions, "Father loves bacon. I want him to be in a good mood. I have things to discuss with him."

"There's lots of bacon. We'll serve it with the ham," Sandy says as he points to two big hogs in the corner. "Grab those two, Carter, and then we can all have a helping of bacon."

"We plan to eat in the early afternoon after church. Will you be ready?" Charles questions.

"We'll slow-cook the hogs all night," Sandy assures him. "We're going to have a sunrise service, then breakfast. Plenty of time before your family's Easter meal."

"Might stop by for a taste before I head to church," Charles muses, already picturing it.

Carter uses a switch to guide the last two hogs out of the pen toward a small barn for slaughter. Charles approaches him with a bag of clothes.

Carter hesitates. "Are you sure this'll be okay with Miss Perkins and…?"

Charles cuts him off. "Doesn't matter what people think. We'll be gone soon. I'm going to tell my father I'm going to California tomorrow during dinner. It will be best if I tell him with everyone there. We'll leave in a few weeks. Will you be ready?"

Carter exhales. "I guess. I've read about it in the papers, sounds like gold's just lying on the ground. Shouldn't take long to find it."

Charles smirks. "Papers stretch the truth. There's gold, but we'll have to work for it." He pauses as he thinks, then adds, "Father loves turkey. I'd like you to get one as a special surprise. Can you shoot a couple in the morning?"

Carter tilts his head. "I'll have to go into the neighbor's woods at sunrise to find turkeys. What if they catch me? And how am I supposed to kill one?"

"The neighbors won't be up that early. I'll leave a shotgun in the stall by my horse. You can ride him."

Carter sighs. "I'll get a couple of turkeys."

"Thanks, Carter."

Carter helps Sandy slaughter and prepare the hogs, then drags himself toward the cabins in the moonlight. He usually enjoys helping to slow-cook hogs overnight, but he's too tired. His legs feel like lead tonight. The hum of crickets barely registers in his weary mind his thoughts are tangled between the hunt at dawn, serving at Easter, and the weight of leaving.

As he walks to the row of cabins, he spots Peg asleep on her cabin steps, head tilted down. The sight of her brings a broad smile to his lips. Her face is soft and peaceful even after a long day's work.

He steps closer and whispers, "Peg. Wake up, Peg."

Her eyes flutter open. "Carter!"

He places a finger to her lips. "You shouldn't have stayed up. You need sleep."

"I didn't know you'd be this late." She rubs her eyes as she lifts a bowl for him. "I saved you a bowl of chicken soup, but it's cold."

Carter sinks onto the step, takes the bowl, and slurps.

"You and your mama know how to make chicken soup," he says between slurps. "You need to sleep. I need your help tomorrow. Master Charles wants me to serve the family and the guests, and I don't know what I'm doing."

Peg straightens. "I'll help you. I'll always help you." Her voice is soft and steady. She closes her eyes and tilts her face, lips pursed for a kiss.

Carter smiles, gently brushing his fingers against her cheek before kissing her forehead. He caresses her and turns her toward the door. "Get some sleep. Tomorrow's a big day."

She lingers a moment before slipping inside.

Carter watches the door a second longer, his chest still tight. He cares for Peg, but she's younger, and nothing is certain. She could be sold tomorrow. Plus, the thought of California still has his mind in a whirl.

Finally, he forces himself to move. His cabin is far away, and the rough wooden floor creaks beneath his weight when he enters. He weaves through a maze of men sleeping on straw cushions covered in coarse cotton cloth, finally reaching his corner.

He curls up on his straw-filled cushion, already dreading the morning. He needs to be up before sunrise, but sleep is restless every half hour, he wakes and checks the dark sky, willing dawn to hold off just a little longer.

CHAPTER 4
TROUBLE IN THE WOODS

Charles, dressed in his Sunday finest and sporting his bright white, broad-brimmed straw hat, saddles Star in a large stable. A dark bay horse is saddled and tied to the stall nearby. Carter walks into the barn.

"Morning, Carter," Charles announces with a broad smile.

"Morning, Master Charles. I didn't expect to see you."

"Don't call me Master," Charles says with a smirk. "At least when nobody's around. We've known each other way too long."

Carter looks at the dark bay horse and asks, "Are you riding with Master William? It seems early for him."

"I'm riding with you. You're riding Father's horse," Charles replies, picking up a double-barreled shotgun and shoving it into a leather sheath on his father's horse. "The shotgun's loaded." He turns and hands Carter a small canvas bag. "Here's more black powder and shot. Just in case you miss." He laughs.

Carter hesitates as he grasps the bag. "But this is Master Williams' horse. I can't ride him."

"Father is taking Mother and the family in carriages to church. He won't be needing his horse. He's all yours this morning. Hop on. We're going for a ride."

"But you wanted me to get turkeys."

"There's plenty of time. The turkeys are still asleep. Follow me."

Charles mounts Star and nudges his heels into Star's ribs. Star leaps into action, prancing and darting out of the barn toward a gravel road. Charles struggles to hold on as Star rears.

Carter climbs on William's horse and races out of the barn, following Charles. They gallop past cattle and hog pens as Carter tries to catch up.

They pass the magnificent Perkins main house, with its white Grecian pillars framing a spacious porch. Charles reflects on its beauty and his father's ambition to build it as a symbol of wealth and power. The two-story mansion gleams in the pre-dawn light, its large windows shining between black shutters. Two imposing double doors create a grand entrance.

Carter gazes at the mansion, recalling his childhood spent playing with Charles in the house when they were young boys. He hasn't been allowed inside for years. Now, it feels like he's looking at a monument. The bright morning sun highlights its grandeur, yet it feels cold and forbidding to Carter. He knows it was built with his family's blood, sweat, and tears, along with those of the other slaves.

Charles and Carter gallop down a road flanked by freshly planted cotton fields, the young plants just beginning to push through the soil. They ride toward a pyramid mound—the highest point overlooking Choctaw Bend—where the Mississippi River curves around the Perkins plantation.

At the top of the mound, they rein in their horses and face the rising sun. The vast cotton fields of the Perkins plantation stretch toward the horizon. Behind them, the Mississippi River glimmers in the morning light, its surface rippling with streaks of red, orange, and gold.

Charles takes in the familiar landscape, his thoughts drifting to the summer before he left for college. His father had taken him to New Orleans to negotiate the sale of a massive shipment of cotton. After unloading the bales, they visited the bank to review the plantation's finances. Then came the shopping, fine suits, elegant dresses for his mother and sisters, and gifts for everyone. That night, they dined at a lavish restaurant in the city and slept in a hotel so grand that Charles was barely able to close his eyes.

Beside him, Carter sees the land differently. He imagines the empty fields swelling with white cotton under the brutal summer sun. He sees himself and the others bent low, their fingers raw from plucking the bolls, the weight of full sacks dragging at their shoulders. He can already feel Nick and Daniel watching, their presence a constant threat, their whips always within reach.

For a long moment, they sit in silence, two young men who grew up together, staring at the same view but seeing two different worlds.

Finally, Carter speaks, his voice soft and thoughtful. "Things haven't been the same since you left."

Charles exhales and grips the reins, his mind already stretching toward California. "Things are never the same. Every day is different. Everything should be different. And everything should be better."

Carter shifts in the saddle. "You could make things better here."

Charles shakes his head. "It's a big world. I've got to make my mark." He scans the land, from the muddy Mississippi to the plantation house, to the barn, to the distant slave quarters barely visible in the morning haze. "I'll come back with a fortune and change everything. I have dreams."

Carter hesitates. "You could lose everything. Even your life."

"Every day could be our last. Life is shorter than we think." He exhales and catches his breath as he turns to Carter. "California will be dangerous, but it's worth the risk. It'll be an adventure." He pauses, studying Carter. "Are you ready?"

Carter gazes out over the land, reminiscing about Peg and the faces he has always known. He and Peg have talked about their future, but she's still young. And California… It's farther than he's ever imagined going.

"I guess," he says, trying to be positive.

Charles reads the hesitation in his face and tries to reassure him. "Chances are, we'll be fine. And we'll come back. The plantation will always be here."

The Mississippi gurgles softly behind them as Charles and Carter sit atop the mound, watching the sun climb higher over the fields.

Charles exhales. "You have to take risks to get ahead. That's how my family got to where we are today." He glances at Carter. "My great-great-grandfather arrived in America as an indentured servant, bound to an English landowner in Virginia over a hundred and fifty years ago. He worked for seven years before earning his freedom."

Carter frowns. "I didn't know White people could be slaves."

Charles shrugs. "People have always tried to control others. It comes down to greed, I guess. The Egyptians and the Romans used slaves. Now it's the Spanish, the Portuguese, the French, the English, and now us Americans. "Sounds like you've learned a lot in college. How did Master William get this plantation in the first place?"

Charles straightens with pride. "My ancestors worked hard, farming and buying land, spreading from Virginia to Tennessee. When my father was young, he took a big risk and bought land here in Mississippi. He kept expanding, kept making money."

Carter breathes in deep, his chest tightening. He knows exactly what that "hard work" means generations of men and women bent under the sun, hands raw from picking cotton, bodies broken by whips and exhaustion. He should hold his tongue, but he can't.

"More land means more slaves," He says to Charles as he looks out over the endless rows of planted cotton.

Charles hesitates, then nods. "More land means more work. More work means more workers."

Carter wants to say it outright—that more land and more slaves mean more wealth for the Perkins family, while slaves like him gain nothing. But he doesn't speak out. Now is not the time.

They sit in silence as the sun rises.

Charles shifts in his saddle. "Do you know what this hill is?"

Carter glances down. "Just a hill."

"It's a Choctaw burial mound."

Carter's head jerks up. "You mean there are Indians buried under us?

Charles nods. "I always wondered about it. It turns out that the Choctaw lived here thousands of years before us. They built these mounds for burials and ceremonies." He scans the horizon. "I've been trying to picture what it must've been like."

Carter tries to imagine it, too, and asks, "How did they live? What did they eat?"

"They lived in huts made of mud and straw. They fished, hunted, and grew corn." Charles gestures toward the river. "They weren't so different from us."

Carter imagines the land before the cotton fields. "Must've been something." He scans the river beyond. "I bet they loved this land. I bet the river looked the same."

"I bet it did. It's looked like this forever."

"What happened to the Choctaw?"

Charles' voice flattens. "The government forced them out—gave them land east of the river, then pushed them hundreds of miles away to a place called Oklahoma." He shakes his head. "Seems like everyone's moving west."

A long silence stretches between them, the sun warming their backs.

Charles finally speaks. "I think my father will understand why I must go to California. It's the chance of a lifetime."

Carter stays quiet. He knows William Perkins won't approve. The family won't want Charles to leave again, especially not his mother or sisters. But Charles doesn't see that yet.

Carter adjusts his reins. He'd rather stay, but he has no choice. "I'd better go hunt those turkeys for Master William. They're up by now."

Charles nods. "I'm going to ride a while, then meet you at breakfast. I want to taste the hogs and check on the turkeys."

Carter nudges his horse and gallops toward the sunrise. He rides down the road past the Perkins plantation to the neighbor's plantation. He dismounts William's horse and ties his reins to a tree.

He moves through the tall brush, shotgun raised. The turkey ahead of him suddenly ducks and runs. Carter takes off after it, dodging trees and bushes, feet kicking up damp earth in the glow of dawn.

Charles' cousins are dressed for an Easter Sunday ride on a dirt road near where Carter is hunting turkeys.

A.G. "Green" Perkins, twenty-two, a sharp-eyed, ambitious slave owner, sits tall in the saddle. Hardin Scales, twenty-three, a hardened overseer always looking for a fight, rides beside him.

Hardin raises a hand. "Look." His voice drops to a low drawl. "There's a runaway with a gun."

Green reins in his horse beside him.

"We could get a reward," Hardin says as his fingers brush the pistol at his side.

They dismount, weapons drawn, and move through the trees, stalking Carter as he weaves through the brush.

Hardin motions to Green and points with his index finger. "You circle behind him. I'll run down the road and head him off."

Green nods. They split, closing in.

At the same time, some distance away on the Perkins Plantation, Charles rides past rustic wooden slave cabins and a blossoming apple orchard. He leads Star up a gentle rise, pausing at the crest to take in the view below.

In the grassy meadow, the Perkins' one hundred and sixty slaves are gathered for their Easter brunch.

Charles dismounts and guides Star to the top of the hill, watching the morning service unfold. Sandy and his wife, Patience, stand before the assembled crowd. Many are dressed in bright white, ready to serve at the Perkins' celebration later that day. The others wear their best work clothes, pressed and cleaned with care. Young girls wear vibrant flowers in their hair.

Sandy closes his Bible, and the crowd falls silent. He turns to Patience. "Let's sing."

Patience smiles and lifts her voice to sing "Amazing Grace."

"Amazing Grace, how sweet the sound,

That saved a wretch like me.

I once was lost, but now I am found,

Was blind, but now I see."

The hymn rises into the morning sky, washing over the fields and river.

As the last note fades, Sandy looks out over the gathered faces. "Let us pray and bless our meal."

Heads bow. On the hill above, Charles removes his hat and bows.

Sandy's voice carries through the clearing. "Holy One, you have made us witnesses to the gospel's good news, that Jesus Christ, our flesh and bone, is risen from the dead. Open our minds to understand these things and let your word be fulfilled so we may share the bread of life with a hungry world and live in peace. Amen." Silence follows for a few seconds until Sandy lifts his head and grins. "Come on, everybody, let's eat!"

Laughter ripples through the crowd as they break into cheerful chatter, gathering plates and forming lines at the buffet tables. Charles leads Star down the hill toward the feast.

Sandy stands by a roasting pit, carving a perfectly cooked hog. Charles approaches, plate in hand.

"What do you recommend?"

Sandy slices off a thick piece of ham and lays it on Charles' plate. "This is the best."

Charles takes a bite and nods with satisfaction. "My father will love this. What about bacon?"

Sandy gestures toward a nearby platter.

Charles picks up a strip and bites down. His eyes widen. "This is fantastic! Why have I never tasted this before?"

Sandy chuckles. "It's Patience's recipe. She calls it spicy bacon."

Charles grins. "Tell Carter to serve this to my father, it'll make him incredibly happy. Speaking of Carter, did he get a turkey?"

"So that's where he went. He didn't say anything." Sandy frowns as his brow furrows. "He isn't here."

Charles takes a deep breath and glances toward the road. "That's not like him. I'll check on him on my way to church."

He grabs a handful of bacon and strides to Star. Sliding his boot into the stirrup, he swings smoothly into the saddle. His fingers tighten around the reins.

Star senses Charles' mood shift, snorting and shifting on restless hooves. Though they've already had a long morning ride, Star is ready. Charles doesn't need to spur him.

They launch forward, thundering across the plantation at full gallop.

Sandy and Patience exchange uneasy glances, a quiet worry settling over them.

Hardin creeps through the bushes a distance away in the neighbor's woods, stalking Carter.

Carter moves through the underbrush, shotgun in hand, eyes locked on a turkey scampering between the trees. He crashes through a thicket, keeping pace with his prey.

Hardin watches from the shadows, then takes off at a sprint, angling ahead.

Suddenly, he leaps into Carter's path, pistol drawn.

"Drop it," Hardin growls, his voice low and steady.

Carter freezes. His mind races. His grip tightens on the shotgun.

From the side, another figure emerges—Green Perkins. His pistol rises, aimed squarely at Carter's head.

"I'll drop it," Carter says carefully, voice tight. "But it might go off."

He slowly points the gun away from Hardin and lets it fall.

The shotgun hits the ground—

BOOM!

The shot echoes through the trees.

Startled, Green flinches. His finger jerks on the trigger.

BANG!

The bullet whizzes past Carter's head, missing him by inches.

Carter takes a deep breath as Hardin steps closer, still aiming the pistol at his head. Hardin's steely blue eyes peer into Carter's chestnut brown ones as he vents, "How dare you run away on Easter Sunday!"

Carter stands frozen, still reeling from the shock of the gunfire. As his vision clears, he recognizes his captors.

"I know you, Master Hardin," he says. "It's me, Carter Perkins. I wasn't running away, I was out hunting turkeys."

Hardin's grip on the pistol eases as he studies Carter. A slow, wicked smile creeps across his face. "Well, well. I haven't seen you in years. Thought you were real smart back then. More like a smart-ass." His voice hardens. "You need to be taught a lesson, boy."

Green, sensing the tension, lowers his pistol. "Let's take him to the Perkins," he pleads. "We've got time before church. We'll see what they say."

Hardin keeps his gun trained on Carter's forehead. "You belong to Charles, don't you?"

Carter nods. "Yes, sir. Master Charles sent me to get a turkey for Easter."

Hardin snorts. "Nobody eats turkey for Easter."

"Master William likes turkey," Carter says cautiously. "Master Charles wanted me to get some."

Hardin glances at Green and scoffs. "Charles is too soft. This isn't Perkins' land. No slave should be running around with a gun." His face darkens. "If you were running, I'd be the one to break you. You'd never run again."

Before Carter can speak, Hardin and Green seize his arms and drag him through the underbrush. Without a word, they bind his hands in front of him with a length of rope.

Hardin swings into the saddle and grips the other end of the rope. "Let's move."

They ride slowly, but Hardin digs his heels into his horse, forcing Carter to jog behind.

Green cautions. "You're working him too hard."

Hardin grins. "Let's see how fast he can run."

Carter stumbles on the rough dirt road, struggling to keep up.

Hardin glances back. "Don't fall, or I'll drag you."

A cloud of dust rises in front of them. It's Charles. He barrels toward them at full gallop, Star's hooves pounding the earth.

Hardin and Green rein in their horses. Carter gasps for air as Charles pulls up beside them, his face red with fury.

"What the hell is going on?" Charles shouts.

Hardin glares back. "We caught him running with a gun. Thought he was escaping."

Charles' jaw tightens. "He was hunting turkeys!"

Hardin scoffs. "You Perkins' are too soft. You let a slave roam with a gun—on someone else's land! What were you thinking?"

Charles' voice is cold. "That's none of your business."

Hardin leans forward in the saddle. "Slaves with guns are everyone's business."

Charles swings down from Star, strides past Hardin, and unties Carter's hands. He scans Carter's face. "Are you alright?"

Carter dusts himself off, catching his breath. "I'm okay. They ran me a bit, though." He forces a slight grin. "Looks like you got here just in time. Again."

Charles exhales sharply, shaking his head. "I didn't realize things had changed this much." He meets Carter's eyes. "Things will be different in California. I promise."

Carter can only nod.

"Go home. Get something to eat and rest," Charles tells him. "You don't have to serve this afternoon if you don't want to."

"I'm okay," Carter assures him. "I'll be ready."

Charles scans the road. "Where's Father's horse?"

"Tied to a tree, a quarter mile up," Carter says.

"I'll take you to him."

Charles offers a hand, and Carter climbs onto Star behind him.

Before leaving, Charles reins in beside Hardin and Green. He looks them over with disdain. "You two better get to church and pray like hell."

Hardin smirks. "What did they teach you up North, cousin? We weren't doing no harm. Just keeping things the way God intended."

Charles' expression hardens. "This isn't what God intended."

With a sharp nudge, Star surges forward. Carter grips Charles tightly as they ride away, leaving Hardin and Green in the dust.

CHAPTER 5
BREAKING THE NEWS

Carter walks down the path from the slave cabins toward the sounds of the Easter celebration. He is dressed in a white cotton jacket, shirt, and pants. He walks carefully to avoid dirtying the polished black dress shoes that Charles gave him.

Peg approaches him wearing a bright white dress. Her deep, dark eyes shine with excitement as she smiles. "I knew the clothes would fit you perfectly."

Carter looks down at the fit of his suit. "It's great. I was planning to wear the clothes Master Charles gave me, but I'm wearing his shoes."

"Miss Perkins wants us to wear white when we serve, and white gloves, too. We're not supposed to touch anything with our bare hands, our dirty black hands, I heard her say once," Peg complains as she hands Carter a pair of gloves. "You're nervous. I haven't seen you like this before."

"I've never served important people before."

"My momma told me to think of rich white people like they are two-year-olds with soiled pants. Sometimes, when I look at them whining and fussing, wanting this and wanting that, demanding this and demanding that, I see them as two-year-olds who crapped their pants and are whining about sitting in their poop."

Carter snickers. "I'm not sure how that helps, but I'll try. I'm worried about how to serve a fine dinner."

"It's easy. Serve drinks from the right. Serve food from the left and clear food from the left. Do not clear a plate from the table until everyone has finished that course. Only take two plates at a time."

"How do you know when people are done eating?"

"They follow what they call etiquette; they put their knives and forks to the side with the fork pointed down. If you're not sure, you can always extend your hand and say, 'May I?'" Peg articulates as she bats her eyes and delicately holds out her white-gloved hand to show how it should be done.

"I want to hear what Charles tells his father. I'm going to need your help."

"Of course I'll serve Master Charles' table with you and help keep you close to him," Peg assures him as she holds her white-gloved hand for Carter, who grasps it. They walk a few steps, then Peg stops as she pulls out a fine cotton wrap. "I almost forgot. All of us women must wear white headwraps. Will you help me?"

Carter helps Peg tie the headwrap over her neatly braided hair before they walk between beautiful magnolia trees. The sun shines on a crowd of guests dressed in their Sunday finery, all gathered for the Easter feast on the back lawn. They are bathed in sunlight beneath towering oak trees and magnolias blossoming in shades of pink and white. The soft music of a violin and cello adds to the festive atmosphere.

The women are dressed in white and floral bell-shaped skirts with ruffles. They mirror Queen Victoria's fashion, made famous in newspapers, photographs, and paintings. Their shoulders are bare. Risqué for the time. Their hair is parted in the center and looped into a plaited bun at the back, decorated with flowers. They wear imported silk and satin scarves because cotton is too common, mundane, and too ordinary for them.

The men are dressed in a fashion made famous by Prince Albert, Queen Victoria's husband. The Queen influenced him, and the Southern gentlemen's wives have now influenced their husbands. The men wear tight-fitting dark frock coats with high waists. The coattails extend to their calves. Bright bow ties, cravats, and silk scarves complement their bright white cotton shirts.

William raises his hands and announces, "Greetings to all our friends and family on this glorious Easter Sunday." The crowd hushes. "I've asked our neighbor and esteemed Senator Jefferson Davis to lead us in prayer."

Senator Davis strides towards the front of the gathering. He is in his early forties with long locks of light brown hair and dazzling blue eyes. Strands of grey thread through his hair and his scruffy goatee.

"Thank you, William, and thank all y'all for being here on this glorious day," Senator Davis begins in a high-pitched voice with a long Southern drawl. He bows his head, prompting the crowd to do the same, before delivering the prayer:

"Almighty God, who has given us this good land for heritage; We humbly beseech Thee that we may always prove ourselves a people mindful of Thy favor and glad to do Thy will. Bless our land with honorable ministry, sound learning, and pure manners. Save us from violence, discord, and confusion, from pride and arrogance, and from every evil way. Defend our liberties and fashion into one united people, the multitude brought hither out of many kindreds and tongues. Endow with Thy spirit of wisdom those to whom in Thy Name we entrust the authority of governments that there may be justice and peace at home and that through obedience to Thy law, we may show forth Thy praise among the nations of the earth. In time of prosperity, fill our hearts with thankfulness, and in the day of trouble, suffer not our trust in Thee to fail; all of which we ask through Jesus Christ our Lord, Amen."

"Thank you, Senator Davis. Thank all y'all for coming. Please take your seats and enjoy our Easter feast," William proclaims with heartfelt gratitude.

The attendees chatter as they herd themselves to their carefully arranged places.

Carter and Peg stand at a distance as men swarm around Senator Davis.

"Who is he? Why all the fuss?" Peg asks.

"He's Senator Davis," Carter explains. "He and Master William have been friends for years. His plantation is just up the road, his brother's, too. He was a colonel in the war against Mexico. Now, he's Mississippi's senator in Washington."

Peg wrinkles her nose. "What's a senator?"

"They make laws and decide things."

"How do you know all that?"

"I've known about him and his family since I was little, but mostly, I read about him in the newspapers."

Peg shakes her head. "You and your reading. It'll get you into trouble someday."

Carter chuckles. "Might keep me out of trouble."

"It's time to go to work." Peg nudges him. "I'll stay close."

"I need to make sure I don't spill anything on Master Davis," Carter jokes as they head toward the tables.

Carter has read about Jefferson Davis's achievements. His Brierfield plantation is just a few miles north, where he owns sixty slaves and leases additional land from his eldest brother, Joseph, who is twenty-three years his senior and owns thousands of acres and hundreds of slaves.

He recalls reading how Davis fought in the Black Hawk War under Zachary Taylor, who is now the President of the United States. Davis led troops during the Mexican War, helping win the battles of Monterrey and Buena Vista. After the war, only two years ago, Carter remembers how Davis was offered a promotion to brigadier general but turned it down to pursue a Senate seat.

Carter has also read that he is fiercely advocating for the expansion of slavery into Western territories, arguing that they belong to the nation as a whole and therefore cannot ban slavery. He insists that slaveholders have the same rights as any other citizens to settle there with their property, including their slaves.

He has seen Jefferson Davis as a legendary figure in the news, but now he finds himself standing in front of him. This unexpected encounter could be a chance for Charles. It's a remarkable coincidence that a man who aims to transform California into a slave state is present on the same day that Charles plans to discuss a trip there with his father.

Carter and Peg move between the tables, pouring drinks and serving plates of food. Peg keeps him near William and Charles, allowing him to overhear their conversation.

When the main course is served, Carter approaches William with a plate of bacon.

"Master William, we know you like bacon," he says, carefully offering the plate.

William takes a slice and savors it. "This is delicious. Whose recipe is this?"

Carter straightens. "It's my Gram's recipe—I mean, Patience's. She calls it spicy bacon."

William nods in approval. "We'll have to get that recipe from you, Carter. We could have it for breakfast sometimes, right, Mother?"

Jane Perkins, seated beside William, wrinkles her nose. "I'm sure it's lovely, but I don't care for spicy foods." She glares at Carter and adds sharply, "Thank you for serving us."

"I'd love to try that spicy bacon," Senator Davis interjects.

"I'll have some, too," Daniel chimes in.

Carter walks around the table, carefully serving each of them a slice.

Davis takes a bite. "This is the best bacon I've ever had," he declares, savoring the flavor. He turns to Carter. "I must have this recipe."

"I'd be happy to write it down for you, sir," Carter replies with a proud grin.

Davis raises an eyebrow. "You can write?"

Carter stiffens. "I—I meant, I'll tell Master Charles the recipe. I'm sure he'll write it down for you."

Charles steps in quickly. "Of course, Carter. I'll gladly write it down."

Carter risks a glance at Jane Perkins, who is staring daggers at him. Her face is tight with embarrassment and anger, offended that a slave is speaking so freely with the senator. Carter lowers his eyes and quickly moves away, biting back a grin as he remembers Peg's words. He pictures Miss Perkins as a wailing toddler, red-faced and whining, stuck in her own mess.

Across the table, Daniel takes another bite of bacon and tries to stifle a grin, but he can't. "This is amazing," he admits reluctantly.

Charles smirks. "I told you. You owe me two gold pieces."

Daniel laughs, pulls two gold coins from his pocket, and slides them across the table.

As the feast continues, the guests talk and laugh, finishing their meal with warm peach cobbler and scoops of ice cream.

Charles senses the moment is right. He pulls a newspaper from his coat and slides it across the table, pointing excitedly at the bold headline:

"GOLD! GOLD! GOLD! CALIFORNIA GOLD IS INEXHAUSTIBLE."

"You said you'd consider my plans for the future once I finished college," Charles presses. "California's a huge opportunity, and I need to stake my claim now!"

William's response is firm. "This is where you belong. You're the eldest—we need you here. I thought you'd want to help build the plantation. I've been looking to buy more land."

A tense silence settles over the table. Jane, Daniel, Green, and Hardin continue eating their dessert, listening closely. Carter stands a few feet behind, waiting to clear the plates.

Charles squares his shoulders. "The cotton's planted. I can find gold. I'll send money back to help the plantation. And if I don't strike it rich, I'll return in a few months. Our family has always taken risks. Our great-great-grandfather came to America as a slave with nothing but a dream. You left your family and built all of this. This is my chance."

William's expression hardens. "Your great-great-grandfather didn't come here as a slave. He came as an indentured servant. There's a difference. Every generation has worked hard. We are a family of adventurers and risk-takers—but going to California alone is reckless. You have no idea what you're walking into."

"I've traveled back and forth to New Jersey on my own. That's a long way," Charles counters. "And I wouldn't go alone. I'll take Sandy, Robert, and Carter—maybe two or three more. I've saved enough to pay for it all."

The tension thickens until Jefferson Davis breaks the silence. "I've been East many times. Did you travel back and forth from college by ship or rail?"

"I've traveled both ways," Charles answers. "I took a ship to school in New Jersey, but returned by rail, stopping in Tennessee."

Davis nods and picks up the newspaper to skim the article. "I prefer to stay in the South. I usually sail from New Orleans to Savannah, then take the train to Washington. Rail travel is by far the most comfortable."

"Too bad there's no railroad to California," Charles says.

"There will be someday," Davis says. "We're talking about it in Congress. How do you plan to get to California?"

"By ship from New Orleans to Panama, then a ship to San Francisco," Charles says confidently.

Davis strokes his goatee. "That's the best route. Sailing around South America is longer and treacherous. Going overland is even worse; it takes months, and the western tribes are most unruly. And the weather… the Donner Party's fate was appalling."

Charles leans forward. "I've read about the Indians. You fought them, right?"

Davis's lips curl slightly as he tugs his goatee. "I fought against them in the Black Hawk War. My brothers fought with them against the British in 1812. Your father was there. You can ask him about it. I just fought with them in Mexico. They can be great allies—or great adversaries."

Charles turns to William. "You never talk about fighting in the War of 1812. Why not?"

William exhales. "That was years ago. I did what was asked of me— to keep our country free."

Charles looks back at Davis. "Why do you say you fought with them and against them?"

Davis leans forward. "Tribes have warred for centuries. When their enemies were our enemies, we fought together." He pauses. "That's still true in the West. We need to fight with those who align with us."

William studies Davis, his fingers drumming against the table. He isn't just weighing Charles' plans—he's thinking ahead. "Do you think there's opportunity in the West?" He hesitates. "Do you think California will become a slave state?"

"There is a great opportunity—not just for gold, but for agriculture," Senator Davis declares, his voice dripping with confidence. "We have fifteen slave states and fifteen free. We need California to join us as a slave state. We must ensure that our right to own slaves is never compromised. I am committed to doing whatever I can to protect that right, and many in Washington feel the same. President Taylor agrees. The South has many settlers in the new territories, and slaves are essential to taming the land and reaping the rewards."

A few feet away, Carter and Peg stand silently behind Charles. The conversation makes their blood boil, but they don't dare speak. Peg gives Carter a subtle kick to the shin. He bites back a smirk and nudges her in return, exchanging a glance unseen by the others.

Charles leans in and seizes the moment. "See, Father? This is an opportunity I can't afford to miss. It's important, not just for our family, but for the South."

William picks up the newspaper and scans the article.

Jane leans toward Charles. "You've been gone for four years. It's time to take your place in this family—and on this plantation."

"I will always be part of this family, but I need to make my mark," Charles insists.

Jane's eyes shift to William. Her voice tightens. "You can't be considering letting him go to California."

"He's a man," William says flatly. "Men must think about these things. We take risks."

Jane scoffs, shaking her head. She turns to Senator Davis's wife, Varina. "I think I'll check on the children. Please excuse me."

Varina Davis shoots her husband a cold glance. "I'll join you, Jane."

The two women walk briskly toward the children playing on the lawn in the distance.

Davis watches them go, then shrugs. "Women shouldn't concern themselves with politics, business, or the future. Poor souls—they simply don't understand the world."

Charles leans in. "Is it safe to take slaves to California?"

Davis folds his hands together. "Our Constitution protects our rights in all U.S. territories. As free men, we must be able to take and hold our property wherever we choose, including our slaves."

Charles turns to his father. "Father, I must go."

William doesn't answer right away. He exhales, reading the paper. "I need to think about it."

Senator Davis leans back. "The desire for gold is not for gold itself. It is not the love of wheat, wool, or household stuff, it is a means for freedom and benefit."

Charles' face lights up. "That's a great statement. I must write that down."

"No need," Davis replies. "Ralph Waldo Emerson wrote it. He is a strong writer and speaker, but unfortunately, he is an abolitionist."

"I read some of his work in college. I believe he also wrote, "Do not go where the path may lead, go instead where there is no path and leave a trail," Charles adds with a smile.

Senator Davis laughs. "They taught you well at Princeton."

Charles beams. "I learned a great deal. I took geology classes. I will have an advantage in finding gold in California."

William folds the paper and hands it to Charles. "We'll talk about this later." He turns to Davis. "I believe you wanted to discuss politics with the gentlemen. I have whiskey from our cousins in Tennessee and cigars from our cousins in Virginia."

Senator Davis grins. "I never turn down whiskey, cigars, or politics." He shifts his gaze back to Charles. "Good luck. You can count on me as your Senator and friend, whether you go or stay."

Then, turning to the younger men, Senator Davis raises his voice and adds, "Your future is bright. The future of this country is bright. Keep fighting for our freedom. Are you boys up for a fight?"

They all chime in, "Yes, sir!"

William and Davis walk toward a group of older men gathered around a table, cigars smoldering, whiskey glasses in hand.

The guests break into smaller groups. The older gentlemen sit together in deep conversation, while the women gather separately. The young men and women mingle at their tables, their laughter rising above the hum of discussion. In the distance, the children play under the watchful eyes of their nannies.

Charles sits at a table with his neighbors, Jonathan and Stephen Kirk, along with Daniel, Hardin, and Green. A newspaper is spread between them, the pages curling at the edges from the evening humidity. They slam down whiskey shots, cigars smoldering in their hands. Carter stands nearby, silently refilling their glasses, listening to every word.

"How many Darkies are y'all takin'?" Green asks, exhaling a thick plume of smoke.

"Five or six," Charles answers.

Daniel scoffs. "No way in hell Father lets you take that many."

"I'm going with or without them," Charles shoots back, glaring.

Hardin leans in, eyes gleaming with ambition. "Can all y'all spot me some money? I'll go. I know how to work Darkies hard. Been a foreman and a driver for years."

Charles' expression hardens. "Work them and whip them until they drop and die. That's what I heard."

Hardin bristles. "That's a foul-mouthed lie. I wouldn't have worked him so hard if I knew he was sick. You have to whip to make sure they know who is boss—leave a mark so the others don't forget."

Hardin takes a deep puff of his cigar. He points at Carter, who is cleaning a table nearby, and says with smoky breath, "Y'all treat your Darkies too soft. Just this morning, he was running around with a gun. When's the last time you whipped one?"

"I don't believe in it," Charles snaps back. "If you treat them right, they get the work done."

Daniel puffs his cigar and exhales into the air like a chimney. He leans toward Charles and says, "I'm not sure what you learned at college, brother, but it doesn't sound like you learned about running a plantation. Like Hardin says, you need to make an example of anybody who runs or doesn't work. You need to whip them and leave scars. Then the others know what happens when they step out of line."

Charles fumes that his brother has grown into a monster and glares at him. "Your horse, Thunder, ran off a few years back. Did you whip him when you found him?"

"Horses are wild," Daniel says defensively. "They want to be free. We found him, and he was glad to be home. He minds me just fine."

Charles leans into Daniel, their blue eyes meeting in a cold steel stare. Charles' voice drops to an icy tone as he says, "Maybe I should whip your horse Thunder—make sure he knows who the boss is. Or better yet, Hardin can do it."

Hardin huffs. "I don't whip horses."

Charles turns his blazing blue eyes to Hardin. "But you whip men."

Hardin glares at Charles, his nostrils flaring as he struggles to control his anger. "Horses and animals are different; they're wild and free. They don't know any better." He takes a long puff of his cigar and adds, "Slaves know better. They know they work for us. When they don't, they need to be taught a lesson."

Charles' jaw tightens as he barks at Hardin and Daniel, "They know better, don't they… Don't you think they're like us… Don't you…?"

Jonathan clicks his glass with his knife and interrupts, "Brothers and cousins shouldn't fight. We all handle things our own way. As long as the work gets done, it doesn't matter." He points to Carter, who has been monitoring the conversation and lingering nearby. "Pour us all a drink, Carter. Bring the bottle that Senator Davis left on the table."

Carter brings a bottle from a nearby table; his face is unreadable. He pours them all a glass and steps back. Charles and Carter's eyes meet for a split second, but they quickly turn away.

Jonathan raises his glass. "Enough talk about what was. Let's talk about what is, and what's gonna be. Charles is headed to California, and when he strikes gold, we'll follow him and be rich."

They clink their glasses, shout, and cheer.

Charles places his glass down, glancing at Carter, who shrugs and smirks, going unnoticed by the others. No further words are needed. Their understanding runs deep. They are embarking on a grand adventure, and nothing else matters.

Later that afternoon, guests depart on horseback and in carriages, the sounds of hooves and wagon wheels crunching over gravel. The slaves move in to clear the tables, gathering empty glasses and folding linens.

Near the edge of the back lawn, Charles stands in the shade of a grove of trees, facing his seventeen-year-old neighbor, Emeline "Emmy" Mobrey Adams. She is the picture of Southern grace, dressed in a bright blue gown, with white gloves covering her delicate hands. Her dark hair is braided, ringlets framing her face, and her emerald-green eyes are sharp beneath arched brows.

Charles has known her since childhood. She was a tomboy once— riding horses, climbing trees—but now, she's a young woman, refining her manners, shaping herself into the proper lady society expects her to be. Yet, beneath the layers of etiquette, she is still the girl he grew up with, the one who shares his thoughts before he can even say them.

Emmy's voice is smooth, carrying the slow, sweet cadence of the South. "You were away at college for so long. I thought when you came back, we would spend time together."

Charles interrupts as she pauses. "I thought that, too. But I must go. Opportunity's knocking. I must make my fortune."

Her hands tremble as she grips the folds of her dress. "I don't know how much longer I can wait." She hesitates, voice breaking. "It's just me and my mother running the plantation. Don't you care?"

Charles gently cups her face, his thumb brushing against her cheek. His steely blue eyes look deeply into her emerald ones. "I care. And I'll come back." He leans in, kissing her softly. "You've got the right people working your land. I will be back before you know it."

She searches his eyes. "Do you love me?"

"I love you," he says without hesitation, then kisses her again. "I'll come back. When I do, we'll live like a king and queen."

A short distance away, Carter and Peg watch them as they finish putting away the last tables and chairs.

"I can't believe he's leaving again," Peg says. "I didn't think he'd leave Emmy."

"He's going," Carter assures her. "That's one thing I know for sure."

"Are you gonna go, too?" she asks, her voice breaking.

He exhales. "I go where he tells me to go. You know that."

"I know." Peg's voice is barely above a whisper. "But I was hoping you might say or do something—so you wouldn't have to leave."

Carter smiles. "You need to get some sleep."

"So do you," she counters.

"I'll walk you home." He places a gentle hand on her back, guiding her toward the slave cabins.

She frowns. "You don't have to work tonight, you've been working all day. No one expects—" She stops mid-sentence, realization dawning. "Wait a minute. You're gonna spy on them, ain't you?"

Carter's lips twitch. "If I happen to hear something…"

They reach Peg's cabin, and he walks her to the door.

"I hope you stay," she says softly.

They share a long kiss, and then Carter gently twirls her toward the door. She opens it, turns back with a bright smile, and disappears inside.

The last light of day clings to the sky as Carter walks toward a large outhouse near the slave cabins. He sits on a wooden bench next to Sandy alongside three other slaves.

Sandy grunts and rips a few pages from a newspaper—the one with the Gold Rush headline.

"You think we're all gonna go?" Carter asks, keeping his voice low.

Sandy shrugs. "Not sure about us. But Charles, he'll go. No matter what."

"I think that, too," Carter pauses. "What does it mean that California's a territory?"

"It means it's a lawless free-for-all," Sandy replies. "Men do whatever they please."

The man beside Carter cuts in, shaking his head. "Y'all shouldn't be readin'. Ain't nothin' White folks hate more than an educated Darkie."

Sandy snorts. "Ain't nothin' worse than ignorance."

The man yanks the paper from Sandy, tears off a strip, and uses it to wipe himself. "White words is lies. Only good for wipin' my ass."

Carter quickly snatches back the remaining paper before more can be destroyed. He folds it carefully, keeping the front-page article on gold in California intact.

Later that evening, Carter moves through the halls of the Perkins mansion, dusting and polishing. He wears dark dress pants and a crisp white shirt, one of Charles' hand-me-downs.

It's the first time he's been inside the house in years. Every creak of the floorboards, every corner, every flicker of the oil lamp brings memories flooding back—of childhood games, of sneaking cookies, of running wild until Miss Jane put an end to it.

He pauses outside the study, where voices drift through the half-closed door. He presses close, listening.

Inside, William and Charles sit facing one another at the large desk, cluttered with newspapers. Charles pours another splash of whiskey for his father.

"I know I'll find gold," Charles says, energized. "I'll send money back. I want to take Carter, Sandy, Robert, and three more strong men. That should be enough to start."

William hesitates. "We can't afford that. I rely on Sandy. He keeps things running. He's been with us a long time."

"But they're mine," Charles insists. "You gave them to me."

"I did, but that was for the plantation," William replies, his voice now firmer. "I expected you to be my right hand when you came home."

"I will come back," Charles says quickly. "I can find gold fast. Give me a few months—if I fail, I'll return for good."

William leans back, thinking. "Have you spoken to your cousins? They may want to go."

"They don't have the money," Charles says. "And I'm the one who studied geology. I know where to look."

William nods slowly, a smile spreading across his face. "That's the Perkins spirit." He raises his glass. "You can take Carter. That's my final word. Daniel will help keep things in order here."

Charles forces a smile. He'd hoped for more, but Carter would be a good start. "Gold will flow from California like manna from heaven," he says with a glimmer of hope.

William chuckles. "Your Princeton education finally paid off."

Just outside the doorway, unseen, Carter listens in silence. He can't help the small smile at the thought of the adventure ahead—but deep down, a knot of worry grows. Life is about to change.

He slips away and resumes cleaning the entryway.

A short while later, just as Carter gathers his things to leave for the night, he hears voices rising in the study again. He stops near the doorway, just out of view.

Inside, Jane sits stiffly across from William, her mouth set tight, her brow furrowed.

"I can't believe you're letting Charles go to California," she snaps.

"He needs another adventure," William replies. "He wants to make his mark. He'll see the hell of the world and come back ready to settle down and run the plantation."

"He won't be safe in California."

"He and Carter will look out for each other. They're like brothers," William blurts without thinking.

Jane slams her whiskey glass on the table. "They're too much like brothers," she says bitterly. "It's a good thing he looks like his mother."

William straightens in his chair. "Leave that alone. Slaves are my business."

Jane bites her lip and storms out of the room. Carter struggles to process what he's just heard. He grabs a cloth and pretends to dust as she brushes past him, her perfume lingering for a moment before fading.

William steps into the hallway, spots him, and gestures. "I'd like to see you for a minute."

Carter follows him into the study, standing stiffly by the doorway, unsure of what's coming.

"Charles is going to California," William says firmly, "and I've agreed to let him take you."

Carter nods and says nothing, trying to hold his thoughts and emotions. They gaze at each other in silence. Carter senses William's deep blue eyes trying to pry into his soul.

William takes a sip of whiskey. "You're like family to me. I trust you with Charles' life."

The weight of the words lands on Carter's shoulders. Could William really be his father?

There have always been whispers. He'd been teased as a boy for his lighter skin. He'd seen it happen to others—children born from masters and slaves. He draws a slow breath. Maybe it's true. But it doesn't matter. Not really. His skin is still dark. He is still a slave. No name, no bloodline, can change that.

"I'll watch out for him," Carter manages to choke out. "I'll keep him safe."

William nods and stands up. He reaches into his pocket and pulls out two gold coins. He walks over to Carter, hands them to him, and says, "Take these, just in case."

Carter looks at the coins in his hand—the first real gold he's ever touched.

"If you and Charles get into trouble, use them. Best to keep 'em in the soles of your shoes," William says as he puts his right hand on Carter's shoulder. "You boys will be leaving soon. I want you both to come home safe. You're like family to me."

"I'll do everything I can," Carter replies.

"I know you will. That's all I can ask," William says, giving him a gentle pat on the back.

Carter trudges back to the slave quarters, his thoughts spinning. The night air is heavy, and each step feels heavier still. This journey was going to change everything—he could feel it.

In the dark cabin, men are asleep on cots, mats, and the floor. Carter steps over them carefully until he reaches his corner. He curls up, pulling a thin blanket over himself, but sleep doesn't come.

William's voice lingers: *You're family to me.* Was that true?

It would explain things. The way the family treated him—especially Miss Jane. And Charles. Charles has always felt more like a brother than a master. Maybe that's why.

But even if it were true, none of it changes how the world sees him. None of it changed his skin. He bears the Perkins name, but he's never truly belonged to the family. Not like *that*. Not in the way that matters.

He closes his eyes and thinks of Sandy and Patience—the ones who raised him, taught him right from wrong, and kept him grounded. No secret bloodline could ever replace them.

His mind drifts to happier times. Riding horses with Charles, racing through the fields like wild boys. Their favorite spot was by the river, where they'd fish, laugh, and read. Carter smiles at the memory.

Charles risked everything to teach him to read, and Carter will never forget it. It was the best gift someone could give another. They were always careful, especially around Miss Perkins, who believed teaching slaves to read was a sin.

They'd made a pact never to tell. It was their secret—one of many. Like the day they snuck into town and saw bodies hanging. Slaves and Whites both were punished for rebellion. The Whites were accused of teaching slaves to read and helping them dream of freedom.

He wonders how different California will be. The newspapers claim it is a free territory, free for the taking. Will it be a place of secrets and lies, like Mississippi, where no one is truly free? Perhaps it will be different with just the two of them. Perhaps they can be free.

He shuts his eyes and lets the darkness take him.

CHAPTER 6
OFF TO CALIFORNIA
JUNE 1849

As the day of their departure approaches, Carter becomes acutely aware of how quickly time slips away. Each day has carried a mix of excitement and unease. The air is thick with anticipation, and his mind buzzes with thoughts of the journey ahead.

A wave of emotion swept over him as the reality sank in—he was about to leave Peg and the only family he had ever known. The thought pierces him like a cold wind, leaving a hollow ache in his chest. Every moment with them played in his mind like fading snapshots. Life has been hard, but it is his life.

Charles spent weeks in New Orleans preparing for the journey. The only available ship was scheduled to depart in mid-June, later than he hoped, but it gave him time to gather supplies and information. Though determined to seek his fortune, doubts linger. Leaving the plantation—and failing to meet his father's expectations—weighs on him.

He shared the details of his plans with Carter when he returned from bringing newspapers from across the country. Carter had studied them, absorbing every word about the journey: from New Orleans to Panama, a brutal trek through the jungle, and then a ship north to San Francisco.

On the morning of his departure, Charles sits on Emmy's porch, finishing breakfast across from her.

She gazes into his blue eyes and says, "Are you sure you have to go? Can't you stay?"

Charles holds her gaze. Everything he had ever felt for her was shining in her warm emerald eyes. He sighs. "I have to listen to the wind of my soul. I have to go."

"Mother and I need help on the plantation. You can be happy here, with me. Can't you?"

Visions of a future with Emmy swirl in his mind: a house filled with laughter, the chaos of children, shared mornings on this same porch. It is a beautiful dream—but it has to wait. First, he needs gold. He can't let this chance pass him by. He is lost in his thoughts when Emmy interrupts.

"Will you think of me?" she asks, handing him a black-and-white photograph of herself in a white dress and floral hat. "I had it taken in New Orleans. I thought you might want to take it with you."

"I'll never forget you," he says, kissing her gently. "You and I are not over. They say gold fades, and love is forever. I'll come back."

"I'll be waiting," Emmy whispers, her tears falling freely.

Charles rushes away and mounts Star in one smooth motion, and waves. "Next time you see me, I'll be rich with gold!" he calls, spurring the horse into a gallop.

Near the slave cabins, Carter stands in front of Peg.

"You're coming back, right?" Peg asks, her voice low and mournful.

Carter's heart tightens. "I'll be back if Master Charles comes back. But...there's a chance I won't. We've talked about that."

Peg hands him a charcoal drawing she made using a mirror. "Do you like it?"

"It's beautiful. Looks just like you," he says, voice catching in his throat.

"I have to work tomorrow. I won't be able to see you off. I guess this is goodbye," she sighs, trying to hold back tears.

Carter pulls her into a gentle embrace and kisses her. "It's goodbye for now. I'll be back before you know it." Then he turns and walks away.

Later that morning, Charles enters his father's study, a weight of sadness on his chest. The room hangs heavy with silence, thick with everything they don't want to say.

"I'm ready to go. I'll pick Carter up on the way."

William nods and retrieves a small wooden box from his desk. Inside is a Colt pocket revolver.

"I hope you never need this," William says, handing it to him. "But it's better to be safe."

"I'll use it if I have to," Charles replies, eyeing the weapon.

They knew the dangers and the odds, but neither wanted to speak them aloud. William trusted Charles to care for himself and knew that Carter would help keep him safe.

As Charles stands to leave, William surprises him with an embrace. It has been years since he last felt his father's warmth.

"Take care of yourself. Take care of Carter," William says quietly. "This is your home. You can always come back. I hope it's soon."

They walk out the front door together. A wagon loaded with luggage waits at the end of the gravel driveway.

The Perkins family stands by the wagon, gathered to bid him farewell. His older sister, Jane P., seven years his senior, stands with her boyfriend, S.B. Curry. His other sister, Louisa Ann, is there with her husband, Dr. Joseph Pugh, and their small children. Charles has never been close to his older sisters, primarily due to their age difference.

They exchange pleasantries, and each wishes Charles well.

Louisa Ann's six-year-old son, J.J., hands Charles a small gold coin.

"This is for good luck. I hope you find gold in California," He says with a broad smile.

Charles kneels and accepts the coin with a grin. "I'm sure this is lucky, and I will find gold. When I come back, I'll give you ten of these."

J.J. smiles and wraps his arms around him.

Charles turns and spots his youngest brother. Ten-year-old William races toward him, followed by eight-year-old Nolan. Two-year-old James toddles to Charles and clings to his leg, his eyes full of wonder.

Charles has missed this—missed them—during the years he has been away. He pulls them into a hug.

"I'll bring back gold for you, I promise. Then we can play all day. I'll buy each of you a horse."

Daniel walks to Charles and extends his hand for a formal shake, his expression unreadable. Charles accepts the handshake, and Daniel pulls him close.

"Don't worry about the plantation. Take your time. I'll manage it," Daniel whispers with a sinister grin.

Charles places his left hand on Daniel's shoulder, leans in, and replies quietly, "I'll return with more money than you could ever imagine."

They tighten their grip. Their eyes lock in a cool, wordless standoff.

Charles pulls away and turns to face his mother. She offers a handshake, but he surprises her by pulling her into a full embrace, something he hasn't done in years.

"I'll be back," he promises.

They separate, still holding hands. Jane struggles to hold back tears.

With a final wave, Charles climbs onto the wagon. "I'll be back before you know it."

He slaps the reins, and the horses lurch forward, pulling the wagon down the gravel road toward the slave cabins beneath the blazing Mississippi sun.

Charles sits quietly as Carter approaches, accompanied by Sandy and Patience. Their sons and families follow behind, Wake, Simon, and Robert among them. Wake's wife, Matilda, holds the hands of their fifteen-year-old son, Sandy II, and his younger sister, Sophia. Robert uses a cane to hobble to the wagon with his wife and family.

Dozens of slaves trail behind to see Carter off.

"You might need something to read," Sandy says, handing Carter a small pocket Bible.

Carter holds it in awe. "This was your father's Bible!"

The leather cover is worn and cracked, and a tarnished metal clasp holds it closed.

"It's yours now," Sandy says, voice quivering. "You can read it to me when you return."

Tears run down Carter's face as he hugs his family, knowing it might be for the last time. No words are exchanged as he climbs into the wagon beside Charles.

Charles offers him a handkerchief. Patience begins to sing softly:

"Everywhere I go, there's an angel there.

My God, my God, he never leaves me alone.

Everywhere I turn, there's an angel there..."

Neither Charles nor Carter looks back. The singing follows them down the road.

A few days later, on June 23, 1849, Charles and Carter board the two-masted sailing ship *Octavia* in New Orleans. The docks teem with noise and movement—young men packed with ambition, all hoping to strike gold. Some are accompanied by slaves who walk solemnly beside them.

At the boarding ramp, Charles hands documents to the ship's purser, who confirms that he owns Carter. The purser examines the papers closely, asks a few questions, and finally motions them through.

Carter carries Charles' suitcases as they move through the crowded ship with over a hundred passengers. They descend multiple flights of stairs into a narrow hallway and enter a small cabin furnished with only a bed and a desk. There is barely space for one person to stand.

"It's not much," Charles admits as he unpacks, "but it's only for a few days."

Then he leads Carter down another cramped passageway, down two ladders, and into a storage compartment at the bottom of the ship. A dim lantern reveals boxes of supplies and twelve hammocks, eight already occupied.

Charles frowns. "I apologize, Carter. Let's go get some air."

They return to the deck as the *Octavia* pulls away from the dock. Her sails catch the wind, and the ship slips out toward the Gulf of Mexico. Charles and Carter stand side by side, watching the bustle of New Orleans fade into the horizon. They don't speak, but they both understand how far they will travel and how long it might be before they return—if they return at all.

That evening, dressed in his finest clothes, Charles returns to Carter's cramped quarters. Carter is asleep in a hammock along the far wall. Charles gently shakes him awake.

"Carter. Carter. Wake up."

Dazed and tired, Carter sits up.

"Come with me, Carter," Charles tells him.

Carter follows as Charles leads him up to his cabin.

Once in the cabin, Charles unwraps a bundle of cornbread and dried meat. "You need to keep your strength. I'm going to play poker. You don't need to go back down there tonight. You can sleep in my bed until I get back, and then on the floor. You don't have to go back to stowage. You can stay here with me."

Around two in the morning, Charles stumbles into the cabin, drunk and grinning, slamming the door behind him. The noise startles Carter awake.

Charles holds out a bulging bag of coins. "I won! Look!"

"That's great," Carter says, blinking. "But you need rest."

He helps Charles onto the bed, then curls up on a blanket on the floor. In minutes, both are asleep.

As Charles groans awake the next day, Carter walks in with a pot of coffee and two cups.

"Where did you get that?" Charles asks, blinking.

"I bought it." Carter laughs. "Figured you won enough last night to deserve it."

"Where did you get the money?"

"Master William gave me coins for emergencies. This is our first emergency."

Charles laughs as he sits up, reassured but ashamed that he asked. He knows Carter will never steal from him.

Carter pours a cup. Charles takes a long sip, then stares into the mug, lost in thought.

"They went easy on me," he says. "Too easy. It was a setup. They let me win. They're planning to take everything before we reach Panama. They may even try to break in. I've got to get my gun."

"Who are they?"

"There are two men and a woman. I'm sure they're working together," Charles says, pulling a small bag from under the bed. He lays its contents across the bed: a Colt pistol, a powder flask, six percussion caps, and six lead balls.

"You know how to load a pistol?"

"Like a shotgun, I guess," Carter replies.

"I'll show you. From now on, it stays loaded." Charles holds the barrel pointed up. He cocks the trigger and spins the cylinder. "First, half-cock it so the cylinder spins free."

He picks up the flask and pours powder into a chamber. "One quick pour—too much or too little can be deadly." He spins the cylinder and repeats the step in each chamber.

"Now, the balls." He places a lead ball in a chamber, pushes it down with his finger, and then does the same for the rest.

He pulls down the loading lever beneath the barrel. "Then you press each ball down snug against the powder." After loading all six, he turns the gun muzzle down and picks up the caps. "Last step—one cap per nipple." He carefully fits the percussion caps and gently returns the hammer to its resting position. "That's it. Think you can do it?"

"I can. Almost like a shotgun."

"Good. We'll take turns guarding the room." Charles' tone is deadly serious. He reaches into his suitcase and retrieves two large knives in leather sheaths. He tucks one into his boot and hands the other to Carter, then slips the pistol into his jacket pocket. "I'm going to fetch us some food. If anyone tries to break in, stab them. We'll get you a gun in California."

Carter stands for a moment, stunned. They haven't traveled far, yet everything feels completely different. He slides the knife into his boot. He expected change, but not this soon, and not like this.

Charles and Carter guard the cabin in shifts for three days and nights. They eat their meals in the cramped room, venturing out only for fresh air and short walks along the deck as the ship sails across the Gulf of Mexico. The unease lingers. The thieves don't make a move against them—but they know they are still out there.

Charles carefully arranges his belongings on the bed as the *Octavia* reaches Panama. He opens a hidden leather-lined compartment in his suitcase, revealing gold coins and paper banknotes. He fills two money belts.

He hands one to Carter. "Wear this under your clothes. Don't let anyone touch that suitcase."

Carter straps the belt around his waist and tucks it beneath his shirt. It is surprisingly discreet. They grab their bags and hustle off the ship. Charles spots the thieves in the distance and steers Carter into the crowd to avoid being seen.

The port of Colón, Panama, swelters under the blazing sun. Sweat pours from their bodies. Carter dons a wide-brimmed felt hat for protection, while Charles—still dressed as if heading to a garden party—wears white cotton and a straw hat.

Vendors shout from small stands selling fruits and vegetables. Native Panamanians and Spanish locals mix with clusters of White Americans. Carter and Charles follow a group of Americans, some accompanied by slaves, all trying to reach the muddy banks of the Chagres River, the next step on their journey to California.

Twelve wooden canoes—bungos—line the shore, each swaying in the river's lazy current. They vary in size, holding anywhere from four to eight people.

A large, unkept man in a worn dark hat greets them. "I'm Joe. People call me Mississippi Joe. It's twenty dollars each for food, tents, and a mule for the jungle."

"The ad said five," Charles replies, frowning.

"Prices changed. Take it or leave it," Mississippi Joe says as he shrugs.

Charles sighs and pulls gold coins from his pocket. They are soon introduced to Juan, an older Native man who will guide them.

Charles smiles. "I'm Charles, and this is Carter."

Juan nods, picks up one of the bags, and leads them to their bungo. It is just big enough for the three of them and their gear.

Charles slaps the back of his neck, scowling at a bloody mosquito splattered on his hand. "Damn these mosquitoes."

Juan hands Carter a paddle. "You front. Paddle right." Then he gives one to Charles. "You middle. Paddle left. Juan steer."

Carter takes the front seat, the cool wood pressing against his legs. Charles settles in behind him. With a mighty shove, Juan launches them from the shore. The three begin paddling in rhythm, pushing through the murky brown water tinged with a green shimmer. Dense bushes flank the banks, giving way to towering trees that reach toward the sky.

Above them, lime-green parrots with red cheeks dart through the canopy, and their shrill cries echo through the air. Carter, mesmerized, watches the birds glide overhead, forgetting the dangers for just a moment.

Juan shouts, "Paddle on the left!"

Charles and Carter dig their paddles into the water, veering the bungo right as five alligators slide off the bank and vanish beneath the surface. Their hearts pound. Adrenaline surges. They paddle furiously, eyes scanning the dark water. The alligators don't resurface.

They paddle furiously until the river widens and the danger passes.

Hours later, Juan guides the bungo to a gentle stop beside a clearing along the bank. Grateful for the break, Charles and Carter climb out and stand in silence, savoring the feel of solid ground.

The other bungos arrive one by one. Mississippi Joe passes out beef jerky, hard biscuits, and gourds full of water. Everyone tries to drink enough to wash down the dry food and to cool themselves, but the heat clings to them.

Charles eats little and keeps wiping sweat from his brow. Carter watches him with concern. It is more humid than a Mississippi summer—but not by much.

"You okay?" Carter asks.

"I'm fine," Charles replies, trying to sound steady. "I guess I spent too much time back East. I'm not used to this heat. We have hotter days in Mississippi."

Minutes later, they are back in the bungo, paddling upriver as the sun dips low. Juan steers them up a narrow tributary flanked by thick, tangled foliage. As dusk deepens, they reach a wide clearing. Colorful grass huts stand on stilts above the forest floor.

The village is alive with laughter and movement. Native men in bright robes work alongside women dressed in vivid clothing adorned with beadwork. Children play near a fire while food cooks over open flames.

"We spend the night here. We leave at first light, so get some rest," Mississippi Joe says.

"How much longer until Panama City?" Charles asks, exhaling heavily.

"A few more days upriver, then a couple of days by mule through the jungle."

Charles shakes his head and slumps onto a fallen tree, wiping his brow.

"You sure you're all right?" Carter asks.

"Just tired. I need to rest."

As villagers prepare dinner, Juan approaches with two steaming cups of dark liquid and hands them over.

"What is this?" Charles coughs after a sip.

"Coffee," Juan replies, smiling.

They take another sip, and their expressions shift to surprise and delight.

"This is the best coffee I've ever had," Charles says.

"It's more than coffee—its heaven," Carter adds, inhaling the aroma.

"Good for you," Juan says as he nods.

"We're going to need a lot more," Charles chortles.

Soon, the guests line up to eat. The feast includes roasted chicken, or at least a bird of some kind, grilled fish, beans, squash, mangoes, bananas, papaya, and passion fruit. Carter walks behind Charles, piling food onto his plate. Charles picks at his meal while the others devour theirs.

Darkness falls fast. Campfires light the clearing, casting flickering shadows. The travelers sit quietly, exhausted from their journey.

An ominous growl pierces the silence.

Mississippi Joe stands up and bellows, "Best get to your huts and stay there. Jaguars have been spotted nearby. And the snakes here are deadly."

"What's a jaguar?" someone asks.

"It's a big cat, like a lion. You don't want to meet one. It will be the last thing you see."

"I ain't goin' anywhere," a traveler says as they all get up and rush to their huts.

Carter and Charles climb the stairs into their hut. Carter pauses to admire the craftsmanship—woven grass walls, reed frames, a palm leaf roof.

They stow their luggage in a corner. Charles pulls out his pistol and slides it under his pillow.

"Just in case," he says.

Carter nods in approval as four other travelers join them and settle down. The sounds of parrots and monkeys fade, giving way to sleep.

Before dawn, the loud chatter of parrots jolts them awake. Juan enters with two steaming mugs of coffee. Charles blinks and takes a long sip.

"Ah, just what I need."

Juan grins. "More outside. Food's ready. You need to be strong."

Charles and Carter grab their gear and step into the fire-lit clearing. A long table brims with breakfast. Carter notices that Charles eats very little.

"We gotta get moving!" Mississippi Joe calls. "Long day ahead."

They pack up and push off once again, paddling upriver. Carter marvels at the rainforest—the towering trees, the bursts of color, the stillness broken only by bird calls. When they stop for lunch, Charles barely touches his food, sipping only coffee.

"You need to eat," Carter says.

"Don't feel like it. I'll eat later."

They paddle up the muddy river, feeling like they have paddled forever, before finally coming ashore and walking to a large village.

The light of day fades as they are greeted by Natives who tend large fires. The smell of the grilled food fills their nostrils and lifts their spirits.

"Welcome!" one shouts in broken English.

Mississippi Joe turns to the group. "I told you we'd make it for dinner."

Juan walks beside Carter and Charles as they hustle to the food. "This is my home," he says, beaming. "You are welcome."

Charles is soaked in sweat. "I'm not hungry, Carter. You eat. I need to sleep."

"I'll bring you fruit and water. I can bring you some coffee," Carter suggests.

"Okay," Charles mumbles as he drifts off to sleep.

Carter joins the others by a large fire. Villagers serve grilled fish, fruits and vegetables. Carter eats quickly, then returns with a plate for Charles. He tries to wake him, but Charles only moans and turns over.

Carter props himself against the wall, watching over Charles, trying to stay awake. But exhaustion wins out. He falls asleep.

Before dawn, parrots' chatter wakes him. Carter sits up and glances over.

Charles is drenched in sweat. His body radiates heat. Carter touches his forehead, then quickly pulls his hand back. It's burning hot.

"Are you all right? Can you hear me?"

"Mom? Is that you?" Charles mumbles.

"It's me. Carter."

Charles opens his eyes wide, confused. "Where am I? What's happening?"

"We're in Panama."

Charles groans. "I want to go home."

"You've got a fever," Carter whispers.

Others in the hut watch with alarm. One man stands. "He's got the fever!"

They grab their gear and flee.

Moments later, Mississippi Joe appears in the doorway with Juan.

"I hear he's sick," he says flatly.

Charles moans and shivers.

"His temperature is high," Carter says. "It's bad."

Mississippi Joe frowns. "He's not coming with us. I've seen this before. His chances are slim. Are you coming with us—or staying?"

"I'm staying," Carter snaps. His voice cracks with anger. He can't believe anyone would even ask.

Charles stirs, trying to rise. "We have to find our ship… our gold…"

"You need to rest," Carter says gently, easing him back. "We'll find gold when you're better."

Charles nods weakly. "Okay… Father."

Then he shivers and closes his eyes.

"My village," Juan chimes in. "I'll stay and take care of him."

"You're going with us," Mississippi Joe tells Juan firmly.

"I'll get help," Juan assures Carter as he rushes out of the hut.

"We'll check on him in a few days on our way back," Mississippi Joe says. "If he doesn't make it, I'll take you back with us."

Carter stares blankly. The idea of returning to Mississippi without Charles sends a chill down his spine.

A short while later, Juan returns with his wife, Rosa, and two teenage daughters. Their long black hair is adorned with bright flowers, and they wear colorful dresses.

"My wife and daughters will help him," Juan tells Carter.

Carter props up Charles' head and sits beside him as his body shakes with chills and sweat.

"I'm Carter. This is Charles," Carter says.

Rosa nods and smiles at him as she kneels beside Charles. She gently touches his forehead, then looks at Juan. They step outside and speak quietly in their native language.

Juan returns as Rosa, and his daughters leave the hut. "They will help. I must go," he says as he walks out.

Moments later, Rosa and her daughters arrive with bowls of water. Rosa takes a sponge from the bowl and gently dabs it on Charles' forehead. His eyes flutter open, and he gives Rosa a worried look before turning to Carter, his face filled with uncertainty.

He tries to sit up and coughs violently. He falls back down.

"You've got a fever. They're here to help," Carter tells him.

Charles nods, then closes his eyes.

Rosa unbuttons his shirt and sponges his chest. Her daughters soon return. One carries a cup with a strong, bitter odor, the other offers Carter a mug of hot coffee.

"Thank you," Carter says, smiling as he sips.

Rosa motions for Charles to drink the foul-smelling liquid and tries to speak in Spanish. Carter doesn't understand her words, but her meaning is clear enough. He helps prop up Charles so he can drink.

Charles is groggy but sips hesitantly from the mug, recoiling at the smell.

"You've got to drink it. They're trying to help," Carter says.

"What is it?" Charles asks.

"I have no idea, but they know what they're doing. It'll make you feel better."

"Tastes like dead frogs," Charles mutters.

"Si. Rana," Rosa says she and Carter help Charles drink more of the frog juice.

Charles coughs and sputters as he looks at Carter. "I smell coffee. I need some."

Carter raises the mug to his mouth.

Rosa cautions and puts her thumb and index finger together, making a small sign. "Poquito!"

Carter nods and gently puts the mug to Charles' lips, "Sip just a little for taste."

"Thanks. It's better than frog juice, " Charles says as he falls back on his pillow.

Carter stays by Charles' side through the night. Rosa brings water bowls and gently dabs Charles' forehead, and Carter takes over when she is not there.

During the night, Charles' breathing becomes heavy and labored. His face appears pale, ashen, and gray.

The possibility of Charles dying strikes Carter. What will he do?

He remembers how Charles said life was shorter than people think. He considers his options as he dabs Charles' forehead with a cool cloth.

If Charles dies, he could go back to Mississippi. He envisions Peg and the rest of his family, but things would be different without Charles. Daniel would still be there, and so would the overseer. And who knows what they'd say—what they'd think. Would they blame him for Charles' death? He promised William he would bring Charles home safe.

He could hide in Panama, where the jungle is wild but free, but that feels like a last resort. He would be free, but he would be lonely and lost, too.

California—now that's something. Everything he's read says it's a free territory. The risk might be worth it. There's gold, too. He could use Charles' money to pay his way. Plus, there's the gun. The knife. He could make it to California. Maybe even Oregon. Or Canada. He remembers reading that Canada is a free and open country. Perhaps he could find a way to buy Peg and his family and take them there.

He's lost in his thoughts when Charles' coughing snaps him back to the moment near dawn. At first, his coughing is light. Then it builds into a fit—deep, hacking coughs that shake his whole body. Carter holds him steady as Rosa and her daughters rush in.

Rosa crushes leaves in her hand and cups them to Charles' nose. His coughing slows. His eyes flicker open.

She looks into Charles' eyes. "Baño de sudor. Baño de sudor."

She turns and gestures to Carter, trying to help him understand.

Charles looks at Carter. "They want to sweat it out of me. Might as well try," he croaks.

Carter and Rosa help him stand. Two men rush in and take over, leading Charles to a mud-covered hut as smoke pours from its entrance. Inside, it's close and hot, with a ring of fire and glowing rocks in the center.

Carter and Rosa sit beside him, propping him up as the heat and steam build.

Native men pour water from gourds onto the hot rocks, and steam fills the hut. Charles coughs and breathes heavily as the men place aromatic leaves on the fire, filling the space with a sharp, earthy scent. Charles breathes deeply, coughs, and spits.

Charles bends forward, filling his lungs with steamy air, again and again. He chokes and coughs. He smiles at Carter. "I can breathe!"

"I'm glad," Carter says, his voice tight with relief. "I was worried about you."

Rosa gestures, and two men help Charles to his feet. They guide him to a bathtub carved from a tree trunk as the morning sun breaks through the clouds.

They ease Charles into the water. He shudders. Though lukewarm, it feels like ice after the heat of the hut. They bathe him gently. Rosa cups aromatic leaves in her hands and crushes them under his nose as he breathes.

"Gracias," Charles says in full voice as they help him dress in fresh clothes—a white shirt and a brightly colored wrap. Still groggy, he leans on them as they lead him back to the hut.

He sleeps through the day, with a fever rising and falling. His coughing eases, though it returns in the night. Carter stays close, watching over him. Rosa is always nearby, nursing him and urging him to drink more water or broth.

Days pass. Carter watches the village, helping where he can, but never strays far. When it rains, he reads from the Bible, Peg's self-portrait tucked inside as a bookmark.

Days later, Charles stirs and sits up. He squints at Carter. "Is there anything in that book for me?"

"It's for everyone," Carter says with a soft smile. He flips to Isaiah 38:16-17 and reads aloud: "'Lord, by such things people live; and my spirit finds life in them too. You restore me to health and let me live. Surely, it was for my benefit that I suffered such anguish. In your love, you keep me from the pit of destruction; you have put all my sins behind your back.'"

Charles nods. "That's a good one." He holds out his hand. "May I?"

Carter passes him the Bible. Peg's picture slips out. Charles catches it and smiles before tucking it back in and turning the pages. He finds Isaiah 40:31 and reads: "They who wait for the Lord shall renew their strength; they shall mount up with wings like eagles; they shall run and not be weary; they shall walk and not faint.'

Carter smiles as Charles flips pages to Matthew 10:8. "'Heal the sick, raise the dead, cleanse those who have leprosy, drive out demons. Freely you have received; freely give."

He slips Peg's picture back as a bookmark and returns the Bible. "Thanks, Carter. I wouldn't have made it without you."

Carter takes the Bible and turns to Matthew 6:34. "'Therefore do not worry about tomorrow, for tomorrow will worry about itself. Each day has enough trouble of its own."

Charles chuckles. "Every day presents challenges, but we will soar like eagles."

The next day, Charles asks for his bag and pulls out newspapers and notes. He finds the picture of Emmy and studies it. Carter watches and smiles, thinking of Peg. They are truly like brothers.

As the days pass, Charles regains strength and begins helping with meals. He and Carter try to learn bits of Spanish and the native Panamanian language. One afternoon, Mississippi Joe returns with the next group of travelers.

"I wasn't sure you would still be with us," he says as he sees Charles sitting outside the hut.

"I'm here," Charles replies. "I wasn't sure I would be a few days ago. I'll be ready when you come back."

"That's in six days. You sure?" Mississippi Joe questions.

"I'll be ready."

The days pass quickly. Charles is thin and pale when Mississippi Joe arrives with the new group, mostly young men, one of them a slave owner with five slaves. When they learn Charles had the fever, they keep their distance.

The next morning, Mississippi Joe visits their tent as they pack.

"They've heard you had the fever," he says. "I told them you'll keep your distance. Juan will guide you. Stay far behind, but within sight."

"No problem," Charles assures him.

They wait with Juan before starting upriver. The river winds through thick greenery, resembling a narrow canyon. Juan maintains a safe distance between them and the others.

They stop for lunch and stay twenty yards from the rest. Late in the afternoon, they reach the final river stop. Juan helps carry their gear toward a nearby tent. As they pass a corral of mules, wranglers speak Spanish and wear white cotton shirts, denim pants, and straw hats.

Juan offers Charles his hand. "Good luck."

Charles blinks, surprised. "Mucho gracias. You're not going with us?"

"No. We go back home." He turns to Carter and shakes his hand.

"Mucho gracias," Carter echoes. "You helped us so much. Please thank Rosa and your daughters."

Juan clasps both of Carter's hands. "You are welcome. Please come back to see us." He hugs Carter, then walks to the bungos as the other natives prepare to leave.

Mississippi Joe keeps his distance. "You know how to ride mules?"

"We know how to ride," Charles replies.

"Good. None of the wranglers wants to go near you. You'll ride behind us. Don't lose sight of us. If you get lost in that jungle, you're done."

He points to a small tent in the distance. "You're sleeping there tonight."

That evening, they ate outside. Dinner is rice and beans with gray meat that tastes like chicken, but it is not. Charles pokes at it and groans. "I was getting used to fruit."

The following morning, they set out on their mules. A third mule, guided by Carter, carries their supplies. Riding a short distance behind the group, they keep them in sight. The path meanders through dense vegetation, as they navigate streams and ascend hills where the mules hesitate and slow down. Frequently, they have to dismount and urge the animals onward.

They pause for lunch by a stream, give the mules a break, and then continue. By evening, they arrive at a clearing. Everyone is tired and silent. Carter and Charles are given a tent distant from the rest.

Before dawn, shouting wakes them. They rush outside to find men running toward the jungle with torches.

Mississippi Joe yells, "We're only waiting till sunrise! If you're not back by then, we're leaving without you. You're on your own."

"We'll be back. He couldn't have gone far!" one of the men shouts.

Carter and Charles walk up but stay far from the others, keeping their promise to avoid spreading the fever.

"What's going on?" Charles asks Mississippi Joe.

"One of the slaves ran off," he says, disgusted. "The owner's offering a reward, but the poor man won't get far in this jungle. We don't have time for this."

Back at their tent, Charles and Carter sit down for a quick breakfast. Just after dawn, voices rise from the jungle. Two slaves emerge, carrying the runaway between them. The slave owner and several others follow.

They drop the limp body near the fire. The slave owner's face twists in fury as he examines the injured leg.

"God damn it! Snake bit him!"

Mississippi Joe kneels beside the man and examines his swollen, blackened ankle. He lifts an eyelid, then looks. "Viper. No saving him now. He'll be dead within hours."

The owner's frustration boils over. He turns to his four slaves. "I told you boys not to run! Why'd you let him?"

"We were asleep, Master," one replies. "Didn't know he was gonna run."

Mississippi Joe stands up. "We have to leave now. We're behind schedule. It looks like rain is coming. It could slow us down."

One of the slaves looks at the dying man. "What about him? He's still breathing."

The owner scoffs. "Tie him to a mule. We'll bury him in Panama City." His voice is cold. The others look away and say nothing. They pack their gear in silence.

Charles feels a tight knot in his chest at the thought of the rain slowing them down. Their ship departs in two days, and any delay risks losing everything.

"We must make it. We can't miss our ship," Charles blurts.

"We'll make it, as long as the weather holds," Mississippi Joe reassures him.

The day drags on, burdened by silence. By nightfall, the snake-bitten man has found his maker, enveloped in white cloth.

The group rises early, though not early enough for Charles. "If we push hard, we can make it," he says.

But the jungle has other plans. By late morning, the rain returns, turning the trail to mud. Mules slide and stagger.

Mississippi Joe stops at a small clearing. "We'll camp here. Rain's not letting up."

Charles urges his mule forward, Carter close behind. "We can't stop. Our ship leaves tomorrow!"

Joe points down the trail. "Listen."

Charles strains to hear—rushing water.

"That's usually a stream. Now it's a river."

"Is there a bridge?"

"No. It will be impassable till tomorrow morning. Maybe longer."

"That's too late!" Charles looks down at the soaked path, caught between fear and resolve. After a long pause, he turns back.

They pitch their tent under thick brush. Rain pounds the canvas all night. Near dawn, the storm breaks. Charles pokes his head out.

"The rain's stopped. We're going."

Carter emerges, groggy. "What about the river? The trail?"

"If we wait, we miss the ship. We've already lost time."

Carter thinks of his promise to William. He should stop him from taking such a risk. Still, Charles has a point. They pack in the dark and mount the mules.

Mississippi Joe's voice breaks the silence. "Where the hell are you going?"

"We'll make it to our ship, whatever it takes," Charles snaps.

"Don't be a fool," Joe warns. "You're lucky to be alive after that fever."

"If we run into trouble, we'll wait for you on the trail."

"We're not coming to find you," Joe says sharply—then notices the mules. "You can't take my mules."

"I'll give you seventy-five for all three," Charles says, pulling out coins.

Joe snorts. "Hundred fifty. Take it or leave it."

"That's robbery!"

Joe smirks. "Wait till you get to California. You'll see real robbery."

Charles curses under his breath and hands over the gold coins. Without another word, Charles leads Carter and the mules into the jungle.

The trail is slick and steep. Clouds loom, yet faint light breaks through. At a bend, a clearing reveals the raging, muddy river.

"Looks bad," Carter says.

"It's fast but not deep." Charles points to a fallen tree that is damming and slowing the river. "We can cross here," Charles decides, heading for the bank.

He dismounts and guides his mule into the water. The water rises past his waist, and he swims. The mule struggles and swims behind.

Charles disappears underwater. He pops to the surface, gasping for air, "Come on, Carter! The water's getting deeper." He manages to use the branches on the fallen tree to help him across. He yells again to Carter, "Come on!"

Carter dismounts, leading his mule into the raging river, urging it to swim while pulling the pack mule behind. It's all or nothing. He struggles against the current but goes under. He resurfaces, gasping for air.

Carter reaches the middle as a surge of water pulls him under, trapping him between the mules as he struggles to swim.

"Carter!" Charles screams. He rushes to the fallen tree trunk and crawls on his hands and knees to reach Carter. The water almost pulls Charles into the river, but he makes it to the mules and grabs Carter's hand, holding the reins of the closest mule.

He pulls Carter's hand with all his might. Carter surfaces, gasping.

"Climb on the mule!" Charles yells.

Carter manages to climb onto the mule. Charles pulls the mule by the reins as he makes his way back down the log. Carter pulls the other mule as they swim ashore.

They collapse exhausted, soaked, and shaking.

After a long silence, Charles turns to Carter. " I thought I was going to lose you there."

Carter gasps, "Thought I was a goner. You saved me."

"You saved me back at the village," Charles chuckles. "I guess we're even."

"I suppose we'll have to cross a river or two in California." Carter groans.

"I'm sure we will. We'll be smarter next time," Charles assures him with a laugh. "First, we've got to get there."

Charles stands up, reaches for Carter's hand, and pulls him to his feet. They check the mules to ensure they are sound. Without wasting any time, they continue their journey.

They remount the mules and press on. The jungle becomes hotter and more humid. The trail narrows and becomes slick with clay, and the pack mule stumbles and tumbles off.

"No!" Carter shouts as he is dragged down with her, barely freeing himself. He skids to a stop and watches the pack mule crash into rocks below.

Charles slides down beside him. The mule blinks slowly, her hind legs broken. Carter kneels beside her.

"She's done for," Charles says, drawing his pistol. "Do you want to do it?"

Carter shakes his head. "I can't."

"Stand back." Charles fires a single shot. Then silence.

"She was a good mule," Carter chokes as he strokes her neck.

"One of the best," Charles agrees. "We've got to keep moving."

They load their gear onto the remaining mules and resume their journey down the trail, leading the mules. Charles walks at a quick pace. Nothing will stop him from missing the ship.

Hours later, Charles sniffs the air. "Smell that? The ocean."

They follow the scent through the brush—and there it is: the Pacific.

"It's the ocean, Carter! We're almost there!"

They rush down the trail. The jungle thins. Fields appear. Then a gravel road. Then a village.

Panama City rises ahead, sprawling along the coast.

They start jogging, pulling the mules behind.

CHAPTER 7
TROUBLE IN PANAMA

The sun hangs high in the clear blue sky, casting golden rays over Panama City as they step into its bustling heart on the afternoon of July 14, 1849. The lively sounds of market vendors fill the air—shouts of haggling, bursts of laughter, and the rhythmic clatter of carts on cobblestone.

A mix of aromas surrounds them. Fragrant spices—cumin, garlic, and chili peppers—blend with the smoky scent of grilled meats. The sizzling street food tempts their senses. Their stomachs growl in protest, but Charles urges them forward, leaving behind the enticing pull of the market as they head toward the waterfront.

Charles leads Carter and the mules away from the busy streets toward the harbor. Fishermen, their hands weathered and skilled, work quickly to unload the day's catch. Fish with shimmering scales glint in the sunlight as they are tossed into wooden carts. Seagulls circle and squawk overhead, drawn by the promise of an easy meal.

The air is thick with the briny scent of the sea, mixed with the sharp aroma of fish, an unmistakable sign of the ocean's presence. Despite the flurry of activity, the dock is empty of large ships.

"Our ship should be here," Charles tells Carter as they quicken their pace toward a small building with a ticket window. He pulls out his papers, hands them to the ticket agent, and tries to catch his breath. "We have passage on the SS *California*."

The ticket agent glances at the papers and points to a column of grey smoke rising from a speck on the horizon. "That's the SS *California*. Your ship has sailed."

"But I paid to be on this ship," Charles says, his voice rising.

"You weren't here. We have schedules to keep. People wait for months. You can put your name on the waiting list," the ticket agent replies.

"How long's the wait?" Charles asks.

The ticket agent scans papers and meets Charles' gaze. "If you put your name on the list, there's a slim chance for November, a better chance for December."

"But that's months away," Charles says, trying to contain his anger.

"That's the way it is. Everybody's going to California. This is the only way to get there," the agent replies as he shrugs.

"What about the money I paid for the tickets?"

"We can give you half credit if you buy passage now. You'll have to pay for January and be on the waitlist for the earlier ships," the agent advises.

Charles takes a deep breath. "Alright, I'll do it." He reluctantly pays for the tickets.

Depressed and discouraged, they trudge back to Panama City.

"We've got to find a place to stay and get something to eat," Charles complains. He looks visibly thinner and weaker from the fever and their long journey. Carter can only imagine how Charles must feel—he can barely drag himself down the street. They walk side by side, each holding the reins of a mule carrying all their possessions.

They hurry through the bustling streets to a row of businesses, restaurants, and hotels near the beach. The buildings are distinctly Spanish, characterized by their white walls and red tile roofs. They stop at a stable, where Charles arranges for the mules to be fed and watered.

Carter watches as the stable manager admires the mules. Charles tells him he'll sell them for $150. After some haggling, they settle on one hundred and twenty dollars.

Carter and Charles change into fresh clothes in a stable stall, then sit on a porch outside, trying to figure out their next move. Charles points across the street to a large white stucco hotel with grand arches. "I'll see if we can stay there."

"Do you think they have rooms?" Carter asks, doubting anything will be available.

"I'll find out. Money talks," Charles says as he gets up and walks through the wide-open lobby doors. Carter can smell food and hear voices from the hotel restaurant, which faces the ocean.

Charles bargains for a room in a mix of broken Spanish and English. The answer is no, no matter how much money he offers. The front desk clerk tells him rooms might be available on the outskirts of town, likely in a tent camp. Charles asks if they can at least stow their gear while they look for a place to stay. A few coins cross the counter, and the clerk agrees.

Charles returns to Carter, dejected. "Let's get something to eat. More importantly, let's get something to drink." He pulls out the suitcase with all their money and his gun. "We'll keep this one," he smirks as they check the other bags.

They walk through the hotel's bustling restaurant. Exhausted, they sit quietly, gazing at the white-capped waves crashing against the deep blue sea. Palm trees sway gently in the breeze.

Carter absorbs it all. He read every newspaper he could find, but none captured the beauty of the Pacific Ocean. He realizes they never could—not the scent of salt in the air or the way the beach kisses the surf and pulls away like a whisper. He loses himself in the moment.

"I've never seen anything like it," Charles says, his voice rising excitedly. "I've seen the Atlantic and the Gulf of Mexico, but they're nothing like this. Words can't express it."

Carter chuckles. "I was thinking the same thing."

"We think alike. I bet you're thinking what I'm thinking. I'm starving," Charles says as Carter smiles and nods.

They glance back at the restaurant. It is chaotic. Patrons argue with the wait staff, and several storm out while waiters shout after them.

Carter notices that the customers are White, while the staff are Panamanian and African. Back in Mississippi, he could never sit in a restaurant with Charles or any White man or woman. But here, no one seems to care. It feels good. He wonders if California will be the same.

"We've got to get something to eat and drink," Charles says as he stands and walks to the bar to place an order. Carter turns back to the ocean, aware that Charles will pay whatever it takes to get them fed.

Charles returns with a bottle of water, whiskey, and glasses. He pours them each a shot of whiskey.

"I'm not supposed to drink," Carter says, hesitating.

"We're not in Mississippi," Charles replies, raising his glass. "We saw our first elephant and survived."

Carter raises his glass but looks at Charles in confusion.

"You don't know what that means, do you?" Charles questions.

"No idea. I've seen a drawing of an elephant in a newspaper once, so I guess I've seen one."

Charles laughs. "It's a saying. It means you've been through something that changes you."

"You mean the fever? The alligators, the snakes, the jungle, the river?" Carter asks.

"Exactly."

"We definitely saw the elephant."

"I've seen a live elephant. And a lion," Charles adds.

"You've seen a real elephant and a lion? Where?"

"Back East, in a circus. This was the first time I've seen alligators. We're going to see a lot more elephants."

They sip their whiskey, letting the ocean breeze wash over them.

"It'll be months before we can get on a ship to California," Charles says. "When I was sick, I thought I was going to hell. Now I think my hell is never getting to California."

"I'm sure you'll get us there," Carter replies, drawing in a deep breath of the salty air. A few months in Panama don't sound so bad.

When their food arrives—grilled fish and a variety of tropical fruit— they take one bite, smile, and devour their plates.

"Everything's expensive. I need to save enough to buy our gear in California. We need to make money while we're here," Charles says, eyeing the restaurant and bar.

Carter watches a waiter struggle with a tray of drinks. "I can serve better than that. I can make money."

Charles' eyes light up. "I can manage this restaurant and bar. You can work the tables. I might be able to convince them to give us a room."

A short time later, Charles and Carter sit across from Carlos, the hotel manager, a distinguished elderly man with a heavy Spanish accent. He shuffles a stack of papers and signs one before turning to Charles.

"I'd like to talk to you about managing your restaurant and bar," Charles says firmly.

"Do you have experience?"

"I know how to get things done. This is Carter, he's a waiter," Charles replies.

"How long will you be in Panama City? Please don't lie to me. Everyone's going to California. I lost my last manager a couple of weeks ago."

"The ships are full. We'll be here at least four, maybe six months," Charles assures him. "I like it here. If things work out, we might stay. This is better than California." The lie slips out smoothly.

"You're hired. We pay fair wages. If the bar isn't running smoothly in two weeks, I'll find someone else," Carlos says.

"We need a room too. Rent free," Charles adds.

Carlos leans back in his chair, thinking. "I can only spare one small room."

"That's fine," Charles replies, standing and shaking his hand.

Moments later, they enter their room—a small stone bungalow behind the hotel. It has a bedroom with two beds and a tiny kitchen. A window over the sink faces the ocean. Charles opens it, and the sea breeze fills the space. They stow their gear, and Charles hides their coins, bills, and treasury notes between the rafters. They wear their money belts, only removing them when they sleep.

Charles wastes no time. The next morning, he gathers the staff—a mix of African, Spanish, and Panamanian workers. He quickly realizes he and Carter need to learn more Spanish. As Charles speaks to each person individually, Carter moves alongside him, offering assistance and the etiquette he learned from Peg about serving guests.

Charles assigns Carter to manage the waitstaff while he takes on guest relations, bar oversight, and the cash. Lunch runs more smoothly, and dinner service is even better.

Carter hustles, training the servers as they work. Charles observes closely, shifting people into new roles where their strengths can shine. Within days, the restaurant and bar are running smoothly. Carlos watches behind the scenes as the restaurant and bar become packed with customers.

The food also improves. —Carter spends time in the kitchen, collaborating with the cooks and adjusting the menu. They offer breakfast, with spicy bacon as the highlight. Charles tracks the days in the ledger and studies the ship schedules, hoping to find a way to secure passage to San Francisco.

Weeks later, on a sweltering afternoon in late August, Charles is behind the bar during a quiet lull between lunch and dinner. A few guests linger in the restaurant.

A hardened seaman in his forties, rugged as the oceans he crosses, strides to the bar, tugging at his short red beard as he sits. Charles approaches from behind the bar.

"What'll you have?" Charles asks.

"Scotch would make me happy," the man answers in an unmistakable Scottish accent.

Charles turns and grabs a bottle of Scotch and a glass from the shelf. As he turns back, the man holds up a hand to stop him.

"Not that stuff. The Scotch under the bar," he says firmly.

"That's only for the owners…" Charles begins, then catches himself. He doesn't know for sure, but rumors have floated through the hotel that

Captain Forbes of the SS *California* has a stake in the hotel. The realization clicks. "Wait—you're Captain Forbes, aren't you?"

Captain Forbes nods and motions for the Scotch.

Charles reaches under the bar and pulls out a bottle with an ornate Scottish label. "I've been wanting to talk to you," he says, pouring the drink.

"Don't tell me—you want passage to California," Captain Forbes says dryly.

Charles smiles. "That's where the gold is."

"Gold's everywhere," Captain Forbes replies. "That's why I bought into this hotel. Look around—people keep coming, and the money keeps flowing. Carlos tells me you've turned this place around. We need someone like you. Looks like you can manage more than a bar."

"I'll pay double to get on your ship," Charles blurts.

Captain Forbes takes a long drink and stares across the bar, considering. "My ship's fully booked for the next few months, but I'll make you an offer. I can't keep workers on board, —everyone wants to head to California. I'll take your money if you run my galley. You'll be in San Francisco in six weeks. Or stay here and keep running the bar. Either works for me."

"I'll run your galley, but I need passage for two." Charles points to Carter, who moves swiftly between tables. "He's with me. He'll do anything I ask."

Captain Forbes turns and watches Carter work, then looks back with a steely expression. "On my ship, he does what I ask. I need crewmen. I'm the captain. My men work for fair wages—and they keep them.

You'll share a cabin in the crew quarters. Everyone's equal on my ship. Do we have a deal?"

Charles reaches across the bar and shakes his hand. "We've got a deal."

CHAPTER 8
WORKING TOWARD CALIFORNIA

Charles and Carter hustle down the dock, carrying their luggage. They arrive at the gangway of the majestic SS *California.* The ship is painted deep black and red, featuring a gleaming gold wooden deck. On either side, two large black wooden semicircles conceal the paddle wheels, enhancing the vessel's commanding presence.

Dark smoke billows from the tall smokestack at the ship's center. Its boilers rumble to life, signaling that it is preparing to set sail. Three towering masts stand proudly, their sails neatly wrapped, ready for the wind's call. A grand American flag, marked by thirty stars and thirteen stripes, flutters at the stern, dancing in the ocean breeze.

An impeccably attired Black sailor in a crisp white and blue uniform stands guard at the gangway.

Charles greets him. "I'm Charles Perkins. Captain Forbes asked me—"

The sailor cuts him off. "Captain's been expecting you. Stow your gear in cabin thirteen and report to the galley immediately."

Charles and Carter make their way into the belly of the ship. They stow their gear in a small cabin with two beds.

Within minutes, Charles assumes command of the galley staff, precisely directing their movements. Carter supervises the waitstaff in a compact, bustling dining area at the ship's heart.

As the ship makes steady progress north, they work tirelessly. One evening, Carter pauses and watches Charles from across the dining room as he keeps the staff moving efficiently. He reflects on how they embrace hard work, finding satisfaction in accomplishing every task.

A week into their journey, the ship rocks with a heavy storm. Charles, feeling seasick, goes to the cabin before dinner. Carter stays behind to manage the staff. They serve cold meals to the crew and a few brave passengers as the ship battles the wind and waves. Carter ensures the kitchen gear is secured.

After dark, Carter opens the door to the deck. Instead of weaving through the ship to reach his cabin, he faces the storm head-on. Rain pours and wind howls as he steps outside. He tries to hold the door open, but it slams shut behind him. Suddenly, the ship lurches, throwing him to the deck.

He grabs the railing and pulls himself upright. He sees Captain Forbes at the base of the main mast with three crew members, all in rain-soaked coats and hats. Carter, in only a shirt and pants, is already drenched.

Clutching the railing, Carter fights the wind and rain as he moves across the slick deck. The crew stares up at the mainsail, barely holding on as it whips violently with each gust. The *California* groans and lurches, rocking from side to side in the storm.

"We have to cut the sail loose!" Captain Forbes shouts. "If the wind gets any stronger, we could capsize!"

"I'll do it, Captain," Carter says without hesitation.

Captain Forbes turns to one of the crewmen. "Give him your slicker and knife."

The crewman objects, sneering. "But he's a—"

A sudden gust slams into the ship, forcing everyone to brace themselves. "Give it to him now!" Captain Forbes barks.

Reluctantly, the crewman complies. Carter puts on the slicker as the ship rocks beneath him. The only way to reach the rope holding the sails is by climbing a narrow rope ladder. Battling the storm, he ascends the rigging toward the highest yardarm.

The wind and cold rain cut deep. He pauses, looking down at the deck where the captain and crew watch from below. The ship pitches and rolls, tossing him like a rag doll as he grips the rigging with all his strength. The wind screams, and the ropes sing a mournful tune.

He looks up at the rope holding the sail. The thought of climbing another fifteen feet chills him. He has never experienced anything like this. As he holds tight to the rigging, his thoughts drift back to Mississippi. Nothing like this happens there.

He considers climbing down. But the ship might not survive, and everything would be lost. He grits his teeth and reaches for the next rung with no other choice. He struggles to hold on with his left while extending his right to the next grip, using only his fingertips to keep hold of the knife.

Slowly, he climbs to the top of the mast. He can only brace himself with his left foot and hand as he leans out to slash the rope. Suddenly, the wind shifts. The sail snaps back and its rigging strikes him in the face, nearly knocking him off the ladder. He dangles in the air, holding on with one hand as the ship tosses him back and forth with each violent sway.

He slashes at the rope with each pass, every cut tearing it further. The ship rocks, flipping him over the mast. As he swings back, he takes one final, forceful swipe, severing the rope. The sail drifts off like a gray ghost over the ocean, vanishing into the white-capped waves.

The violent heaving caused by the massive sail stops, but the *California* still rocks in the wind and heavy seas. Carter clings to the rigging, shivering. His fingers barely respond as he inches his way down the rope ladder.

At last, he reaches the deck, soaked to the bone and trembling. Captain Forbes meets him with wide eyes. "Bravest thing I've ever seen. Come with me."

He turns to the small group of stunned crewmen. "Fire up the boilers! Turn the ship into the wind and against the waves!" The men snap into action and scatter across the deck.

Captain Forbes and Carter struggle through the storm, slipping and bracing against the wind as they make their way to the bridge. Inside, the first mate grips the wheel. Rain batters the windows, and thick black smoke pours from the boilers.

Captain Forbes grabs the wheel and helps steer. "Keep her steady into the waves," he orders.

The engines roar to life, and the paddle wheels churn as the ship turns. "Keep her steady," Captain Forbes repeats.

"That'll take us west. We need to go north," the first mate protests.

"Mother Nature's forcing us west," Captain Forbes replies. "The seas will calm by morning. Then we'll turn north, with the wind at our backs. I know someone who can help us replace the mainsail."

He glances at Carter with a sly grin and motions to a small table.

Captain Forbes opens a cabinet, pulls out a pair of wool blankets, and wraps them around Carter's shoulders. Then he fetches a bottle of Scotch and two glasses.

"This'll warm you up," he says as he pours. "That was one of the bravest things I've ever seen. I could use a man like you."

He raises his glass.

"I can't drink," Carter stammers. "I mean—I'm not supposed to drink. And I don't want to."

"Well," Captain Forbes says, downing his whiskey, "you're a stronger man than me. I can pay you well to work on this ship."

"Charles is taking me to California."

"You don't have to go anywhere you don't want to," Captain Forbes replies. "You could slip away in Panama. It's a free world—everywhere but the United States and the Caribbean. You need to steer clear and find safe water. We stop for fuel, food, and water before California. I can arrange for you to leave the ship quietly. Pick you up on the way back."

"Charles and I are like brothers," Carter says, hesitating. "I promised William—his father—that I would keep him safe."

"I admire loyalty," Captain Forbes says, nodding. "But no one should belong to anyone. I come from a family of fighters. I've traveled the world. If there's one thing I've learned, it's this—things change. Especially when you fight to change them."

"Things are changing," Carter says, "but there's a lot more to it. I'd better get back. Charles must be wondering where I am."

He stands, tightens the blankets around himself, and turns toward the door.

"Things will change," Captain Forbes assures him. "Just remember, you have the power to change things. You're always welcome on my ship."

Carter steps onto the deck, bracing against the wind and rain. Wrapped in blankets, he makes his way to the cabin. The sharp smell of vomit meets him at the door. Charles lies in bed, his head hanging over a bucket.

Charles looks up, pale and drawn. "I've been worried about you," he says hoarsely. "I barely made it back. I guess I'm not cut out for the sea."

"Captain needed help," Carter replies calmly, as if he hadn't just faced death high above the deck. "You gonna be okay?"

"If the world stops rocking, I'll be fine," Charles groans.

"Captain says it'll be calm by morning. I'll run the galley. Get some rest."

The next day, Carter directs the galley crew without issue. A day later, Charles appears in the dining room, moving slowly. Carter brings him a bowl of chicken soup and a glass of water.

Charles takes a sip, then looks up. "Thanks, Carter. This always reminds me of home."

The following day, Charles takes over the galley. They work hard for weeks, cooking and serving meals. But every day between lunch and dinner, they take a break to stand on deck, soaking up the sun and the sea air. They watch whales breach the surface. Dolphins leap and play in the waves alongside the ship.

Charles grins. "Told you we'd see more than elephants."

"They're bigger than elephants," Carter muses, watching a whale flip up its massive tail and dive beneath the water.

"Much bigger," Charles says, then points to the right. "Look there—hundreds of dolphins."

"I have never seen, read, or heard about anything like this."

The ship's steam paddles require vast amounts of wood, so they must stop frequently to refuel. Carter helps with the loading and welcomes the chance to set foot on land.

He is awed by the changing coastlines and vibrant ports. In Acapulco, golden beaches sparkle beneath the sun. In San Blas, lush green hills roll toward the ocean. In Mazatlán, music and laughter float on the breeze.

Each stop on the journey reflects a mix of cultures—Mexican, European, Spanish, Native, and African. No one cares about the color of his skin. For the first time, he moves freely without fear. In Mississippi, he was constantly being watched. He couldn't travel alone without papers. Even then, he was stopped and checked constantly.

The ship continues north to San Diego, where the sun sets over a harbor lined with whitewashed buildings. From there, it proceeds to the quiet beauty of Monterey, the final stop before reaching San Francisco.

In Monterey, Carter is caught by the beauty of the redwood logs he loads onto the ship. They have a distinct, earthy, spicy fragrance. He pauses and looks at the mix of workers loading the ship. People from everywhere, of every color, are happily working together.

"I feel free," he thinks to himself. "Truly free."

CHAPTER 9
CALIFORNIA, FINALLY!

The SS *California* docks in San Francisco late at night in early October 1849. Charles and Carter prepare breakfast for the passengers and crew. After cleaning up the galley, they leave the ship in the late morning.

Captain Forbes meets them at the gangway. "I wish you both the best of luck. But if you don't find gold, you're always welcome to work on my ship—or at the hotel." He glances at Carter, and they share a quiet smile, unnoticed by Charles. "Always a possibility," Captain Forbes adds, "even if you find some gold."

"I'm sure we'll find gold," Charles replies. "I appreciate you letting us work and getting us here on time. At least we made it before winter."

They walk down the pier into a city brimming with ambition and deceit. Con artists line the docks, ready to trick, swindle, and steal from gold seekers carrying their life savings. The air rings with clinking coins and cheers. Roulette wheels spin, and card games lure newcomers with promises of riches, no shovel or pick required.

They push into the heart of the city. The streets are a chaotic patchwork of canvas tents and rough wooden shanties. Vendors hawk everything a miner might need—picks, shovels, pots, pans, food, even livestock—all at outrageous prices.

Charles has read that Sutter's Fort in Sacramento offers better deals but worries that high demand has already driven prices beyond his budget. As they delve deeper into the city, the tents give way to wooden structures—hotels, restaurants, stores, and saloons.

They stop in front of a small building with a wooden sign that reads *Alta California,* the city's most prominent newspaper. Copies hang on a rack outside. Charles buys the latest issue along with several past editions. They find a bench nearby and sit down.

Charles hands Carter the older papers and unfolds the new ones. "We need to figure out the fastest way to Sacramento. Maybe there's a boat up the river. See if you find anything worth buying here in San Francisco before we head out."

Carter skims the papers, folding a few pages to show Charles later. As he looks up, he notices a group of men watching him from across the street, their expressions hard.

He leans toward Charles. "Maybe I shouldn't be reading in public. What will people think?"

Charles glances at the ragged group, then turns back to Carter. "I don't care. I'm not sure those idiots can even think, let alone read."

Carter holds the paper up to hide his smirk and continues scanning. He holds out an article for Charles. "Look, there's an ad for a steamship. Says it sails from San Francisco to Sacramento on Wednesdays and Fridays at one o'clock—from Pier Three."

Charles turns to a man at a nearby newsstand. "What day is it?"

"It's Wednesday," the man replies with a smirk.

Charles pulls out his pocket watch. "We can make it. Let's go."

They grab their bags and rush toward the harbor.

They sprint toward the *Pioneer,* a tiny side-wheel steamship with smoke billowing from its stack as the crew prepares to sail. The ship was brought from Boston in pieces and launched in August 1849. It can carry forty passengers and make four knots against wind and tide.

The vessel is full, but Charles refuses to take no for an answer. After some haggling, he secures them standing-room-only passages.

Carter packed food from the SS *California*, and they snack as they made their way up the river that afternoon and into the evening. As night falls, they find a spot on the deck to curl up among the other weary travelers.

After arriving at the Sacramento dock, they bypass the crowded waterfront and join other new arrivals heading toward Sutter's Fort. Wagons and mules laden with goods follow close behind.

The fort's white adobe walls gleam in the hot afternoon sun. Wooden buildings and tents shaded by massive oak and sycamore trees line a dusty path to the front gate. Bastions loom from each corner.

Construction is underway just outside the fort. Workers shout over the sound of saws and hammers. They pass blacksmiths at blazing forges, shaping metal with rhythmic clangs. Chickens squawk and peck at the dirt. In the distance, horses whinny and cows bellow from their pens.

Charles and Carter enter through the large wooden gate. In the center of the fort, a giant American flag flutters atop a towering pole. At its base sits a cannon, a Mexican-American War relic that John Sutter purchased for special occasions.

They pause in the middle of the fort, taking in the movement, noise, and smells. Shops and stores line the interior walls. Smoke drifts from campfires and an open-pit barbecue, where a side of beef slowly turns and is basted by a grinning cook.

The smell is irresistible. A line forms near the grill, where a buffet of beef, corn, and beans is served. The price is steep, but Charles doesn't hesitate. "We may not get another chance at beef for a long time," he tells Carter.

Carter's mouth waters. He can't remember the last time he had a meal that smelled this good.

As Carter waits in line, he looks around the fort. It stretches over 400 feet wide and 175 feet deep. The thick adobe walls stand eighteen feet high. The perimeter is packed with shops, restaurants, a jail—everything, a growing town needs.

But it is the people who fascinate him most. Languages from every corner of the world surround him, but he doesn't understand them. Everything is warm, alive, and full of hope. Everyone seems busy, eager, and full of anticipation.

He watches the cooks at the fire. Some are fair-skinned, others are bronze. He recognizes Spanish words in their chatter. They might be Spanish, Mexican, or maybe Indian. He wishes he understood more. He makes a quiet promise to learn.

Nearby, workers carry lumber into a carpenter's shop. Their features are unfamiliar to him. He figures they must be Chinese. He has read about them, but this is his first time seeing any in person. He hopes to learn more.

Scanning the crowd, he notices something else—he is the only Black man in sight. There have been others on the trip through Panama. Maybe they are already working claims or keeping a low profile. Still, it makes him feel out of place. There are a few women here, too—maybe one for every ten men.

Behind him, a group of six men chatters in a flowing, melodic language. Carter leans in, trying to understand. Their voices rise and fall, carefree and lyrical. It sounds like music.

He recalls hearing the language as a child. Back in Mississippi, Master Perkins purchased slaves from Louisiana who spoke it. They were compelled to learn and speak English, but at night, Carter sometimes heard them talking and singing. He remembers that the language was French.

His thoughts wander back to Mississippi.

"Carter. Carter!" Charles nudges him. "Aren't you hungry?"

Carter snaps out of it. Charles is ten feet ahead. Smirking, Carter hurries to catch up. They load their plates with beef, beans, and corn.

After devouring the meal, they head to a general merchandise store, where they meet the owner, Sam Brannan—a sharp-dressed man in his thirties with an air of authority. Three young women in white full-length dresses move between the shelves, arranging clothes. Their hair is braided and pinned in tight buns.

"What can I do for you?" Sam asks.

"We need everything," Charles replies, pulling out a folded paper. "Trousers, shirts, pans, picks, shovels—all of it."

"You've come to the right place. We've got it all," Sam says, then glances at Carter. "But I'm afraid he'll have to wait outside."

Carter gives Charles a disappointed look and steps outside. Maybe California won't be so different after all.

He stands just beyond the door and can still hear Charles inside.

"I need heavy cotton trousers," Charles says. A pause, then a sharp exclamation: "How much? That's robbery!"

Sam replies calmly, "This is California. If you want to find gold, you've got to pay the price."

Carter lingers, listening as Charles tries to barter.

"I've got clothes to trade," Charles offers. "I'll trade you my shoes for a pair of boots."

"It's hard for me to sell dress shoes," Sam replies.

"They're custom-made calf leather."

"They won't last a week here. I'll have to try to sell them in San Francisco."

"Add up the cost for my list, and we'll see," Charles mutters, disgusted.

Carter steps away from the door and sits on an empty wooden crate nearby. From there, he watches the lively fort bustle with life—figures moving in every direction, laughter drifting through the air, the occasional metallic clang ringing from the blacksmith's forge. He lets it all wash over him.

An old miner approaches the store, leading a mule weighed down with supplies. Despite his years, the man is rugged and strong, his weathered face marked with deep creases from a life spent outdoors. He rubs his gray, scruffy beard and dusts off his tattered clothes.

"That's a fine mule," Carter remarks, rising from the crate and walking toward the animal. She reminds him of the mule they lost in Panama.

"Her name's Sarah," the miner says proudly. "She can climb anything and carry everything."

Carter steps closer and gently strokes her neck. Sarah gives a contented nod and soft whinny.

"You know much about mules?" the miner asks.

"I know a thing or two," Carter says, rubbing her neck.

"Where are you from?"

"Mississippi. Where'd you get her?"

"Bought her off a fur trapper a few years back. You need a mule?"

"We need everything," Carter laughs. "Just got here."

"You're in luck, I'm selling everything." The man extends his hand. "Name's Bill."

"I'm Carter. Why are you selling?"

"I'm not spending another winter here. Found enough gold to set me up. There are too many people, and the gold's drying up."

"Where are you headed? San Francisco?" Carter questions.

"Hell no!" Bill snorts. "Winters in San Francisco will freeze your balls and suck 'em up into the back of your head. I'm goin' someplace warm."

"We just came from Panama City. It was great."

"That's my first stop. But I'm lookin' for a warm island in the Caribbean," Bill says, patting Sarah's side. "I want a good home for her. I was gonna sell my stuff to Sam, but I think you'd be good for her. Interested? Got pretty much everything else you'll need. I'll make you a deal on the whole lot."

"Might be. I'll get my master—I mean, Charles." Carter corrects himself, turning toward the store.

Bill's face twists in surprise. "Wait a minute. You mean he owns you?"

Carter hesitates.

"Nobody's supposed to own anybody," Bill says firmly. "This is free territory."

"We're just here to find gold, then we're headed back to Mississippi," Carter tells him as he walks toward the store, moving slowly, still turning over Bill's words. He read about California's push toward becoming a free state, but he and Charles never discussed it. He knows he will go back to Mississippi. His fate is sealed.

Carter peers into the store. Charles is hunched over a pile of clothes and gear.

"There's someone outside you should talk to," Carter says. "Might be a better deal."

"I'm trying to close a deal, Carter!" Charles snaps, frustrated with the prices. But he catches the seriousness in Carter's face—he wouldn't interrupt without good reason.

Charles turns to Sam. "Hold on a minute." He follows Carter outside and stops short when he gets a whiff of Bill. The miner hasn't bathed in months.

Charles looks over Sarah and the pile of gear, sizing things up quickly. "I'm Charles. What are you selling?"

"Name's Bill. Selling everything. I've already told Carter that Sarah can climb anything and carry everything. You won't find a better mule. I'll give you a better deal than Sam will. But I'm not sure I'm gonna sell to you. This here's free territory."

"California is part of the United States," Charles replies coldly, handing over his list. "The Constitution guarantees my rights and property. I wasn't sure about buying a mule yet, but we need everything on the list."

Bill takes a deep breath, pondering the situation, unsure if he wants to sell to a slave owner as he looks at the list.

Charles walks to Sarah and strokes her neck. He turns to Carter and says, "She looks like the mule in Panama."

"Her name's Sarah," Bill says as he looks up from the list. "I want her to go to a good home."

"We treat our animals like family," Charles assures him.

Bill looks at Charles with concern. "Things don't feel right. I'm not sure I want to sell her." He looks questioningly at Carter and then turns to Charles, watching him stroke Sarah's neck.

Carter feels the heat from Bill's look. "We'll treat her like family," Carter blurts. "Charles is a good and fair man."

Charles looks at Carter, puzzled at first, but then smiles. Carter shrugs.

"Fine," Bill huffs. "I'm done with California. Done with the United States, too. Headed to the Caribbean. Got pretty much everything you need."

Bill opens his packs and spreads his gear on the ground. "You'll need to buy clothes—mine are worn thin. Not much food left, either."

He stands and looks at Charles' dress clothes. "Are you looking to sell your suit and shoes? I was planning to buy myself some fancy duds in San Francisco."

"We might be able to make a deal," Charles says. "Let's see what you've got."

Charles and Carter pick through the gear. Carter raises a shovel, and the handle falls off.

"Stuff's a little used," Bill admits, "but it's everything you need. I'll throw in the shotgun and one of my pistols. They come in handy."

"How much for everything, including Sarah?" Charles asks.

Bill rubs his beard, thinking it over. Then he says, "I'll take three hundred for everything."

"That's a lot of money," Charles complains.

"I can get more. Sarah alone is worth that much. Mules like her don't come easy," Bill replies. "It's your call. I can find someone else."

Charles takes a long breath, looks over the gear again, and checks it against his list. A few people gather, eyeing Bill's equipment.

"Tell you what," Bill adds. "Make it two ninety and throw in your clothes and suitcase." He points at Charles' wide Panama hat. "I want the hat, too. Perfect for where I'm headed. You'll need a felt one anyway. Rain and snow are coming."

Charles frowns. "How about this one?" He rummages through a travel bag and pulls out a smaller straw hat—the one the Natives gave him in Panama. "I'll keep mine, but I'll throw in this one. It's brand new."

Bill looks it over, throws his dirty, worn hat on the ground, and tries it on. "You've got yourself a deal."

"Give me a minute," Charles says. He darts back into the store.

A few minutes later, he emerges wearing a flannel shirt, cotton jeans, and a fresh pair of boots. He carries a stack of supplies and clothing, with his shiny black dress shoes perched on top of the stack of clothes.

Charles hands Bill his suitcase and shoes. Bill opens the suitcase and inspects the clothes. "These will suit me fine," he proclaims as he closes the suitcase. He removes his boots, revealing filthy socks with toes sticking through large holes. He puts on Charles' dress shoes and chortles, "They fit perfectly."

"I'm glad they'll get some good use," Charles smiles as he hands the money to Bill.

"You seem like honest fellers. I'll give you some advice," Bill says as he pulls out a large, tattered map. "Here's my map. If I were you, I'd head to Coloma on the American River. Set a base camp, and then you can work the rivers and creeks. There's a lot of gold there."

Charles and Carter lean in close to examine the map. They exchange glances, noticing Bill's odor, and step back as he points to a location along the river. "This is Coloma," he says. "I've marked the spots where I've had good luck and a few others that seem promising. I believe there's gold up Mosquito Creek."

"That's mighty helpful," Charles says.

Bill folds the map and hands it to Charles before picking up the suitcase, still wearing Charles' shoes. "I'm going to take a bath and shave," he says. "But first, I need a moment with Sarah." He walks over and gently strokes her neck. He brushes tears and walks away quickly.

"Enjoy Panama," Carter calls out. Bill doesn't turn back, but he waves in acknowledgment.

Charles looks over his list as they pack the gear and load it onto Sarah. "We still need beans, cornmeal, and coffee. We'll get as much food as Sarah can carry."

Carter walks beside Charles and leads Sarah as they make their rounds through the stores inside Sutter's Fort. After gathering the rest of their supplies, they prepare to leave. As they load Sarah, they spot a clean-shaven Bill approaching. Dressed in Charles' clothes and topped with the Panama hat, he looks younger, almost unrecognizable.

Charles and Carter smile. "You clean up well," Charles laughs.

"I'm not sure Sarah recognizes you," Carter adds.

Bill chuckles as he playfully rubs Sarah's nose. "Bet you've never seen me look or smell like this, have you, girl? You take care." He turns back to them, his voice tight with emotion. "I need to get to my ship." He strokes Sarah's nose one last time before walking briskly away.

Charles and Carter grab a bite to eat as they exit the fort. It's late evening. They find a flat ground to set up their tent and gear. Struggling with the tent in the dark, they eventually get it upright. Exhausted from the day's events, they fall asleep on the uneven ground.

They rise before dawn and start up the trail to Coloma, following the American River. Sarah knows the trail well and seems eager, despite her load.

They pass small encampments scattered along the riverbank, where gold panners sift through gravel. The weather is hot and dry, climbing into the high 80s. Carter wears his Panama hat, its beaded band catching the light, while Charles sports the white straw hat from Mississippi.

By late afternoon, they reach the crest of a Sierra foothill overlooking the American River. The river glimmers like a blue sapphire, sunlight dancing off its surface. They pause, captivated by the sweeping panorama. After a moment of quiet awe, they set up camp.

Before dawn, they eat a quick breakfast and continue. The river winds through golden hillsides dotted with evergreen shrubs. Along the bank, trees and bushes blaze with fall color—yellow, orange, and scarlet leaves flutter in the breeze. In the distance, two gold seekers pan in the shallows.

Charles breaks the long silence. "I think we've already found gold," he says. "Isn't it glorious?"

"I can't believe it. Everything's gold—the hills, the trees..." Carter replies, marveling at the scene.

"Let's get our share," Charles says, picking up the pace.

As they near the river, they pass a small Native American village. The huts are made from cedar bark, tree limbs, grass, and mud. Women grind acorns into flour on a stone slab while children play nearby. Two elders tend to salmon that are smoking above a low fire.

The trail hugs the river until it reaches Sutter's Mill. Large timbers support a high plank roof above the water. Four men maneuver a massive log toward an eight-foot saw blade, powered by a towering water wheel. The blade buzzes, cutting the trunk into smooth planks. Workers load the boards onto a wagon pulled by four mules. More logs sit stacked along the bank, ready to be milled. The sawmill runs nonstop to meet demand.

Charles turns to Carter. "We're here. That's Sutter's Mill."

Carter nods, watching the diverse crew at work—White, Mexican, Spanish, Asian, African, and Native men laboring side by side. He thinks of the lives they left in Mississippi. California is different. He wonders what the future might hold.

They continue for a short distance to the small yet growing town of Coloma along the American River. The first building is constructed of stone. Out of curiosity, they peek inside—the store bustles with activity.

A line of miners waits at the counter to buy medicine. A Chinese man carefully weighs white powder on a scale while another helps a customer choose a ladle from a rack of spoons. The store sells porcelain dinnerware and cooking utensils, but most customers are there for medicine.

They move deeper into Coloma, which spans only four blocks and consists of brick buildings, tents, and wooden plank structures. They pass a hardware store crowded with gold seekers purchasing shovels, picks, and, most importantly, guns.

A gunshot cracks from beside the building. A salesman demonstrates handguns, shotguns, and rifles on a large table. A customer reloads a rifle short distance away, takes aim at a wooden box across the river, fires, and hits a bullseye dead center.

They continue down the street and pass a blacksmith shop, where workers hammer metal above a glowing fire. The fruits of their labor, every metal good imaginable, are displayed for sale. A miner inspects a large, gleaming knife.

"I think we've got everything we need, but it's good to know all this is here. We need a place to sleep and use as our base camp. And we need a place for Sarah, too," Charles says as they pass several more stores.

They follow the road to a row of large tent camps by the river. It's quiet, with only a few miners moving about. Charles leads them to a scruffy young man sitting on a log, tending a fire in front of a tent.

"My name's Charles. Do you know anybody with a place for two and a stable for my mule?"

"Name's Archibald. My friends call me Archie. I got space for you, and there's room at the stable," he replies in a thick Southern drawl. Then he points at Carter. "We ain't got room for him. Nigger tents are down the river." He jerks his thumb toward a row of ramshackle tents far away. "That's where mine would be if he were still alive. The son of a bitch caught the fever and died right after we got here."

Carter tries not to react and turns to stroke Sarah. Charles thinks for a moment.

A few tents away, a miner in his early thirties with a scraggly beard and long hair has been listening. "We might have room for you," he says with a distinctive Northeastern accent.

Charles looks back at Archie. "I'll think about it."

Archie shrugs as Charles leads them toward the other miner.

"We lost two fellas who couldn't pay. Everybody pays their fair share for food and supplies," the miner says.

Charles nods. "Sounds fair."

"Name's George. Do you own him?"

"I'm Charles, and this is Carter. And yes, I do."

"We all come from free states. We don't believe in slavery," George says. "This is free territory. If you want to share our tent, you must work the same and pay the same. Can you agree to that?"

"We can agree to that," Charles replies.

George turns and points to Carter. "I figured he'd say that. Does he pay you, or will you get your share fifty-fifty?"

"We work together. We're like brothers," Carter says, glancing at Charles, who fights to hold back a smile.

"That ain't good enough," George scoffs.

"I pay him fair wages," Charles insists, meeting Carter's eyes.

Carter is caught off guard but doesn't let it show. He's not sure Charles will pay him—but it doesn't matter. What would he do with the money, anyway? "He pays me, and he's a fair man," Carter tells him to secure the deal.

George studies their faces, still skeptical, but he reads their sincerity. "All right, grab your gear and come on in. We work from before sunrise to after sunset," he says. "We take turns with the chores. Today's my day to cook dinner. You'd better like it." He cackles.

The tent has twelve cots. George leads them to the last two in the back.

"You can stow your gear under your cots. Nobody steals around here. A few have tried, but justice is swift. We take it into our own hands, so don't worry. Your mule can stay at the stable out back. We all chip in for food. You're lucky to have a fine mule. They're getting scarce. A few guys in our tent have them. They let us rent them when they're not using them."

"We plan to use her often, but renting sounds fair," Charles says. "We want to make sure she gets her rest and stays healthy."

They walk out of the tent as George admires Sarah. "Where did you get your mule?"

"Bought her at Sutter's Fort from an old miner," Charles replies.

"Hell, it's Sarah! You bought her off old Bill," George exclaims, stepping up to stroke Sarah's neck. "Heard rumors he struck it rich. He must have if he sold Sarah and skedaddled. She's the best mule in California. Bill was in our tent before he went off on his own. Wish I knew where he found the strike."

Charles and Carter exchange a look. They bought the right mule, and have the right map.

"We serve breakfast before dawn, and dinner an hour after sunset. We'll work you into the schedule," George says.

Charles and Carter unload their gear and stow it in an empty tent under their cots.

Charles faces Carter and says, "I meant what I said, Carter. We're in California now. Things are different. I've thought about it. I'm going to pay you a fair monthly wage."

"I don't know what I'd do with money. I guess I can pay my fair share for food—and pay you back for the supplies, Sarah, and the cost to get here…"

Charles is taken aback. "You don't owe me anything. You saved my life in Panama. I know you could've run, but you didn't. That one night when I was sick, I tried to tell you to take everything and be free if I died. I'm telling you now—if I die before we make it back to Mississippi, everything I own is yours. You can be free."

"You saved my life on the river," Carter says, his voice tight. "I could've drowned. You don't owe me."

"We're even. We'll start fresh here in California. I'll pay you fair and square—but I'm taking the risk, and the gold is mine," Charles says, then laughs. "But if I die, it's all yours. Don't go back to Mississippi."

They face each other for a long moment.

"I mean it," Charles says, "I know you helped with Bill. We wouldn't have Sarah or the gear without you. Or the tent." He takes a deep breath before adding, "I feel free here. I don't have to worry about my family or who I'm supposed to be. This is it. This is freedom. I can do what I want. Don't you feel it?"

Carter hesitates. "I know you'll make the right choices. Freedom seems to have a very high price. No one needs to die. I'll feed and water Sarah."

Carter leaves the tent, then returns shortly after to find Charles asleep on his cot. He crashes on the cot beside him.

They wake to the smell of food as the sun sets.

George and the other ten tentmates greet them outside as they dig into a meal of rice, beans, and salmon.

"These are our new tentmates, Charles and Carter," George announces. Two miners glance up and nod, but the rest stay focused on eating.

"Thought you were going to miss dinner. The salmon are running. This'll be the best food you'll get for a while," George says.

He loads their plates. They sit by the fire and eat while the others finish their meal and quietly head back into the tent.

"You'll get used to it. It's every man for himself," George remarks.

"Can you teach us how to pan for gold?" Charles asks.

"Well, Charlie, I'd be happy to teach you," George replies. "But it'll take up my valuable time. If you find gold while I'm teaching you, we split it. Deal?"

"That's a fair deal," Charles agrees.

After breakfast, George helps them sort through their gear to find pans and small glass jars. Then he leads them down a narrow trail to the American River, where miners are scattered along the banks.

Most are White, but several Black men pan nearby while their owners sit on the shore, watching them work. A few slaves dig sand and gravel with shovels and dump it into a sluice box, while another pours water over the mixture.

"What's that?" Carter asks.

"That's a sluice box," George replies. "I'll show you how to use one in a few days, but today we're panning."

George leads them to a quiet stretch of the river, a bit removed from the others. He tells them to grab their pans and follow him to the shallow edge.

"We had a big rain the other day," George says. "That usually washes gold loose."

He wades into the water and fills his pan two-thirds full of sand, gravel, and water. Charles and Carter follow his lead, mimicking his movements as he swirls the pan. He lowers it into the water again and keeps swirling.

"Mix it up good with your fingers," George instructs.

He uses his right hand to stir, pulling out larger rocks and inspecting them one by one.

"Check the rocks carefully. Don't toss away a nugget by mistake."

George demonstrates how to tilt the pan and let the lighter material wash away.

"Use the riffles to sort out the lighter stuff. Gold's heavy—it'll sink to the bottom. Shake it side to side."

They follow his guidance, swirling and shaking their pans until only fine, dark sand remains at the bottom.

"You boys see anything?" George asks.

"I got some—I've got gold!" Carter shouts.

George and Charles rush over to look. Charles leans in and grins. "By God, that is gold!"

"Shhh!" George hisses. "You don't want the others to hear. Rule number one: keep your finds and your spot to yourself. I told you—rain shakes gold loose. This is a good place."

He pulls out a small jar and carefully lifts several gold flakes from Carter's pan, placing them inside.

"Let's keep working this spot," he says.

They get back to work. A few minutes later, Carter wades over, holding something in his wet, muddy hand. It's a gold nugget, easily over half an inch wide.

"Look at this," he whispers.

Charles blurts, "Oh my God!" Then he quickly lowers his voice, asking, "How much is that worth?"

George examines the nugget closely. "It's worth plenty. You've had a lucky first day. But keep your voice down. And remember—we split what you find."

He drops the nugget into the jar.

They work all day, panning steadily through the afternoon. By evening, their jar is glinting, heavy with gold.

As they arrive at their tent, their tentmates barely glance at them, too occupied with eating and talking around the fire.

After dinner, George pulls a small scale from under his bed. He, Charles, and Carter sit at the table by candlelight. George pours the gold onto one side of the scale. He adds small weights on the other side until it balances. The gold catches the glow of the candle flame bright and sharp.

"It's just over eight ounces," George says as he grins.

"How much is that worth?" Charles asks.

"Going rate's a little over twenty dollars an ounce. So, about a hundred and sixty," George figures. "We'll split it three ways. But don't count on this happening again. You're lucky to get half an ounce in a day—maybe a full one if you strike a good spot."

"How about I pay you your share in coins?" Charles says. "I want to keep the first gold we found in California."

"Suits me fine," George replies.

Carter knows his share won't ever really be his. Charles promised fair wages, but Carter doesn't expect to see it. Best to say nothing; he figures things will settle in time.

Day after day, Charles and Carter work the river. From sunrise to sunset, they pan the cold water. Some days, they find a little gold, and some days, none. Charles keeps a log of each location and marks their finds on Bill's old map.

One evening, they eat around the campfire with other tentmates. Charles talks while Carter listens. He thinks about how strange this life is. Here, White men share tents and meals with him like he's one of their own. Back home, no White man would dream of it. There's a kind of freedom in that, and it feels right.

But just a few tents over, things are different. Southern men won't look his way, and their slaves are camped far down the river in makeshift shelters. It's like walking a line between two different worlds. The tension's quiet, but it's always there.

A few days later, under the heat of the sun, Charles and Carter sift through sand and gravel with a crowd of miners along the riverbank. Suddenly, an older miner shoves a younger miner hard, knocking him into the icy current.

"That's my gold! It fell out of my pan!" the old man shouts.

The younger miner scrambles up, drenched and holding a nugget the size of a marble. "It's mine now!" he shouts back.

The old man snarls, pulls a pistol, and fires.

The shot cracks through the air. The bullet hits the young man square in the chest. He falls back into the river. Blood spreads beside him, dark and wide, as his body floats downstream.

No one moves. No one speaks.

The old miner steps into the water, bends, and picks up the nugget. His gun is raised as he turns to the other miners.

"This is mine. Anybody got a problem with that?"

Heads lower. Pans dip back into the water. No one answers.

Carter leans toward Charles and mutters, "Law seems to be whatever a man says it is. Guess that's freedom."

Charles whispers, "I guess the law's what you make it."

He sets his pan aside, dries his hands, and pulls out the map. His eyes follow the slope of the hills above—up to a creek and a line of dry ravines. He makes a few new marks.

"That was a big nugget," Carter says. "Think it came from up there?"

"Could've floated down from upriver," Charles says. "But more likely, it washed out of one of those creeks."

Carter goes back to work. Charles draws lines on Bill's map as he studies the landscape, trying to find the gold's source.

"We'll head up those creeks and ravines," Charles says. "But we'll do it at night."

A few days later, the three men walk back to their tent in the dark, passing near the Black miners' camp. Two slave owners step out from the trees, carrying a dead slave tied to a pole between them like a hog. They drop the body beside a fire as a crowd gathers.

One of the slave owners says, "We tried to bring him back. But he fought. If you run—and fight—this is what happens."

Charles, Carter, and George turn and walk on.

"I can't believe there's no law here," Charles complains.

"You get used to it after a while," George replies. "But that just ain't right."

CHAPTER 10
NEW FRIENDS

Charles and Carter toil day and night, scouring hills, mountains, and streams in search of a big strike. Charles marks Bill's map and takes notes, tracking the areas they've covered and identifying promising spots.

Sometimes they load Sarah and spend days in the Sierra Nevada mountains. They sleep under the stars, but rain and snow begin to fall as winter sets in. Coloma and its surroundings see little snow but plenty of rain. Higher in the Sierra, the terrain turns dangerous. Several feet of snow can fall in hours.

Charles often ventures into the mountains, leaving Carter to pan the American River and its tributaries. He stays alert, especially when he finds gold. Many disapprove of a Black man working alone. He keeps his gun and knife close but avoids trouble, choosing to pan with his tentmates or in secluded areas.

Charles believes he's found a claim on a mountainside a few miles from Coloma. They load their gear onto Sarah and begin working the site. Using pickaxes and shovels, they chip at a promising outcropping near the top of a ravine. They battle rain and occasional snow flurries.

When the weather clears, Carter and Charles swing their pickaxes under a bright afternoon sun. The ravine is scattered with broken rock. Carter sweats heavily and staggers as he lifts his pickaxe.

Charles looks up. "Are you okay?"

Carter's eyes flutter before he collapses, tumbling down the steep slope.

Charles scrambles after him. He glances back at Sarah, who stands uphill. "Come on, Sarah!" he calls, waving. She slowly begins picking her way down the ravine.

Carter lies still, face down in the dirt. Charles reaches him and rolls him over. His face is scraped and bloody. His eyes flicker open.

"Carter! Carter! Are you okay?" Charles pleads.

Carter's voice is faint. "I feel awful."

Charles places a hand on Carter's sweaty, bloodied forehead.

"You've got a fever. Why didn't you say something?"

"I didn't feel that bad this morning."

"We've got to get you to a doctor," Charles says, helping Carter sit up. Sarah walks over and leans in to nuzzle him. Charles steadies Carter to his feet and helps him onto Sarah's back.

"Do you think you can hold on and ride?" Charles asks.

"I'll manage."

They descend the mountainside, following a trail back to Coloma. The only doctor for miles is Doc Hill—just twenty-six, yet relied upon by gold seekers for every injury and illness. They'd heard of him but had never met him.

Charles guides Sarah to the front door of a rustic cabin made of plank wood and logs. He helps Carter down carefully and supports him to the door. Charles knocks. A young Black woman opens the door.

She locks eyes with Carter. He tries to smile through the pain as he looks into her dark eyes, which remind him of Peg. A jolt of surprise passes through him—she's the first Black woman he has seen in California.

She smiles back and gasps. "Oh my. Let me help you. Let's get him over there." Her Southern accent is as thick as Georgia molasses. She helps Charles ease Carter into a chair in the main room.

Doc Hill hurries in. "How long have you been sick?"

"Just started feelin' bad today," Carter mumbles.

A patient groans loudly in the next room.

Doc Hill runs a hand through his light brown hair and looks at Charles. "Is anyone else sick? How did he get those cuts on his face?"

"Don't know anyone else who is sick," Charles replies. "We were working, and he passed out and fell."

Hannah steadies Carter in a chair as Doc examines him. Carter sweats and coughs. Hannah dabs the scratches on his face with balls of cotton.

Doc Hill glances at Charles. "Cholera, dysentery, and typhoid are rampant. I think it's the flu, but it's a bad case. Are you boiling your water?"

"Sometimes we drink straight from the river," Charles says with a shrug.

"Boil it!" Doc Hill warns.

Carter slumps in the chair. Hannah catches him, and they all help carry him to a nearby cot.

Two men walk past, carrying a body wrapped in white cloth. The room falls quiet until the door closes behind them. Attention shifts back to Carter.

"He needs to stay here for a few days," Doc Hill says. "He should recover, but we don't want it spreading. Hannah will take good care of him."

A short while later, Carter's eyes flutter open. Hannah dabs a cool cloth on his forehead. Her eyes glow in the lamplight.

"How ya feelin'?" she asks.

"Like I'm being boiled in water. My name's Carter."

"I'm Hannah. I'll take good care of you, Carter," Hannah assures him. "You need rest. I gotta help the others."

That night, Carter awakens coughing and choking. Hannah rushes to him from the rocking chair she was sleeping in by his bed.

She grabs a bucket, helps him vomit, wipes his face, and tucks him back under the blanket.

He remains feverish and delirious for days. Hannah stays by his side, tending to him day and night.

Late one afternoon, Carter sits up in bed as Hannah enters.

"You're lookin' better," she chirps.

Carter smiles. "Feelin' a lot better."

"Think you can handle chicken soup?"

Carter nods. "I can handle chicken soup."

She leaves and returns with a bowl. Carter takes it in both hands and slurps it down. In no time, it's gone.

"Do you have more?" he asks, holding out the empty bowl.

Hannah returns with another. As Carter eats, he remembers the soup Peg and her mother made in Mississippi.

When he finishes, he holds the bowl out again. "Can I have more?" he asks sheepishly.

Hannah takes it with a grin. "You'd better slow down. Let that settle, and then we'll see," she says as she walks out.

Carter realizes it's the first time he's thought of Peg or Mississippi in a long while. It feels like a lifetime has passed, though it's only been six months. Hannah reminds him of Peg. She has spark. He wonders how Peg and his family are doing. Lost in thought, he drifts off to sleep.

The next morning, he wakes to find Doc Hill and Charles at his bedside, with Hannah standing behind them.

"You're lookin' good, Carter. Time for you to go home," Doc Hill says.

"I could use more chicken soup," Carter says with a grin.

"I'll bring you some tomorrow," Hannah purrs with a smile.

"Can't remember the last time I had chicken soup. I'll pay if you bring me some, too," Charles jokes.

"I'll bring all y'all a pot tomorrow mornin'," Hannah laughs, emphasizing her Southern drawl.

The next morning, she dishes soup from a pot over a fire in front of their tent. Charles and his tentmates slurp it down for breakfast.

"Best soup I've ever had," George says.

Another tentmate lifts his head from his bowl. "Tastes like home."

"This is my grandma's recipe," Hannah says, turning to Charles. "How's Carter?"

"He's better. We let him sleep in," Charles replies.

Hannah fills a bowl, steps into the tent just as Carter stirs, and sits on the edge of his bed, wrapped in a blanket.

"How are you feelin'?" she asks, handing him the bowl.

"Much better," he says, grabbing it and slurping it down.

"You need to rest for a few more days. Doc Hill says you need beef, beans, and vegetables. I'll bring some by this evening," she promises.

"Are you Doc Hill's…?" Carter begins.

"Nobody owns me," Hannah chides. "I work for Doc Hill. He pays me. Carlton Davis brought me here from Georgia. He got sick. He set me free before he died. I've been working for Doc ever since."

"It must be great to be free."

"I still gotta work, but I get to choose what I do," Hannah replies, looking at Carter. Then she asks, "I take it Charles is…?"

Carter nods. "He's a good man. After Charles finds enough gold, we'll be heading back to Mississippi."

Hannah tilts her head. "Y'all don't sound like you're from Mississippi."

"I guess I picked it up from Charles. He went back East for college and kind of sounds like them."

"Can you teach me how to talk proper?" she asks, her drawl thick but playful.

Carter smiles. "I can teach you—but I like how you talk. It's like a bird singing."

"Doc says he's gonna help me learn to read, but he's too busy," she says as she sighs. "They say California's gonna be a free state. I want to be educated so I can do what I want."

"There've been rumblings," Carter agrees. "Does Doc Hill have any newspapers? I haven't read the news in weeks."

"You can read?" Hannah's eyes widen.

"Keep it a secret. Not good if people know."

"I'll find papers if you help me learn to read, and talk proper." She beams.

"As long as I get chicken soup now and then," Carter laughs.

"I'll give y'all more than chicken soup," she teases, then corrects herself, trying to suppress her accent. "You are going to like my cooking. Now, get some rest. I'll come back this evening with fried chicken."

That evening, Hannah returns to the tent with a small basket. Finding it empty, she shakes her head and smiles, guessing Carter returned to work. She places the basket under his pillow.

Later that night, Carter knocks on Doc Hill's cabin door. He answers, surprised.

"You're up and about already?"

"I'm feeling fine," Carter says. "Charles needed help. The chicken was great. Is Hannah here?"

"Wait in the front room. I'll get her."

Hannah rushes in. "I stopped by, but you weren't there. I hope you weren't working too hard. Are you okay?"

"I'm fine," he says with a smile.

"Hope you liked the chicken. I've got a surprise for you."

She leads him to a small table where a stack of newspapers sits beneath a glowing kerosene lantern. The top headline reads, *Delegates Debate California's Freedom.*

"This looks interesting," Carter says.

"You said you'd teach me. I want to know what these words mean," Hannah insists.

"I'll teach you, but it's not easy. Let me read this one out loud, and then I'll show you some of the words."

He pulls up a chair beside her and flips through the papers until he finds a recent copy of the *Alta California,* dated November 15, 1849. A large ad catches Hannah's eye.

"What's that?" she asks, pointing.

"It's an ad for medicine—*Sands' Sarsaparilla.* They claim it cures everything."

"Maybe you need some of that," Hannah says with a grin. "Doc might want it for our patients."

Carter chuckles. "Charles says it's snake oil. Makes you feel better while they empty your pockets."

"How come they can say things that aren't true?" she asks.

"People can say what they want. It's up to us to be smart enough to know what's true."

"But how am I ever gonna learn to read? There are so many words... all these little letters."

Carter points to the newspaper's masthead. "This word is California. C-A-L-I-F-O-R-N-I-A." He says each letter clearly, then pronounces, "ka·luh·for·nyuh."

"But if the first letter is C, why isn't it see-a-lie-for-in-ya?" she protests.

"It's complicated," Carter admits. "The sound changes depending on what follows. Sometimes you have to recognize the word. It's ka-luh-for-nyuh."

Hannah slumps back in her chair. "It's too hard. I'm never gonna learn to read or talk good."

"You will. It takes time. Try to find California in the text."

She traces the headline with her finger, then scans the column. "California... California... California..." she reads each one aloud, her confidence growing.

"That's very good," Carter praises. "You're getting it."

"There are so many words. What duh they say?" she asks, catching herself. She pauses, then carefully enunciates, "What do they say?"

"Better," Carter nods, smiling. "The article says politicians are meeting in Monterey to decide whether California should be a free state or a slave state."

"Where's Monterey?"

"Didn't you see it on the way here?"

"I was in a stowage compartment at the bottom of the ship. No daylight for weeks. How did you see it?"

"I worked on the ship. I helped gather wood for the steam engine. Our last stop before San Francisco was Monterey."

"Can you tell me about it? Describe the ocean...and Monterey?"

"Close your eyes," Carter says, leaning closer. "I'll tell you."

Hannah closes her eyes. Carter takes a moment to study her in the candlelight—her dark skin glows, her teeth shine with a soft smile. She is the most beautiful woman he has ever seen, he thinks to himself, before closing his eyes to remember Monterey.

"The ocean is a beautiful shade of bright blue," he begins, his voice low and warm. "Waves crash against dark rocks, making white foam as they hit the emerald sea. Seagulls glide above, circling. Pine trees that are twisted by the wind stand tall on the cliffs. The shoreline stretches farther than you can imagine."

Hannah opens her eyes and grabs Carter's hands.

"We must go there. I just imagined it. Is that what happens when you read words? Do you get pictures in your head?"

"A picture can paint a thousand words," Carter says with a grin, "but a word can paint a thousand pictures."

"That's amazing. I must learn how to read," Hannah says, wide-eyed.

"You will. It just takes time and practice," Carter assures her.

"Tell me what the words say about California becoming free. I'll close my eyes." She leans back and shuts them again.

Carter watches her quietly in the candlelight for a moment, absorbed in her beauty.

Doc Hill walks in unseen from behind. He stops to listen from the doorway.

Carter reads softly, trying to shape the story visually for Hannah.

"There were forty-eight men," Carter begins. "They were called delegates from all over the California Territory."

"How were they dressed? Paint me a picture. Tell me everything," Hannah pleads, eyes still closed.

Carter thinks for a moment. "It doesn't say how they were dressed, but I imagine they wore fine suits. Probably stiff collars and polished boots."

"Tell me how you think it was."

Carter draws a breath and closes his eyes, trying to visualize the scene and search for the right words.

"They met in a large room inside a grand white hotel in Monterey. Chairs and tables lined up neatly, facing a speaker's podium. Henry

Crabb held up a Bible and told them that California was a land given to them by God, and they were to reap its riches."

"What?" Hannah's eyes flash open, anger sharp in her voice. "He thinks God gave White people California?"

Carter opens his eyes and looks at her. "Not just California. The whole country. He quoted the apostle Paul—slaves must obey their earthly masters with fear and trembling, as if they were obeying Christ."

Hannah leans forward, jabbing her finger at the text. "They don't think we're human, do they? Obedient to our human masters—what the—" She cuts herself off, shaking her head.

"Some believe that, but others don't," Carter assures her. "A man named Henry Hill from San Diego quoted the Bible, too. He read this to them: 'There is neither Jew nor Greek, neither slave nor free, no male and female, for you are all one in Christ Jesus.'"

"Does the Bible say all that?" Hannah asks, frowning. "How can it say such different things?"

"Words mean different things to different people," Carter explains. "Some twist them to mean what they want to hear."

"How can I ever learn to read if the same words mean different things to different folks?" Hannah sighs. "How will I know what they mean to me?"

"You'll figure it out. It's like listening to people talk—some lie, some say things you disagree with, and some tell the truth. It's up to you to decide what the truth is and what lies are. Reading is the same. I have a Bible. I read it and try to understand it myself.

"I want to read the Bible," Hannah says with conviction. "I want to understand it for myself."

Carter smiles. "You will. I'll bring my Bible. We'll read it together."

He gathers up the newspapers and folds them. Hannah watches him with admiration, then leans in to kiss him. Carter looks up in surprise—

Doc Hill clears his throat. "It's getting late," he says in a fatherly tone. Hannah pulls back as Carter straightens the papers. "I couldn't help but overhear. I had grand plans to help Hannah read, but I haven't had the time. I'm glad you're helping her. But it's late, and tomorrow's a full day."

Hannah shifts uncomfortably, still feeling flustered. "There's a man named Henry Hill in the paper. Do you know him?"

"He's my brother," Doc Hill says with a shrug. "Not sure why he got into politics. Then again, I'm not sure why I became a doctor. I guess we both wanted to help people."

"Is California gonna be free?" Hannah asks, her voice barely above a whisper.

Doc Hill thinks for a moment. "A lot must happen. They're working on a constitution, but Congress, the Senate, and the President must agree. Still, things are leaning that way."

CHAPTER 11
WORKING THROUGH WINTER

Charles presses on in his relentless search for a big strike. Gold seekers flood the region, increasing prices and crowding the easily accessible riverbanks. With Coloma growing more congested, Charles and Carter pack their gear onto Sarah and head north toward the Yuba River. The crisp winter air bites at their faces as they explore the winding tributaries.

Carter helps Charles build a wooden rocker box to sift through the sediment. Unlike panning, the rocker allows them to shovel large amounts of gravel into it. Then they shake it by hand, letting heavier particles, like gold, settle to the bottom. It's more efficient than panning, allowing them to work dry creek beds and other promising spots, but the rains slow them down.

They take shelter under trees, beneath rocky outcroppings, in caves, and inside their tents. Sometimes, it rains for days. They do everything they can to keep Sarah warm and dry. A large canvas offers her shelter from the cold, snow and rain.

Charles uses the runoff from the rain to power a sluice box. Unlike the rocker, the sluice uses flowing water to separate gold from gravel and sediment, making the work faster and less labor-intensive. They try their luck on every creek and stream, but eventually they run low on food. Still, they press on—until a brutal winter storm sweeps in, dumping inches of snow by the hour. Battling wind and snow, they struggle back toward Coloma.

Late that night, they find an empty cabin. Carter surmises that the miners left only a few hours earlier; the coals in the small fireplace still glow. They build a fire and lead Sarah into the cabin. She curls up in a corner, exhausted.

Their food is nearly gone, but they share what little remains—even with Sarah.

The next morning, the sky is a brilliant blue with no clouds. They pack up and return to the trail. It is quiet—no miners, wagons, or people panning in the stream or river. Charles is itching to try his luck, but they are exhausted and low on supplies.

It's dark when they reach Coloma. Music drifts through the trees—singing and laughter fill the air. A crowd is gathered around a tree glowing with small candles. Miners dance and clap. Voices rise, singing a Christmas Carol above a lively, off-key violin.

Charles and Carter wade into the crowd, blinking at the sudden warmth and cheer.

George spots them and shouts, "Where the hell have you been?"

"We've been all over," Charles replies. "What's all this? What's going on?"

"It's Christmas Eve!" George laughs, clapping him on the back. "Looks like you boys just crawled out of frozen hell. Come on and be saved—we've got whiskey, beer, beef, everything you can dream of. Everyone chipped in. Even got carrots for Sarah. Merry Christmas!"

George leads them to a line of wagons overflowing with food and drink. Carter grabs a handful of carrots and feeds Sarah, then helps her sip from a tin of beer. They eat gratefully but drink sparingly as the celebration begins to wind down.

Soon, the mood softens. Laughter fades into quiet conversation. No one wants to be here for Christmas—not deep down. They all long to be home.

Carter notices Charles looking at Emmy's picture before slipping it back into his pocket.

He wonders how his own family, and Peg, might celebrate Christmas. But the truth is cold and hard. He's not there. He may never be there again. There's one person he wants to see. He's unshaven, dirty, smelly, and tired, but it's not too late.

He leads Sarah toward Charles. "I'm going to the tent. I'll feed Sarah, unpack, and clean up. There's something I need to do."

Charles eyes him knowingly. "It's getting late. I'll take Sarah back and unpack. You look fine. I won't wait up."

Carter shrugs, embarrassed, and pulls his Bible from a pack on Sarah's back. "I won't be too late."

Charles smiles and leads Sarah away.

Carter loads a bag of food from the tables. One of his tent-mates hands him a bottle of apple brandy and says, "Merry Christmas."

Carter grins, takes it, and hurries off.

He arrives at Doc Hill's cabin and knocks softly on the door. There is no answer. He knows Hannah has a small room at the back, so he walks to her window and taps.

Rustling. Then he whispers, "It's me, Carter. Merry Christmas."

"Meet me at the front door," Hannah murmurs.

Wrapped in a wool blanket, Hannah opens the door and hugs him. "Merry Christmas! Where have you been?"

"We were high in the mountains. Got stuck in the snow." He holds out his bag of food. "I brought apples, bread, all kinds of things. Even apple brandy. Merry Christmas."

She leads him into the dark cabin to a small table. She lights a lamp and whispers, "We have to be quiet—Doc and the patients are asleep."

Carter lays the food on the table and sets his Bible near the lamp. Hannah picks up an orange, then a bright red apple.

"I've never seen an apple this pretty," she says.

"They said there are orchards here. Can you believe it? Take a bite. Best apple I've ever tasted," Carter says.

"I haven't had one since I left Georgia. There was a big orchard on the plantation." She bites into the apple, and juice runs down her chin. "Oh, my God," she slurps. "I can't believe it." She takes another bite, then nods toward the Bible. "I want to know about Christmas. We weren't allowed to attend church or discuss it. Can you read it to me?"

Carter picks up the Bible. Its warm leather comforts his hands. As he opens it, a picture slips out—Peg—a sharp reminder of how far from home he really is. Hannah picks it up, holding it in the candlelight.

"She's pretty. Your sister?" she asks.

Carter hesitates. "No, she's, well, she's…"

Hannah smiles softly, reading his face. "Your girl, huh? That's all right. She can be your girl in Mississippi. I'll be your girl in California. Now, tell me about Christmas."

Carter is caught off guard by her honesty but can't help but smile. He slips Peg's picture back into the Bible and reads from Luke 2:9-15.

"And an angel of the Lord appeared to them, and the glory of the Lord shone around them, and they were filled with great fear.

And the angel said to them, 'Fear not, for behold, I bring you good news of great joy that will be for all the people.

For unto you is born this day in the city of David a Savior, who is Christ the Lord.

And this will be a sign for you: you will find a baby wrapped in swaddling clothes and lying in a manger.'

And suddenly there was with the angel a multitude of the heavenly host praising God and saying,

'Glory to God in the highest, and on earth peace among those with whom he is pleased!'"

After a quiet moment, Hannah says softly, "That's beautiful. Back in Georgia, they told us the Bible wasn't for us. Do you think Jesus will save us? Do you think God is pleased with us?"

"I think He will," Carter says, meeting her eyes. "And yes—I think He is pleased."

Hannah gestures toward a stack of newspapers in the corner. "I've been saving those for us to read."

"It's getting late," Carter says reluctantly. "I'll come back in the morning. I want to catch up on the news. Charles said we're taking a few days off." He pulls out the small bottle of applejack. "But first, a toast."

They raise the bottle in the candlelight, share a quick drink, and then Carter slips back into the cold.

The next morning, Carter wakes early. The tent is filled with hungover miners, but the camp is quiet. Charles is snoring, Emmy's picture propped on his pillow.

It's a crisp, clear day. Carter makes a pot of coffee and carries the newspaper bundle to a rocky outcrop overlooking the American River.

He pours a steaming cup, sits down, and begins to sort through the papers. Some are from the East, even a few from Mississippi. Most are from California, especially *Alta California,* which is published three times a week.

He skims the papers, most interested in tracking California's struggle for statehood and freedom. He has read the California Constitution, which prohibits slavery. It is promising, but he knows the battle will be long.

He focuses on an article in the *Alta California* dated December 21, 1849. California elects Governor Burnett—another step toward statehood. Carter reads the article several times, unable to believe it. Burnett makes his stance clear: while the California Constitution prohibits slavery, it makes no provision for settlement by free people of color. The constitution bars them from voting and holding offices of honor or profit under the state.

The paper quotes Burnett:

"For some years past, I have given this subject my most serious and candid attention, and I most cheerfully lay before you the result of my own reflections. There is, in my opinion, one of two consistent courses to take in reference to this class of population: either to admit them to the full and free enjoyment of all the privileges guaranteed by the constitution to others, or exclude them from the state. If we permit them to settle in our state, under existing circumstances, we consign them, by our own institutions and the usages of our own society, to a subordinate and degraded position, which is in itself but a species of slavery. They would be placed in a situation where they would have no efficient motives for moral or intellectual improvement, but must remain in our midst, sensible of their degradation, unhappy themselves, enemies to the institutions and the society whose usages have placed them there, and forever fit teachers in all the schools of ignorance, vice, and idleness."

Governor Burnett further explained that California's only option was to exclude Black people and all people of color from entering the state, claiming their presence would only bring more problems. He envisioned an ideal state—one he would govern—without people of color.

Carter puts down the paper and takes a sip of coffee. The openness of the argument against people of color like him is staggering. California seems different. Many people don't judge him by his skin, but now, to have a newly elected governor confront him with such prejudice is jarring. What does the future of California hold for him?

He sips his cold coffee and gazes at the American River. The river seems truly free; no one can ever stop it. Yet the cold, hard truth is that he might never know that kind of freedom. His hopes for liberty, equality, and freedom are dashed. He remains committed to following California's political developments. He worries about Hannah—will she ever be truly free in California?

CHAPTER 12
GOLD!

Carter and Charles labor tirelessly through the relentless downpours of the rainy winter, trekking miles from their base camp in Coloma—northward to the Feather and Yuba Rivers, and southward to Placerville.

Along the way, they witness the emergence of mining camps and the gradual formation of small towns near every river and creek. In this lawless land, the precious gold lies ripe for the taking, yet once a claim is staked, it is fiercely guarded.

Carter stays behind to pan or pick for gold while Charles rides Sarah into the Sierras, searching for a big strike. Most miners spend the winter in the foothills below the snow levels of the mountains. Charles only ventures higher when he is certain he won't be caught in a snowstorm. He plans to take them deeper into the Sierra Nevada mountains in the spring, once the threat of heavy snowfall has passed.

Carter spends time with Hannah when he can, but she is overwhelmed. The influx of gold seekers brings a host of diseases. Doc Hill erects large tents for patients near his cabin. He is joined by a newly arrived doctor from the East, who hires several women as nurses to assist Hannah.

Carter finds gold in several locations near Mosquito Creek, a small tributary of the South Fork of the American River. It is one of the areas marked with an X on Bill's map. They search the mountain slopes along the creek, taking advantage of the rainfall and using a sluice box where the small streams converge. It proves productive. They find more gold in a day than they usually find in a week.

As the weather grows warmer and drier, they use pickaxes and shovels to work their way down the ravine. The rocker box helps them separate gold from dirt and stones. They find more and more flecks of gold.

"This gold has to be coming from somewhere up this ravine," Charles says as he and Carter rest on a large boulder in the hot sun.

"We'll follow it up the mountain," Charles continues, picking up a large chunk of white quartz. "Keep looking for rocks like this. Gold's usually found in quartz veins." He points across the ravine. "You work that area. Chip at any quartz you see. I'll work this side. There's got to be a large formation."

"How do you know gold's in quartz?" Carter asks.

"Studied it in college and read about it," Charles replies. "Millions of years ago, volcanoes spat out rocks and lava. Sometimes quartz and gold flow together." He points down the ravine. "Wind, ice, and rain broke it all down over time. That's how the small gold flecks and nuggets get into the river."

Carter studies the rock formations and boulders. "The Bible says that God created heaven and earth. How can we ever know how or why? Should we even try?"

"He gave us two hands, two legs, and a brain," Charles answers. "He wants us to figure it out. If we don't try, we won't do. If we don't do, why are we here?" He looks up at the blue sky and puffy white clouds. "We are here to do. It's a glorious day to find gold."

Carter stretches and grabs his pickaxe. He glances down the ravine across the mountainside, then up at the deep blue sky.

"Every day is a glorious day. Gold or no gold," Carter says. "I guess we'll all know what it's about someday."

"We're living in a moment of sunlight," Charles muses. "We must find our destiny before the sun sets."

Carter turns to him. "Is that from the Bible?"

Charles chuckles. "I wrote it for an English class."

They walk to their sides of the ravine and toil for hours under the hot late-winter sun.

Carter picks at a large mound of rocks and uncovers a streak of white quartz. He chips away, revealing more. He swings hard, and the vein of quartz widens.

With a mighty swing, Carter knocks loose a chunk of rock as large as his head. It rolls into the sunlight, revealing an unmistakable vein of shimmering gold running through the white quartz.

"I found gold!" Carter calls out as he admires the rock, tracing a shiny stream of gold with his finger.

Charles scrambles across the mountainside to reach him. He inspects the rock.

"That's gold!" Charles gasps, breathless from the run. "Crack it open."

Carter swings his pickaxe and smashes the rock. They sift through the fragments, gathering every piece laced with gold.

"Where did this come from?" Charles asks.

Carter points to the rock outcropping above. "There."

Charles walks up to the boulders, pickaxe in hand. Carter follows.

Charles runs his hand across the bright white quartz and brushes loose chips away, revealing a gold stream.

"We found it, Carter!" he cries, swinging his pickaxe at the boulder. Shards of quartz fly as he works, pausing only to marvel at the gleaming surface. "Look at this!"

Carter steps up as Charles traces a half-inch-wide line of gold running over a foot long. "This is it. This is our motherload. I'm sure the vein keeps going."

"Take a breather. I got this," Carter says, lifting his pickaxe and striking the boulder.

Jagged chunks of quartz fly like snowballs. Charles picks them up and examines each one—most glitter with gold. The vein thickens.

They take turns digging until dusk, sweat-soaked and aching. Before them lies a shallow mine, its quartz walls streaked with gold. A growing pile of gold-laced rocks shimmers in the fading light. They exchange a look of disbelief.

"We need to stay and work this vein," Charles says. "We'll hide the gold where no one can find it. First, we eat. Then rest. We've got long days ahead."

They make camp near the claim. The hills provide plenty of grass for Sarah, and water pools across the ravine. At night, they sleep with pistols under their pillows, waking at every sound, but each morning brings fresh energy. The gold drives them.

They follow the vein for days, swinging pickaxes under the late winter sun. The gold gradually thins.

They pry the gold from the quartz, carefully removing each chunk. They find clever hiding spots along the ridge under boulders, behind brush, and conceal the gold with fresh dirt and branches. Charles marks each location on his map.

One crisp morning, Charles doesn't stir as Carter prepares breakfast. When he finally rises, Carter hands him a cup of coffee.

"I'm afraid that's the last of the coffee," Carter says as he sighs, pulling six hardtack biscuits from a small sack. "And the last of these, too."

Charles takes a slow sip, steam rising from his breath. "Take Sarah and ride back for supplies. We don't need much. This vein's thinning out. I'll stay and clean up what's left. Then we'll take the gold to San Francisco. I need to send it to my father and get more help. There's more gold."

"How you gonna send gold to Mississippi?"

Charles takes another sip. "There are ways. I could ship it as gold, but most likely, I'll convert it to banknotes."

"You mean turn gold into paper?" Carter questions, frowning in disbelief.

Charles laughs. "More or less. I'll show you when we get to San Francisco."

"Getting the gold to San Francisco could be dangerous," Carter reminds him.

"I'm thinking about that." Charles exhales. "We'll be safer in a group. I might need to hire help. We'll buy more mules."

After breakfast, Carter packs for the ride back to Coloma.

Charles hands him several gold coins. "That should cover it. Don't tell a soul. If anyone asks, we're striking out. Just trying to get by. Be careful—make sure no one follows you. Keep your gun close."

"I won't tell anyone anything," Carter says. "You be careful, too."

"I'll sleep with one eye open." Charles chuckles. "Tell Doc and Hannah I say hi." As Carter rides Sarah down the mountainside, Charles adds, "Take your time. I've got enough biscuits and coffee for a few days."

Carter reaches Doc's cabin early in the evening. He is a dirty mess, but can't wait to see Hannah.

Surprised to see him, Hannah hurries him into the kitchen and sets a steaming bowl of soup, rice, beans, and half a loaf of bread in front of him. He devours it.

She glances at the flecks of gold beneath his dirty fingernails, gleaming in the lamplight. She doesn't say a word.

After a moment, she leaves the room and returns with her hands behind her back. "I've got a surprise," she says, beaming. She holds out a tattered school primer. "Doc bought it for me. He's been helping, and some patients have helped me learn, too."

She sits down and reads slowly, trying to hide her drawl: "In Juan's fall. We sin all. Thy life to mend, God's book attend. The cat doth play, and after slay. A dog bites a thief at night."

"You're doing great," Carter says, glowing with pride. "What are the A, B, C, and D words?"

"A is for all. B is for book. C is for cat. D is for dog," Hannah chortles. "You'll have to help me. I've been saving papers for you."

"I'm only in town for a few days," Carter says, "but I'll help. We can read together tomorrow."

"Are you and Charles having any luck?" she asks, hoping he might open up about the gold shining under his nails.

"No," Carter lies. "It's been rough. Charles keeps looking and looking. I've got to get back soon and help him."

"Lots of people are finding gold. Doc treated a man from the Sweet Vengeance mine the other day. They asked Doc how to get it to a bank and send some home. Do you think Charles could help?"

"I heard people talking about the Sweet Vengeance," Carter replies. "They say it's a group of free Black men with a mine near Yuba City."

"That's right. Rumor is they've found a lot of gold."

"If we find any, I'm sure Charles will know how to keep it safe. Maybe he can help them, too. I'll ask him," Carter says, dodging the question.

Hannah walks into the dark corner of the cabin and returns with a bundle of newspapers.

"I've been saving these for you." Hannah smiles, handing them over. "Don't forget to ask Charles if he can help the men at Sweet Vengeance with their gold."

Carter cradles the papers. "Thanks. I'll be sure to ask," he says as he rushes out the door.

Hannah stands in the doorway, watching him walk away. She hopes she hasn't upset him by bringing up the gold—or the Sweet Vengeance—but deep down, she believes it was right.

Carter is rattled, but more from fear than frustration. He knows she saw the gold under his nails. He worries that someone might catch wind of the rich vein they found. He keeps to himself and speaks to no one.

He buys supplies and, by late afternoon, he swings a pickaxe beside Charles.

They chip at the rock for several days, following the vein, but all they find is quartz. Eventually, it gives way to grey granite.

Charles studies the stone. "I think we've gotten all we can from this spot, at least for now. The vein must continue farther back, but we need help digging it out."

He steps away and sits by the fire, sipping coffee across from Carter.

"What are you thinking?" Carter asks.

"It's time to send money to my father and bring in more help," Charles says.

"Hannah said the men at the Sweet Vengeance found gold and were wondering how to keep it safe and send some back home. She thought you might be able to help," Carter says without thinking.

Charles snaps back, "Did you tell Hannah we've found gold?"

"I didn't tell her anything! I swear!"

Charles' blue eyes dig deep into Carter's dark brown ones.

"Sorry I doubted you," Charles consoles. "We've got to get the gold to a bank in San Francisco as fast as possible. They will exchange it for banknote certificates and send them to a bank in New Orleans. My father can collect it there. I plan to ask him to send more men."

Charles stares into the fire. "The hard part is getting the gold to San Francisco. That stretch is crawling with thieves. We'll need a plan. We need to travel with people we can trust. But who can we trust?"

"What about George and the others from our tent?" Carter offers.

"I've thought about it." Charles pauses, firelight flickering across his face. "But they'll want a share. I'm not sure I trust them."

His voice trails off, and he falls silent, gazing into the fire.

Carter breaks the long silence. "What about the folks at the Sweet Vengeance? They say they found lots of gold. They don't need more. They need help. Maybe they can be trusted."

Charles shakes his head. "I've heard of the Sweet Vengeance mine. Folks say they're tough as nails. Do you think I should team up with a group of free Black men—and maybe some not-so-free ones—to get my money to San Francisco and on to Mississippi?"

"Just figured I'd mention it," Carter mutters as he shrugs.

Charles bites into a biscuit and dips it into his coffee. He chews thoughtfully, then looks up and smiles.

"I guess this is the way it is. Not the way I want it to be, but it is how things are. I'll head to Coloma, get more supplies, and talk to Doc and Hannah. Maybe I can help the Sweet Vengeance men, and they can help us. It might be a few days before I'm back. Do you have enough to get by?"

"There's still some beans, sugar, and flour. I'll try to scare up a rabbit," Carter replies with a grin.

"Or maybe a turkey," Charles laughs.

Carter shakes his head. "I ain't huntin' no more turkeys. They get me into trouble."

They laugh, and Charles stands up from the fire. "I'll head out in the morning and be back in two days."

Carter tends to the claim, mostly standing guard and resting. Days pass uneventfully until one late afternoon, when a sound in the distance causes him to freeze. He grabs the shotgun and crouches behind a rock, aiming toward the trail that leads into camp.

Charles rounds the bend between the trees. He sees Carter and looks at the shotgun barrel. He raises his hands.

"Just me, Carter. Don't shoot."

Carter lowers the shotgun as Charles rides into camp, leading three mules. One carries a saddle, while the others carry supplies.

"Thought you'd never get back. I'm about to starve," Carter chuckles. "What's with all the mules?"

"One's for you. The other two are for the gold. I also brought food and supplies. I'm starving. Let's eat."

They sit by the fire a few minutes later, devouring fresh food. The smell alone lifts Carter's spirits.

He slices into a piece of meat, takes a bite, and sighs. "Can't remember the last time I had beef."

Charles grins. "I hope it's beef. They told me it was, but I'm not sure whether it used to whinny or moo. Either way, it tastes a hell of a lot better than hard tack and beans."

They laugh and dig into the food, washing it down with coffee.

"So," Carter asks between bites, "what's the plan for the gold?"

"I talked to Doc. He says the men at Sweet Vengeance can be trusted. I met one of them. His name is Fritz. He's going to organize a group from the mine and a few men from the Negro Bar tent camp. I'll help them get their gold to the bank in San Francisco."

Carter raises an eyebrow. "That's a lot of folks. And…well, it's just you. You trust them?"

"There's safety in numbers," Charles answers with confidence. "They need me, and we need them."

They fall into silence, the crackle of the fire filling the space. Charles watches Carter's face—thoughtfully, yet troubled.

"I know what you're thinking. It might raise eyebrows that I'm helping them. But nobody can know. Especially not the others from the South."

He leans toward Carter. "I have a perfect plan. We're not going by ship or through Sacramento—too many thieves. We'll head south down the valley, then circle up the west side of the San Francisco Bay. Should be safer."

He unrolls a map and points to a spot southeast of the San Francisco Bay.

"We'll meet the group here in two days. Spend a night with them and another man from Mariposa. Then we'll travel to San Francisco by land, around the bay."

"I'm sure they'll appreciate your help," Carter says with a small smile.

"I'll appreciate their help when we get the gold to the bank in one piece," Charles replies. "We leave first thing in the morning."

CHAPTER 13
IT'S ONLY GOLD

The sun shines on a crisp morning as Charles and Carter leave their claim. Charles rides ahead on Sarah, leading a mule loaded with gold and supplies. Behind him, Carter rides a dark mule and holds the reins of another loaded mule. Both men wear their pistols openly at their waists, and Carter keeps his shotgun in a sheath by the saddle, ready for trouble.

They ride from sunrise to sunset, avoiding well-worn trails. The landscape unfolds in quiet isolation as they enter the Sacramento Valley—no towns, no people, only scattered oak trees, thick brush, and tall grass waving in the breeze. At one point, they spot a group of men on horseback in the distance and duck into the brush, waiting until the riders pass out of sight.

That night, they take turns sleeping, each standing watch with a wary eye on the gold.

The next afternoon, they head toward the spot marked on Charles' map, nestled in the hills southeast of San Francisco Bay. They find a shady rise between two large oaks and stop to scan the valley.

Charles pulls out his telescope, scanning the golden hills and tree-lined ridges.

"I see them. They should be here soon," he says, squinting through the lens. "They're not being followed."

A short while later, Charles and Carter walk down the slope to greet seven men approaching on mules. Each rider leads one or two pack mules loaded with gear.

"So, there are seven?" Carter asks, keeping his voice low.

"Yeah. Three from Sweet Vengeance, three from Negro Bar, and one from Agua Fria near Mariposa."

The group comes to a slow stop as Charles and Carter step forward.

"I'm Charles, and this is Carter," Charles says, raising a hand in greeting.

A stocky man with short-cropped hair and a thick black beard rides at the front. It's Fritz.

"Glad to see you, I wasn't sure," Fritz says in a distinct New England accent. He gestures to the men flanking him. "That's James, and that's William. We're from Sweet Vengeance." He nods toward the others. "That's Carl, Andrew, and Frank. They're from Negro Bar." Then he points to the last man riding up behind them. "And that's Moses. He's from Agua Fria."

"Nice to meet y'all," Charles says in a pleasant drawl.

"Let's make camp and get something to eat. We head out first thing in the morning," Fritz suggests as he dismounts.

The group falls into an easy rhythm, tending to the animals and building a fire without instruction. Each man knows precisely what to do, as if they've ridden together for years. Supper is simple—beans and hard tack—but the food and fire are hot.

Later, they sit around the fire, sipping coffee and swapping stories. Charles and Carter mostly listen.

Andrew Jackson—a tall man with weathered hands and deep-set eyes—shares his story. He was enslaved. His master brought him west, but he died of fever shortly after arriving in California. Left behind, Andrew continued working to support himself, believing he was free. But back home in the South, newspapers claimed he had escaped.

To clear his name and avoid being hunted, Andrew, with the help of friends, wrote a letter to his master's widow, offering to purchase his freedom.

He pulls a folded letter from his pocket. "I can't read, but folks tell me she says I can buy my freedom for fifteen hundred dollars." He hands the paper to Charles. "Can you make sure that's what it says? And help me send the money?"

Charles takes the letter and scans it by the firelight.

"That's what it says. I'll help you." He hands the paper to Carter. "Why don't you read it to him?"

Carter grins and begins reading aloud.

Andrew's eyes widen in disbelief. "You can read? Well, I'll be a son of a bitch."

Once Carter finishes, he hands the letter back. "You're going to be free."

Andrew stares at the paper. "How will I know? How can I be sure no one comes after me?"

Charles leans in. "We'll send the money to a bank back home, with a letter asking her to sign a statement confirming your freedom. When she sends it back, we'll keep a copy in the bank and send you one, too."

Andrew folds the letter and slides it into his pocket. It's worth more than gold.

"I'm going to be free!" he exclaims as he stands, raises his hand to the sky, and walks into the dark.

The others sit in silence, watching the fire, until Carl finally speaks:

"I appreciate you helping us. I want to bank some, coin some, and send some home back East. Can you help me do all that?"

"Sure will," Charles replies. "Do you want to send it home as gold or as a bill of exchange?"

"I'm thinkin' gold," Carl says. "But how does a bill of exchange work?"

The others lean in, listening, all wondering the same thing.

"The bank exchanges the gold for a piece of paper that gets sent to a bank near your family," Charles explains. "They have to prove it's theirs and sign for it. After that, they can keep it in the bank or cash it out."

"How do I know it gets there?" Carl asks.

"Whether you send it as gold or a bill of exchange, it's insured. No one gets the money unless they sign for it," Charles assures him.

"We asked around, trying to figure out the safest way," Fritz adds. "Charles is right—this is the best method we've heard."

The group splinters into small conversations. A few minutes later, Fritz stands and addresses them.

"We'd best get some sleep. We'll be movin' out early, and we need someone on watch." He pulls a stopwatch from his coat. "I'll take the first hour. Who wants the second?"

"I got it," Carl says, raising a hand.

Everyone takes turns standing guard before settling in for the night. Fritz walks over to Charles, motioning for him to step away from the fire.

"Can I talk to you a minute?" he asks, lowering his voice as they move beyond earshot of the others. "Don't take this the wrong way, but the guys and I were talking. California's free soil. We're wondering— do you pay Carter?"

Charles stiffens, caught off guard, but he takes his time answering. He recalls telling Carter he'd pay him wages when they agreed to live in the tent with George and the others, but he hasn't followed through. There seemed to be no need.

"He gets room and board," Charles replies. "I take good care of him."

Fritz nods slowly. "Ain't my place to tell you what to do. But if you were to pay him for his work, it'd help the boys trust you. Might make things smoother down the line." He pauses, watching Charles carefully. "Figured it might be weighing on you."

A flush rises up on Charles' neck. Fritz's remarks haven't caught him off guard—they mirrored thoughts he'd entertained before. He has reassured himself that money won't concern Carter. After all, what use would he have for it? But the moral landscape in California is changing. The opposition to slavery is getting stronger, yet at least half the population endorses it.

Charles has gold now and will soon have more. Paying Carter ten dollars a month is a small price to pay for peace of mind—and loyalty.

"Do you pay folks at the Sweet Vengeance? What are wages like?" he asks.

"Ten dollars a month, plus room and board. That's the going rate."

Charles exhales slowly, feeling the pressure of Fritz's gaze—and his conscience. "Didn't realize labor costs that much," he mutters. After a pause, he adds, "Seems fair. I'll give him ten dollars a month, starting from the day we arrived in California. And I'll keep paying him moving forward."

Fritz extends a hand. "Doc and Hannah said you are fair-minded. Appreciate it."

Charles finds Carter near the trees, laying his bedroll near Sarah and the mules.

"I've been thinking—and had some help thinking," Charles says. He pauses, choosing his words. "You work hard. I told you I'd pay you, and I think it's time I make good on that."

Carter looks up but says nothing.

"I'll pay you ten dollars a month, starting from when we get to California. From now on, every month."

Carter blinks, still processing. "How much do I owe you for food and supplies?"

"You owe me nothing," Charles replies.

"Not sure what I can use the money for," Carter says quietly. "Doubt I'll get to spend it in Mississippi."

"We'll cross that bridge when we get there. For now, you can buy whatever you want or save it." Charles yawns and lays out his bedroll a few feet away. "Get some sleep. Tomorrow's going to be a big day."

In the pre-dawn light, a man steps out from the trees. His face is hidden beneath a wide-brimmed hat and a handkerchief. A double-barrel shotgun hangs in his hands. Frank sits alone, keeping watch by the fire, his pistol resting in his lap. He doesn't notice the man.

Then, three more figures emerge, masked and armed. They move silently into a line behind their leader, revolvers raised. Just ten yards away, the leader steps on a branch—*snap*.

Frank jolts awake, eyes wide, his pistol quickly trained on the bandit.

"Drop the gun!" the bandit leader barks in a thick Southern drawl, leveling the shotgun at Frank's chest.

"Nobody moves, or it'll be the last thing you do!" the bandit shouts to the rest.

Frank stays still, his gun trained on the bandit.

The others stir. Groggy voices, shifting blankets. Confusion.

Charles and Carter lie near the trees at the back of the camp, the mules and gold behind them. Beneath their blankets, each man silently reaches for his pistol.

"There are only four of you," Fritz says, propping himself on one elbow. Beneath his blanket, his right hand holds his pistol pointed at the lead bandit.

Carter, close by, angles his weapon under his blanket toward a second bandit, Bible clutched in his left hand.

"We've got enough bullets. A couple for each of you," the bandit leader snarls.

"You'll never get away with this," Charles calls out, his hand wrapped tight around the grip of his pistol under the blanket.

"What do we have here?" the bandit sneers. "A White man helping niggers. Looks like you picked the wrong crowd. We'll be glad to take your gold."

"You picked the wrong side," Charles shoots back. "It's only gold. Not worth anybody's life. Not even yours."

The bandit laughs. "May not be worth dying for, but it's worth killing for, but nobody has to die. Just put your hands up, load the mules for us, and we'll be gone."

"You plan to kill us anyway," Fritz growls.

"That's option number two. What'll it be? Your lives or the gold?"

A heavy silence settles. The miners glance at one another. A shared understanding passes between them. They will not give up their gold without a fight.

"Now!" Fritz shouts, firing at the lead bandit. The shot hits him square in the chest. He stumbles backward, squeezing the trigger as he falls. His shotgun roars skyward in a wild blast.

Just a few feet away from the bandit, Frank fires and hits him in the chest. The bandit staggers, gasping, then manages to unleash one final shot. The blast catches Frank in the chest.

Gunfire erupts from both sides. Black powder smoke fills the cold morning air, blending with the dawn's haze. Carter aims for the bandit farthest to the right and squeezes the trigger. His bullet strikes the man high in the chest, but the bandit fires back, hitting Carter in the left ribs.

Carter drops his pistol and rolls onto his side, groaning, one hand clutching his ribs. Charles fires at the same man, dropping him where he stands.

The gunfight lasts only seconds, but each shot echoes like thunder. When it ends, smoke hangs low over the camp. The only sound is the metallic click of the Sweet Vengeance miners reloading and cocking their pistols.

Charles rushes to Carter, who lies face down. He rolls him over gently, and Carter moans as Charles opens his jacket. A small leather pouch tumbles from an inside pocket. Gold nuggets and dust spill out, glinting in the early light. A crimson stain spreads down Carter's vest, the blood streaked with flecks of gold.

Charles unbuttons the vest and tears Carter's shirt open. A ragged wound crosses his left side, blood seeping between the ribs.

Carter tries to sit up. "How bad is it?"

"You're lucky you were wearing that vest, and had a pouch of gold. It looks like the bullet hit the pouch and glanced off your ribs," Charles says, inspecting the contents. He holds up a flattened gold nugget with fragments of lead. "The bullet hit this."

He presses a torn shirt on Carter's wound. "I'll take you back to Doc."

"We need to get the gold to the bank," Carter says, grimacing. "We need to help the others. I'll be okay."

Carter grabs the bloody shirt with a shaky hand, gritting his teeth. He presses it to the wound as Charles pulls back. He sits up. They turn toward the group, surveying the aftermath.

The bandit that Carter and Charles shot is lying face up, surrounded by grim-faced miners.

"I've got to see him," Carter says, trying to rise.

"Are you sure?" Charles asks as he steadies Carter and helps him to his feet.

"I'm sure," Carter says, gritting his teeth as they approach the fallen bandit. All the others are dead. On the way, they pass Carl, who kneels beside Frank's body, his shoulders shaking with grief.

They reach the dying bandit just as Fritz yanks off the handkerchief covering his face. The man's breath comes in ragged gasps, blood coating his teeth and dribbling from the corners of his mouth.

"I've seen you before, you son of a bitch," Fritz spits. "You got slaves workin' near Ophir."

"I know him," Charles says coldly. "I recognize all of them."

The bandit's lips tremble. "We weren't as lucky as you. We just wanted more money for our families. We're gonna go back home," he chokes, eyes glistening with pain.

"Your luck ran out today," Carter growls, his hand still pressed to his wounded chest, gaze fixed on the man who shot him.

"I've got gold in my pocket... for my wife and kids. I was writin' them a letter. Will you send it?" He coughs, spitting blood. "I just wanted enough..." His voice trails off.

"I'll make sure it gets to them," Charles asserts.

The man gives a faint, bloody smile. "Thanks. I..." His eyes lose focus. His chest falls still.

Fritz turns on Charles, furious. "What the hell are you thinkin'? He's a lyin', thievin' bastard!"

Charles stands tall. "His family didn't do this. I gave a dying man my word. It's the right thing to do."

The others mutter among themselves. Their voices are tired and angry.

"Let it be," Fritz snaps. "Whatever these other bastards have is goin' to their slaves. We'll make sure they go free." He fixes Charles with a hard stare. "You got a problem with that?"

"I got no problem with that," Charles replies.

Another miner speaks up. "So what now?"

"We take the bodies to the sheriff in San Francisco," Charles says. "Tell him everything."

"He won't believe us," James mutters as he steps forward, clutching his bleeding arm.

"It's the right thing to do," Charles insists.

Fritz scowls. "I'm sick of hearin' about the 'right thing to do.' Maybe they'll believe you, but they won't believe us. The law ain't on our side. Justice has been done. I say we bury the bodies. Nobody needs to know what happened here."

"That's right," Carl agrees. "If anyone finds out, we're done for. They'll come down on us hard."

"You got a problem with that?" Fritz asks, glaring at Charles.

Charles looks at the weary, wounded faces of the men. Carter nods in agreement. After a pause, he says, "I got no problem with that. No one needs to know."

"Good. We'll bury 'em down in the ravine," Fritz continues, but Carl cuts him off.

"I'll take Frank back. Bury him near our claim. He'd want that," Carl says, voice cracking.

"What about his gold? And yours?" Fritz asks.

"My gold'll keep. I'll split his with the others. Far as I know, he ain't got no family."

Fritz nods and turns to James. "Let me look at that arm. Anyone else shot?"

"I was," Carter says. "Bullet glanced off my ribs."

"I've got salve and bandages. I'll fix you both up. Then we dig," Fritz advises.

The men grab picks and shovels. They dig shallow graves in the ravine and wrap the four bandits in blankets. Rocks and dirt pile high over the bodies, enough to keep scavengers away and the secret buried.

"Are we just gonna bury them like this? No words?" Moses asks solemnly.

"They got what they deserved," Fritz scolds.

Carter pauses, feeling the heavy burden of having shot and killed a man. He strides forward, opens his Bible, and discovers bloodstains on its pages—his blood.

"I'll say a few words," he says. "No man should ever have to kill or be killed."

The others remove their hats and bow their heads.

"Dear Lord," Carter begins, low but steady, "we stand before you in grief, with confusion in our hearts. Help us find peace. Help guide us through this darkness. We do not know what led these men to such foolishness and greed. But we ask that you ease the guilt and burden we carry for sending them to you this morning."

He turns to Matthew 6:19-20 and reads: "Lay not up for yourselves treasures upon earth, where moth and rust doth corrupt, and where thieves break through and steal. But lay up for yourselves treasures in heaven, where neither moth nor rust doth corrupt, and where thieves do not break through nor steal. We give these men to you for judgment. Help us to forgive them—and help us forgive ourselves."

He flips to Luke 6:37, where Peg's picture rests as a makeshift bookmark.

"Judge not, and you will not be judged; condemn not, and you will not be condemned; forgive, and you will be forgiven."

Then he begins to recite the 23rd Psalm.

"The Lord is my shepherd; I shall not want."

The men join in, their voices quiet but steady as they follow along with Carter's words.

"He makes me lie down in green pastures; He leads me beside still waters. He restores my soul; He leadeth me in the paths of righteousness for His name's sake. Yea, though I walk through the valley of the shadow of death, I will fear no evil, for You are with me; Your rod and Your staff, they comfort me. You prepare a table before me in the presence of my enemies; You anoint my head with oil; My cup runneth over. Surely goodness and mercy shall follow me all the days of my life: and I will dwell in the house of the Lord forever. Amen."

The men stand in silence, each lost in thought, weighed down by the morning's violence and reminded once again how easily life can be snatched away. Death lingers close in California, and none were strangers to it.

Fritz finally breaks the silence. "We've got to get moving. Grab your shovels." He turns to Carter. "That was a fine prayer. A good friend of mine—Reverend Blue—started a church in Sacramento. I get there when I can. You should go."

Carter glances at Charles, who gives him a nod of approval.

"You can take Sundays off," Charles says.

"I'll get there when I can," Carter assures Fritz.

They walk away solemnly to grab a quick breakfast and load their gear.

Fritz steps close to Carter and pulls him aside.

"We've got to stick together. California's free. If you ever need help, you can come find us."

"I will," Carter says, his voice firm. "I surely will."

It is late afternoon when the group makes its way down a gravel road toward San Francisco. They keep their thoughts to themselves, still overwhelmed from the morning gunfight. Carter takes in the city with quiet astonishment. In just six months, it has transformed. Buildings rise in every direction, and the streets bustle with new arrivals. What once felt raw and scattered now surges with energy and ambition.

Charles leads the group down a crowded street and stops outside a clothing store. "Wait here a few minutes. I'll be right back."

The group fidgets impatiently until Charles reappears in short order, dressed in a dark wool suit. His worn dungarees and trail-stained coat are gone. Black dress shoes gleam where dusty boots had been, though his beard and shaggy hair remain.

Fritz gives a low whistle. "You clean up well." Laughter ripples through the group.

Charles grins. "Figured it might help. Let's head to the bank."

Fritz looks the group over, then eyes the bathhouse across the street. "That's good for you, but what about the rest of us? We're going, too. And you still haven't shaved or taken a bath. We all smell like mules."

He points at the bathhouse. "I say we all get cleaned up and buy new clothes before we walk into any bank."

"What about our gold?" Moses questions.

"We'll take turns. Half stand guard while the rest bathe." Fritz nods toward a group of uniformed policemen down the street. "Our gold's safe here."

Charles negotiates with the bathhouse manager and pays a few gold coins. The Black men are told they have to share the tubs in the back and shave themselves. No one argues.

After scrubbing away the grime and cleaning up, they cross the street to the clothing store.

Carter hesitates. He isn't sure whether they're allowed to buy anything. In California, the rules change from town to town—often depending on who you are and who you talk to. Charles goes in first, clean-shaven now, his long hair trimmed, and his suit pressed.

He emerges moments later. "Carter, Fritz, Moses—you're up first. Then we switch and guard while the rest of you go in."

Carter steps into the store, uncertain if Charles has made some sort of arrangement. But the moment he passes through the doorway, his worries fade. The scent of laundered fabric greets him. Racks of jackets, trousers, and shirts fill the room. Shelves of dress boots line the back wall.

Three clerks approach to help. One of them says, "You're all welcome here. Look around. We have the finest clothes in San Francisco or anywhere."

"I think this one's for you, Carter," Charles says, holding a suit coat.

Carter steps to a full-length mirror. It's the first time he's seen himself head to toe. His reflection stares back—dusty, worn, shirt bloodstained and bandaged.

Like the others, he is used to cotton shirts, a neckerchief to soak up sweat, thick trousers, and a heavy coat. He looks down at his square-toed leather boots, scuffed from miles of trail.

He unbuttons his shirt and checks the wound at his side. The bandage is soaked with blood, but the bleeding has stopped.

Charles steps beside him, eyeing the wound. "You alright? I think it'll heal fine, but we'll get you to a doctor."

"I'm fine," Carter says, buttoning his shirt again.

Charles drapes the dark blue frock coat over Carter's shoulders. It falls just above his knees.

"How often am I going to wear this?" Carter mutters.

"It's wool. You can wear it whenever you like. Wear it to the bank. We'll have a nice dinner this evening. Hannah will like your suit," Charles adds with a wink.

"And how am I supposed to pay for this?"

"I've got it. Save your money. Come on, try on the pants and shoes. I'll get you a couple of shirts."

Minutes later, Carter stands before a full-length mirror in a dark blue suit, a crisp white shirt, and a light blue silk cravat. He looks down at the polished black shoes, so much like the pair Charles gave him back in Mississippi.

Soon after, the well-dressed group arrives at a wooden building flanked by guards holding rifles. A large sign reads: *Naglee and Company. Gold Coined. Bills of Exchange.*

Charles hitches Sarah to a post and dismounts. The men scan the street and position themselves around their mules, hands resting on pistol grips as they guard their sacks of gold.

Fritz walks up to Charles. "You go first. I'll come in with you. Then we can help the others."

Charles and Carter remove the saddlebags from their mules and walk with Fritz to the guards at the front door. One of them holds up a hand.

"No guns inside."

They hand their pistols to Moses with care.

Inside, a rigid man stands behind the counter, sharp-eyed and unmoved. Years of service in the Mexican-American War have carved the soldier into Naglee.

"We've got gold for exchange," Charles says, dropping a heavy bag on the counter.

"We've got gold from men of color like me. Is that a problem?" Fritz adds.

Naglee's voice is firm. "The only color I care about is gold."

Charles opens the bag and pulls out a folded letter from the dead bandit. "I'd like to start with this. I want the gold to go with the letter."

"You want it sent as gold or as a bill of exchange?"

Charles considers, then produces a small picture of the dead man's family. "Send it as gold coins."

He takes a sheet of paper and writes a note to the family, omitting the circumstances of the man's death but making clear that it was his dying wish that they receive the gold.

Naglee passes the gold to an assistant, who weighs it and scrawls a note. "Comes to one hundred and thirty-six dollars. Ten for insurance, five for the letter," Naglee says.

Charles nods and passes over a coin. "I'll cover the cost for insurance and the letter."

He folds the letter and slides it across the table. Naglee passes it to his assistant.

"Who's next?" Naglee asks.

Fritz gestures to Charles. "You go on."

"I guess it's my turn," Charles says, stepping forward with Carter. Together, they unload their vests filled with gold.

Carter, in a clean shirt, still bears the signs of his injury. Blood has seeped through his bandages. He pulls out a bloody nugget, creased by the bullet, and lays it on the counter.

Charles picks it up, studies it, and hands it back. "Keep this one. It's lucky."

Trying to lighten the mood, Carter shrugs. "Fell off my mule. Landed on a sharp branch."

Naglee eyes the nugget and sees the truth. "Gold comes at a high price. Some people will kill for it."

"Some try," Charles replies. Naglee nods and pushes the sacks toward his assistants. Charles leans in. "If it's all the same, I'd like a note on how much there is. No need to share it with the others."

He pulls out a piece of paper and writes a note to his father. Carter peeks but only catches fragments—names like Sandy and Robert. Carter smiles to himself.

The assistants weigh the gold. It takes time. When the note comes back, Charles reads it, smiles faintly, and writes instructions: how much to send to his father, how much to deposit, how much to receive in coins.

Naglee nods. "You'll get a mix—twenty-dollar gold eagles and Mormon twenties."

"That's fine," Charles says.

Stacks of gold coins are pushed across the counter, five hundred dollars' worth.

Charles picks up an eagle, studies the Liberty head, flips it to see the crest, and the eagle with bold letters United States of America and Twenty D written around it. Then he lifts a Mormon coin: TO THE LORD HOLINESS around a crown and all-seeing eye, and on the back, clasped hands beneath the words PURE GOLD. TWENTY DOLLARS. 1849.

"Eagles or Mormons?" Charles asks Carter.

Carter considers. He remembers being turned away by Sam Brannan, the sermons calling Black people cursed, the Mormon prophets who said his skin color bore the mark of Cain.

He picks up an eagle coin again and considers the word Liberty on one side and the eagle on the other—symbols of freedom—yet he has neither.

"I'll take eagles, if it's all the same."

Charles reads his face and nods. "Gold is gold. Eagles, it is."

He counts out one eagle for each month they've been in California, stacking them before Carter. Then he slides over one more.

"That's for saving my life in Panama."

Carter pushes it back. "I didn't save you. You fought the fever. You saved me in the river."

"I wouldn't have made it without you," Charles insists, pushing the coin back.

Fritz watches and smiles.

Carter picks up the coins. "I'll tend to the mules. Guard the others' gold." He beams and heads outside.

Naglee turns to Charles. "Who's next?"

Fritz drops his bag on the counter. "I am."

Outside, Carter stands guard as Charles helps each man exchange and send their gold. By late afternoon, the work is done.

Charles insists that Carter and James see a doctor. But the physician refuses to treat men of color. Charles pleads, and the doctor finally agrees to sell an ointment and a foul-smelling concoction for the pain.

Next, they search for a stable for the mules and somewhere to sleep. They find a stable for the animals, but lodging proves harder. Most inns are too crowded, or don't accept Black patrons.

They end up agreeing to sleep in the stable with their mules.

Hunger sends them into the city, but restaurant after restaurant turns them away.

"We have money," Fritz says bitterly, "but can't even use it to get what we need."

Finally, street vendors charge a premium for their gold. They eat salted fish, roasted beef, and fruit fresh off the ships, then return to the stable and settle into the hay.

Rowdy sounds from nearby saloons fill the air. Charles, restless, convinces Fritz and a few others to join him for a night of gambling and drinking to celebrate their good fortune.

He tries to convince Carter, but he refuses.

"Just take $60," Carter advises. "You've worked too hard to lose your gold to gambling. And watch your drinking. Remember the people on the ship from New Orleans?"

Charles looks at Carter, shocked at his bold direction.

Carter realizes his statement was out of place, and his expression shifts. "I don't want you to get hurt…"

Charles cuts him off with a laugh and taunts, "Yes, Father. I will not gamble away my money, and I will not drink too much. You need to get some rest and care for that gunshot wound."

Carter and several others want nothing more than rest after an eventful day. Most of their gold is safe in the bank, but they still carry dozens of coins. The threat of thieves weighs heavily on their minds.

They stash a few pouches in the hay near where they sleep, keeping the rest tucked deep in their pockets. Each man keeps his pistol close at hand.

Despite their efforts to stay vigilant, they drift off quickly.

Around two in the morning, loud chatter and the shrill laughter of women shatter their sleep. Dark shapes appear in the stable doorway. The men awake and point their pistols at the shadows.

"We brought the party here!" Charles whoops as he, Fritz, and a few others stumble in with women draped on their arms. Several hold bottles of whiskey.

Carter has never seen Charles this drunk. He can barely stand.

Carter lowers his pistol, tucks it into his belt, and then approaches him. "I won, Carter. We're on a winning streak!" Charles slurs, thrusting a bottle toward him. "This is excellent whiskey."

One of the women tugs at Charles' hand. "Come on, Charlie, let's play cards and have some fun."

"You go ahead. I'll be there in a minute," he mumbles, swaying.

Carter takes the bottle and steadies Charles. "You should rest," he says as he guides him toward the straw where he's been sleeping. "It's been a long day."

"You're right, Carter." Charles blinks slowly. "You're too good to me." He mumbles again, then looks Carter in the eye. "You took a bullet to get the gold here. How are you?"

"I'm fine," Carter says as he props Charles up against the stable wall and arranges a straw bed. Opening the luggage bag, he uses clothes to make a makeshift pillow and helps Charles lie down.

"Thanks, Carter," Charles mumbles before falling into a deep sleep, undisturbed by the rowdy laughter echoing from the other side of the stable.

Carter settles into his spot next to Charles. He keeps an eye on the group gathered in the moonlit corner where Fritz and a few others drink and play cards. Carter dozes, drifting in and out of sleep, occasionally waking to see the men and women paired off. Eventually, the stable grows quiet, and he drifts into a deep sleep.

A shuffling noise wakes him.

He watches as three dark shadows creep through the hay where some gold is hidden. Carter doesn't move. He watches quietly and reaches for his pistol.

Moonlight trickles through the windows—just enough to make out their shapes. It's three of the women. They move with intent, sifting through the straw. Carter figures they know exactly what they are after. *Whiskey talks,* he thinks grimly.

He pulls back the hammer of his pistol with a sharp, unmistakable click. The three women freeze.

"Looking for something?" he barks.

The woman in the middle raises her hand and points at Carter. He sees the glint of metal. It's a tiny derringer pistol. She clicks back the hammer.

"It's only gold!" Carter shouts.

The men awaken. The other women aim their pistols, prompting the men to draw theirs. The sharp, metallic sound of pistol triggers reverberates.

Fritz is close to the women. He steps into the moonlight and aims his pistol at the woman in the middle. They stand facing each other. The moment is tense, waiting for the first shot to be fired.

"We've all had our fun," Fritz says calmly. "It's time for you ladies to leave."

"We'll leave when we get our money," the woman in the middle snarls.

"I paid you fair and square," Fritz says.

"You did, but he didn't," she says as she points to Charles, who is groggy and trying to take in the situation.

Carter looks at Charles. "The lady says you owe her money. Do you?"

Charles rubs his head, trying to remember. "Maybe, I don't remember." He falls back on the straw.

Carter looks at the woman and lowers his pistol. "How much does he owe you?"

"He said he'd pay me twenty," the woman complains.

Carter looks at Charles, who can only wave his hand. "Give her twenty."

The woman to her left points at one of the other men and says, "He owes me ten."

The other woman points to one of the men and says, "He owes me twenty," and points to another and says, "He owes me forty."

"Forty?" Fritz says as he glances back. "What the hell did she do for you?"

"I borrowed money from her when I was gambling…"

"Pay the ladies," Fritz demands.

They scramble to pay them, but they all keep their pistols pointed at each other.

One of the men yells, "My money's gone!" He points to the third woman, who has been silent. "She stole my money!"

Fritz aims his pistol at the woman and says, "Did you steal his money?"

The woman hesitates.

The woman in the middle turns to her. "Did you? We don't steal. Give it back!"

The woman reluctantly retrieves a small leather pouch full of coins from a garter under her dress and throws it to the man.

After the money is reconciled, Fritz asks, "Are we square?"

The women look at each other and nod in agreement. The woman in the middle says, "We're square."

Everyone lowers their pistols as the women disappear into the moonlight.

Fritz turns to the group. "I don't think we can sleep now, at least not here. Let's head out."

Everyone agrees except Charles, who moans but manages to answer, "We're going to take the steamship back to Sacramento." He falls back against the straw.

Carter helps the men pack their gear and leave in the pre-dawn light while Charles sleeps.

He props himself next to Charles with his gun in hand, waiting for daylight.

CHAPTER 14
HOT SUMMER OF 1850

Carter and Charles return to Sacramento on the small steamship they took after they first arrived—this time with their mules and money in their pockets. Charles sells two mules in Sacramento at a handsome profit. Carter rides Sarah while Charles rides a dark mule named Jake back to Coloma. The journey is rough and Carter's wound reopens. Despite Carter's protests, Charles insists they stop at Doc's to have it treated.

They both know they need a convincing story about how Carter was hurt. After some back and forth, they settle on a flimsy explanation: Carter fell from his mule onto a sharp branch. It must do. The truth is too dangerous to share.

Hannah greets them with a warm smile and embraces Carter as he steps down. He wobbles into her arms. She pulls back and looks at her fingers, now stained with blood.

"Carter, what happened?"

"He fell off his mule and landed on a tree branch," Charles says.

They hurry Carter into a small room. Doc unwraps the blood-soaked bandages and examines the wound.

"There are metal fragments," Doc mutters, his brow furrowing. "I'm going to have to cut them out. You should probably leave." He tells Charles.

"I'm staying," Charles says firmly.

Doc turns to Hannah. "We need to make sure Carter doesn't feel anything."

Hannah nods and retrieves a bottle of pills and whiskey from the cabinet. Doc pours out several pills from a bottle marked with Chinese lettering.

"Here, take these," Doc tells Carter. "Wash them down with some whiskey."

"What are they?" Charles asks.

"Morphine," Doc replies as Carter swallows the pills and takes a long drink.

Carter lies back on the cot, his eyes already beginning to glaze. Hannah grinds some of the pills into a powder as they wait for the whiskey and morphine to take full effect. She mixes the powder with a salve and dabs it onto Carter's bloody wound.

"This will help with the pain," Doc assures Carter.

A minute later, he pokes lightly at the wound with a pair of forceps. "Can you feel this?"

"Feel what?" Carter mumbles.

"Good. Just relax and hold still. This shouldn't take long."

He looks at Charles. "Can you keep him steady? He might still feel it."

Charles nods and places his hands on Carter's shoulders as Doc raises a scalpel.

Doc works carefully, slicing into the wound. Carter moans and clenches his fists, his face tight with pain. With delicate precision, Doc extracts a gold-tipped bullet fragment and drops it into a metal pan with a sharp clink.

Charles swallows hard. "He had gold in his jacket pocket," he offers, trying to sound casual. "The branch must've shoved some of it into the wound."

Doc pauses, exchanging a glance with Hannah. "Must've been some lead mixed in with that gold," he says dryly.

Neither Carter nor Charles responds.

Hannah places a hand on Carter's clenched fist. "I'm just glad you're going to be okay," she says softly, her voice layered with meaning. She knows it was a bullet. She also knows she might never hear the whole story.

Doc removes small fragments—some gold, some unmistakably lead—then stitches the wound and wraps it in fresh bandages.

"You'll need to take it easy for at least two weeks," Doc says. "No lifting, no swinging a pick. Come by every day so we can apply more salve and change the bandages."

"I'll make sure he rests," Charles assures him.

Carter manages a faint smile in Hannah's direction, trying not to let Charles or Doc notice. Resting and seeing Hannah every day sounds great.

The next morning, Carter lies alone in his tent. The others, including Charles, had left early to work their claims.

A familiar voice calls out, "I brought you something."

Hannah steps in, holding a steaming pot of chicken soup.

"I think I am supposed to come to you," Carter jokes.

"I have to get supplies," she replies with a broad smile. She ladles soup into a bowl and hands it to him.

Carter slurps down several bowls, grateful for the warmth and flavor. Hannah carefully unwraps his bandages and examines his wound.

"That was quite a tree limb you fell on," she comments. Then, more pointedly, "Did everybody's gold make it to San Francisco?"

Carter hesitates, careful with his words. He does not want to lie. "Everybody who made it to San Francisco's gold is safe."

Hannah reads between the lines. "Glad you made it." She steps out of the tent, then turns back at the flap. "Make sure you rest and come see me tomorrow. We've got some reading to do."

Carter spends as much time with Hannah as he can. She is busy helping Doc with every form of disease and wound imaginable, but still, she is always ready to tend to Carter and ensure he is well-fed.

Charles does not return for days. They enjoy their time together in his absence. Carter increases the reading lessons. He guides her through English primers and newspaper articles, and their laughter mingles with stories and small triumphs. With each day, their friendship deepens.

Nearly two weeks pass before Charles finally ducks into the tent.

"How are you feeling, Carter? How's the wound?"

"Fine. Where've you been?"

"Working the claim. I think I figured out how to get more gold." Charles leans forward, eyes bright. "Do you think you're well enough to ride Sarah up to the claim tomorrow afternoon?"

"Sure, but I'm not supposed to swing a pick."

"You won't have to. I want you to see something—you won't want to miss it."

The next day, Carter rides Sarah along the dusty trail to the claim. He stops short, stunned to see more than a dozen men working the site with pickaxes. They are Chinese, Native American, African American, and Mexican. Charles is wearing his Panama hat and stands in the center of the group next to Fritz.

Carter dismounts and walks toward them. Charles scrambles down the slope to meet him.

"You're just in time," he says. "Take Sarah and get behind that big rock over there." He points toward a massive outcropping. "The Chinese crew has packed enough black powder to blow half the mountain."

Carter leads Sarah to shelter behind the rock, followed by the workers. Only two Chinese men and Charles remain behind, adjusting the fuse. Carter shakes hands with Fritz.

"How are the ribs?" Fritz asks.

"They're fine," Carter replies as Charles shouts, "Fire in the hole!"

Carter and Fritz look up. Two Chinese men and Charles scramble toward them, the fuse hissing behind them.

"Get down!" Charles orders as they duck behind the rock. Everyone crouches, bracing themselves.

The blast comes like thunder, shaking the ground beneath them. Dust and rocks fly skyward. The hillside rumbles, and a roaring echo bounces off the cliffs—shards of rock shower down as dense clouds of dust roll over the mountainside.

Charles jumps up first, followed by Carter and the others. They race toward the opening carved into the mountain.

"This beats the hell out of swinging a pick," Charles says as he beams. "Let's see what we've got."

They pick through the rubble. Workers carry chunks of stone to Charles and Fritz, who inspect them closely. Charles turns over a large rock and finds a small vein of shimmering gold.

More rocks come. Charles and Fritz bend over them, searching for clues.

"What do you think?" Charles asks.

Fritz studies a piece of quartz, squinting down at the debris around them. Several rocks glitter faintly.

"There's a vein, but not much," Fritz replies. "You should blast again tomorrow. If you don't find more, it's best to move on."

The next day, they blast the site again. The result is the same—little gold. Carter, Charles, and Fritz examine the fragments in silence.

"I think it's played out," Fritz says, handing Charles a chunk of white quartz.

"We've got more places to look," Charles replies, eyes scanning the hills. "We'll get everything we can get here and then move on."

Carter helps pick through rocks to find a bit of gold, always careful not to reopen his wound.

The weeks pass. He enjoys working with the diverse crew. While working with them, he tries to pick up as much Chinese and Spanish as possible. There are two local Native Americans, and he absorbs as much Nisenan as possible.

He makes his way back to Hannah as often as Charles and the work will allow.

She tends to his wound and ensures he is well-fed. In return, Carter helps her learn to read. They enjoy each other's company while it lasts, knowing that Carter is destined to return to Mississippi.

Charles pays his crew in gold coins after they have cracked every rock and collected every fleck of gold dust.

Charles tells Carter, "I hope you're ready to work. It's just the two of us. There's not much left after expenses. We should have more help from Mississippi soon. Then we'll find more gold."

CHAPTER 15
MISSISSIPPI
JUNE 15TH, 1850

It's a sweltering, humid day in Mississippi as Daniel walks into his father's office. William looks up from a stack of papers.

"Were you able to trade for any workers?" William asks.

"Everyone wants strong young men. There were only old women, children, and old men," Daniel replies, handing him a stack of mail.

"We need more strong men. It's going to be a great year for cotton." William shuffles through the mail.

Daniel hands him a letter that he had been holding. "You finally received a letter from Charles. It's been a year since he left." Daniel's voice carries a bitter edge. "He and Carter should be here. They could help."

William nods and opens the letter. He reads aloud:

"Dear Father,

I've found gold. I deposited money in a bank in New Orleans under your name to pay for the passage of four strong men. I think Robert, Sandy, and two more will do. Perhaps Daniel can escort them. He could use the adventure. If not, Green, Hardin, and the Kirk brothers wanted to come to California. There is more than enough money for their trip. The rest can be used at your discretion and for safekeeping. I've also enclosed a letter to Emmy. Please see that she gets it.

Your loving son,

Charles Perkins."

William reaches into the envelope and pulls out two twenty-dollar gold coins—an eagle and a Mormon—and a small envelope addressed to Emmy.

"Well, I'll be damned," William says. "Looks like Charles found gold." He passes the letter to Daniel.

Daniel smirks. "Do you think he found a big strike?"

"I'm sure he did." William hands him Emmy's letter. "I trust you can deliver this. I know you've been seeing a great deal of her lately. We want to maintain good relations with our neighbors."

Daniel takes the envelope. "I'll make sure we keep good relations. She and her land are more valuable than gold."

William sighs. He has made a point of not interfering with his children's interests or desires. He grudgingly stays clear of their relationships. Who is he to judge?

He realizes that Charles may never return. His doubts have intensified, knowing that Charles has found gold. Daniel has been an immense help on the plantation. He reflects that Charles will likely never want to manage the plantation; if it were his true passion, he would have stayed.

William reconciles to let things be and let Daniel and Charles follow their passions.

Still, he can't help but counsel Daniel: "Land is the most valuable treasure. It lasts forever."

Daniel smiles, but says firmly, "You're not thinking of sending more slaves to Charles, are you?"

"I need to think about it. California presents a once-in-a-lifetime opportunity. He's already found gold, and he might find more. I've heard the land is ripe for the taking."

Daniel paces in front of his desk. "We need more help. And there's talk about California becoming a free state. We could lose our slaves."

"Senator Davis is home from Washington. He'll know whether it's safe. I'll go to the bank in New Orleans tomorrow to secure Charles' gold. I'll visit Jefferson on my way back."

"I'm not going to California," Daniel snaps. "Who will take the slaves?"

"We'll cross that bridge when we come to it," William said calmly. "Your cousins keep talking about going west. There may be others from Mississippi willing to make the trip."

"I can't believe you're even thinking about this," Daniel says, raising his voice. "This plantation is more important."

William raises his hand to quiet him.

"I will not jeopardize the plantation. We must seize every opportunity. Gold—and maybe land—in California might be worth the risk."

"It's too big a risk," Daniel protests as he storms out.

Daniel, impeccably dressed, rides Charles' horse to Emmy's plantation. He stops between two large magnolia trees in full bloom and opens the letter, reading silently:

"My dearest Emmy,

I miss you and think of you often. I gaze upon your picture and reminisce about our time together and your sweet smile.

I found gold. I plan to find more. I know it's been a year, but we have many years to plan our future.

With love,

Charles."

Daniel pulls a gold eagle coin from the envelope.

Daniel scowls, stomps the ground, and mutters aloud, "If you love her, brother, you wouldn't have left her. You value your gold, but she and her land are worth far more."

He tears the letter and envelope to pieces, letting them scatter in the wind. Then he pockets the coin and rides toward her plantation.

As he approaches Emmy's plantation, he spots slaves working a small field behind the house. To his surprise, Emmy is kneeling among them in a white dress. He is shocked that she is working the land with her bare hands, especially alongside slaves.

He stops Star at the edge of the field, dismounts, and inspects the ground. Hesitantly, he walks toward her, trying to keep his boots clean.

She looks up with a warm smile. "I decided to start a garden with vegetables and flowers," she says, raising her hands, covered in earth. "It feels wonderful to plant and nurture life. Would you like to help?"

Daniel looks at his polished boots, now speckled with dirt.

"I can bring more help," he says stiffly.

Emmy stands to face him. "No need. We're almost finished." She wipes her dirty hands on her white dress, then brushes her brow, leaving a smudge. "What brings you here?"

Daniel stammers, knowing that word of Charles' gold strike will spread. He can't afford to be caught in a lie. "We finally got a letter from Charles. He found gold." He reluctantly reaches into his pocket, pulls out the twenty-dollar gold piece, and hands it to her. "You can have this."

Emmy looks at the shiny coin. "Did he say when he is coming home?"

"No. He sent money for slaves, thinking he could find more gold. I doubt he'll come home," Daniel says, masking the lie calmly.

Emmy clutches the coin, looks down, and turns away.

"There's a dance at the Davis's plantation in two weeks. I was wondering if you'd like to go?" Daniel asks boldly.

Emmy turns back, surprised by the offer.

Daniel tries to recover. "My sisters, brothers, and parents are going. You could join us. I'd be happy to escort you."

"I need to think about it," Emmy answers as she returns to the garden. "Are you sure you don't want to help?"

Daniel cringes at the thought of working on his hands and knees next to slaves. "I best be getting home. Think about the dance."

"I will," Emmy says, hesitating as she kneels and continues planting.

A few days later, William arrives at Jefferson Davis's plantation. An impeccably dressed servant ushers him into Jefferson's large office filled with books and memorabilia.

Jefferson shakes William's hand. "It's great to see you, William," he drawls with a buttery-smooth Southern accent. "I have the finest whiskey and cigars. I've been waiting for someone to share them with."

He rifles through crates behind his desk and returns with three bottles of whiskey and two boxes of cigars. He places them on the side of his desk and motions for William to sit.

"You want to go through all of this?" William chuckles.

"We'll see how far we can get," Jefferson replies with a wry smile. "People keep giving me things. I guess they think I can be bribed with whiskey and cigars."

He hands William an ornate bottle. "This one's from Elijah Craig in Kentucky," he proclaims, opening it and pouring two glasses. "They say it's over seventy years old and bottled by Elijah himself. They use it to judge their whiskeys. Let's toast Elijah and the great state of Kentucky."

"And to the great state of Mississippi," William adds as they sip.

Jefferson pulls back his glass and admires the golden amber. "Oh my, that is special."

"It is extraordinary," William agrees.

Jefferson looks at the boxes of cigars. "The question is, what would be the finest cigar to pair with this whiskey?" He opens a wooden box bearing the Por Larrañaga logo. "Have you ever tried a Cuban cigar?"

"No, I have not. I would have thought you smoked American cigars," William says.

"The truth is, we are trying to buy Cuba from Spain. She would make a fine slave state. We need as many as we can get," Jefferson summarizes as he prepares the cigars and hands one to William. "We're also looking at other opportunities for expansion in the Caribbean."

"I didn't realize that. I'm sure there are great opportunities. Speaking of opportunity, my son Charles found gold in California. Quite a find, I might add," William booms as he puffs the cigar.

"That's worth celebrating. Congratulations," Jefferson chortles. "Did he return, or is he still there?"

"He stayed to find more—and now he wants more help."

"How many did he take?" Jefferson asks between cigar puffs.

"He just took Carter."

"I remember Carter," Jefferson reflects. "He was the boy who served at Easter. I have his family recipe for spicy bacon. We keep trying, but it never tastes quite the same."

"I can have Patience teach your cooks to prepare it," William offers.

"That would be wonderful," Jefferson says, taking a sip of whiskey. "Carter seems like a smart boy. I can see why you sent him with Charles."

William redirects the conversation. "The thing is, I am concerned about sending more. They claim California will be a free state soon."

"They agreed to a state constitution, but it is still a U.S. territory. The Northerners are pushing for a vote to make it a free state, but we are pushing to keep it a territory. We need to get more support to make it a slave state. We're fighting the abolitionists at every turn, but they are getting stronger," Jefferson admits.

"The problem is, I could lose my slaves if I send them to California," William says, his voice tight with concern.

"Absolutely not," Jefferson insists. "We are finalizing a stronger fugitive slave law. It even has support from the North. They do not want the darkies taking their jobs or even living in their states. The law has the support of President Taylor. He and I are still very close." Jefferson's eyes grow misty.

William remembers that Jefferson served under Zachary Taylor in Mexico and married his daughter, Sarah. She died of malaria just three months after they wed.

"She was a fine woman. Life can be cruel. It seems the prettiest flowers are the first to go," William consoles.

"It seems like yesterday, but it was so many years ago," Jefferson says, gazing out the window. They share a quiet moment. "We must let the past inform our future. But we must make our future. Expansion is our future. California is our future." He puffs his cigar. "Now, about your concerns."

"We already have a fugitive slave law, but it hasn't always been enforced. Many slaves have claimed their freedom in a free state and have been protected," William complains.

"Our new law requires all local, state, and federal officials—and territories, including California—to assist in the return of escaped slaves. Any federal marshal or official who fails to arrest an escaped slave will be fined one thousand dollars. The law relies solely on the claimant's sworn testimony. A slave can't request a jury trial or speak in court," Senator Davis declares proudly.

"What happens to those who protect and harbor slaves?" William asks.

"Aiding a runaway slave anywhere in the U.S.—including California and all of our territories—will be a criminal offense, punishable by six months' imprisonment and a one-thousand-dollar fine," Senator Davis concludes, his tone laced with arrogance.

"Are you sure it will be enforced?" William presses.

"We've made the penalties severe. It will be enforced. We included provisions for the Justice Department. Federal commissioners will receive five dollars for ruling a person is free— but ten dollars if they rule in favor of the claimant."

"I'm still concerned with what will happen if it becomes a free state."

"There are many of us in California, and we have many friends. Whether it remains a territory or—heaven forbid—becomes a free state, we'll protect our property. They can't take our slaves. The Constitution guarantees our freedom and liberty," Senator Davis professes. "Send Charles more slaves. Help him find gold and buy land. If you and I were younger, we'd go."

"I believe we would. I'll consider sending more to Charles, but I need more fieldworkers. The price for hardworking men is going up, and even then, no one wants to sell."

"I know people in New Orleans who can help. They're bringing in fresh blood—but don't tell anyone," Senator Davis cautions.

"It's risky. It's been illegal to import slaves for forty years," William replies.

Senator Davis leans forward. "We're driving our country's economy. They need us." He taps his finger on the desk. "Go to New Orleans and speak with them. You'll find what you're looking for. There are millions of slaves in the Caribbean and South America for sale. We must keep our economy strong and competitive. I'm afraid Northerners don't understand what it takes to grow cotton, sugar, and tobacco. They don't know how to get things done, but they're happy to reap the rewards of our labor through taxes." He jots down several names on a slip of paper and hands it to William. "Talk to these gentlemen. If I were you, I'd send Charles more help." He scribbles another note, signs it, and passes it over. "This may help you in New Orleans."

William reads the note: *William Perkins is a man to be trusted,* followed by Senator Davis's signature. He looks up. "I will most likely send my nephews and a few slaves. I haven't told them of Charles' success, but I'm sure they'll be excited once they hear the news."

"Let's celebrate your family's good fortune. Here's another fine whiskey from Tennessee. Find some you like and take it home to share with friends and family. Take as many cigars and bottles as you can carry," Senator Davis urges, glancing around at the crates and boxes in his office. "I hope you and your family will attend the dance at my brother's plantation."

"We'll be there," William assures him.

A few days later, William and Daniel arrive in New Orleans. William wrestles with the thought of buying illegally imported slaves, but Daniel is excited by the opportunity. William has not shared how much Charles deposited in the New Orleans bank account, but Daniel knows his father well. He senses it must be a considerable sum. He plans to persuade his father to allocate the funds to purchase the necessary supplies for the plantation.

They walk through the crowded streets, then into the darker, seedier parts of New Orleans. William pulls out Jefferson Davis's note as they step into a large brick warehouse. An armed young man stands guard at the front desk. William hands over the note, and after a brief exchange, he and Daniel are led down a series of stairs to a candlelit room.

A middle-aged Southern man greets them with a slow drawl. "We've received word that you're gentlemen of honor. We welcome you, and we assure you, you'll see the best we have to offer."

He motions to a table and pours whiskey from a cut-glass decanter.

"We have strong men for you. Let's start with Roberto." He signals to the side of the room, toward the small stage. A worker lights floor lamps, revealing iron bars between them and the stage.

"Are the bars necessary?" William asks, concerned.

"Only a precaution," the Southerner assures him.

Roberto walks onto the stage bare-chested, wearing canvas pants. Armed guards on either side instruct him to turn and display his muscles. His back bears several scars from whipping.

Daniel leans forward, excited. "Where's he from? How much is he?"

The Southerner consults his ledger. "Of course, everything we say and do here is confidential. He's from Cuba. Highly valued for his hard work. The price is two thousand."

William scoffs. "Two thousand? Look at all those scars. He looks like trouble. We don't need trouble."

"Think about how much work he can do. We could get a new overseer and drivers to keep him and others like him in line," Daniel urges.

"That's not how I run my plantation," William scolds. "We need men we can rely on—men who won't fight or run."

Unfazed, the salesman waves to the guards, who parade a series of young, strong men onto the stage. They range in age from teenagers to middle-aged. William and Daniel take notes as each one is presented.

After the show, William and Daniel step aside to compare notes. The salesman interjects with a final offer. "You said you're not in the market, but we have some fine young women. You should at least look. With the way the laws are, you ought to consider the future—consider more breeding stock."

"Might as well," Daniel says, glancing at William, who does not respond. Too busy reviewing his notes and prioritizing the slaves he wants, along with their costs.

Women are led onto the stage. One catches Daniel's eye. The Southerner notices and seizes the moment. "She's a very hard worker from Venezuela. Only speaks Spanish, but she'd be a fine addition to any plantation."

Daniel stares at her. "I think she'd be perfect, don't you, Father?" he says, eyes locked on the young woman, who tries to avoid his gaze. "How much?"

The Southerner checks his notes. "They're asking $1,200, but if you buy eight, I'll let her go for a thousand."

William, still adding figures in his notebook, glances at Daniel and recognizes the look on his face.

"Just more trouble," William grumbles. "We don't need any more trouble. You've already caused enough."

"Like he said, we need more breeding stock. The plantation is my future. I've saved money. I'll buy her," Daniel insists.

William says nothing and hands the salesman a note. "We'll take these eight men. That's my price. If Daniel wants her, that's his business."

Daniel shakes the salesman's hand. "We have a deal."

"You should travel back to your plantation at night," the salesman advises.

"We'll leave tonight," William replies. "No one will know."

A few weeks later, in early May of 1850, Hardin arrives at the Perkins plantation, driving a wagon alongside the Kirk brothers. Five of the Kirk brothers' slaves sit in the wagon among several pieces of luggage.

William is waiting out front as they pull into the driveway. He walks up to the wagon. "Hello, gentlemen. I see you're taking a few of your own. Where's Green?"

"He wanted touh go, but his dad and mom are sick. The Kirk boys and I will make sure they get there," Hardin assures him.

"I'm sure you will."

"Are your slaves ready?" Hardin asks.

"Yes, Sandy and Robert are ready. They're at the cabins."

"We've got to get moving," Hardin insists.

"Good luck, boys. Have a safe trip," William says, waving as they pull away.

At the cabins, Sandy and Patience are in tears, hugging their family. All 160 Perkins slaves are gathered behind them.

Sandy's sons, daughters, and grandchildren encircle him. His fifteen-year-old grandson, Sandy Jones II, steps forward. "You can't go, Grandpa. We need you. I've got a lot to learn."

"Master Charles needs me in California. My heart is here. I'll always be here. I'll be back before you know I'm gone. I'll teach you everything I know when I return. I promise," Sandy says as they walk to the wagon. He gives Patience one last kiss before climbing aboard.

Robert embraces his wife, daughters, and sons as they cling to him. His voice cracks. "Take care of your mom while I'm gone." He pulls himself away and climbs in beside Sandy.

"Hurry up! We've got to get going," Hardin snaps.

Patience begins to sing, clapping her hands. "Everywhere I go, there's an angel there." The Perkins slaves join in, answering each line. "Everywhere I go, there's an angel there. 'Cause my God, my God, He never leaves me alone. Everywhere I turn, there's an angel there…"

As the wagon rolls away, Sandy, Robert, and the Kirk slaves clap and sing along.

Hardin turns and shouts, "Stop singing! The gospel ain't for you! God gave us dominion over all creation. The Word of God is for us, not you. You ain't got souls. We're here to take care of all God's creation. That includes you…"

Sandy and Robert sit in silence, exchanging a look with the Kirk slaves. They all know it will be a long, difficult journey to California.

And deep down, they understand they may never see Mississippi, or their families again.

CHAPTER 16
FREEDOM FADES IN CALIFORNIA

Hannah and Carter sit atop a sun-warmed boulder on the mountainside. Below them, the river churns and gurgles, its constant motion a gentle backdrop as they read through newspapers. Down by the water, prospectors crouch in the shallows, panning for gold.

Hannah lowers her paper and glances at Carter. "Do you think California will be a free state? It seems like everyone's fighting each other."

"Half of them want freedom. Half don't." Carter points to an article, then crumples the paper and throws it into the breeze. It floats up and away. "Even the White folks who want California to be free don't want us here."

"Charles treats you all right. Doc Hill treats me fine," Hannah counters. "We have to keep hope."

"Charles and Doc Hill are good men. Some people are good, some are bad. Skin color shouldn't matter, but it does. They use it to control us," Carter says as he stares at the river.

"Things are changing," Hannah insists. "Someday, you're going to be free. I know it."

Hannah reaches for Carter's Bible resting between them. "There must be words about freedom in the Bible," she says as she opens it and scans the pages. Peg's picture flies out.

Carter jumps to his feet and chases it in the wind, finally catching the photo.

He sits back down as Hannah reads Galatians 5:1.

"For freedom Christ has set us free; stand firm therefore, and do not submit again to a yoke of slavery." Hannah hands the Bible to Carter.

"I once thought those words were meant for me, for all of us, but they're not. The world will never let me be free," Carter grumbles.

"They're meant for you," Hannah says softly. "They're meant for everyone."

Carter snarls under his breath. "I'm never going to be free. I know I'll have to go back to Mississippi."

"I'll go with you," Hannah says without hesitation.

Carter steps away, staring down the mountain. "You can't go to Mississippi. You wouldn't be free there. No one is free there. Even Charles isn't free there."

Hannah lets the silence settle for a moment before speaking again. "You said Charles is bringing more help from Mississippi. You said it might be your grandfather and uncle. That should help, shouldn't it?"

"I don't know who's coming. I just know things will change."

"I thought you'd be excited to see your family again," Hannah says, watching him closely. "What's going to change?"

"Things between Charles and me." Carter's voice drops. "I don't think his brother will come, but his cousins will."

"Are they bad?"

Carter nods. "They're bad enough to change things."

He stares into the distance, fists clenched, and breath tight in his chest. Memories rise—the pain in his back from the overseer's whip, Green's gunshot that almost killed him, the sting of insults. He knows what Charles' cousins will bring.

Hannah steps closer, eyes filled with concern. She places a hand on his shoulder. "It'll be okay. I can help you." Her voice is calm and sure. "You don't have to go through this alone. I'm here."

Carter steps away from her touch. "I should've never let this happen," he says out loud without thinking. "It's gone too far. Things can never work between us. You need to be free."

"Things work out if you fight for them!" Hannah snaps, surprised at his tone.

"You're free. I'm not. I'll never be free," Carter insists. "You can't fight the truth."

Hannah's anger boils. "The truth is, you don't care about me. I'm not sure you're willing to fight for anything."

She turns and storms down the trail.

Carter scrambles after her for a few steps and then stops. He watches her disappear through the trees toward the river. His shoulders slump, and tears well in his eyes.

He knows it's the right thing to let her go. To let her be free.

He knows he has no choice but to return to Mississippi.

And there's Peg. He does love her. She needs him.

The closer he gets to Hannah, the more she'll hurt when he leaves.

And the truth is, the closer he gets to Hannah, the more he'll hurt.

It's better this way.

CHAPTER 17
MORE MISSISSIPPIANS ARRIVE
AUGUST 1850

On a scorching 100-degree day, Hardin leads Robert and Sandy through a line of tents in Coloma. The Kirk brothers trail behind with their five slaves. They pass miners busy cooking and enjoying their midday meals in front of their tents.

Hardin stops in front of Archibald, the Southern slave owner near Charles and Carter's tent, who is tending a fire, boiling coffee, and cooking.

"We're lookin' for Charles Perkins," Hardin says. "Do you know him?"

Archibald eyes the group, trying to figure them out.

"I know a slave lover named Charles Perkins. Looks like y'all brought more Darkies for him to love. You a Darkie lover, too?"

Hardin bristles. "I ain't no slave lover. I ain't fond of assholes, either."

The miner lets out a laugh. "That's good to know." He points lazily toward a nearby tent. "We need more Southern boys out here. You'll find Charlie and his nigger over there."

Hardin turns and walks briskly to the tent where George and several tent-mates are eating lunch.

"You know Charles Perkins?" Hardin asks.

George turns toward the tent opening and says, "You've got company, Charlie."

Charles emerges, followed closely by Carter, who rushes up to Sandy and Robert and wraps his arms around them.

"It's great to see you!" he says.

Sandy grins. "Nothing could be better."

Charles greets Hardin and the Kirk brothers with a polite smile. "Thanks for bringing them."

Hardin's expression remains cold. "Maybe we're too late. Don't tell me y'all are sleepin' in the same tent as Carter."

"Things are different here..." Charles begins.

"Thangs ain't different," Hardin snaps. "White men don't sleep with Darkies."

George, who has been watching from nearby, stands and steps forward.

"We're all free here. Ain't got room for the likes of you. Stop bringin' your slaves around."

Hardin narrows his eyes. "Maybe cousin Charles has been spinnin' lies. I guess that's what educated folks do." He jabs a thumb toward Sandy and Robert. "Fact is, he paid us to bring these two."

George turns to Charles.

"Is that true, Charlie?"

Charles hesitates, caught off guard. "Well..."

"Well, what?" George snaps. "Rumor is you've been finding gold and not tellin' us. I didn't believe it. Now I do. You're a no-good, Mississippi, slave-ownin', lyin' son of a bitch."

Archibald and other slave-owning miners burst into laughter down the row of tents.

"It's not like that," Charles protests.

"No, it's exactly like that. You either believe in freedom or you don't. This is free soil. Pack your shit and get," George demands.

Hardin smirks. "Looks like your lies got you thrown out. Your family's been wonderin' what you're doin' in California. We'll straighten you out. Find a place where you can be with us. And we'll find a proper place for Carter and the rest."

Charles breaths deeply, doing his best to hold his temper. He can't afford a fight with his cousins. He knew things might go bad, but not so soon.

Carter steps up. "I know a place for Sandy, Robert, me, and the rest." He points toward the tattered Black camp in the distance.

"Well, Carter, good to know you still understand your place in the world," Hardin drawls sarcastically. Then he turns to Charles. "Pack up your shit. You're comin' with us."

Charles clenches his jaw but remains silent.

Hours later, Charles stands with Carter outside a tent in the Black miners' camp. The tents are old, weathered, and worn. Carter unpacks his gear from Sarah. Sandy and Robert wait nearby, along with the five Kirk slaves. Hardin and the Kirk brothers linger at a distance.

Charles looks around the ragged camp and sighs.

"Sorry, Carter. I guess this is how it's gonna be."

Carter shrugs, trying to lighten the mood. "It'll do. It's good to be with my family. You gonna stay in the tent with your cousins?"

"Maybe for a few days. I'm gonna try to rent a place from Doc. He's got a cabin out back."

"You think your cousins will work your claim?"

"Hell no. We'll teach them to pan. Then they can find their own gold."

The next morning, Charles leads his cousins and their slaves, along with Carter, Sandy, and Robert, down to the riverbank to teach them how to pan for gold. He stops at a shallow bend where the current is slow.

Gold seekers dot the banks, some kneeling in the water, others digging into the muddy slope with pickaxes. A few slaves labor under the sun while their masters lounge nearby, eating breakfast.

"Grab your pans and wade in beside me," Charles says, stepping knee-deep into the river.

Hardin follows him in, but the Kirk brothers stay dry, sitting on rocks to watch their slaves work.

Charles scoops gravel and sand into his pan and lifts it for everyone to see.

"You gotta look close," he says as he swirls the water and sifts through the dirt. A tiny gold flake glints in the sunlight. "See? Just like that."

Hardin's eyes light up. "It's that easy?" He plunges his pan into the river, eager.

Charles drops the gold fleck into a small glass bottle and hands it to Hardin. "This is yours."

Hardin pans in a frenzy. Carter, standing nearby, chuckles under his breath. He saw Charles slip the gold from his pocket into the river by Hardin.

"That first pan was lucky," Charles says. "Take it slow. Gold's heavy—it settles at the bottom. You gotta swish the lighter stuff away."

Carter helps Sandy and Robert with the technique while Charles coaches the Kirk brothers' slaves. A few more flakes turn up, surprising them all. Charles and Carter know the truth: the river has been worked hard by too many newcomers. The gold is mainly gone. But there is still enough to get by.

A scruffy prospector strolls by, takes in the scene, and pauses. He glances at the Kirk brothers perched on their rocks.

"Makin' money off other people's backs is a sin."

Jonathan Kirk sneers. "Ain't no sin. I don't know what Bible you're readin'. Paul says slaves oughta obey their masters with fear and trembling, as to Christ."

The prospector scoffs. "You better reread that Bible. Doesn't matter. Ain't right. Everybody oughta reap what they sow."

Jonathan fires back, "We work with our brains, not our backs."

"You couldn't find your ass in the dark. You're weak in body, mind, and spirit," the prospector mutters as he walks off.

They keep at it, panning hard. Charles and Carter move from person to person, showing them the finer points.

Sandy begins to hum a spiritual, then sings softly:

"Wade in the water,

Wade in the water, children,

Wade in the water, God's gonna trouble the water..."

Carter, Robert, and the others join in, swishing their pans in rhythm. The song carries across the river. Slaves working nearby pick it up. Even a few White miners add their voices.

For several days, Charles and Carter continue to pan alongside Hardin and the Kirk slaves. The gold is scarce, just as Charles hoped.

One evening, Carter, Sandy, and Robert sit around their fire, weary and quiet. The night air is damp, and the river murmurs nearby. One of the Kirk slaves steps out of the tent and joins them.

"We may not be seein' y'all for a while," he says. "We're headed to Placerville."

"Why's that?" Carter asks.

"They say there's more gold there. We ain't had much luck here."

"Is Hardin goin' too?"

"He wants to go the most. Y'all should come."

Carter tries to contain his smile. "We'll keep lookin'. Some days, you get lucky."

Charles appears at Carter's tent at dawn, ready for another day of panning. Carter, Sandy, and Robert are gathering picks and shovels.

"Why picks and shovels?" Charles asks.

"Hardin and the Kirks took off for Placerville before sunrise. They say there's no gold left here. I figured you might want to do more than pan today."

Charles laughs. "You thought right. I don't think we'll be seeing them for a while."

He glances around to make sure no one is listening, then leans in close.

"We'll work the claim."

They load their gear on Sarah and make their way to the claim. They follow the river and climb the mountainside, careful not to draw attention or be followed. Charles and Carter examine the area closely. The boulders and rocks remain undisturbed, showing no signs of being moved.

They pull back the brush to reveal a shallow mine. Carter, Sandy, and Robert take turns swinging their pickaxes at a wall of quartz. They knock loose jagged boulders the size of a loaf of bread. Charles uses a small hammer to crack them open, inspecting each one for traces of gold.

After a quick lunch break, they return to work, taking turns swinging their pickaxes at the granite and quartz. Jagged chunks of rock are scattered across the front of the claim.

Sandy takes a mighty swing and stumbles backward. His left arm is sliced open from the elbow to the wrist. He rolls to the ground, clutching his arm as blood spills across the rocks.

They spring into action, tearing off their shirts to wrap his wound. Blood seeps through the white cloth despite their efforts. Their hands slick with blood, they help Sandy to his feet, but he collapses. Carter and Charles catch him.

"He has to get to Doc Hill. Take Sarah—get him there as fast as you can," Charles orders.

Minutes later, Carter rides behind Sarah, holding Sandy in front of him. Though Sandy sways, he leans forward and grabs Sarah's mane.

"We can make it, Grandpa," Carter says, hugging him tightly as they ride down the trail.

CHAPTER 18
LIFE GETS COMPLICATED

Doc Hill stitches Sandy's arm while Carter sits beside him, supporting him but trying not to look at the blood.

Hannah walks into the room. It's the first time she's seen Carter in months. He looks down, embarrassed. Hannah says nothing and moves to assist Doc Hill.

She smiles at Sandy. "You must be Sandy Jones. I've heard a lot about you."

Sandy hasn't heard anything about Hannah and is surprised she knows who he is. "You have? How do you know about me?"

"Carter told me a lot about you," Hannah replies, shooting a cold look in Carter's direction.

Sandy glances at Carter, who stares at the floor sheepishly.

"Carter was teaching me to read. He knows a lot. Did you help teach him?" Hannah asks.

Sandy glances hesitantly at Doc Hill, uncertain if he approves of slaves being allowed to read or to teach others.

Doc Hill senses his concern. "Carter has been helping Hannah learn to read—until recently," he comments. "Everyone should know how to read."

Sandy casts a brief, silent look at Carter for neglecting to mention Hannah. Carter meets her gaze momentarily before diverting his eyes once more.

"I helped him a little," Sandy says, not wanting to raise any concerns since Charles taught him. "Teaching someone to think for themselves and understand emotions is more difficult." He chides Carter with a grandfatherly smile.

Carter shrugs and turns away. Sandy smiles at Hannah. He senses something has passed between them and maybe remains.

"Tell me all about Patience and your family," Hannah purrs. "Then tell me about Mississippi. I'm from Georgia."

"You don't sound like you're from Georgia," Sandy remarks.

"Carter's been teaching me to read and talk properly." She slips into her Georgia drawl to tease him. "I'm a-learnin' real good. Ain't I, Carter?" She chuckles and winks at Sandy.

Carter exhales a soft laugh and smiles. He shakes his head and looks back down. He misses Hannah. But what will Sandy think? What about Peg?

After bandaging Sandy's arm, Doc Hill asserts, "He's lost a lot of blood and needs rest. No swinging picks or lifting for two weeks."

"I'll bring you chicken soup in the morning," Hannah promises Sandy. "Carter says it reminds him of home. Maybe we can talk more about your family."

"That would be lovely." Sandy smiles. "But I don't want you to get into trouble."

"I make a lot of chicken soup for our patients. I'll bring some for the whole tent—even Carter," she says as she smiles.

Carter lets out a long breath and mirrors her smile.

Sandy and Carter are silent as they leave Doc's cabin and head to camp. Carter holds Sarah's reins.

"Are you sure you don't want to ride?" Carter asks.

"Feels good to walk. Maybe I'll ride in a bit."

An awkward silence stretches between them. Sandy has a thousand questions about Hannah and hasn't been honest about Peg. Neither knows how to begin.

Sandy finally breaks the silence. "Hannah's very nice. I'm glad you helped her learn to read. Why'd you stop? Sounds like you haven't seen her in a while."

"I know I've got to return to Mississippi," Carter laments. "Hannah's free, and I'll never be. Things will never work out with her. And there's Peg. I promised Peg I'd come back."

The trail leads to a high point overlooking the American River, with the small, growing town of Coloma spreading along its banks. Gold seekers pan in the water, while Sutter's Mill operates at full steam, cutting timbers as smoke from cook fires rises into the evening sky.

They pause to catch their breath and take in the view.

"Could you have imagined we'd be here a year ago?" Sandy wonders aloud. "Where will we be in a year? We don't even know what'll happen in the next few minutes. Let's sit for a spell."

They sit on a large rock as Sarah grazes nearby. Sandy stares into the distance, searching for words, then turns to Carter.

"I was going to tell you when I first got here, but the time never seemed right," Sandy begins, his voice catching. "I knew you had feelings for Peg, but I didn't know how deep. I guess I was hoping…"

"Is she okay? Did they sell her?" Carter interrupts, his voice sharp.

Sandy hesitates. "I have to give it to you straight. Peg is dead."

Carter fights back tears. "I can't believe it. How did she die? She was so young."

"The thing is…she died in childbirth. The baby didn't make it, either."

Carter trembles. "I can't believe it. Who was the father?"

"It doesn't matter," Sandy replies, attempting to calm him down.

"It matters. I want to know. Was the baby Black or White?" Carter's voice shakes with rage. "It had to be Daniel—that bastard. When I get back, I'll find him and—"

"You'll do nothing of the sort," Sandy interrupts. "You need to move on. It'll take time."

Carter stands up and paces. "I can't believe it. She is about the only thing that mattered back home."

"You've got friends and family there," Sandy encourages. "I'm sorry I didn't tell you when I first arrived. It just doesn't seem like the right time."

Carter stares at the river, lost in thought. "That doesn't matter. I'm not sure what matters anymore."

"What matters is here and now," Sandy counsels. "We can't take anything for granted. We don't know what's ahead. But I do know this—there's a beautiful, smart young woman who loves you. And I'm pretty sure you love her."

"I can't love her," Carter protests. "I've got to go back to Mississippi. Hannah is free. I have to let her be free. I'll never be free."

Sandy takes a deep breath, reflects on his relationship with Patience, and says, "Love is bigger than you think."

Carter drops his head. "I don't want to break her heart."

"You're breaking it now. She'll never truly be free without you. They can try to chain our bodies, but they can't chain our hearts or souls. They can't chain our love."

"We're going back to Mississippi. She can't go back there. She wouldn't be free."

"Love's greater than all that. Love doesn't know Mississippi from California. It doesn't know right from wrong. You've got to follow it—wherever it takes you. If you don't, you'll regret it forever." Sandy's voice softens. "I'm sorry about Peg. But she's gone, and Hannah's here. She won't be here forever."

Carter sighs. "I guess I should…" His voice trails off as he looks back toward Doc's cabin.

"I think you should," Sandy says with a quiet smile. "Help me up onto Sarah. I'll be fine. You go do what you need to do."

As he walks to Doc's cabin, Carter picks a bouquet from the hillside. The sun sets as he knocks on the door, the wildflowers hidden behind his back.

Hannah answers. "Is Sandy okay?"

"He's fine. I came to say…well, I…" Carter stammers.

"I saved newspapers for you. Come in."

He stands in the doorway, then reveals the bouquet. "I brought these for you. The thing is…" His voice cracks. He shakes and breaks into sobs.

Hannah steps forward and holds him, guiding him to the couch. She waits patiently as he gathers himself.

"What's wrong? What happened?"

"It's about Peg." Carter chokes on the words. "She's…she's dead."

"Oh, Carter." Hannah wraps her arms around him. "I'm so sorry. That's awful."

They embrace until he settles himself and wipes his tears. "I just wanted you to know. I still want to be your friend. I know that since you're free, we can never…"

Hannah gently places a hand on his cheek. "I've missed you so much." She wipes a tear from his face. "I know you loved Peg. I know you always will. Let's not think about the past. Let's think about the future. I'll always be your friend. No matter what."

Early the next morning, Hannah arrives at the Black miners' camp with a pot of soup. Carter and the others enjoy it before heading off to work. Sandy stays behind to rest and spends time talking with Hannah. She asks him everything she can about Carter and Mississippi.

A few days later, Carter and Robert work the claim, chipping away with pickaxes to build a growing pile of stone. The shallow tunnel gradually transforms into a genuine mine. Nearby, Sandy examines chunks of rock for any sign of gold, his bandaged arm still in a sling.

Weeks pass. Charles and Carter take Sandy to see Doc Hill for a check-up. Doc is pleased with the progress and tells him he can return to work.

A loud knock resonates at the door.

Hannah opens it to find Jonathan Kirk and Hardin assisting a very ill and weak Stephen Kirk. A slave supports him from behind. Stephen is pale and soaked in sweat, struggling to stand.

Doc Hill rushes over and guides him to a chair while Charles, Carter, Sandy and Hannah watch in silence as he examines Stephen. Then, with a serious expression, he steps back.

"Is he gonna be okay, Doc?" Jonathan asks, panic creeping into his voice.

"He's very sick. When did it start?"

"A couple of days ago," Jonathan says, trembling. "He started coughing but said he was fine. Yesterday, he could barely move. We took him to a doctor in Placerville, but he couldn't help. We heard you might be able to."

Doc nods solemnly. "I'll do what I can. Get him into the next room."

The next day, Carter and Charles return to Doc Hill's cabin to check on Stephen.

They find Jonathan sitting on the porch, shoulders hunched, face streaked with tears. Hardin sits beside him, staring at the ground.

Jonathan looks up, his eyes red, his voice low and bitter. "I wish we'd never come here. This was your idea," he says to Charles as he points a trembling finger. "My brother's dead. They're trying to take our slaves. This ain't a place for a Southern gentleman. I'm going home. Are you coming?"

"I'm staying."

Jonathan sneers. "Figures. You've become one of them. Aren't you worried they're going to take your slaves?"

"I came here to find gold," Charles replies, steady and calm. "And I'm going to stay."

Jonathan turns to Hardin. "What about you?"

Hardin shrugs. "I don't own any slaves. I'm staying to find gold."

CHAPTER 19
BAD NEWS FROM MISSISSIPPI

Weeks later, Carter, Robert, and Sandy sit around the campfire in front of their tent. The night air is cool and quiet, but something heavy clings to it. Charles approaches slowly, clutching an envelope. His shoulders sag, and grief pulls at every step.

Charles' voice is rough and distant. "I got a letter from my father."

He sinks onto a log beside them, takes a shaky breath, and reads aloud. His voice cracks under the weight of the words.

"Dear Charles,

I hope you're doing well. I'll get straight to the bad news. A disease has swept across Mississippi, taking many of our friends, neighbors, and workers. Our entire family became sick. Unfortunately, your brother William did not make it.

I hope you've found more gold. If not, perhaps it's time to come home and lend a hand.

Yours truly,

William Perkins

P.S. Patience and Robert's son were among those who passed away. We had to trade women and children to secure stronger field workers. It was necessary to trade Robert's wife and daughter."

Silence falls like a hammer. The fire crackles, but none of them move. Each man stares into the flames, the letter echoing in their minds.

Sandy's voice trembles. "How could this happen? How can so much devastation fit in one letter?"

Carter stares at the dirt, barely whispering, "I can't believe it. Grandma Patience… she's gone."

Robert stands abruptly. His eyes gleam in the firelight, burning with fury. He points at Charles, every rippling muscle tense.

"My mom's dead. My son's dead. And they sold my wife and daughter?" His voice thunders. "You owned them. Why'd they sell them?"

Charles steps back, hands raised in alarm. "I don't know," he says, shaking his head. "I don't know why. I don't know what's going on back home. I'm…I'm sorry."

Robert's voice drops to a near whisper. "I'll never see them again." He turns and disappears into the darkness, swallowed by grief.

Charles' face is twisted with sorrow. "We need time," he finally chokes out. "We'll take a few days off."

Without another word, he walks into the shadows.

Sandy and Carter remain silent by the fire. The crackle of burning wood fills the space between them as their thoughts drift across thousands of miles to Mississippi. They both see Patience's warm eyes in their minds—her steady hands, prayers, and strength.

Sandy wipes his eyes and stands. "I'm going to turn in," he says hoarsely, then disappears into the tent.

Carter stays behind. For the first time, he feels a flicker of anger toward Charles. This journey, once filled with promise and adventure, now feels like endless labor for someone else's gain. They left everything behind, and for what? His hands are raw, his spirit worn, and nothing is left in Mississippi but ghosts.

He stares into the fire, jaw clenched, bitterness creeping into his heart.

Carter can't sleep and rouses early the next morning. He walks to a spot on the hillside to watch the sun rise over the river. He thinks about Patience and all the love and care she has shown him. She was his grandmother, but she was the only mother he's ever known. *What is Mississippi like?* he wondered. *No Peg. No Patience. Disease. What others were sold or traded?*

He can't imagine what Sandy and Robert are feeling. Their loss is profound, perhaps even deeper than his. He knows they will need time to themselves to cope with their grief.

He spends the day walking quietly in the woods, trying to remember how things were and not to think about how things are or will be.

Carter spends the next day alone again, walking in the mountains. He takes time to read the Bible. In the evening, he visits Hannah and shares the news with her.

"I'm so sorry, Carter," Hannah says as she sits beside him in Doc's cabin. She takes his hand and gently strokes it.

"There's nothing left for me in Mississippi," Carter grieves. "I'll never see Patience again."

"How are Sandy and Robert taking the news?"

"Sandy's been very quiet. He doesn't want to talk. He seems lost. I've never seen him like this."

"And Robert?"

"He's mostly angry. It looked like he was going to hit Charles when he heard the news. I felt like hitting Charles, too."

"What are you going to do now?"

"I guess we'll go back to work in a few days."

"I think it's time you found a way for you and your family to be free."

Carter's brown eyes flash with anger. "You know there's no way to escape. If we run, everyone will be looking for us. I know Robert wants to, but we can't let that happen. Things would only get worse."

Hannah takes a deep breath. "There has to be a way, Carter."

Carter shakes his head. "It's just how things are."

Carter, Robert, and Sandy spend the next few days processing their loss. They haven't seen Charles and haven't gone looking for him.

One morning, as they finish breakfast, Sandy asks, "Has anyone seen Charles?"

Robert grunts and sneers. "Who cares?"

"I haven't seen him," Carter replies. "I bet he's working the claim."

"It ain't doing us much good sitting around. Let's get to work," Sandy says, running a hand through his white cotton hair and putting on his hat.

Robert glares at him. "I say we don't work for him anymore. He can't force us. It's time to escape. I know some people who are talking about it. It's a big territory."

"Charles is a decent man, but he'll put a price on our heads if we run," Sandy says. "There are plenty of men eager to hunt us down. They've caught everyone who has tried. He can make us work—and he can sell us. You want to end up working for someone like Hardin?"

Robert throws the rest of his coffee into the fire and storms into the tent.

They reach the claim by mid-morning and find Charles swinging a pickaxe. He turns and reads their grim expressions. Holding a smile, he says, "Glad to see you guys."

Carter, Sandy, and Robert nod but remain silent as they start their tasks. They observe that Charles' face shows signs of exhaustion and sorrow. He must have been working the claim alone for days.

They pick up pickaxes and shovels and get to work.

They break for lunch. Charles breaks the awkward silence, overwhelmed with guilt.

"I don't know what's going on back home. If I'd stayed…" Charles starts as he looks at their solemn faces, then corrects, "If *we* had stayed. Perhaps things could have been different. Maybe we could have gotten Patience and the others' help from a doctor. I would have never sold your family, Robert."

There is dead silence.

Robert throws his plate of food to the ground. "It don't matter anymore. They're gone."

He walks a few feet away and grabs a pickaxe. He glares at Charles and then walks to a rock wall. He swings the pickaxe with vengeance.

Charles looks at Sandy and Carter. "I know you're hurt. We're all hurt." He takes a deep breath and pauses. "The thing is that the gold is playing out. I've got to find a big strike. Then we can all go home. I've got to keep searching."

"You keep searching and we'll keep working," Sandy says fatherly. He gets up and returns to work. Carter follows without saying a word.

Charles leaves the digging to Carter, Sandy, and Robert and spends the next few weeks riding Sarah up and down the gold fields. He studies his maps and marks promising areas.

The work is grueling, but it keeps them from thinking about their family in Mississippi. They camp by the mine and fight rainstorms to keep working.

Carter travels to buy supplies and visit Hannah whenever possible.

One evening after a brief reading lesson, Hannah gazes at Carter. She looks at his hand and runs a finger over his calluses. "Why do you work so hard? It's all for Charles and his family."

"The sooner we find gold, the sooner we go back to Mississippi," Carter blurts.

"Is that what you want? Do you want to go back to Mississippi and pick cotton?"

Carter controls his feelings and manages a smile. "That's the way it is. I promised Master William I would bring Charles home safe, and I will. You don't understand, they're like family."

"They're not family. Families don't treat each other like that. The men at Sweet Vengeance are working for themselves. They keep their money. People are saying they are finding more and more."

"I know they are, but they're free."

"Someday. Someday you can be free. Lots of folks are talking about it."

"Folks talk about. They write about it. But they don't do anything."

"You can't give up hope, Carter. They can't take that away from you. They can't take your soul. You told me, Sandy said, 'They can't chain love, and they can't take it away.'"

"They can't take it away, but they can destroy it. They can kill it."

"They will never take the love I have for you. They can never kill it. Do you love me? Are you going to let them kill love?"

Carter takes a deep breath. "They will never take that, but they will take everything else."

"Promise you'll never give up. Never give up hope. Never let them take your soul. Never let them kill love."

"I promise," Carter says as he kisses her.

Day after day, the routine remains the same—leave the tent, swing pickaxes, and shovel rock. After weeks, Carter brings his pickaxe down hard, his frustration flaring.

He spots a chunk of quartz glinting with gold. He kneels to pick it up and sees more gold-flecked quartz. He yells at Sandy and Robert, "Look! Gold!"

They sift through the rocks and build a pile containing shimmering bits of gold.

"Finally!" Sandy exclaims. "We found gold."

"Do we have to tell him? Can't we keep it?" Robert questions as he examines the gold. "He doesn't need to know. We can run. We can buy our freedom."

"Robert! You can't think like that," Sandy says sharply.

"He's never around, and he—" Robert begins, but Carter cuts him off.

"We work for him, and this is his. That's the way it is," Carter growls. "We're not thieves."

Robert sulks back to work.

They work the claim for days, pulling in a fair amount of gold.

Charles returns, worn and tired, unshaven and rugged. Sarah's exhausted, too.

Carter is surprised to see him in this state. His thoughts flash back to Mississippi, and he remembers the day Charles returned and saved him from the whip.

The next morning, Charles was proud and dressed in his Sunday finest. The Mississippi was gleaming, and the rows of cotton were freshly planted.

He was beaming about his plans to find gold in California. Carter felt it, too. The promise seemed so grand—that was just a year ago.

Now here they are. Worn and broken. Picking through rocks on a dusty mountainside.

Still, Carter is excited to show him the gold. Perhaps it will change things.

He pulls out a sack of gold and hands it to Charles.

Charles beams. "Good job, men. This won't get us back to Mississippi. But it's a start. It will pay the bills." He turns to Carter. "How much more do you think there is?"

"I think she's played out."

"Probably is, I'll look. It's okay. I've found another strike that's not far away."

Charles picks the rocks and searches. There's not much left and little potential.

After a hearty dinner, he tells them he will take the gold to the bank in Sacramento and return in a few days. Then they will move to a new claim.

Carter knows they found a lot of gold. Enough to buy passage to Mississippi, but he knows Charles won't leave until he finds his big strike. *Maybe he is sending more back home,* he considers. *Maybe to get more help.*

When Charles returns, they pack and move a short distance away to try their luck again. After a few days, they uncover a modest amount of gold. Charles stays with them this time, and they sleep in tents pitched on the mountainside to guard their claim.

One night, Carter awakens to the soft clink of metal. He sits up, attentive, and looks toward their claim. A brief flicker of light captures his attention, prompting him to rouse Charles.

"There's someone out there," Carter whispers.

They move cautiously through the darkness with their pistols drawn. Near the old claim, they spot a figure hunched over, chipping rocks with a pickaxe. A small lantern casts a faint glow, illuminating the man's back.

"Stop right there," Charles commands, raising his pistol. "Put your hands up and turn around."

The man freezes, then slowly straightens and turns. In the weak light, Hardin's startled face comes into view.

"Looking for something, cousin?" Charles sneers.

"Just thought I'd try a little diggin'," Hardin replies as he shrugs.

"This is my claim, and you know it," Charles says, his pistol trained on Hardin. Carter also keeps his pistol steady, pointing at Hardin's face.

"No need to get so upset. No reason to point guns," Hardin says, raising his hands. "Ain't fair that you've got free labor. I'm just tryin' to scratch out a living."

"I can pay fair wages if you work for me," Charles offers, trying to de-escalate.

"There's nothin' fair about that," Hardin snaps, grabbing the lantern. "I thought blood was thicker than water. Thicker than gold. You've changed, cousin. You can keep your claim. I'll find my own."

He turns and stumbles down the rocky hillside, the lantern swinging wildly.

Before disappearing into the dark, he shouts, "You shouldn't let Carter play with guns. One day, he'll point it at the wrong man. That'll be his last day."

CHAPTER 20
CALIFORNIA BECOMES FREE
OCTOBER 1850

Carter, Charles, Sandy, and Robert head toward Coloma on a sunny afternoon, looking to resupply and take a few days' rest. As they near the town, they hear shouting and gunfire, Miners fire their pistols into the air. Some dance with glee. Others shout angrily and storm off in disgust.

Charles nudges Sarah and rides ahead toward the crowd. He spots George approaching with several of their old tent-mates and reins in his horse.

"What's this all about?"

"California's a free state, Charlie!" George exclaims and points to Carter, Sandy, and Robert in the distance. "They're free. We're on equal ground now. You're on free soil."

George rushes to join a cluster of cheering miners.

Charles dismounts and walks to a nearby newspaper vendor. Bold headlines scream the news—*California Admitted as a Free State.* He buys several papers: the *Alta California, The Republic* out of D.C., and even a Mississippian newspaper buried in the stack. He steps away from the noise, flipping through the pages, unaware that Carter, Sandy, and Robert have come up behind him.

The town is in chaos. Some miners celebrate, others argue. Southern miners yell at people of color. Some of their slaves taunt them.

A stern-faced Southern miner approaches Charles. "Politicians are coming tonight. There's a meeting. They're going to talk about the compromise. We need to stick together. Nobody's taking our slaves. Are you with us?"

"I just heard about California being free," Charles replies. "I'll be there."

He scans the headlines, pulls a few gold coins from his pocket, and walks to Carter.

"Get supplies and camp near Doc Hill's place tonight. I've got to talk to some people. I'll come by later," he tells Carter as he hands him the newspapers. Without another word, he heads to a gathering of Southern men.

That night, Carter sits with Hannah, flipping through the newspapers. She scans the *Alta California,* eyes catching the headline. She reads aloud: "'California Admitted to the Union as a Free State.'" She sets the paper down. "You're free," she says, her voice rising.

Carter lowers *The Republic,* its page marked with the subhead "The California Compromise."

"I wish it were that simple. They passed a new Fugitive Slave Law. Remember when I told you about Senator Davis from Mississippi?"

"I remember. He's your neighbor—and a bad man."

"He helped push through a compromise. Slave owners can claim slaves in any state—even free ones. I'll never be free."

"It's time to get free! We could go to Oregon. Or Canada. Or even Panama. Everybody's free there."

"I can't. They'll catch me. People now get paid to turn in runaways. And anyone who helps runaways faces fines or jail time. Every law is against me. If I run, it'll only be worse."

"What does Charles say?"

"He just found out today. He's going to a meeting tonight with the pro-slavery men. I'm going, too," Carter says, resolute.

"You can't go," Hannah pleads. "It could be dangerous."

"I'll stay out of sight. I have to hear what they say," he replies, rising. "I'm going now."

She grabs his hand. "Promise me you'll be careful."

"You're the one who was just telling me to run," he teases as he grins, gently caressing her hand before kissing it. "I'll be careful."

He slips out into the night.

Carter moves through the woods into the darkness, approaching a clearing lit by a fire. A large bonfire crackles, casting flickering light over a crowd of angry men. He crouches between two boulders, hidden but close enough to hear.

Henry Crabb stands atop a makeshift platform, arms raised.

"I've just come back from D.C., and I assure you—we fought hard to keep the balance of power," Crabb declares.

A voice from the crowd shouts, "You failed! You failed us. Sixteen free states now. Fifteen slave states!"

Grumbling ripples through the gathering.

"We're not giving up," Crabb bellows. "We're working to bring more territories into the slaveholding fold. We won't let Northern high-mindedness—or abolitionists—take our freedom!"

The crowd erupts in cheers.

"You have friends in Washington and California," Crabb continues. "We fought for and passed a new fugitive slave law. It's stronger than ever. If anyone helps or hides a runaway, they'll be punished. Even here in California. You're safe here. Your property is protected."

Applause roars from the crowd.

"I will continue to be your champion. I will make sure California protects you. Vote for me for the California Senate!"

Crabb steps down, and the crowd surges toward him, shaking his hand and clapping him on the back.

Carter watches silently for a moment, then slips away into the darkness.

The next morning, Hannah arrives at Carter's tent with breakfast. They sit outside, the morning sun glinting off the pines.

"What did you hear last night?" she asks, her voice tense but hopeful.

Carter stares at the ground. "It was just like I thought. The politicians are on the slave owners' side. I won't be free—not here, not anywhere."

Hannah sets her jaw. "Things have to change."

CHAPTER 21
THE LONG HARSH WINTER

California's population is surging, and new towns are emerging across the Sierra foothills. Doc has moved his practice to the growing settlement of Auburn, not far from Coloma and the American River. The road between East and West is becoming a well-worn crossroads for travelers.

Gold seekers have learned the hard way that heavy winter snow and spring rains often lead to flooding. Tent camps near rivers and creeks are usually wiped out, forcing miners to higher ground.

Doc has partnered with another young physician and hired a team of assistants. Hannah remains Doc's most trusted aide. They became overwhelmed by a surge of illnesses from around the world. Mining accidents are on the rise, and with the territory still largely lawless, Doc has grown skilled at treating stab wounds and gunshots.

Cabins and tents dot the Auburn landscape as if they'd appeared overnight. Charles has secured a small, snug cabin near Doc's place and found a larger one for Carter, Sandy, and Robert a short walk away. Carter cherishes the nearness to Hannah. Though both are busy, they make time for each other whenever possible.

Carter, Sandy, and Robert work steadily, moving from one claim to the next, following Charles' instructions. Now and then, Charles joins them, but most days, he disappears into the Sierras, riding Sarah to scout areas he believes might yield a major strike. He often stays out for days, braving rain and snow.

Carter worries about him. Even in the worst weather, Charles always returns, but something has changed. He is quieter—more withdrawn and distracted. The letter from Mississippi shifted something between them. Carter feels the distance. He suspects Charles, Sandy, and Robert think so, too.

Waves of Southerners arrive with their slaves, taking advantage of the compromise. They want to seize the opportunity and shape California's future. Politicians, including Davis, push for the expansion of slavery at all costs.

Carter watches as Charles falls in line to uphold the Southern social order they'd brought with them. Hardin hasn't let up, either. He knows Charles worries about what he might say to his father and family back home. The South has arrived in California.

Charles pushes to find gold despite the weather. They pan through the rain, working the lower slopes of the Sierra Nevada below the snowline. When the skies are clear, they push higher into the mountains. They work the ridges and rugged mountainsides when the weather allows. Several times, they've been caught in a sudden snowstorm. One was an all-out blizzard, but they managed to pull through.

CHAPTER 22
GLIMMER OF FREEDOM
SPRING OF 1851

The rivers and streams roar with runoff from the heaviest snow and rain anyone can remember. There are no reliable records to predict the weather since few people have lived in the region long enough to know what to expect. They have since learned how fast the weather can change, but this winter is especially harsh.

The spring runoff forces a pause. It is too dangerous to pan or travel along the riverbanks. News comes that Sacramento has been hit hard, its businesses and tent camps swept away by the flooding.

They wait, knowing the surging water might loosen fresh gold from the mountains. Even so, Charles rides into the Sierras alone on Sarah. Nothing will stop him from seeking his fortune.

Hannah has been busy helping Doc, but Carter spends as much time with her as he can. He helps in the kitchen and sometimes with patients, though he has to look away from the blood.

Their quiet moments come late in the evening. Hannah's reading has improved remarkably. They read newspapers together and share the most compelling articles.

One evening, Hannah's eyes light up. "Look, Carter!" she says as she holds up a paper and reads aloud: "'Slave Set Free—Judge Rules Federal Fugitive Slave Act Does Not Apply in California.'" She turns to him, eyes bright. "You're free?"

Carter shakes his head. "It's not that simple."

Hannah points to the article. "He's just like you. Brought to California, didn't run away. The judge said he wasn't a fugitive, and the law doesn't apply."

"I can't fight the law."

"This is the law, Carter! Laws change. I know people at Sweet Vengeance are helping others like you. I'll talk to them."

"What about Charles?" Carter growls.

"You don't owe him anything. Look at all the work you do for him. What do you have to show for it?"

"We are like brothers…but now…" Carter trails off. "I know things will change. Laws are changing in California, but not in Mississippi. Charles can't change. There's too much pressure from his family and all the rest of them."

"He's part of a wolf pack. They use people for control and power. Charles tried to resist them, but now he's running with them. Maybe he's tired. Maybe he's scared."

Carter smiles, impressed by her insight. "You amaze me. I've been trying to figure out what's happening with Charles. We were close when we got here. Like a couple of wolves."

"You don't belong to his pack. All the gold is for himself and his family. They're not just a pack of wolves. They're a pack of thieves. There's nothing for you and your family."

Carter takes a deep breath, her words settling in his chest as he stares into the candle flame.

Hannah looks into his eyes lovingly. "Things are changing. You can be free. We can be free together." She pauses and then adds, "I know you and Charles are like brothers. You're both trapped. But when you're free…maybe you can help him find his way, too."

Carter leans back, letting her words sink in. "How do you know all this?"

"It's been a long winter. I've read everything I could get my hands on. It's helped me think."

She turns to a pile of books on the table and restacks them individually. "These are the ones you need to read." She calls out the titles as she sets them down: *The Count of Monte Cristo* by Dumas, *The Pilgrim's Progress* by Bunyan, *David Copperfield* by Dickens, and *Pride and Prejudice* by Austen.

Carter is astonished. He picks up *David Copperfield.* "You've read all these?"

"I've read them. I'm still working to understand them." She reaches for one last book and holds it out to him. *Narrative of the Life of Frederick Douglass.* "You must read this," she says, opening to Chapter Eleven.

She reads aloud: "He told me, if I would be happy, I must lay out no plans for the future. He said if I behaved myself properly, he would take care of me. Indeed, he advised me to complete thoughtlessness of the future and taught me to depend solely upon him for happiness."

"I don't understand…Who is he?"

"He was a slave. Now he's free. He wrote this book. There's a lot to learn."

She flips to a marked page in Chapter Seven and reads: "I would sometimes feel that learning to read had been a curse rather than a blessing. It had given me a view of my wretched condition without the remedy. It opened my eyes to the horrible pit, but to no ladder upon which to get out."

Hannah pauses, her gaze steady. Carter's eyes widen as the weight of the words settles.

"He broke free from slavery ten years ago. Now he's living free. You can, too."

"I can't run. I can't escape," Carter fumes.

"You don't have to run. You can use the law. I'll talk to Fritz and the men at Sweet Vengeance. They'll know people who can help. They'll know a lawyer."

Carter takes a deep breath, absorbs his situation, and exhales. "Let's take this one step at a time. Things are what they are—we can't control everything. I'll talk to Grandpa."

Hannah meets his gaze and squeezes his hand. "Things are what you make them," she insists. "You can shape your future. We can be free— together."

Carter shakes his head. "Lawyers cost a lot of money. I can't afford that."

"I've saved money. I can help."

Carter squeezes her hand. "One step at a time. Find out what you can about the lawyer and how much it might cost. But be careful. Don't tell Fritz or anyone else it's about me or my family."

Late that night, Carter, Sandy, and Robert huddle around a fire in front of their tent at the Black miners' camp. Flames flicker in the cool air as Carter unfolds the newspaper and reads aloud about the recent court ruling that freed a man held as a slave in California.

"I'll be damned," Sandy says, eyes wide. "I've been prayin' the law might help us one day."

"What about Charles?" Robert scowls. "He'll never set us free."

"He might not have a choice," Carter says. "This ruling—if it holds—means we don't need his permission. Maybe we can be free. And maybe...maybe we can partner with him."

Sandy looks at Carter and shakes his head. "Charles is a good man, but he ain't that good. How much gold do you think he shipped back to Mississippi?"

Robert lets out a bitter laugh. "More than I'll ever see. They're all in this together, like a pack of thieves."

"Hannah says they're like a pack of wolves," Carter adds. "But maybe we can be our own wolf pack."

Sandy looks over his shoulder at the men gathered around their campfires—some cooking, some talking, all watching the night.

"We can be a wolf pack," Sandy advises. "And it's not just the three of us. I'd rather it be in court if it comes to a fight. But we'll fight them in the streets if we must. Let's see what Hannah finds out about a lawyer. She needs to keep quiet. The Southerners are like a swarm of hornets. They're mad as hell."

CHAPTER 23
DEVASTATING NEWS
APRIL 1851

Carter, Sandy, and Robert sit in front of the fire outside their tent on a chilly, clear evening. Carter looks up at the shadowy outline of Charles riding Sarah, leading another mule loaded with supplies. They haven't seen Charles in weeks—not since he went to San Francisco to handle banking.

Charles' hat is pulled low, his shoulders hunched as he walks into the firelight. His eyes are red from tears.

"I got supplies," he says, his voice rough. "The thing is..." He reaches into his coat pocket and pulls out an envelope. He struggles to open it and then drops it. He picks it up with shaky hands and gives it to Carter. "The thing is...I don't know what to think anymore."

He turns and walks into the darkness.

"Never seen him like this before," Sandy says, uneasy. "Read the letter."

Carter opens the envelope and unfolds the letter. "It's from Miss Perkins." He reads it aloud:

"Dearest Charles,

This is our third letter. We truly want to hear from you and hope you come home soon. Your father became ill and passed away months ago. We are managing the affairs, but we need to know if you will return to take your place with the family or if you plan to stay in California. If we do not hear from you in two months, we must assume that you will not be coming home, and we will take care of your affairs accordingly.

Sincerely,

Jane Perkins."

Carter lowers the letter and stares into the flames. "Can't believe Master Perkins is dead."

"Guess we're heading back to Mississippi," Sandy mourns.

Robert scowls. "I'm not going back. I'm going to Canada."

"You'll never make it," Carter says, sharper than he means. "Everything's against us. If it were possible, we'd all go tonight."

"What about the lawyer? Getting free by the law?" Robert asks.

"Doubt there's time for that. Master Charles will take us back as soon as he can," Sandy moans.

"We don't know what he's thinking. Let's give him a few days," Carter says. "When he decides what he's going to do, then we'll decide what we're going to do."

Carter's mind wanders back to Mississippi, reflecting on William's death, the plantation, and Jane's sharply worded letter. It's more than mere sorrow—it feels like an ultimatum: return home or sever all ties forever.

Carter feels a heavy burden of grief. He reflects that William was a good man, perhaps just running with his pack and making his place in the world. The fact that William might be his father closes in around him, adding layers of confusion and uncertainty.

He knows Charles' pain must run deep. He and William were a great deal alike. They were close. William was the only person Charles was close to in his family. Maybe Charles will stay in California. Or maybe he will seize the opportunity and go back and take control of the plantation.

Carter's feelings are tangled with grief, anger, confusion and fear. He knows he must make hard choices, whatever Charles decides. If he stays in California, Charles cannot keep him enslaved forever. They have to come to some agreement.

The thought of going back to Mississippi sends a shudder down Carter's spine. Things might be different with Charles running the plantation, but things in Mississippi have not changed. There's Hannah and there's freedom. Carter knows he can't go back.

Charles stays secluded in his cabin, unseen for days. Carter respects his need for solitude, recognizing that the news has profoundly affected him.

A few evenings later, Carter watches Hannah ladling chicken soup from the pot.

She hands him a bowl and says, "What are you going to do? You can't let him sit in that cabin forever."

"He needs time to think," Carter says.

"He's had time. You've had time, too," she replies, her voice steady but firm. "We could leave now for Oregon, Canada, even Panama. You don't owe him anything."

Carter sips the soup, then lowers the bowl. "You don't understand...Father's dead—" He catches himself, the word slipping out too easily. He looks away. "Master William is gone. Nothing will ever be the same."

"Nothing's ever the same," Hannah says. "And things shouldn't stay the same."

"Charles said that, too, back when we were leaving Mississippi," Carter reflects. "He said he would get rich and go back to Mississippi and change everything."

"If he goes back to Mississippi, are you going with him?"

"I'm not going back to Mississippi!"

Hannah fills another bowl and hands it to him. "Go talk to your brother. Take this to him."

Carter manages a half smile and takes the bowl to the cabin.

He knocks. No answer. He knocks again, louder. "I've got a bowl of soup. I'm worried about you. We should talk."

The door creaks open. Charles answers with a scraggly beard and a blanket draped over his shoulders. He says nothing, just motions for Carter to come inside.

The room is dark until Charles lights a lamp. Carter hands him the bowl. They sit across from each other at the small table. Charles doesn't speak. He eats spoon after spoon, fast and hungry, while Carter sits quietly, watching his brother come back to life—one bite at a time.

"Hannah makes the best soup," Charles says with a faint grin, slurping from his spoon. "Almost as good as back home."

Carter waits patiently as Charles finishes. He has a million questions, but he knows better than to push. He wants Charles to speak first.

Finally, Charles finishes slurping down the soup and breaks the silence. "I don't know what's right anymore. We should probably go back to Mississippi. We could take Hannah, but..."

"Hannah won't be free back home," Carter interrupts. "The laws are changing here in California, and we've been talking..."

Charles raises a hand, stopping him. His throat tightens. "We should go back, but the truth is, I don't have the money. Father's gone, and I need to go home as soon as I can."

His voice catches. Despite trying to hold it back, tears slip from his eyes. He reaches under the table and pulls out three envelopes with trembling fingers.

"I'm going back to Mississippi to find out what's happening—and then I'll come back," he says, voice cracking. "I know the laws are changing. We'll figure it out when I return. If I don't come back in six months...I've written each of you a letter of freedom. I told Doc. He'll help you."

He hands the envelopes to Carter, who stares at them, stunned. It isn't what he expected.

"What are we supposed to do for six months?" Carter asks.

Charles reaches down and opens a leather satchel beside his chair. He shuffles through papers and pulls out a map. He spreads it across the table. Lines, X's, and circled X's mark various locations. He points to one of the circles.

"Keep looking for gold where I circled the X's," Charles rasps. Then, with shaking hands, he digs out a small metal flask and two glasses, pouring shots.

"What do we do if we find gold?" Carter asks.

"Keep it. Buy what you need. Do what you must." Charles pauses. Then, more quietly, "If I don't come back in six months, everything I own belongs to you. You can share it with Sandy and Robert however you like."

Carter hesitates. "I told Master William I'll keep you safe and bring you home."

Charles gives him a weary smile. "I'm glad Father asked you to keep me safe. You kept me safe. But he'd want you to be safe, too." He swallows hard. "Nothing's certain in life. I always thought I'd see him again...but now I never will. And maybe...maybe we will never see each other again, either."

Charles raises his glass for a toast. Carter does the same.

Charles looks into Carter's eyes and smiles brightly. "To the chapters we read together...and the stories still to write. Here's to new chapters and adventures yet to come."

They sit silently for a moment, the weight settling between them.

Charles stands and extends his hand. "I've got to pack. I'm leaving first thing in the morning."

"I can ride to San Francisco and see you off," Carter offers.

"I hired a carriage. Take good care of Sarah." Charles' voice wavers as he turns away.

Early the next morning, Carter, Hannah, Sandy, Robert, and Doc stand near the waiting carriage. The driver adjusts the reins as the sun rises.

Charles steps out of the cabin, freshly shaven and dressed in his suit. He tosses his bag into the carriage, then turns to the group. His eyes land on Carter, who holds his Bible.

"I'm late. I have to go. I'll be back. So...goodbye for now," Charles says quickly, as if saying it fast might make it easier. He climbs into the wagon, then turns back. "Is there anything in the book for me?"

Carter opens the Bible. Peg's picture slips out. Hannah stoops to pick it up as Carter finds the verse.

"Philippians 3:12," Carter says softly. "Not that I have already obtained this or am already perfect, but I press on to make it my own because Christ Jesus has made me his own. Brothers, I do not consider that I have made it my own. But one thing I do: forgetting what lies behind and straining forward to what lies ahead, I press on toward the goal for the prize of the upward call of God in Christ Jesus."

They stand in reverent silence. Charles smiles, turns away, and rolls down the road.

Hannah is still holding Peg's picture. She studies it for a moment, then hands it to Carter. "She was beautiful."

"She was, and you are," Carter says quietly. He returns the picture to his Bible. "I try to forget what lies behind and press toward the goal and the prize."

He leans in and kisses Hannah. They walk away together.

That afternoon, Carter, Sandy, and Robert look over Charles' map, tracing the lines and examining the marked spots. The gold they find will be theirs now—entirely theirs. A new sense of excitement stirs in them, lifting the burden they have carried for so long. They decide to pan for a few more days, then pack up and head into the Sierras to try their luck at the circled X's.

Sandy and Robert look to Carter for direction. He has earned their trust and is now the leader.

One evening, as Carter prepares dinner by their tent on the mountainside, he stirs a pot over the fire while gazing across the valley. His mind drifts to Charles and the lengthy return to Mississippi. He recalls the challenges of the journey west and anticipates how tough the trip back alone may be.

Charles intends to depart San Francisco on the SS *Oregon* on May 1st. The *Oregon* is a sister ship of the *California* and follows the same route. Carter reflects on this date and understands that Charles won't be back in Mississippi until mid-June if everything goes smoothly. He expects to spend a few weeks there organizing his affairs before returning. The soonest he can return is mid-August, making it three and a half months. Any minor delays could extend his return to over six months.

Hannah wants him to move on, someplace safe and free, but he just can't. *What happens if he comes back after six months?* Carter wonders. Maybe they should go somewhere else as soon as they are free in six months.

After weeks of hard work and numerous X's checked off, Sandy and Robert dig and swing pickaxes in a shallow rock tunnel while Carter examines the rocks.

The sun beats down as they pause to rest. Their bare backs, covered in sweat, glisten in the sunlight. Carter's lash mark, stretching from shoulder to waist, is still visible, though faint. Robert's back bears long welts from Nick's whipping.

Sandy picks up a chunk and turns it over. "I don't know why Charles thought gold was here. There's nothing but rock."

Carter nudges stones with his boot. "Charles knew what he was doing. This is the right kind of rock—it's quartz. He learned about it in college."

He walks to the shallow mine and slowly rubs his hand on the wall. He picks flecks of rock and points to the right. "We need to go this way."

Carter grabs a pickaxe and chips at the wall. Robert and Sandy reluctantly get up and start swinging again as rock splinters fly. They work for hours. Finally, Carter stops them and picks up a small stone. The glint of gold is unmistakable.

"We found it!" Carter exclaims.

Sandy and Robert crowd around to examine it while Carter uses a small pick to chip at the wall. A narrow vein of gold glimmers through a sheet of white quartz.

"There's a lot more here," Carter says as they get back to work.

Sandy and Robert strike at the wall, revealing more of the gold while Carter gathers rocks. He carefully chips away at the rocks to uncover the gold.

They work for days, eventually collecting a small pile of gold. They decide to head home when the small vein disappears into solid quartz. They're short on supplies, anyway. They load Sarah with their gold and gear, then make their way down the mountain, following the American River back to Auburn. Along the way, they stop at the river to bathe, shave, and wash their clothes.

Once they're back at the cabin, Carter takes a small jar of gold to Hannah. She admires it in the lantern light. "What are you going to do with all this gold?"

"We've been talking about that, and I want to know what you think. Gold's going to run out. We got lucky. It's getting harder to find. We're thinking about buying a wagon and mules—starting a hauling business."

Hannah studies him. "What about Charles? What if he comes back? He might try to take everything. You need to talk to a lawyer and make sure you can be free."

Carter stays optimistic. "Charles said we'd figure it out when he gets back. Maybe we'll all work together."

"Do you think he's coming back?"

"I'm not sure. I know he planned to, but he was worried about what's happening in Mississippi," Carter replies. "Things will be different without William. I know he cares about Emmy, but I doubt he'll bring her here. It's going to be hard for him to leave her again."

Hannah pauses. "I have a feeling Charles isn't coming back."

"Why?"

"The way he was acting those last few months was strange. He was frustrated about not finding a big strike. I think he was homesick—maybe about Emmy. And I'm sure his family will pressure him to stay. They'll want him to take over for his father."

Carter chuckles. "I know Charles. Nothing will stop him if he wants to come back and gold."

"Maybe. But I still doubt it. I think your hauling business is a good idea. Gold's bound to run out."

They take Sundays off and make early morning trips to Sacramento to attend services at the Colored Methodist Episcopal Church, California's first and only Black church. The congregation has grown to over a hundred members and has moved from the basement of Daniel Blue's home to a building on Seventh Street in the expanding business district.

Fritz and others from the Sweet Vengeance mine often attend services. Carter and Hannah usually make a full day of it, enjoying lunch with friends and shopping for food and supplies, now more plentiful in the growing city.

The church is a central gathering place for the Black community. Most of the congregation are free Black people, but a few remain enslaved. Some of their masters allow them to attend services and grant Sundays off.

The fellowship provides a sense of hope and unity in the face of racism and the divisions they have endured throughout their lives. They look out for one another and offer support.

They are not alone. People seeking freedom pour into California. They include free-soilers, who resist the expansion of slavery, and staunch abolitionists committed to abolishing slavery at all costs.

They come from diverse backgrounds, races, creeds, and colors, representing every part of the United States and the world. Most understand that protecting the freedom of others is essential to safeguarding their liberty. Nonetheless, racism and prejudice cloud their judgment.

The lines continue to be drawn. Carter and the Black community sort through allies and enemies. Many of their enemies make their positions painfully clear. They all follow the political and moral battle as it rages in California.

CHAPTER 24
CHARLES RETURNS TO MISSISSIPPI
JUNE 1851

Charles drives a carriage toward the plantation on a hot Mississippi afternoon. He didn't send a letter and no one knows he is coming or when he will arrive. There was no point in writing; the letter would take just as long to reach home as it took him.

He stops in front of the mansion, now looming cold and unfamiliar. It no longer feels like home.

He sits still, staring at the house, trying to collect his thoughts. He wants to speak to his father but knows he isn't there. The weight of his loss presses down on Charles, clouding his mind. After a moment, he turns the carriage toward a distant hill—the Indian burial mound that was once his and Carter's favorite spot. A tall monument with a cross marks his father's grave.

Charles stops the carriage and walks up the gravel path. A black, spiked iron fence encloses the monument and his younger brother's headstone. He opens the gate, steps inside, and kneels before his father's grave, overcome with emotion.

"I tried, Father...but I failed," he chokes. "If I hadn't tried, I'd be a bigger failure."

He kneels in silence, the breeze stirring the grass around him. After a while, he stands and looks out over the plantation. The Mississippi River shimmers in the distance.

He thinks of the mound beneath his feet, once a Choctaw burial site. How many lie buried below? How many more of his family will join them? Thoughts of his mortality creep in as he recalls how close to death he came in Panama.

Turning away, he descends the hill with a single thought; He knows who he wants to see.

Back at the plantation, he quickly unhitches the horse from the carriage, leads it to a stall, and fills the trough with water and feed. Then he saddles Star and rides toward Emmy's plantation.

He ties Star near the front porch, climbs the steps, and pounds the brass lion-shaped knocker. Carl opens the door and tells him Emmy is in the back garden.

Charles strides through the house and into the garden, where Emmy kneels, planting flowers with several young slaves. Older men and women work nearby, hoeing and tending vegetables. He rushes to her. She looks up and rises to her feet, her hands and clothes covered in dirt.

"I thought I'd never see you again," she gasps.

"I sent you letters. I told you I'd come back!"

"I didn't get any letters. I thought you'd forgotten me," Emmy replies, her voice rising. "Daniel said you were staying in California."

Charles takes a deep breath, fury simmering. Daniel. Of course. He must've destroyed the letters and courted her while he was gone.

"You said you loved me. I said I loved you. I thought that was enough." Charles' blue eyes pierce into Emmy's green ones. "Have you been seeing Daniel?"

"He's been a big help around the plantation. He's taken me to dances. I didn't think you would ever come home." She blushes. "But I love you. I will always love you."

They embrace and kiss. After a moment, she pulls back.

"I guess that means you love me," she says softly.

"That means I love you," Charles whispers, kissing her again.

"Are you here to stay? Or are you going to leave me again for gold in California?" she asks, her eyes locked with his.

"We'll decide our future together," Charles promises.

"I need to finish planting. If you don't plant and care for things, they won't grow."

Charles drops to his knees beside her, his fine clothes quickly covered in dirt. He digs a hole and plants a flower. A young boy helps him, their hands working side by side in the soil.

"You shouldn't get your best clothes dirty," Emmy says as she laughs.

"They'll clean up fine. Let's finish your garden."

The next morning, before dawn, Charles and Emmy wake in the barn, covered in straw. Charles stands up, naked. "I've got to go."

Emmy reaches out, opening her arms. "You don't have to go anywhere. It's just you and me. My mother's away. No one knows you're here."

Charles hesitates, then falls into her arms.

Hours later, Charles stirs under a blanket in the straw, still naked. He looks around for his clothes, but they are nowhere to be found. He goes to Star, puts the saddle on, and prepares him for the ride back home.

As Charles cinches the saddle, Emmy walks in, carrying his freshly cleaned clothes, a pot of coffee, and a bag of rolls. She pauses to admire him before he notices and turns, startled, covering himself.

She smiles and walks toward him. "Are you planning to ride off in your birthday suit and leave me behind?"

"I need to get home. It's already mid-morning. I'm sure they saw my horse and carriage. They'll be looking for me."

"Your clothes are clean and pressed," she coos, holding them out in both hands—ensuring he takes them with both hands so she can admire him. "I like your birthday suit."

Charles takes the clothes and meets her gaze. "Your birthday suit is better than mine."

Emmy pulls out the photo she'd given Charles before he left. "I found this in your suit."

He smiles and holds it up as he looks at her. "It kept me going through the hard times."

Charles dresses, and they share coffee and fresh rolls in the barn.

"Promise me you'll never leave me," Emmy says, her voice barely above a whisper.

"I won't," Charles replies. "We'll talk about our future. But first, I need to see my family—figure out what's going on." He kisses her gently. "I'll come back soon."

"Come back for dinner," she says. "I'd like you to talk to Mother. We need help with the workers and crops. And our finances...I think we're struggling, but Mother won't admit it."

"I'll be back for dinner," he promises as he kisses her and rushes to Star.

Later that morning, Charles arrives at the Perkins plantation barn. He unsaddles Star, gives him food and water, and notices the empty carriage he'd driven from New Orleans. He assumes someone has moved his luggage to his room.

As he steps out of the barn, Daniel approaches. "Long time no see, brother. Where've you been? We were worried."

Charles meets his cold gaze. "I went to see Emmy."

Daniel hesitates. "You spent the night?"

"I did. She's doing well." Charles doesn't hide the edge in his tone.

Daniel clenches his jaw but holds back. "We heard from folks in New Orleans that you were on your way. Judge Yerger's here. We're getting ready to finalize Father's affairs."

They walk in silence to the study. Jane sits behind William's desk, her posture stiff. Across from her sits Judge Yerger, a grim-faced man with iron-gray hair and a stack of papers in hand.

Jane doesn't rise. "Welcome home, Charles. We saw your carriage yesterday. I trust you found somewhere to sleep."

Charles glares at Daniel. "I stayed at Emmy's."

Jane and Daniel exchange a glance. Daniel tries to look indifferent.

"Are you here to say, or are you returning to California?" Jane asks.

"I haven't decided," Charles adds as Judge Yerger stands and extends his hand.

"You remember Judge Yerger," Jane says. "We nearly gave up on you. He brought the will and estate documents. Would you like him to read them aloud?"

"I'll read them," Charles says as he takes the papers from Judge Yerger.

He reads slowly, page by page, frowning as he turns over the last one. "I don't understand. Why did Father split the plantation? It makes no sense."

"That's what he wanted," Jane says. "He wanted me and the children to receive equal portions of land and slaves."

"It's carved into pieces," Charles snaps. "How am I supposed to run the plantation?"

"You're not going to run it," Jane snarls. "Your father left me in charge. Daniel has been helping manage things while you were off in California. He and I will run it."

Charles sits back, stunned. This wasn't what he envisioned. He assumed he would take over the plantation. Now, everything seemed to be slipping away.

He flips back through the documents. His finger lands on William's signature. Judge Yerger and Jane are the signatory witnesses on the document.

"What about the money I sent back?" Charles asks, his voice sharp. "I sent a lot of gold."

Judge Yerger interjects, "All funds became part of the estate."

Charles scowls and scans the page listing the assets. "This can't be right. There should be more cash than this." He turns to Daniel. "Where did my money go?"

Daniel stiffens, eyes narrowing. "We needed it for the spring planting. Last year was rough for cotton. We lost too many workers to disease. We had to replace them—good field hands cost more. We traded women and children for strong men. We had to pay extra."

"You're the one who sold Robert's wife and children!" Charles chastises.

"Father agreed on who should go and who should stay," Daniel snarks.

Charles' voice drops, low and menacing. "Robert is mine. His family is mine. You had no right. The money was mine. You had no right!"

Daniel raises an eyebrow, challenging him. "You weren't here. Robert wasn't here, either. Where is he? And where are Carter and Sandy? They're property of the estate. Where are they?"

"They're mine! They're working my claim in California," Charles replies bitterly.

"Are you going back, or will you bring them here?" Jane asks coldly. "They're assets for the estate."

"You've all seen to it that I've got no money to go back—or to bring them here," Charles growls.

Judge Yerger places a sheet of paper on the table before Charles. "There's one last thing. We need your signature to finalize the estate."

Charles stares at the document. "What happens if I don't sign?"

"Your portion of the estate will be divided among your family," Judge Yerger replies.

"What about Carter, Sandy and Robert?" Charles demands.

Jane leans toward him. "If you sign, you get your fair share of slaves. They will count as yours. You'll need to figure out how to work your section of land. You need to get them back."

Charles grabs the pen and signs, eyes burning into Daniel and Jane. "I hoped things would be better. They're worse," he says as he storms out.

Jane watches him go, her expression blank. "He needs time to think."

Charles rushes to the barn, saddles Star, and rides out at a full gallop toward his favorite overlook of the Mississippi. The wind on his face does nothing to calm the storm brewing inside. He rides the plantation grounds, taking in the familiar fields and buildings, memories from childhood washing over him with every turn.

Later, he finds himself at the Indian mound, sitting beside his father's grave. He pulls Emmy's picture from his coat. He takes a long moment as he searches his soul. There is no question. He rushes to Star and rides to Emmy's plantation.

That evening, Charles, Emmy, and her mother sit down to a fine supper, both women eager to hear his stories of California.

After dinner, Emmy turns to her mother. "Charles says he'll help with the plantation. Maybe you could talk to him about that?"

"That would be lovely, Charles, if you don't mind," Emmy's mother says. "I've just finished a summary of the accounts. Perhaps you could take a look and offer some advice?"

"I'd be happy to. I could take a look now, if you would like. No time like the present."

She smiles. "Come with me to the study. You, too, Emmy."

"You two go on. I've got a few things to take care of. Besides, numbers always make my head spin."

In the study, Emmy's mother hands him a stack of papers and an old leather ledger. "We're so relieved you made it back. Emmy was hoping for a letter from you every day."

Charles glances up. "I wrote. I don't know why they never reached her."

"Just glad you're here. I've never seen her so happy. Do you plan to stay? California sounds dangerous."

"Emmy and I are talking about it. We'll decide together."

"I know things have changed, including your father's passing. He was such a good man."

"He was a good man. Things have changed. More than I imagined."

"There will always be a place for you here. You can help manage the plantation. We can pay you. We don't have an overseer. His house is open. You can stay there."

"Sounds perfect. You will never regret it."

She clasps his hands. "I will never regret it."

CHAPTER 25
FREEDOM AT LAST
NOVEMBER 1851

Carter, Sandy, and Robert work every site Charles marked on his map. They find gold and save enough to buy mules, a wagon, and a cabin in anticipation of starting their hauling business.

They wait for six months, uncertain about Charles' return. They keep their gold hidden in several secret caches high in the mountains, where no one can find it.

They become self-sufficient and take pride in their freedom. Gold isn't making them rich, but it is enough to buy everything they need and save for the future. Prejudice is all around, but they know who they can work with and who they can trust.

Prospecting for gold becomes less of a task and more of an adventure. They work hard and remain driven, but the thought of Charles returning to claim their gold weighs heavily on their minds. The idea of returning to Mississippi fills them with dread. They just can't.

Hannah urges Carter to talk to lawyers and make legal preparations if Charles returns, but Carter remains confident. "We'll deal with him if he comes back," he tells her.

Hannah doesn't press. In her heart, she doesn't believe Charles will return.

They take Sundays off and faithfully attend church in Sacramento. The concerns for long-term freedom linger. Blue and several leaders work with lawyers and sympathetic politicians to build support. Their allies align with them.

One ally is Mark Hopkins, a Sacramento grocer with a law degree. He arrived in 1849 and is a staunch abolitionist, active in the Free-Soil movement, opposing slavery's expansion.

He and Carter become friends and speak often. Mark encourages him to start a hauling business and promises to send him as much work as possible.

Each day brings Carter closer to freedom. Hannah crosses dates off on the calendar. Carter quietly does the same, tracking every passing day of the six-month promise.

The day finally comes—November 15th—still no word from Charles.

Doc Hill gathers Carter, Sandy, and Robert in his cabin in the afternoon. Hannah stands beside Carter, holding his hand.

"We've heard nothing from Charles. We hope and pray he is all right," Doc says solemnly, before a slow smile creeps across his face. "He told me he gave you letters of freedom if he didn't return in six months. You are free!"

Relief and joy sweep through the room. Carter and Hannah embrace in a long kiss. Doc shakes their hands and offers heartfelt congratulations. He and Hannah secretly prepared a special dinner to celebrate the occasion.

Afterward, Carter and Hannah walk together under the moonlight.

"How does freedom feel?" Hannah asks gently.

"I feel numb. I can't believe it," Carter says, pausing. "I still wonder…"

"I know you're worried about Charles," Hannah says. "I'm sure he's fine."

"I thought he'd come back." Carter sighs. "Now, I don't know. I guess there's always a chance."

"I don't think he's coming. And even if he does, you're free. It's time to think about the future. Our future."

"I want to make sure we have steady income, a house, and land. I want to be ready before we"

"Our future is now, Carter," Hannah interrupts, her voice tinged with frustration. "I've been saving and waiting…"

"I just became free today. There's a lot to think about. We need to buy mules and a wagon. We'll keep renting for now, look for land, build when the time's right."

Hannah draws a slow breath. She knows she needs to be patient. Carter needs time to let the weight of his freedom settle. But she has her plans.

"I've been saving, too. There's something I want to show you tomorrow morning."

"Of course," Carter says, realizing he's been making plans without her.

Hannah leads Carter to a small apple orchard near Auburn the next morning. The bare trees cover a gentle hillside.

"They planted these a few years back," she says with a smile. "They had lots of apples this year."

Carter looks around, trying to remain optimistic. "I didn't know this was here. It's certainly something to think about."

"There's plenty of land," Hannah says, leading him down a row. "We can grow more than apples. Berries, vegetables. We can grow anything."

"There's a lot to figure out. You know how hard it is for us to buy land," Carter cautions.

"We can save. Some of this land's just sitting here," she says brightly.

"It's not just money. The laws are against us. Some folks won't sell to us."

Hannah's shoulders slump. Carter turns to face her.

"I'm not saying no. I'm saying we have hurdles. A lot of them."

"I know, but isn't it worth dreaming about? Isn't it worth fighting for?"

"It is," he says, kissing her. "We'll plan. We'll fight. But first things first. We've saved enough to buy three mules and a wagon. No one can stop us from starting a business."

"There are plenty who won't hire you," Hannah warns.

"And plenty who will. The Sweet Vengeance boys need hauling. So do folks from church. And there's Mark Hopkins. I'm sure we can make it work."

"I know you will," Hannah says with a smile. "But we can still dream, can't we? We can make this our land."

"Of course. And we'll own the finest orchard in California," Carter says, embracing her.

Carter, Sandy, and Robert return to the mountains and retrieve their hidden gold. They have enough to buy three strong mules. Wagons are scarce, but they eventually strike a deal for a new one. They hope this winter isn't as harsh as the last. Either way, they are prepared. They still have a few hidden caches to carry them through the following year.

They rotate duties: two haul freight while the third searches for gold. The weeks pass quickly. They are busy every day. The winter proves milder than the one before, and business booms. The rains come and go, enough to churn fresh gold into the rivers without halting their work.

They rent a larger cabin near Doc Hill and Hannah. Carter leads the planning of a grand Christmas celebration to mark their freedom. Their new home, warmed by a stone fireplace and decorated with a fresh pine tree lit by candles, is the perfect setting.

They invite friends from church, old companions, the men from Sweet Vengeance, and new customers from their growing hauling business.

Their business thrives. They have more work than they can handle. And they're still finding gold. Life is good, and the future is bright.

Still, freedom is not certain. They follow the news as lawmakers in California pass restrictions on people of color, even as others fight back.

CHAPTER 26
CALIFORNIA ALLOWS SLAVERY

The pro-slavery Democrat politicians in California keep busy during the long winter. Crabb and his southern-born allies work to push a more punitive fugitive slave law—stronger than the Federal law that Senator Davis and his cronies pushed through as part of the California compromise.

The California Fugitive Slave Law will allow masters to hold their slaves in California legally. It will criminalize any slave who resists and severely punish anyone who protects them or helps them escape.

Anti-slavery and abolitionists maneuver to add a "sunset clause" giving slave owners one year to claim their slaves and remove them from the state.

In late February 1852, Henry Crabb addresses the eighty members of the California Congress. He reads through the bill with passion, ending his speech declaring, "To sum up, I am asking for your vote on this crucial bill that grants slave owners one year to reclaim their slaves and send them back to their rightful homes in the South."

Crabb is convincing, but he and his cronies are already plotting to extend the law to carve the state into slaveholding counties.

Moderates, hopeful that the law will strike a careful balance between protecting slaveholder rights and preserving California's antislavery constitution, join the pro-slavery legislators. The bill gains support from many who want people of color out of California. They want it to be free for Whites.

The bill passed in February and will become law on April 15, 1852.

On a rainy Sunday morning in late February, Carter and Hannah leave early for church in Sacramento. They arrive late and slip into the back. Reverend Blue is already in the middle of a booming sermon. Crabb's new slave law rattles the entire community—not just Black families, but anyone who values freedom in California.

"To steal a man or rob him of his liberty is a greater sin than to steal his property or to take it by violence. To hold a man in slavery who has the right to liberty is the greatest sin," Reverend Blue bellows from his pulpit.

The congregation roars in unison, "Amen, amen!"

A young woman rises and leads the choir:

"Go down, Moses.

Way down in Egypt land.

Tell old Pharaoh,

To let my people go.

Oh, when Israel was in Egypt land..."

The congregation joins in full voice:

"Let my people go!

Oppressed so hard they could not stand—

Let my people go!

So the Lord said:

Go down (go down), Moses (Moses),

Way (way) down (down) in Egypt land—

Tell all Pharaohs to let my people go!"

As the final note fades, a hush falls over the room.

Reverend Blue steps forward. "We will fight for our freedom. It is what the good Lord intended."

The congregation erupts in cheers.

Carter and Hannah join their church family for a picnic. It is a warm, sunny February day, a welcome break from the long stretch of rain that has left the grass lush and green.

Majestic oaks spread their branches overhead, casting dappled shadows across the field. The air buzzes with laughter and shared stories. For a short time, the weight of the new slave law lifts. They are together. They are united. And they will protect one another.

After lunch, Carter and Hannah find a quiet spot beneath the trees. Carter unfolds the *Alta* newspaper and reads the latest article about California's fugitive slave law. He lets the paper fall to his lap.

"I can't believe it," he says. "I can't believe they can do this."

Hannah caresses his hand. "We're free, Carter. We can help free others."

Carter pats her hand gently. "We will. We will help free others."

CHAPTER 27
SLAVERY REACHES FOR HANNAH

On a sunny April morning, Carter sits in a chair in front of his cabin, sipping coffee and opening the *Nevada Journal*. News of California's Fugitive Slave Law has spread across the nation. The law encourages Southern slaveholders to expand their wealth in California by using enslaved labor.

The article focuses on a large group from North and South Carolina preparing to bring their slaves. It quotes Madison Walthall, a Mississippi assemblyman who owns slaves in California. Walthall confidently predicts the state will embrace slavery. He points to the presence of enslaved people and influential Southerners in California as evidence of its inevitable future. "Despite opposition," he declares, "it will be a proud day for the South when our institutions reach the shores of the Pacific."

Carter sets the paper down and takes another sip of coffee. Is there truth in Walthall's words? Can slavery take root in California? He thinks of his friends at Sweet Vengeance and the threat their former owners might still pose. He takes a deep breath and vows he'll do everything he can to protect them. He is grateful that he and Hannah are free and safe.

It is his day to pan for gold, but that can wait. He picks up a copy of the *San Joaquin Republican*. The headline stops him cold. A slaveholder named Lathrop has tracked down his former slave in Sacramento and brought him before Justice Frye, a well-known proslavery judge. The paper reports the incident with approval.

Judge Frye ruled that Lathrop provided sufficient proof of ownership and returned the man to him. The article quotes Henry Crabb: "Everything passed off with quiet and order—nothing like resistance being made to the due execution of the law," Crabb gloated.

Sandy and Robert had left early with the wagon and mules for a hauling job. Carter decides to pick some wildflowers for Hannah before heading down to the river. But as he turns toward the cabin, he freezes.

Two deputy sheriffs stand on the porch.

Hannah burst through the door, shouting, "You can't do this! I'm free!"

Carter watches, stunned, as the deputies grab her. She fights with everything she has, but they slam her to the ground and cuff her hands behind her back.

He drops the flowers and newspapers and runs to her. He yanks one deputy off her, but the other strikes him hard in the jaw, knocking him back. The deputy pulls his pistol and aims it squarely at Carter's face.

"You want to eat a bullet?" he sneers.

Hannah stops struggling when she sees the gun.

"No, Carter! That's what they want," she pleads. "We're free. You're free."

Carter glares at the deputy, fists clenched. "Freedom's worth dying for," he says through gritted teeth, "but not today. Not like this." He slowly backs away. "She's free. I'll make sure she stays free."

The deputy lowers the pistol. "The law will decide who is free and who ain't."

Placer County Sheriff Samuel Asten steps out from the doorway, followed by Carlton Davis—a White Southerner in his forties, the son of Hannah's former owner. Doc Hill rushes outside behind them.

"You can't do this," Doc warns.

"I've got papers that say I can," Carlton replies coldly. "She's mine now."

"She's free!" Doc protests.

"Not anymore," Carlton shoots back.

Doc turns to Sheriff Asten. "This can't be legal."

"I've got my orders. The judge decides tomorrow morning," Sheriff Asten growls in his Southern accent, thick and slow.

Carter and Doc watch helplessly as the deputies shove Hannah into a wagon.

"Get Cornelius Cole! He's helped the guys at the Sweet Vengeance. He's the lawyer I talked to!" Hannah cries.

"I'll get him! You're free. They can't do this!" Carter shouts.

"We'll get Cole. You will be free, Hannah!" Doc adds.

They watch the wagon pull away, flanked by the sheriff and Carlton Davis on horseback.

"Come on. No time to waste," Doc says. "We've got to get Cornelius Cole. We'll take my carriage."

They arrive in Sacramento late that afternoon. In Cole's office, Doc and Carter sit across from the young lawyer, who listens intently. Although Cole is only thirty, he exudes confidence. He brushes his dark hair and tugs on his goatee, thinking.

"I've read the Fugitive Slave Law," Carter says, leaning over the desk. "It doesn't apply to her. She was already free."

Cole is impressed that Carter can read and looks through the papers on his desk. "I'll make that argument, but the judge is tough. He's ruled in favor of slaveholders before. We'll need proof, Where was she freed?"

"In Placer County," Doc says. "I signed the papers myself."

"Let's hope they were filed. I have court tomorrow morning." He scribbles a note and signs it. "Take this to the courthouse. Get the documents. I'll meet you there in the afternoon."

Early the next day, Carter and Doc arrive at the Placer County Courthouse, a shabby twenty-by-twenty-foot stone building with a tin roof. The clerk can't find the documents, but allows them to search the chaotic filing system themselves. After hours of digging, they find the paper they need—Hannah's proof of freedom.

They wait outside the courthouse. Cornelius arrives and reads the documents.

"They have no case," Cornelius assures them.

As they approach the entrance, Henry Crabb and Carlton Davis arrive.

Crabb sneers. "Cornelius Cole. I should've known you'd stick your nose in this. You're barking up the wrong tree. She's going back to Georgia, where she belongs."

"She's free," Cole snaps, "and she'll go wherever she pleases."

Crabb points at Carter. "Who are you? What's your business here?"

Before Carter can speak, Doc steps forward. "He's a free man—and Hannah's friend."

Crabb narrows his eyes. "People of color aren't welcome in court unless they're defendants. Stay outside."

Crabb and Davis storm past them into the building.

"Who the hell is that?" Carter mutters.

"That's Henry Crabb," Cole says with a scoff.

Carter blinks. "Henry Crabb the politician?"

"The same," Cole replies. "Helped push through the Fugitive Slave Act. Now he's here to enforce it."

Carter's voice rises. "We can't let them take Hannah."

"We've got a strong case. But you should stay outside," Cole says gently. "I'm sorry, but it might help her."

Carter nods and watches them enter. He wedges the door open with a piece of wood and stands where he can see and listen. His fists clench as he sees the sheriff bring Hannah in, her wrists still cuffed behind her back. She looks exhausted—broken.

Crabb and Davis approach the judge. Crabb hands him a stack of documents.

Cornelius Cole and Doc Hill stand a few feet away, silent but steady.

The judge reads through the papers, then passes them back to Crabb.

He turns to Cornelius. "Mr. Cole, what is your defense?"

Cornelius steps forward and hands the judge his documents. "Mr. Davis's father, who held legal title to Hannah Mason, signed these papers attesting to her freedom. Doctor Hill, standing beside me, witnessed the signing."

Judge Frye reviews the documents, but his expression is unreadable. "Doctor Hill, was Mr. Davis of sound mind when he signed these documents?"

Before Doc can answer, Carlton Davis says, "He was ill! He didn't understand what he was doing!"

Judge Frye slams his gavel down. "I'm not asking you, Mr. Davis. I'm asking Doctor Hill."

Doc Hill steps forward, his voice calm and firm. "I was his doctor. He was of sound mind when he signed the papers. Hannah has worked for me ever since. She's been a blessing."

The judge cuts him off with another rap of the gavel. "I see your signature, Doctor Hill. I know your reputation. You are known as a man of honor." He pauses, then declares, "The case is closed. Hannah Mason is free."

Crabb strides forward in anger. "I'll take this to a higher court."

"You do what you must," the judge replies as he stands. "But a higher court has already ruled in a similar case. The precedent is clear. These documents are legal. The case is closed." He bangs his gavel and walks off.

Sheriff Asten uncuffs Hannah. She turns and sees Carter watching from the doorway. She rushes into his arms, and they embrace in a long, tearful kiss.

"I was in a cell with no windows," she whispers. "I thought I'd never see the sun again. I thought I would never see you again."

"You're free now. No one's taking you again," he says as he kisses her.

Cornelius and Doc Hill leave the courtroom, smiles spreading across their faces as they watch Hannah and Carter.

Crabb storms past, his glare fixed on Cornelius. His lips curled in disgust, and his voice is low and venomous. "This isn't over."

Cornelius faces him calmly. "Yes, it is. You're barking up the wrong tree."

"I'll appeal and win. I'll see you in court!" Crabb shouts.

Cornelius walks away without turning back. "Looking forward to it. You'll lose again."

CHAPTER 28
THE SOUTH TAKES ADVANTAGE OF LAWS

Back in Mississippi, Charles diligently works on Emmy's plantation and becomes a trusted advisor to her mother. He uses his and Emmy's enslaved workers to tend his section of the Perkins plantation. Charles labors alongside them, and Emmy often joins in, getting her hands dirty as they work together.

He spends most days and nights at Emmy's plantation and rarely visits his family. He and Emmy grow close and make plans for their future. Though he hasn't formally proposed, they both know marriage is inevitable. Charles wants to ensure their crops are successful before proposing in the fall.

One afternoon, Charles and Emmy are planting cotton with their workers when Daniel appears dressed in a suit. He rides up to them, trampling through the freshly planted rows.

"Mother called a meeting," Daniel announces, his lips tight as he glares at Charles. "You've got to come now. We have things to talk about."

Charles' eyes widen in disbelief.

"Now?" he protests. "We're in the middle of planting."

"This can't wait. Senator Davis is here. If you don't come, it'll be your loss," Daniel sneers before turning his horse and galloping off, tearing up more of the newly planted cotton.

Charles and Emmy watch him ride away.

"I don't know what this is about, but we've got to go," Charles says, brushing dirt from his pants.

"We?" Emmy questions as she glances down at her dusty dress. "I can't go looking like this. It's Senator Davis! You should clean up and go."

"I want you to hear everything they have to say," Charles says firmly. "We work hard in the fields. There's no shame in that. Let them see us as we are."

He takes Emmy's hand, and together they march from the field to a shabby wagon hitched to an aging horse. Minutes later, they arrive at the sprawling Perkins plantation. After brushing off as much dirt as possible, they step inside and walk down the hallway to the study.

Charles' mother sits behind his father's desk, sorting a stack of papers. She barely looks up.

"Good afternoon, Charles," she says. She glances at Emmy but doesn't acknowledge her.

Charles turns and is surprised to see Green standing beside Daniel.

"Hi, Green." Charles greets him with a wave. "What brings you here?"

"I'm here to support the family and the South," Green drawls.

Senator Davis rises from his chair and greets Charles with a handshake.

"Good to see you, Charles. It's been a while. Haven't seen you since you left for California," he says before turning to shake Emmy's hand, noticing the dirt under her nails. "Emmy, it's been some time since the ball. How is your mother?"

Emmy's cheeks flush before she responds, "She's doing well. I apologize for my appearance. We were planting. I find working in the fields rewarding. It's amazing to watch things grow. Sometimes the wind carries seeds, and they grow where God wills. Don't you think that's beautiful?"

"God puts us on this earth to decide where things should grow," Senator Davis replies flatly, then turns to the man beside him. "Charles, I believe you know Judge Yerger."

They exchange handshakes without speaking. The tension in the room grows thick.

Jane gestures toward an empty chair.

"Please sit, Charles," she says hoarsely.

Emmy steps back.

"I should probably go," she says and turns to leave.

Charles catches her hand, gently pulling her to stand beside him. He remains standing and glares at his mother. Senator Davis and Judge Yerger also stay on their feet. Daniel and Green stand behind Charles and Emmy.

"What is this all about?" Charles demands.

Jane looks at Senator Davis, who clears his throat.

"You left valuable property in California. It must be returned. You must do this for your family and Mississippi."

Charles stiffens.

"California is a free state. They're free."

"You need to read the papers and stay informed," Senator Davis growls. "There's a new law. Southerners have the right to reclaim their property."

"I don't believe it," Charles says.

"Perhaps you've been too busy tending your garden," Senator Davis mocks. "California passed a Fugitive Slave Act. We have the right to our property and must give no ground to the abolitionists and their sympathizers."

Judge Yerger picks up a set of papers and reads aloud, "The laws that existed in California before its admission to the Union are not superior to the Constitution of the United States, which recognizes property in slaves." He puts the papers down, then adds, "You have a year to reclaim your property."

Jane stands and faces Charles.

"The time is now, Charles. You have to do this!"

"I gave them my word. I set them free!"

"I'm surprised, Charles. Your loyalty should lie with your family and Mississippi. Your father would have expected no less," Senator Davis chides.

"Did you file papers?" Judge Yerger presses.

"There was no need. I gave them letters stating they'd be free if I didn't return in six months. It's been a year. They're free," Charles snaps.

"A letter isn't a legal document. I have a legal one giving you the right to claim Sandy Jones, Carter Perkins, and Robert Perkins as your property, and authorizing their return under the California Fugitive Slave Act," Judge Yerger replies with disdain.

"I can't go back now. I don't have the money—thanks to my family," Charles growls, glaring at his mother before turning to Daniel with a burning stare. His eyes lock with Green's.

"I'll go get them for you," Green offers, unable to hold back.

Daniel places a hand on Green's shoulder in agreement and solidarity.

He stares at Charles and says, "We've got the money. It's the right thing to do. They don't belong in California. They could be starving or in trouble. I thought you cared about them. You and Carter are like brothers. Don't you want him here? Don't you want him safe?"

Charles pauses, weighing his options. He can return to California, but he can't leave Emmy. The journey is too grueling. Even if Green goes, there is no guarantee he'll survive the trip.

Charles wants to believe everything is fine in California, but things might have changed with the new law and the pressure from slaveholders. Carter, Sandy, and Robert might be in trouble. *Perhaps they will be better off in Mississippi,* he thinks, before he answers.

"Let me check on their well-being before I decide," he says, trying to buy time. "I'll write and find out what's happening in California."

"We know what's happening in California. Mississippi must secure all of her property. The law may give us a year, but the time is now. We must set a precedent. Southerners must stand together," Senator Davis warns. "You must decide where your allegiance lies. If your father were here, I'm certain he would want you to support your family, the great state of Mississippi, and our way of life."

Judge Yerger slides a small stack of papers across the table. "This document gives Green the power of attorney to claim your property and arrange for their safe return to Mississippi."

Charles reads slowly as the others sit in tense silence. His mind races, searching for options. He knows he's trapped—boxed into a corner with no good choices.

His mother places a pen in his hand.

Charles turns to Green, his voice cold. "When do you plan to leave?"

"In a few days. I'll meet up with Hardin. We'll take legal ownership and make arrangements for their return. I plan to stay and find gold," Green replies matter-of-factly.

"You were planning to go whether I signed or not, weren't you?" Charles asks, his tone sharp with accusation.

"As a matter of fact—" Green begins, but Daniel cuts in.

"They're your slaves, Charles. Don't you want them? They'll be better off here. If you don't sign, Mother will. If she signs, they won't be yours anymore. Green can go get them. Right, Judge?"

"Yes," Yerger confirms. "They're designated as part of the estate. She has the authority to sign, and they will become hers. But the right thing for you to do, Charles, is to sign. Every Mississippian must protect their rights and property."

"It's the right thing to do," Senator Davis adds. "It's just that simple."

Charles hesitates, torn between anger and obligation. The room closes in around him. If he signs, he might be able to protect them. If he doesn't, they will not be his.

He signs.

He passes the documents to Judge Yerger, then turns to Green, his voice like ice. "I hope you're all happy. When they return, they'll be mine—and they'll work for me."

He grabs Emmy's hand and storms out of the room.

"He just needs a little time," Jane mutters.

That night, Charles sits across from Emmy on the veranda, a single candle flickering between them.

"I wish I knew how Carter, Sandy, and Robert are doing," he says quietly, anxiety tightening his chest. "I've sent letters to Doc and Hardin. I haven't heard a word."

"Maybe the letters never reached them," Emmy replies gently.

"Probably not. I don't trust Hardin. Or Green. Or my brother." Charles sighs, rubbing his forehead. "Honestly, I don't trust my mother."

"You've helped my mother so much," Emmy says, threading her fingers through his. "Your place is here. This is our future. Carter, Sandy, and Robert's place is here, too."

Charles searches her eyes, then leans in and kisses her. After a moment, he pulls back, the weight of his thoughts still heavy.

"As soon as they return, I'll set them free," he says firmly. "I gave them my word. That's the only reason I signed. You heard them. If I hadn't, my mother would've signed instead. Then they'd belong to her."

Emmy's face brightens. "They can work here as free men. We'll pay them wages. They can take their time deciding what they want to do. I'm sure they'll be happy here."

Carter squeezes her fingers in his hand and leans toward her. "I hope so, but Carter has a girlfriend. He won't want to leave her behind."

"She can come, too," Emmy says with a smile. "You told me about Hannah. I think she'd be a big help."

Charles nods. "I just don't know. We'll figure things out once Carter and the others arrive."

CHAPTER 29
CARTER IS CAUGHT IN THE WEB
MAY 1852

Carter, Sandy, and Robert continue building their hauling business, searching for gold whenever they find the time. Carter spends most evenings with Hannah. Her arrest shocked her, and it has taken her time to recover her spirit.

As the sun's golden light bathes the evening sky, Carter and Hannah sit comfortably on Doc Hill's porch, surrounded by the peaceful sounds of nature. A quiet sense of contentment settles between them.

"The hauling business is doing well," Carter says. "We still have time to look for gold; there's more out there. I'm thinking—it's time to start planning for our future."

"Our future is every second, every moment, every day. Are you ever going to ask me?"

Carter smiles. "I want to do it properly. You'll have to be patient."

Hannah smirks and presses on. "I talked to Doc about starting an apple orchard. He thinks it's a great idea and says he'll help. I also met folks nearby who started their own. I know where the best land is. Not far. We can grow just about anything there."

Carter chuckles. "People need to eat. More folks keep coming. Most everything grows here. It'd be better to strike it big with gold, though."

"You can always keep looking for gold," Hannah replies. "But will you at least look at the land with me? We could visit some orchards and find out how to get started. The trees take a few years, but once they start bearing fruit, we'll have a crop every year."

"I'll follow you into the apple orchard," Carter laughs, kissing her and gently taking her hand. "Are you trying to make me bite the apple, Eve?"

"We're going to have to read more of the Bible. You're the one who's helping to educate me," she says, trying to contain her laughter.

"I think we're even on teaching each other," Carter chuckles.

They share a kiss as Sandy and Robert ride up in their wagon, pulled by Sarah and three other mules. Their clothes are streaked with mud and sawdust, a testament to a long day of hauling lumber. They slouch in their seats, but their tired smiles speak for themselves.

"How's the hauling business?" Carter calls out as they stop in front of the porch.

"Good. Really good," Sandy says with a broad smile.

"How's the gold panning?" Robert asks, glancing at Carter's muddy boots.

"Not great," Carter admits.

"Gold's gonna run out eventually," Sandy says. "But the hauling business? It'll always be here."

"People gotta eat, too," Carter adds with a grin. "They're gonna need apples."

"Are you two planning something we should know about?" Sandy asks with a grin.

"Just thinking about the possibilities," Carter replies.

"Apples sound good. They're gonna need to be hauled." Sandy chuckles. "You two keep thinking," he jokes, snapping the reins as the wagon rolls on.

They have no way of knowing that Green Perkins has already arrived in California and met with Hardin. In short order, they have found Henry Crabb, who has eagerly agreed to help reclaim what they see as their property.

On May 31, 1852, in the Placer County courthouse, Green stands silently as Henry Crabb hands Judge Frye the signed documents from Charles authorizing Green to take Carter, Sandy, and Robert back to Mississippi.

After a cursory review, Judge Frye returns the documents and scribbles a note. "Everything is in order, Mr. Crabb." He hands the note to Green. "Take this to the sheriff. It permits him to use any necessary force to reclaim your property. They must be brought before me. I'll finalize the matter then."

Green and Hardin waste no time. They deliver the judge's order to Sheriff Asten, who is eager to assist. Together, they hatch a plan to act that very night.

Under the cover of darkness, the group creeps toward the small cabin. A faint flicker of lamplight glows through a side window. Sheriff Asten leads the way with Green and Hardin close behind. Three deputies take positions behind trees and brush, awaiting the signal.

Sheriff Asten draws his pistol. Hardin does the same.

"Are guns necessary?" Green whispers, trying to keep things calm. "We need them alive. I don't think they'll resist."

"The order says all necessary force," Sheriff Asten growls, then kicks the door in with his boot. Hardin and Green follow, hearts hammering.

Inside, Carter sits near the fire reading a book while Sandy and Robert play checkers at the table.

Sandy jumps to his feet, stunned. "What's this all about? We ain't done nothin'!"

"Hands up," Sheriff Asten barks, pistol raised. He sneers as Carter puts down his book. "Well, lookie here. A boy who can read."

Green steps beside the sheriff and holds out the signed documents. "Charles gave me legal authority to take you back to Mississippi."

Carter's face twists in disbelief. "We're free. We've got letters from Charles. He wouldn't do this."

Green points to the signature. "That's his name, plain as day."

Carter stares at it, horror sinking in. "I don't believe it…"

Hardin strides to the desk and yanks open a drawer. He grabs a handful of papers and maps. "We can use these maps," he says with a smile. Then he opens the letters Charles wrote authorizing their freedom. He crumples them and throws them into the fire.

"No!" Carter lunges forward. "You can't do that! Those letters are our freedom!"

A sheriff deputy grabs him and throws him down.

Hardin sneers, "Just scratches on paper."

"We're free! Everything belongs to us!" Carter shouts. "We'll get a lawyer."

Green scoffs. "We already saw the judge. You're headed to jail tonight, court in the morning, then Mississippi."

Hardin returns to the desk and rifles through another drawer, pulling out a pouch of gold nuggets and coins.

"That's ours!" Robert shouts, lunging. "We worked hard for it!"

Before he can take another step, Sheriff Asten grabs Robert and slams the butt of his pistol into his face. Robert collapses, unconscious.

Sandy cries out, trembling. "You didn't have to do that!"

Sheriff Asten smirks. "You boys ain't gettin' the message. You ain't free. All y'all are goin' back to Mississippi. I was hopin' we could do this the easy way…" He pauses, his voice dropping to a deadly growl. "But you wanna fight. We'll do it the hard way."

The deputies move in, shackling Carter, Sandy, and Robert as Sheriff Asten keeps his pistol trained on them.

Hardin rummages through the rest of the cabin. He pulls out Carter's Bible and holds it up.

"That's mine!" Carter yells.

Hardin flips through the Bible. Peg's picture slips out. He picks it up and stares for a moment. "I remember her."

"Give me my Bible!" Carter shouts.

"Your Bible?" Hardin jeers. "This Bible ain't for you."

He turns to Genesis 1:26-28 and reads aloud: "'And God said, Let us make man in our image, after our likeness: and let them have dominion over the fish of the sea... and over every creeping thing that creepeth upon the earth.'" He slides Peg's picture into the crease to mark the page and closes the Bible. "God made us in His image—people like Green, the sheriff, and me. Not you. You're just one of them things that creepeth on the earth."

Carter wrenches his right hand free and slaps Hardin. The deputies pounce, beating him to the floor. He staggers up—fighting back, —but they beat him down again.

Hardin strides to the fireplace, Bible in hand.

"You can't burn a Bible!" Green barks.

Hardin hesitates and throws the Bible on the floor.

The deputies force Carter, Sandy, and Robert toward the wagon. Chains around their feet and hands clank and grind.

"You boys help each other climb in," Sheriff Asten orders, pointing his pistol at Carter.

Carter turns to Sheriff Asten. "This is our wagon!"

"It's ours now. Everything you had belongs to me and Hardin," Green laughs.

Hardin growls, "I'd love to work your asses for gold, but you're goin' back to Mississippi where you belong."

Bruised and bloodied, Carter, Sandy, and Robert collapse into the wagon bed. Hardin climbs beside Green and snaps the reins. Sheriff Asten and his deputies follow on horseback.

After they arrive at the jail, the deputies haul Carter through a dank, dim hallway flanked by iron bars. He fights, his chains clanking, blood trickling down his face from fresh cuts.

They throw him into a cell.

"You can't do this. I'm free!" he yells.

"You ain't free no more. You're going back to Mississippi, where y'all belong," Sheriff Asten says in his slow drawl as he slams the door, leaving Carter in complete darkness.

"I'm free! You can't cage me!" His voice shatters the silence, echoing through the jail. He sighs as tears stream down his bloody cheeks. The chains around his legs rattle as he stumbles back to his cot.

The next day, Hannah arrives at the cabin and knocks on the door. The broken latch gives way, and the door creaks open. She steps inside and gasps.

The place is ransacked. Everything is gone—except Carter's Bible, lying on the floor. She picks it up, holds it to her chest, and runs.

A neighbor stands at his cabin and raises his hand to stop her as she runs past. She halts, breathless, as he points toward the cabin.

"I heard them last night," the neighbor says. "The sheriff came and took them away in chains."

"Oh my God," she screams as she races to Doc Hill's cabin.

She bursts in, gasping for air. Doc Hill looks up from his writing desk.

"They took them," she says between ragged breaths. She drops to her knees.

Doc Hill rushes to her side. "Who? Who took who?"

"The sheriff," she says, slipping into her Georgia accent. "They took Carter, Sandy, and Robert away in chains. Their cabin's empty. Everything's gone."

Doc Hill steadies her. "I'll get the carriage. We'll find out what happened."

Meanwhile, Green and Hardin arrive at the Placer County Courthouse with Crabb.

"No one else can come inside," Crabb commands. "Make sure there are no interruptions."

Hardin draws his pistol. "I'll guard the door."

Green and Crabb enter the courtroom. Judge Frye sits waiting.

It is June 1st, 1852.

Carter, Sandy, and Robert stand in chains at the side of the courtroom. Deputies flank them. Carter and Robert's injuries are still bloody and raw.

"We had papers from Charles Perkins. He owned us but set us free!" Carter shouts.

Judge Frye bangs his gavel. "The law is clear. No one of color can speak in court or testify."

The judge looks at Green. "Are there any such papers, Mr. Perkins?"

"No, Your Honor."

"That's a lie!" Carter shouts.

"I warned you," the judge growls, pounding the gavel. "You are not permitted to speak. That is the law!"

Crabb steps forward. "Charles Perkins would not have sent his cousin to retrieve them and return them to Mississippi if he had truly freed them."

"I agree," the judge says. "I find for Charles Perkins. The defendants will remain in custody until arrangements are made for their return to Mississippi. Case closed."

The judge bangs his gavel and leaves.

Crabb looks at Carter. "Told you I had my eye on you," he sneers. "Still have my eyes on your girlfriend, too."

Sheriff Asten and his deputies take Carter, Sandy, and Robert out the back door.

Outside, Crabb, Green, and Hardin walk into the street.

Just then, Doc Hill's carriage comes careening around the corner. He pulls the reins hard and stops beside them. Hannah jumps down and faces them.

"Where are they?" she demands, her voice trembling with fury.

"They're headed back to Mississippi," Hardin replies with steely resolve.

Doc Hill's voice rises. "That's outrageous. They're free men."

Green squints at him. "Who are you?"

"I'm Doctor Hill. Who are you?"

"I'm Charles' cousin, and he authorized me to take custody and ensure they return to Mississippi, where they belong," Green says with an air of indignation.

"That doesn't sound like something Charles would do," Doc Hill challenges.

"Charles signed the documents, and the judge has ruled. The case is closed," Crabb cuts in sharply, eyes narrowed, brow furrowed.

"We'll get Cornelius," Hannah declares.

"Oh, the great Cornelius Cole," Crabb sneers. "He can't help with this one. And I haven't forgotten about you, either. I'll get you out of California."

"We'll fight this. And I will fight to stay free," Hannah shoots back.

"Don't make trouble," Hardin warns. "I've heard enough from Northerners. Y'all are tryin' to take everything from us. That ain't gonna happen." He turns to Doc Hill with a scowl. "Besides, he ain't much of a doctor, and you ain't much of a nurse. Y'all killed our cousin Stephen."

Hannah slips back into her Georgia drawl with a vengeance. "Y'all are nothin' but low-down sons of bi—"

"Hannah!" Doc says as he pulls her back. "We'll fight them in court, not in the street."

Hardin leans forward, glaring at Hannah. "Watch yourself. I'm going to keep an eye on you—both of you. Try to interfere, and it'll be the last thing you do."

Hannah storms back to Doc's carriage.

"We'll get Corneilius Cole. You won't win this fight," Doc Hill says as he snaps the reins, and they ride off in a cloud of dust.

Green turns to Crabb. "Can that lawyer really do anything?"

Crabb shrugs. "He might try to clog things up with an appeal. You need to get them out of California fast."

"We will. Thanks for your help," Green says.

"No problem. I'm always available. Tell your friends I can help them recover their property, too." Crabb grins, already thinking of the business ahead.

"How many slaves do you think are in California?" Green questions.

Crabb thinks a moment. "At least a thousand. Maybe two."

Hardin's eyes widen. "I knew there were a bunch, but not that many. They must be worth a fortune."

"A strong, hardworking slave can fetch fifteen hundred dollars or more," Green contemplates. "That's over three million dollars' worth in California alone."

Crabb's eyes gleam. "I plan to help men like you reclaim every bit of their property."

They shake hands. Crabb departs, eager to round up more slaveholders and make a sizable profit by helping them recover their property.

"We've got to find Mississippi Joe," Hardin says. "I heard he's the best. He can get them back to Mississippi. We got Charles' maps. Those boys were finding gold. We can get rich."

Green nods, smiling. "We'll find Mississippi Joe, or someone else in San Francisco. Let's go!"

Doc Hill and Hannah are only a short distance away when she turns toward him, tears welling in her eyes. "I have to go back and see Carter. It might be the last time."

Doc Hill gives her a long, sympathetic look and turns the carriage around.

They arrive at the Placer County Jail, a grim stone structure with iron-barred windows.

"They probably won't let us see him," he says, eyeing the cold, forbidding building.

"We have to try. I have an idea," Hannah says, a mischievous grin spreading across her face. She takes a deep breath and begins to cry—at first forced, then real tears spill down her cheeks.

"What on earth are you doing?" Doc Hill asks, bewildered.

"Just follow my lead," she whispers, her voice shaky with emotion.

She walks briskly into the jail, approaching a young deputy seated behind a desk.

"I've got tuh see Carter Perkins," she drawls, thickening her Southern accent until it is nearly unrecognizable. Tears roll down her cheeks.

The deputy looks up. "Nobody's supposed to see him," he says as he offers her a handkerchief.

Doc Hill strides beside her and wraps a protective arm around her shoulders. He clears his throat and lays out a clumsy Southern drawl:

"This here's Carter's sister," he says solemnly. "It'd be the right thing to let her see her brother one last time before he's sent back to Mississippi. I doubt they'll ever see each other again."

"Do you own her and trust her?" the deputy asks, a tinge of empathy in his voice.

"I duh, and I duh. You can trust her," Doc Hill assures him.

"It must be hard. I have a sister. I can't imagine what this must feel like. I guess it would be okay for a few minutes," the deputy replies with a nod of understanding. "You wait right here, sir. I'll take her back to see him—but just for a few minutes," he adds, grabbing a set of keys and unlocking a steel-barred door.

Hannah follows him into the cave-like jail lit by sunlight filtering through small windows.

The deputy leads her down a hallway lined with iron-barred cells. The floor is dark gray stone, with a white, foot-wide strip running down the middle.

"You have to stay on the white stones. His cell's on the left, at the end of the hall," the deputy says, pointing ahead.

Hannah's footsteps echo as she moves down the corridor. She passes cells holding ragged, weatherworn gold seekers—some sleeping on narrow cots, while others sit on their cots in silence, their eyes hollow with defeat. One young man stares at her blankly, as if seeing straight through her.

She passes Sandy, asleep in his cell, and then sees Robert lying on his cot in the cell across from him, his back to the world.

At the end of the corridor, she stops in front of Carter's cell. He sits hunched on the bed, hands over his head, staring at the floor. He doesn't notice her.

Her tears—once feigned but now painfully real, —slide down her cheeks. She manages to whisper, "Carter."

Carter looks up in disbelief. He jumps to his feet and grabs the bars. "I was afraid I'd never see you again," he says, trembling. He reaches his arms through the bars toward her.

Hannah steps forward to meet him, but the deputy calls out, "Stay on the white stones."

She halts, stepping back in line with the white stone.

Carter takes a deep breath, trying to compose himself. "They had Charles' signature. He's taking us back to Mississippi—to slavery. I can't believe he'd do this. Why would he? He set us free." Carter's voice breaks. "Why?"

"We've got to fight back," Hannah says.

"The sheriff put us in chains. I've never been in chains before." Carter shakes his head. "There's no way out. The whole world's gone mad."

"Charles gave you freedom letters. Where are they? I'll find them. I'll take them to Cornelius," Hannah says.

"Hardin burned them," Carter chokes out. "He burned them!"

Hannah's face crumples in disbelief. "There still may be a chance. Cornelius will know what to do. If you're going back to Mississippi, then

I'm going, too. I've got money. I can find work. We can be together there."

"There ain't nothing in Mississippi for you or me. It's time to fight. They can try to take my freedom, but they can't take my heart and soul." Carter's voice grows stronger. "Charles isn't like a brother to me anymore. He's one of them now. Something's changed. I will be free— no matter what."

Hannah rushes to him and wraps her arms through the bars. "Don't do anything foolish." They press together, lips meeting through cold iron.

"Get Cornelius," Carter pleads. "Tell him we will fight. The law calls us people of color. We've got to change the law. All colors matter. Everyone should be free. That's what the Constitution says."

"We'll fight. We'll find a way," Hannah promises.

"They took all our gold. Our mules. The wagon. We've got nothing," Carter says bitterly.

"I've got money. And we've got friends. People will help. We'll all fight. We'll find a way," Hannah says again, firmer now.

"That's enough," the deputy barks. He strides over and pulls Hannah gently but firmly from the bars.

He escorts her out of the jail. Outside, Doc Hill helps her down the dusty street, catching her as she sobs.

"This is all wrong," Hannah says, wiping away her tears as anger rises again. "They were free."

"We'll go to Cornelius right now," Doc Hill says, helping her into the carriage. "He'll know what to do."

He snaps the reins, and the carriage speeds from the Placer County jail, heading for downtown Sacramento.

CHAPTER 30
CARTER FIGHTS FOR FREEDOM
JUNE 1852

On the afternoon of June 1st, 1852, Hannah and Doc Hill make their way to Cornelius Cole's office on K Street in Sacramento. The city buzzes with life, growing and sprawling from the Sacramento Riverfront to Sutter's Fort and beyond. Tents give way to permanent buildings. Workers bustle in the hot, mid-afternoon sun. Across the street stands the Sacramento County jail; just blocks away is the courthouse. Next door, a general store offers nearly everything one might need.

Inside Cornelius's small, cluttered office, Doc Hill and Hannah quickly explain the situation. Books and papers are stacked on every surface. Cornelius listens intently, then sifts through a pile of notes. He leans back in his chair, thoughtful.

"This won't be an easy case," he says at last. "Are you certain there are no documents confirming their release?"

"Carter says they burned them," Hannah replies, her voice tight with frustration.

"Were the documents ever filed? Did either of you see the letters?" Cornelius presses.

"Charles told me about them," Doc Hill says, then admits, "but I don't think he ever filed them."

"I saw them," Hannah says, her eyes lighting up. "Carter read his to me. I read it, too."

Cornelius lets out a slow breath. "I'm sorry, Hannah. You can't testify in court."

"But I'm a free woman!" she cries.

"Crabb and his cronies pushed a law through barring anyone of color from testifying in court," Cornelius says apologetically. "Many of us fought against it, but...it passed. It's the law now."

Hannah's face burns with anger. "Are there really laws in California? They change all the time. Is anybody free? Will we ever be free?"

"Hannah," Doc Hill says sharply. "He's trying to help us."

Cornelius leans forward, attempting to calm her. "It's a struggle," he reassures her. "Many of us are fighting for California's freedom—for everyone's freedom—but the opposition is powerful and well-funded. There is a great deal of money and power coming from the South."

Hannah's tone shifts from anger to desperation. "Is there anything that can be done?"

"I can file an appeal with the District Judge in Sacramento," Cornelius contemplates, twirling his beard in thought.

"Will that set them free?" Hannah asks, her hope flickering.

"Possibly," he says. "But it will go in front of Judge Aldrich. He's unlikely to grant our plea. In fact, I'm sure he won't. He's a Southerner to the bone."

"And if he doesn't?" she presses. "What can we do?"

"The case can be appealed to the California Supreme Court."

"Would they be free then?" asks again.

"If the California Supreme Court rules in their favor, then yes. Carter, Sandy, Robert, and everyone of color will be free in California.

We are all people of color." He puts his hand on a white paper and says, "They call me White, but I'm not white. I'm a shade of color."

Hannah flashes a knowing smile. She places her hand on a black Bible resting on the corner of Cole's desk, her bronze, brown skin and pink nails shimmering in contrast. "I'm not Black."

Corneilius smiles. "We are all people of color, from white to black and everything in between. It is what nature intended, what God intended. Certainly not to shackle and enslave each other for the color of our skin or our beliefs. Our constitution guarantees it. We must live up to it."

"Will you help?" Hannah asks, her voice shaking. "Will you take the case to the California Supreme Court?"

Even though his words were full of conviction, he hesitates and takes a deep breath. "My reputation—and my career—will be on the line. I will need to bring in other attorneys. There will be legal fees —a lot of them." He pauses, weighing the risk. "The argument would have to be that the law violates the California Constitution *and* the United States Constitution. I'd have to try every angle. It will be costly."

Doc Hill swallows hard. "How much will you need?"

"I must move fast. I will need at least a thousand for the appeal alone. That must happen in the next few days. It must be compelling. No matter, I'm sure it will be denied by Judge Aldrige in Sacramento. To appeal and fight at the California Supreme Court, I will need thousands more to start and ensure cash flow."

Doc Hill and Hannah share astonished glances.

"I know people who want to be free," Hannah asserts. "And others who will help." She thinks of the friends she and Carter had made—of Reverend Blue and the church members.

"I know people," Doc Hill echoes. "We can find the money. I can give you a hundred now. Can you get started with that?"

"I'll get started on the appeal and send it to the Supreme Court," Cornelius says with conviction. "I can't raise funds myself, but I know people who will help. Most people want California to be free. Carter's not alone."

Doc Hill hesitates, then asks, "I must ask, —do you consider yourself an abolitionist? I mean, I was just wondering..."

"It's all right," Cornelius says, offering a smile. "I'm not a radical abolitionist, but I believe slavery is wrong. I'm confident others will come to that conclusion in time. We must fight for the Declaration of Independence and the Constitution. All men..." He pauses, glances at Hannah, then corrects himself. "All people must be free. I take those words seriously: We are all created equal. We must fight for everyone's freedom. Until everyone is free, no one is free."

"I know people who will fight. Lots of people," Doc Hill says.

"We will need support. We must sway public opinion in our favor. I'll give you a list of people I believe will support the case. It's not my place to ask for money, but you can approach them," Cornelius says as he writes a list.

"I know people who will help. All the folks at Sweet Vengeance. All the people at church," Hannah gushes.

"I know them, too," Cornelius says, looking up from his writing. "I've helped them. They'll fight." He hands Hannah the note and adds, "The first person you should talk to is Mark Hopkins. He runs the store down the street. He's antislavery. He's—"

"I know him! Carter knows him!" Hannah exclaims. "Carter's been hauling for Mr. Hopkins for a long time."

"I know him, too. We'll start with him," Doc Hill adds, taking the list from Cornelius.

Doc and Hannah rush down the block. They find Mark Hopkins working in his office behind a bustling warehouse filled with meat and produce. They explain the situation and the need for money to help Cornelius hire additional attorneys for the case.

"We will fight," Mark Hopkins says. "This is extremely important. We must set all Californians free, once and for all. I know many who will help, and I'll organize a fund. I'll tell Cornelius he will get the money."

"Thank you," Hannah says, thrilled by his support.

"It's the least I can do. They're good, honest, hardworking men. We need more people like them in California," Mark adds.

Doc Hill and Hannah return to Auburn. They decide that Doc will focus on raising funds from the White community while Hannah concentrates on the Black community.

Doc spreads the word and invites those he believes will support the cause of freedom to his cabin. He builds a massive, blazing bonfire to draw attention.

Gold seekers and businessmen gather around the fire, talking, laughing, and bantering. Doc raises his hands to quiet them.

"Can I have your attention, please?" he calls out.

The crowd falls silent.

"I invited you here because we all believe in freedom. We fought hard to make California free—but she isn't," Doc proclaims.

"What do you mean? California's a free state," a miner yells.

"California's not free! Three free men you know, —Carter, Robert, and Sandy, —have been captured and are being forced back into slavery in Mississippi. It's a new law, and we need to fight it," Doc urges.

The crowd murmurs, and they talk among themselves.

"Southerners should've never brought their slaves here," someone shouts.

"California's freedom is for Whites only!" another adds. "Send them back!"

"Until everyone is free, no one is free. Slavery is a disease, and we need to stop it from spreading," Doc calls out.

George steps forward from the crowd and joins Doc.

"Doc Hill's right. They're good men. The goddamn slave owners would turn us all into slaves if they could," he says with conviction.

The crowd breaks into loud conversation and argument.

"We have a chance to set everyone free," Doc continues. "We've got a lawyer willing to challenge the slave owners and their immoral laws. He'll take the case to the California Supreme Court. We need your help!"

"They work as hard as any man. They're my friends. I'll give you some money," George exclaims.

A voice booms from the back, "Too bad for them. I'm keeping my gold. I hope the Southerners take all their slaves back South—and go to hell. Let's get out of here."

He stomps off, and a dozen others follow him into the dark.

George turns back to Doc Hill, followed by several gold seekers and businessmen.

He reaches into his pocket and pulls out a bag of gold. "You can have all of this. There's more if you need it."

The men behind him step forward, pulling out bags of gold and coins, forming a line in front of Doc Hill.

Doc takes out a pad and pencil.

"I'll keep track of your donations. If there's a way to pay you back, we will," he assures them, accepting George's gold.

"No need. Seeing them free will be reward enough," George says, full of heart.

Only a mile away, Hannah stands in front of a campfire at the Black miners' tent camp along the American River.

"This is about your freedom. This is about all of our freedom," Hannah pleads.

"Will we all be free?" a miner asks.

"If the California Supreme Court agrees, everyone in California will be free," Hannah replies, her voice firm with conviction.

"We've had enough of California politicians. We can't vote, and we can't trust them!" a Black miner snaps, shaking his head.

Many in the crowd murmur their agreement.

"There's no guarantee, but it's worth a fight. Isn't it?" Hannah says, urging them on. She raises her fist. "Are you ready to fight for Carter, Sandy, and Robert? Are you ready to fight with me? Are you ready to fight for yourselves?"

A miner steps forward. "It's worth a fight. I've got gold. Let's fight the bastards. We'll fight their laws."

The crowd cheers as he pulls out a bag of gold and holds it high.

Others rush to Hannah, reaching into their pockets and pulling out coins, bags, and jars of gold. Hannah is overwhelmed.

A few days later, Doc and Hannah return to Cornelius's office. They find him hunched over his desk, writing. Papers and books are stacked on his table and the floor.

He looks up as Hannah drops a bag of gold coins on his desk.

"We've raised over a thousand dollars. We can get more," she says.

"I knew you'd get the money," Cornelius replies with a broad smile. "I pulled some strings. The appeal is set..." He shuffles his papers and scans his notes. "It's set for June 7th."

"That's just a few days away," Doc says.

Cornelius glances at his calendar. "I'll be ready. I'm sure the judge will side with the prosecution, but I'm already working on the appeal to the Supreme Court," he says. "I'll meet you at the courthouse early that morning."

On the morning of June 7th, Cornelius, Hannah, and Doc Hill walk toward the Sacramento courthouse. Green, Crabb, and a herd of angry slave owners and sympathizers wait for them.

Green strides up to Cornelius, Crabb at his side.

"You're interfering with our rights," Green snarls through gritted teeth, standing inches from Cornelius's face as the armed thugs behind him brandish their weapons.

"This was supposed to be a legal matter. Now it's personal," Green says coldly.

"Freedom was, is, and always will be personal," Cornelius replies, stepping forward and forcing Green to yield. "We must decide this as gentlemen."

Crabb moves in beside Green, blocking Cornelius.

"Gentlemen have already decided. You're outvoted and outnumbered," Crabb growls.

Just then, George and Fritz round the courthouse corner with a group of miners, —Black and White, —many carrying pickaxes. They head straight for Doc Hill.

Doc Hill smiles and locks eyes with Crabb. "We'll see who's outvoted and outnumbered."

George and Fritz walk shoulder to shoulder and brush past Crabb and Green. They lead their men up the steps. George turns to Hannah with a confident smile. "Figured you might need help."

Hannah glances at the opposing group of slaveowners and their sympathizers closing in. "We'll take all the help we can get," she says as she beams.

The courtroom is packed. Daniel Blue and church members join George, Fritz, and their friends. They sit behind Cornelius. Hannah clutches Carter's Bible and sits beside Doc Hill, just behind the defense table.

On the other side, Crabb and Green sit at the prosecution bench. Hardin sits behind them, surrounded by rowdy slaveowners and their sympathizers.

The rear door swings open. Sheriff Asten and his deputies march Carter, Sandy, and Robert into the courtroom in chains. They look haggard and sleep-deprived. Shouts erupt—some cheering, others protesting.

Hannah stands and yells to Carter, trying to raise her voice above the din of the crowd. He hears her, glances at the crowd, but doesn't see her. He keeps his head down, attempting to block out the noise and confusion.

The bailiff raises his voice. "All rise!"

The courtroom settles as Judge Aldrige walks in and bangs his gavel. "Court is now in session," Judge Aldrich announces, his Southern drawl unmistakable. Perhaps emphasized for show.

The silence doesn't last. Chants and jeers rise again as the judge flips through his papers.

"Your Honor!" Cornelius shouts above the noise. "You must bring order!"

Judge Aldrich rises and slams his gavel. "There will be order in my courtroom, or I'll clear it!" The room quiets. "You all came to hear this— so let us proceed. Mr. Cole, what is the basis of your appeal?"

Cornelius stands. "Your Honor, the California Fugitive Slave Act violates the state constitution."

Judge Aldrich cuts him off. "I'm not here to rule on the California constitution, Mr. Cole." He turns to Crabb. "What is your argument, Mr. Crabb?"

Crabb rises. "Your Honor, the California Congress, Senate, and Governor passed the Fugitive Slave Act to protect our great state. It is legal and valid."

The judge scans the documents before him.

"The law stands. I find for Charles Perkins," Judge Aldrich declares, slamming his gavel. "The defendants will remain in custody and be returned to their rightful owner in Mississippi."

Cheers erupt behind Crabb, Green, and Hardin. Boos and shouts follow from the other side. The two sides cross the aisle. They shove and yell at each other. Some brandish guns.

Carter lifts his head. Through the chaos, his eyes find Hannah's. She's crying, clutching his Bible. For a moment, the crowd fades.

"I love you," she mouths.

"I love you," he replies silently. "Don't follow me. You must be free."

Before she can answer, the Sheriff shoves Carter and forces the men out through a back door.

Cornelius rises, shouting, "Your Honor, I must protest! I haven't finished my argument!"

Judge Aldrich bangs his gavel repeatedly. "This court will come to order!"

The noise fades to a quiet rumble.

"Do not challenge me in my courtroom, Mr. Cole, or I will hold you in contempt! If you want to pursue this, take it to the California Supreme Court. This case is closed!"

"I will file an appeal!" Cornelius calls out.

"Then file it, Mr. Cole. Court is adjourned."

Judge Aldrich exits through the rear door. The courtroom erupts again.

Outside, the two factions pour into the street. Miners, church members, and Sweet Vengeance allies gather around Cornelius, Doc Hill, and Hannah, shielding them as Crabb, Green, and Hardin approach with a hostile mob.

"You're on the wrong side of the law," Green threatens, pointing at Cornelius.

Hannah steps between them. "You're on the wrong side of humanity. You're nothing but a"

Doc Hill gently pulls her back.

"They want a street fight," Cornelius says firmly. "We'll fight them in court."

"You just did. And you lost," Green snaps before turning away.

Crabb steps up. "Tuck your tail and run, Cornelius. You've stirred up a hornet's nest."

Cornelius meets his glare. "So have you. And we'll win in court."

Fritz, George, and their supporters close ranks, helping Cornelius push through the crowd.

"What happens now?" Hannah asks as they walk.

"Now the California Supreme Court," Cornelius replies. His eyes burn with resolve. "The paperwork is ready. I will file the appeal tomorrow."

Across the street, Crabb, Green, and Hardin confer in hushed tones.

"Think he'll appeal?" Green asks.

"I'm sure of it," Crabb says. "But I doubt the court will hear the case. We can't take any chances. If they're not in California, there's no trial. This isn't about their freedom—it's about ours."

"I promised my family I'd bring them home," Green says firmly.

Hardin looks at Green. "We'll get them out of California, dead or alive."

Green glares at him. "Alive! We get them back alive."

That night, under the cover of darkness, Green and Hardin arrive at the jail. Sheriff Asten brings Carter, Sandy, and Robert in chains and gags to the front.

Without a word, Green and Hardin drag them to a waiting wagon, toss them in, and throw a canvas over them.

CHAPTER 31
CARTER TAKES HIS CASE TO COURT

A few days later, in early June 1852, Cornelius arrives at a hotel in downtown San Francisco. He enters an empty ballroom that has been turned into a makeshift courtroom.

Justice Alexander Wells—young, clean-shaven but with dramatic sideburns and long wispy hair—sits alone behind a desk as Cornelius steps into the room carrying a stack of papers.

"Cornelius Cole, I presume? It's nice to meet you," he says with a grin. "I've heard about you."

"Thank you for seeing me on such short notice, Your Honor," Cornelius replies, handing over the documents.

"I'm intrigued by your appeal," Justice Wells says as he looks up, apologetic. "Sorry about the conditions. We're building a proper courthouse, but it'll take time."

Cornelius smiles. "The law can be practiced anywhere."

"True enough," Judge Wells says with a chuckle. "But where can it be perfected?"

"Hopefully here, Your Honor," Cornelius says with a grin.

"We do our best in an imperfect world," Judge Wells laughs, flipping through the papers. Cornelius waits silently as the judge reads his notes and looks at Cornelius's appeal.

"Your appeal has merit, Mr. Cole. We will hear your appeal on July fifth," he announces, stacking the documents neatly.

Cornelius blinks, surprised by the swift decision.

"I hope you'll be ready to present your case by then?" Justice Wells asks, his tone both hopeful and firm.

"I'll be ready. Thank you, Your Honor," Cornelius says, steadying his voice.

He turns and walks out into a busy street. He can't contain the smile that breaks across his face. He takes a deep breath of the salty breeze from the San Francisco Bay. The sky is a beautiful deep blue. Seagulls circle looking for a snack from a street vendor.

This is a perfect omen, —a perfect day. Cornelius ponders as he weaves through bustling streets, finally making his way to a small storefront next to a stable filled with horses.

A young clerk greets him, "What can I do for you?"

"I need to send a letter to Auburn. How long will that take?" Cornelius asks.

"You're in luck. We started a new express line two weeks ago," the clerk says proudly. Riders are posted every twenty miles. We could have it there by late afternoon—but it's expensive." He checks his pocket watch. "There's just enough time."

"I want to send it now," Cornelius says quickly. "Give me a piece of paper."

Just as the sun dips low that evening, a courier arrives at Doc Hill's cabin. Dust clings to his clothes, and his white horse stands lathered and trembling from the hard ride. The courier strides up to the porch and knocks.

Hannah opens the door.

"Letter for Doc Hill. From San Francisco," the courier pants, catching his breath.

Hannah's face lights up. "I'll take it," she says, reaching for the envelope.

The courier pulls it back. "He's got to sign for it."

"He's busy," she protests.

"If he can't come now, someone can bring it back tomorrow," the courier offers.

"Wait here. I'll get him," she says and disappears into the cabin.

The courier waits at the door.

Doc Hill emerges from the back, hands stained with blood, dabbing them dry with a towel. Hannah trails behind him.

"You could've let my assistant sign," Doc Hill complains as he signs the courier's ledger.

"Is she your..." the courier begins.

Hannah cuts him off and snaps, "Am I his slave? Is that what you were about to ask?"

Doc Hill smirks as his bloody hands exchange the signed ledger for the letter.

"Didn't mean anything by it," the courier stammers. "Ain't nothing wrong with that."

"There's plenty wrong with it," Hannah shoots back.

"She's my assistant. She's a free woman," Doc Hill says calmly as he reads the letter.

"I'm sorry. Hope it's good news," the courier says as he leaves.

Doc Hill looks up, "It's good news from Cornelius. The California Supreme Court will hear their case on July 5th. He's staying in San Francisco until then."

Hannah bursts into tears and throws her arms around Doc Hill. "I've got to tell them!"

"They probably won't let you see them," Doc Hill warns as he hands her the letter. "But take my carriage. Carter will want to read this himself."

Hannah races to the Placer County jail. She pauses to compose herself before entering. The same deputy who let her in before sits behind the desk.

Slipping into a thick Southern accent and fake sobs, she cries, "I come touh see my brother, Carter Perkins. I have the most devastatin' news."

"Oh, yeah. Your brother," the deputy says as he smirks. "You're too late. He's gone."

She drops the act and scowls. "You're lying. I want to see him now!"

The deputy pulls a paper from the desk drawer. "Their rightful owner, Green Perkins, claimed them. They're gone."

Hannah flies out of the jail, unable to contain her tears and sobs. She jumps into the carriage and drives off in a cloud of dust.

It's dark when she bursts into the backroom as Doc pulls a bullet from a man's chest. He turns to greet her as he plunks it into a metal tray.

"They're gone," she gasps. "Green and Hardin took them."

"Oh God," Doc Hill says. "I can't leave now. We'll go to San Francisco in the morning and tell Cornelius."

"They might already be on a ship!" Hannah cries.

"I doubt it," Doc contemplates. "They'll need to hide them first. Maybe someone saw them or knows where they went. Take my carriage. Ask around, but be careful."

Before he can say more, Hannah is racing out the door.

Hannah drives her carriage by the river in the dark, guided by moonlight along the narrow path between rows of miners' tents. She stops the carriage beside George, who is tending a fire and talking with several miners.

"Green and Hardin have taken Carter, Sandy, and Robert," she says urgently. "The court's going to hear their appeal for freedom. We've got to find them. Have you heard anything?"

"Those dirty bastards." George shakes his head. "I ain't heard nothing." He turns to the men around him, who shrug. "We'll spread the word and snoop around, but they may already be on a ship to Mississippi."

"I'm afraid so, too," Hannah says, holding onto hope. "But Doc Hill doesn't think they've had time to get them on a ship."

"Probably right," George replies. "We'll do everything we can to help find them."

Hannah cracks the whip, and the horse bolts. She rides off in a cloud of dust.

Minutes later, she pulls into the Black miners' camp. Lanterns flicker. Men look up from fires and cooking pots, gathering around her as she stops.

She repeats the story, voice steady, eyes scanning their faces.

"Those men ain't nothin' but low-down bastards," one miner growls.

Another miner spits in the dirt and says, "Green and Hardin are bastards. I don't think they have mothers. I think they were born in the pits of hell."

An older miner steps forward. "Is what you said true? The California Supreme Court—will they decide if those fellows are free? And if they are… does that mean we all are?"

"Yes," Hannah says firmly. "It's the California Supreme Court. Everyone is free if they decide that Carter, Sandy, and Robert are free."

"Even if they're gone? Will the court still decide?"

"I don't know," she admits. "I don't think so. Doc Hill and I are going to San Francisco in the morning. We'll do everything we can to find them."

"We'll help." The older miner turns and calls out, "Gather round! We've got to find Carter!"

Doc Hill and Hannah sit in Cornelius's room at the Parker House Hotel in San Francisco the next day. Cornelius tugs at his beard, contemplating the news, and stares at the ceiling.

Cornelius struggles as he looks into Hannah's eyes. "Without defendants, we don't have a case."

"They couldn't have gotten them on a ship this fast," Doc says, thinking aloud.

"We've got to stop them," Hannah pleads. "Aren't there laws against this?"

"It's unlawful to abduct defendants and prevent them from appearing in court," Cornelius affirms, already shuffling through papers. "I'll file a motion. They must be found." He looks up. "I'll get you rooms here. Stay until we track them down."

That evening, Hannah and Doc Hill search the streets of San Francisco. The town has grown—wood-plank sidewalks now line the muddy streets, and brick buildings stand beside rough timber storefronts. They pass bars, restaurants, and gambling houses, all glowing with the flicker of kerosene lamps.

"What are you thinking?" Hannah asks Doc. "Where do we start?"

"The harbor," Doc says. "We'll find out if any ships have left, or if any are about to."

The salty wind stings their faces as they reach the waterfront. Tall ships rock in the bay, their masts swaying like dark skeletons in the gloom. They spot a small ticket booth near the wharf, where travel posters flap and sailing schedules are posted on the wall. The ticket agent looks up as they approach.

"Can you tell us if any ships left or are leaving for Panama or around the Horn in the past few days?" Doc asks, breathless.

"No ships have left," the agent replies. "The *California* sails the day after tomorrow. There are plenty of tickets left—everybody's coming here, nobody's leaving. I've got First Class, Second Class, and Steerage."

"We're looking for someone. Who keeps the passenger list for the *California?*"

"The ship's purser logs the names when folks board."

"Thank you." Doc nods, and they hurry back toward the city.

Hannah faces Doc. "We need to find them before they get on that ship."

"I doubt Green and Hardin are taking them themselves," Doc replies. "They will hire someone—someone who won't ask questions, someone willing to smuggle them aboard for enough gold. We'll check the bars. Sailors talk."

They rush into the heart of San Francisco's nightlife. Kerosene light spills onto the streets from the saloon doors and windows.

Drunken miners and sailors stagger past. Laughter and shouting echo through the night. Prostitutes lean from balconies and stoops, calling out, their painted faces catching the lamplight.

"How is that going to work?" Hannah asks.

"We'll find sailors and get them drunk. Loose lips sink ships," Doc Hill replies.

"Their lips are loose, and their ships have already sunk," Hannah says with a bitter laugh as she looks at sailors staggering in the street.

Doc Hill leads her toward two unsteady sailors leaning against each other for balance. "You wouldn't happen to have sailed on the *California,* would you?" he asks.

They laugh, swaying on their feet. "We did sail on the *California*— but we're not sailing anymore. We're here to strike gold."

"We're trying to move some cargo onto the ship, but we don't want it on the manifest. Know anyone who might help?" Doc asks.

"A couple of men asked us the same thing," one sailor answers. "But we ain't going back. We're staying put."

"The captain would never allow it, anyway," the other slurs. "He'd hang us."

"What did the men look like? Who did they talk to? Do you think anyone agreed to help them?" Hannah asks urgently.

"Don't remember. They were in that bar," the sailor says, pointing to a rowdy bar.

His friend wobbles up, adding, "They talked to Moses for a long time. You should ask him."

"Who's Moses?" Hannah asks.

"You can't miss him—scraggly beard, sitting in the back," the sailor slurs.

"They all have scraggly beards," Hannah complains.

"Come on, Hannah, we'll find him," Doc says as they walk into the bar. The air smells of whiskey and sweat. Their eyes scan the room before landing on a scruffy, middle-aged man at a corner table, his cheeks flushed from drink.

"I bet that's him," Hannah whispers to Doc.

She leads the way into the bar, weaving and shoving through drunk men and a few ladies of the night. "Mind if we sit?" she asks Moses as she pulls out a chair.

He nods and gestures for them to sit. "It's a free country."

Moses' glass is empty. Doc flags down a waitress and orders a bottle of whiskey. "Looks like you could use a refill," Doc offers.

Moses slides his glass forward as the waitress arrives with a bottle, "I hate drinking alone," he says, nodding toward the other empty glasses.

Doc obliges, pouring all three.

"We need a reason to drink," Moses says. "What's the occasion?"

"Let's drink to freedom," Hannah suggests.

Moses pauses, eyeing her—aware she's the only Black woman in the bar. He feels the intensity in her eyes. A slow smile spreads across his face.

"I like that. To everybody's freedom." He throws back his drink and motions for another.

Hannah sips hers and coughs at the bite of the whiskey.

Doc pours another round for Moses. "We'd like to ask you a few questions."

Moses eyes the fresh pour. "Figured there was a catch."

"We've heard folks are trying to smuggle passengers onto the *California*. Word is, you might know something," Doc says.

A flicker of amusement crosses Moses' face. "Something like that could get a man in trouble. Sounds like information worth paying for."

Doc slides a gold coin across the table.

Moses taps it with a finger on the coin. "Now that you mention it... Two men asked me. Offered good money. But I told them no—I'm staying here. Besides, I'm an honest man."

"Do you remember their names?" Hannah asks, leaning in.

Moses raises his glass. Doc pours and slides another gold coin across the table.

"They had strange names," Moses says slowly, brows furrowed.

"Was one of them Green?" Hannah asks, her voice tight and urgent.

"Yeah. What kind of name is that?" Moses scoffs. "The other feller was Harley... or something."

"Hardin?" Hannah says.

Moses nods. "That's it. I turned them down, but I heard others making a deal. They're sneaking them on the night before the ship sails."

Doc Hill and Hannah exchange a look. They've found their lead.

Doc Hill pleads, "It's a long story, but we need your help. Will you tell your story to one of our friends?"

Moses holds out his glass. Doc Hill slowly pours the whiskey.

"It could get me in a lot of trouble," Moses mumbles.

"Our friends are already in trouble," Hannah says, her voice tight with desperation. "Green and Hardin have kidnapped them and are trying to smuggle them out of California. Please help us."

Moses sighs. His eyes meet Hannah's. For a moment, the gravity of the situation sobers him. He takes a long breath. "I know what's going on. I'll talk to your friend. Everyone should be free."

Doc Hill and Hannah lead Moses to the Parker House Hotel. He passes out in Doc's room.

The next morning, Hannah, Doc Hill, and Moses sit around a small hotel table facing Cornelius. Moses sips coffee while Cornelius scribbles notes as fast as he can.

"Do we have what we need?" Hannah asks.

Cornelius nods, finishing the page, then turns it so Moses can read. "You must sign this affidavit and testify before Supreme Court Justice Wells today. You need to be sober."

A cold wave of sobriety hits Moses. He rubs his face, suddenly wide awake.

"Wait a minute," he says, uneasy. "I don't want to go in front of a judge. People will find out."

"It'll help everyone," Hannah urges. "They're free men, and bad men are trying to turn them back into slaves."

Moses looks at her—really looks—and nods. "Slavery's wrong. I'll do it. No one should have this happen to them."

"Let's get you cleaned up," Doc Hill says. "You can wear some of my clothes."

Doc Hill shaves Moses while Hannah trims his hair. Cornelius returns with a pressed suit that fits Moses almost perfectly. They waste no time getting to the hotel that houses the California Supreme Court.

They stand in the back and patiently wait for their turn.

Justice Wells looks up. "Please come forward, Mister Cole."

Cornelius hands Justice Wells the papers as they all stand before his bench. Doc Hill and Hannah steady Moses between them. Moses reaches to tug his beard nervously, but it's gone. He's clean-shaven and rubs his chin.

Justice Wells studies the document, then lifts his eyes to Moses.

"Step forward, Moses," Judge Wells commands. "Do you swear your testimony is true and confirm your signature on this affidavit?"

Moses shifts his feet, glances down, then straightens. "All of it is true. I signed it. I hope you can help them."

"Thank you for your honesty," Justice Wells says, his voice measured as he signs a note. "Based on your testimony, I can and will issue a warrant for Carter, Robert, and Sandy. When they are found, they will remain in custody until the court decides their case."

Hannah steps forward, voice sharp with resolve. "What about Green Perkins and Hardin Scales? They should be arrested!"

Doc Hill places a hand on her shoulder. "Hannah—"

Justice Wells raises a hand to calm the room.

"As you surely know, people of color cannot testify or speak in court under California law," he says. "I know of no statute that allows me to bring charges against those men."

"Your Honor," Cornelius interrupts, "they abducted the defendants before a hearing. That's illegal."

"There is no proof they were aware of the appeal or court proceedings," Justice Wells replies. "The defendants are Charles Perkins' rightful property, and Green is his lawful agent. The San Francisco police will help you locate and detain the defendants. But there will be no case if they are not in court on July fifth."

"Thank you, Your Honor. We'll find them," Cornelius replies, steering the group out of the courtroom.

They walk into the street. Hannah pulls out several gold coins and holds them out for Moses. She looks into his eyes. "That was very brave, thank you."

Moses smiles and closes the coins into her palm. "I didn't do it for money. I did it for the truth."

Cornelius steps up. "We may need you to appear at the hearing. Where can we find you?"

Moses looks down the street at all the workers pounding nails and raising buildings.

"My father was a carpenter. He taught me well. You won't find me in a bar again. You can find me here, building."

Cornelius, Hannah, and Doc take Wells' signed order directly to the San Francisco police.

The following morning, Doc Hill, Hannah, and four officers walk down the San Francisco pier toward the SS *California*. A line of passengers waits to board. One of the officers steps ahead and hands the warrant to the purser.

Moments later, Captain Forbes appears and reads the document with a scowl.

"This is highly irregular," he says. "We're about to sail. I have a schedule to keep." He turns to the purser. "Are any of these names on our manifest?"

The purser scans the warrant, then checks his list. "No, Captain. None of them."

"They're likely not using their real names," Doc Hill insists. "This is a matter before the California Supreme Court. These men are free citizens being taken back into slavery. We have a witness who says someone is trying to sneak them aboard."

Captain Forbes narrows his eyes at the paper. "I remember a young man named Carter Perkins. He sailed with me a few years ago. His master was Charles Perkins. Is this the same man?"

"That's him!" Hannah beams. "He talked about you. Said you were a fair man. He helped on your ship."

"Carter's not on our list, but we can look. I owe him that much," Captain Forbes vows.

Captain Forbes leads the group below deck, lantern light flickering against the ship's narrow passageways. They descend through tight stairways and dim hallways until they reach a locked door. Captain Forbes unlocks and opens it.

Inside, canvas hammocks are slung wall to wall—each one occupied.

"Carter Perkins, are you here?" Captain Forbes bellows.

"I'm here, Captain," Carter croaks, clearing his dry throat.

Captain Forbes raises the lantern as Hannah rushes to Carter. His wrists are shackled above his head. She throws her arms around him, weeping. Nearby, Sandy and Robert are cuffed in separate hammocks.

"This is outrageous!" Captain Forbes roars. "I'm not running a slave ship! I want to know who did this. I want them arrested!"

A police officer steps forward. "We have a warrant to arrest these three. No one else."

"I'll take care of the matter myself," Captain Forbes growls. "There are rats on my ship—and they won't last long. Rats can't swim in the ocean."

Back on deck, sunlight pierces the gloom. Carter flinches at the brightness and he stumbles. Hannah catches him and guides him up the final steps. He blinks against the sun his first glimpse in days. Behind him, Sandy and Robert shield their eyes as they emerge. Their handcuffs and chains rattle.

Carter steadies himself, then walks on his own. He raises his handcuffs to a police officer.

"Can't you take the cuffs off of us?" Carter pleads.

"Our orders are to arrest you and take you to jail," the officer answers coldly.

"I don't understand why we have to go to jail to be free," he complains to Hannah.

"It's to protect you from Green, Hardin, and the rest," Hannah says, holding his arm. "Your case is going to the California Supreme Court. They can set you free. They can set everyone free."

"How long are we gonna be in jail?" Sandy says through a clenched jaw as he rubs his neck.

"The trial is on July 5th," Hannah says, trying to be positive.

"We are never going to be free." Robert sighs as his shoulders drop and his pace slows. "Just more White lies."

"It's just a few days. We can make it," Carter offers.

"We can't give up hope," Carter tells Robert.

"I gave up hope a long time ago," Robert complains as he trudges forward.

At the gangway, Captain Forbes pauses and turns to the police officer. "I need a word with Carter."

The officer nods. Carter follows Captain Forbes a few paces away.

"I'm glad you're all right, Carter. Focus on getting free," Captain Forbes says. "Whatever happens, you've always got a place on my ship. Panama is free. The sea is free. If you need to be freed, find me. I can set you free."

Carter, Sandy, and Robert are booked into San Francisco County Jail. Hannah watches them, fearing it might be the last time she sees them before the trial. The jail is dark and dank, and she can hardly bear the thought of Carter suffering more.

She and Doc Hill return to Auburn with heavy hearts and a vow to raise more funds for their defense and gather support.

It is now July 1st, 1852.

Cornelius Cole sits on a wooden chair in the jail hallway, facing Carter through the bars. Inside the cell, Sandy and Robert sit beside Carter. Law books, some with bookmarks, are scattered across the floor.

Carter picks one up, opens it to a bookmark, and tells Cornelius, "The California Fugitive Slave Act contradicts the California Constitution. No law can override the Constitution."

"You're right." Cornelius smiles. "The Legislature can't override it, and the California Supreme Court's job is to defend the California Constitution. They must strike the law down."

"Everyone wants freedom," Carter complains, "but no one gives it to you. You have to fight every day."

"Every day and every night," Cornelius echoes.

"Are the judges fair?" Sandy asks.

"Justice Wells issued the warrant and granted your hearing. That's promising. But Justice Anderson is a slave owner from Tennessee."

"How's that fair?" Sandy snaps.

"All judges take a solemn oath to rule by the law," Cornelius says carefully. "They have agreed to protect and defend the Constitution and rule impartially."

"They twist the law the way they want," Robert snarks, staring out the small window.

"Sometimes they get it wrong. That's why we must fight to make it right," Cornelius says. "Chief Justice Murray is young—only twenty-seven—and new to the court. He's from Missouri."

Sandy scowls. "That's not comforting. I've heard and read about Missouri. Folks aren't free there."

Robert turns and glares at Cornelius. "How is it fair that three decide whether we are free or not?"

"Not just you—this case affects everyone in California," Cornelius replies. "It is vital, and I will do everything I can to win. I've hired the best attorneys and assistants to help. We are gaining support. Everyone is watching."

"If we win, do we get our money and property back?" Sandy asks. "They took everything."

"How much did they take?" Cornelius asks.

Carter replies without hesitation. "We had $426 in gold dust combined. Sandy had $230, Robert had $200, and I had $343. And we had four mules and a wagon—worth around $700."

"When we win, I'll pursue restitution," Cornelius promises. "But first things first."

On the night of July 4th, 1852, Carter, Sandy, and Robert stand on a cot, peering out a barred window, watching fireworks burst in the sky. A band plays the national anthem as the crowd in the street sings in unison:

"Oh say does that star-spangled banner yet wave,

O'er the land of the free and the home of the brave?"

The final explosions flash in the night sky. Carter stands between Sandy and Robert, watching the crowd disperse.

"This is our home. We're brave. If the judges aren't blind, we'll be free," Carter says, trying to believe it.

Robert steps down from the cot. "We're in jail. That song's not about us—it's about them. We'll never be free."

Sandy tries to calm him. "Let's wait and see. At least we're alive. Worst case, we go back to Mississippi."

"There's nothing for me in Mississippi," Robert says as he sits and stares at the floor. "Everything I care about is gone."

"We still have our hauling business," Carter says. "We'll find more gold. We can build a life here."

"We don't have a hauling business. They took our gold. They took our mules. Took everything," Robert says bitterly. "No matter what they say tomorrow, they'll find a way to keep us slaves. White folks treat us like shit on their shoes."

"They probably won't decide tomorrow," Carter says. "It could take days—maybe weeks."

"You mean we have to be here for weeks?" Robert seethes. "I told you we should've run while we had the chance."

"Let's rest," Sandy mumbles as he sighs. "Tomorrow's a big day."

Carter gazes through the window one last time. "We've got to be free. I need to be with Hannah—no matter what."

Finally, it's July 5th, 1852. Carter has spent a sleepless night waiting in anticipation, excited about the prospect, trusting Cornelius, but knowing it will be a hard fight.

Cornelius Cole walks alongside Doc Hill and Hannah toward the hotel where the California Supreme Court will hear the case. A large crowd has already gathered. Reverend Blue stands with members of his church. Fritz and his partners from the Sweet Vengeance mine are also there. Mark Hopkins and a large contingent of White supporters join them.

Crabb, Green, Hardin, and a mob of pro-slavery supporters approach from the opposite direction.

"You're in for a fight," Crabb hisses.

"We'll fight it in court," Cornelius snaps back, brushing past him.

Hardin opens his coat just enough to show a pistol tucked inside. "We'll fight in the streets, too. You'll never win."

Fritz and the others step forward. The two sides square off in the street, taunting each other as the courthouse looms.

A clerk opens the door and scans the rowdy crowd. He yells, "Will Mister Cole and Mister Crabb please come forward?"

They enter as two sheriff's deputies exit and take positions to guard the door.

Moments later, Crabb and Cornelius emerge. Cornelius looks defeated, but Crabb announces, "The hearing is delayed until July 29th. We will win!"

The crowd erupts.

Cornelius Cole raises his hands and tries to shout over the noise. "That's not true! We will win!"

Cornelius pushes into the crowd and gestures for his supporters to follow. A short distance away, near his hotel, he turns to face them.

Before he can speak, Fritz shouts, "Is it true? Are we going to lose? Are they going back to Mississippi?"

Cornelius raises his hands to calm the crowd. "They're busy with other cases. Nothing has changed. We have more time to prepare."

"So do they!" Fritz snaps.

"We'll be ready!" Cornelius shouts back. "We'll fight! And we will win!"

Cheers erupt once more. Hannah and Doc follow Cornelius back to his room at the hotel, where they sit at a small table.

"Will they be free?" Hannah pleads.

"That's up to the judges," Cornelius says gently. "But we have more time. I will hire the best lawyers, but they'll cost much more."

"We'll find the money. They must be free. Everyone must be," Hannah says. "I have to see Carter. I can't wait any longer."

"I'm the only one allowed to see them, but I'll find a way," Cornelius assures her. "I'd like them to look their best for the hearing. Maybe you could bring them clothes. I might be able to get you in the evening before the trial."

Hannah's eyes brighten. "I'll find the best clothes."

Doc Hill and one of his assistants—now his girlfriend—help Hannah choose fabric in San Francisco. Hannah painstakingly tailors each piece using the men's worn garments as patterns. She admires the result. The clothes are as fine as any lawyer's, perhaps even finer than Crabb's.

On the afternoon of July 28th, 1852, Cornelius brings Hannah to the jail. After a lengthy discussion, the guards agree to let her in. They search her and the basket of clothes thoroughly, but refuse to let her into the cell.

Carter rushes to the bars when he hears her voice. Hannah drops the basket and runs to him. They embrace and kiss through the iron bars.

The guard hurries over and pulls her back. "That's enough. You need to step back or leave," he warns.

Hannah steps back from the cell and tells Carter, "I brought you all clothes for tomorrow. Try them on!"

The guard intervenes again. "You need to stand at the end of the hall. You can come back when they have their clothes back on."

Hannah and Cornelius wait. After several tense minutes, the guard nods and waves them forward.

Carter, Sandy, and Robert stand proudly, wearing their new clothes. Each outfit fits perfectly.

"These are perfect, Hannah!" Carter exclaims.

Robert shifts uncomfortably. "This isn't us. Maybe we should wear our work clothes. We shouldn't look like them."

Hannah looks at Cornelius. "Maybe he's right. They might get more sympathy."

"We're not asking for sympathy," Cornelius says. "We're demanding equality. The Justices need to stare equality in the face." He looks each man in the eye. "We're ready."

The next morning, July 29th, the makeshift California Supreme Courtroom is packed and noisy. The clerk steps forward from the back.

"All rise."

The room quiets as the crowd stands.

Justice Wells enters, followed by Justice Andrew "Outlaw" Anderson—a weathered man of fifty-eight with long gray sideburns and wispy hair. Last comes Chief Justice Hugh Campbell Murray, just twenty-seven like Wells. He is tall, bony, and cold as he ascends to the raised bench between the others.

Chief Justice Murray pounds his gavel. "The Supreme Court of California is now in session. Mr. Cole, you may present your case."

The Justices take their seats. The crowd settles into an uneasy silence.

Cornelius turns to Carter, Sandy, and Robert as he steps behind their table. Holding a stack of papers, he meets each man's gaze with a steady smile. Then he surveys the hushed courtroom, pausing on Hannah and Doc seated behind him.

Across the aisle, Crabb and several prosecutors sit stiffly—Green and Hardin glare.

Cornelius walks to the podium and places his notes down with care.

"Thank you for hearing this case on such a glorious day. We recently celebrated our independence. Over seventy-five years ago, our forefathers declared: 'We hold these truths to be self-evident, that all men are created equal…'" He pauses. "I will prove to you that these men are free."

Cheers rise from the defense's supporters. The prosecution's side jeers.

Chief Justice Murray bangs his gavel. "There will be quiet and order in this court, or I will clear it." He fixes a stern eye on Cornelius. "We are familiar with the Declaration of Independence and the Constitution, Mr. Cole. This hearing regards the California Fugitive Slave Act. Please confine your argument to the matter at hand."

"Of course, Your Honor," Cornelius says, suppressing a smile. It was the response he had hoped for. "I'd simply like to remind the court of Marbury v. Madison, where it was found that the courts—not the legislature—determine the law."

Chief Justice Murray smirks, pleased. "That is why we are here. To ensure our legislature passes just laws," he declares. "That is why we are the Supreme Court."

Cornelius winks at Carter and begins to pace slowly in front of the bench.

"The California legislature created the Fugitive Slave Act in violation of the state's constitution," he says. He pivots and gestures toward Carter, Sandy, and Robert. "It criminalizes what was not previously a crime in California—refusing to return to slavery."

The crowd murmurs again. Murray silences them with another gavel strike.

"The Act impairs California's contractual obligation to secure liberty for all its residents," Cornelius continues, voice rising with conviction. "It violates the contract clause of our Constitution."

The Justices shuffle their notes.

Chief Justice Murray looks up. "Are you saying California has a contract with slaves?"

"I'm saying California has a contract to secure every resident's freedom and liberty," Cornelius replies, steady. "It's detailed in my written argument."

"We will read it carefully, Mr. Cole," Justice Murray says, tapping the papers in front of him. "Please continue."

Cornelius breathes deeply and presses on.

"California's Act directly conflicts with the Federal Fugitive Slave Act. A state has no authority to legislate on matters of fugitives from labor. That power belongs to the national legislature—and the Constitution." He turns and looks directly at Crabb. "California—or any other state—has no authority to legislate on the issue. California cannot return even a fugitive from labor, much less compel the return of a slave brought within its borders by the free will and consent of their master."

Crabb glares at Cornelius. He wants to speak but bites his tongue and says nothing.

Carter jots notes at his table while seated between Sandy and Robert. The Justices take notice that Carter can read and write.

Cornelius becomes animated as he addresses the Justices. He paces before the three defendants, his voice rising with conviction.

"Most importantly, the California Fugitive Slave Act conflicts with the very spirit of the antislavery clause in the California Constitution.

That provision unshackled the servant and severed the tie that bound him to his master," he declares, his tone defiant and passionate.

The crowd erupts. Chief Justice Murray bangs his gavel to restore order.

Cornelius continues, "The good people of the United States hoped and prayed that the fires of sectional jealousy had been extinguished when California became a state. But this legislature fanned the flame when it enacted this law. They have set a spark to powder, and we stand on the edge of danger once more."

Cornelius walks to his table and picks up a document. The courtroom falls silent.

He holds up the paper and faces the bench. "This is the California Constitution, ratified by the people of this state. It is the law. "I quote." he says while pausing before reading in a booming voice. "Neither slavery nor involuntary servitude, unless for the punishment of crimes, shall ever be tolerated in this state."

He points to Carter, Sandy, and Robert.

"That clause means exactly what it says. Slavery cannot exist in California. Every enslaved person who set foot here became—ipso facto—a free man. These men are free." Cornelius stands tall, meeting the Justices' eyes. "The legislature acted without authority. Some would tear this nation apart. But this Court, on this hopeful day, has the power to preserve the noblest form of government ever to grace the Earth." He returns to his desk, gathers his papers, and lifts his chin. "The right of man must be upheld, and this disgraceful law must sink into its merited oblivion."

The courtroom erupts. Supporters behind the defendants rise and cheer while Crabb's followers boo and jeer.

Chief Justice Murray bangs his gavel. "Come to order, or I will clear this courtroom!"

The noise surges. Murray bangs again, louder. "This court will come to order!"

Gradually, the room settles to a low murmur.

"We all want to hear this case," Chief Justice Murray says firmly. "We have heard a great deal. We will thoroughly digest what we've heard and review Mr. Cole's argument. We will reconvene in the morning. If there are any outbursts, I will clear the court." He bangs his gavel once more. "This court is adjourned until tomorrow morning."

The crowd erupts again as the Justices rise and exit quickly. Deputies escort Carter, Sandy, and Robert out of the courtroom.

The next morning, as proceedings resume, Carter hands Cornelius his written notes.

Cornelius scans them and nods. "Thanks, Carter. I'll use these."

The courtroom falls silent as Cornelius begins his final argument. He holds the room in his grip for two and a half hours. The Justices rarely interrupt. He paces with energy, voice rising and falling with careful rhythm.

At last, he nears his conclusion.

"No legislature can override the Constitution," he says, sauntering in front of the Justices, and no power can put shackles on a man in California."

He pauses before his final words.

"In sum: California is a free state. The moment a slave steps onto California soil, he becomes a free man. The legislature acted beyond its power, yet this Court can restore justice. The right of man must prevail, and this shameful law must vanish into deserved oblivion."

He returns to his seat beside Carter, Sandy, and Robert, who struggle to hide their smiles.

Across the aisle, Crabb quietly takes notes, his jaw tight. Cornelius sees the flicker of doubt in his eyes. He glances at the gallery—his supporters beam with hope, while Crabb's faction sits subdued, their confidence shaken.

"Thank you, Mr. Cole," says Chief Justice Murray. "We will review the matter and issue our opinion. The defendants will remain in custody. This court is adjourned."

He bangs his gavel. The crowd files out in silence. Neither side is sure of the outcome.

Outside, Cornelius walks alongside Doc Hill and Hannah. A large, mixed crowd of Black and White supporters claps and cheers. Cornelius nods to them. Hannah beams.

"It's over," she says with a crackling smile. "They'll be free."

Cornelius looks down the street. Crabb is in a heated conversation with Green, Hardin, and a group of slaveholders and their sympathizers.

"Freedom will always be a battle," Cornelius says as they walk away from the crowd.

CHAPTER 32
THE CALIFORNIA SUPREME COURT RULES

Carter, Sandy, and Robert spend two more months in a damp, dimly lit San Francisco jail while they await a final decision. Visitors are not allowed, and they are moved to windowless cells. Despite the conditions, Carter clings to hope. Cornelius visits when he can, though there is little more he can do.

Carter thinks about Hannah and would give anything to see her. With each passing day, his confidence in a favorable outcome wanes. Still, thoughts of freedom—and the dream of a life with her—help him endure.

He does everything he can to avoid thinking about being forced back to Mississippi. But some nights, those thoughts won't let him sleep. He knows Hannah can't come with him if he is sent back to Mississippi. He has never loved anyone or anything as deeply as he loves her. And yet, he understands—if you truly love someone, you must let them go and set them free. She cannot be free in Mississippi.

On August 30, 1852, Hannah and Doc Hill sit behind Cornelius as the California Supreme Court is called to order. The courtroom is packed, and crowds spill into the street. They are silent. Both sides believe they might prevail, but the verdict is anything but certain.

Three heavily armed sheriff's deputies bring Carter, Sandy, and Robert into the room. They wear the suits Hannah has cleaned and pressed, but the men look worn. Their hair is uncombed, their beards scruffy—razors have been denied. They are in handcuffs.

Sheriff deputies take them to the side of the room, not the defendant's table.

Hannah tries to manage her emotions. Carter attempts to control himself, but when their eyes meet, their restraint falters. Hannah smiles through a tear, and Carter wipes away his own. They turn away.

The room falls quiet as Chief Justice Murray and Justice Anderson enter. Murray strikes the gavel. "The California Supreme Court is now in session."

Cornelius stands. "Your Honors, where is Justice Wells?"

"He was here on a temporary appointment," Murray replies. "He is no longer on this court."

"I must object," Cornelius said. "Three men heard this case. Three men should decide it."

"Justice Anderson and I are in agreement. Even if Justice Wells held a different opinion, it would not change the outcome. You may be seated, Mr. Cole."

"I must demand that the defendants be unshackled and sit with me at the defendant's table," Cornelius barks.

"Control your temper, Mister Cole. Is that a demand or a request?" Chief Justice Murray scolds.

"It is a request, Your Honor. These men are innocent until proven guilty. How can they be shackled in a free state without committing a crime or breaking the law? That is why we are here."

"Watch your tone, Mister Cole," Chief Justice Murray admonishes as he turns to the deputies. "Uncuff them and seat them."

The courtroom is dead silent as they are uncuffed and seated.

Chief Justice Murray breaks the silence. "We will summarize our opinion. The full written opinion will be made available and is a matter of record." His Southern drawl is unmistakable, and he plays it for effect. "You argued that the act criminalized a previously lawful act. It did not. It allows for the removal of slaves brought here before a specific date."

"But Your Honor—" Cornelius stands and pleads.

"We heard your arguments, Mister Cole. We've read your appeal," Murray interrupts, his voice sharp. "The time for debate is over. You are here for our ruling."

Cornelius sits back, deflated. He truly believed they might win, but his hope has vanished. Carter, Sandy, and Robert feel it, too. Murray's tone says it all.

Murray turns to his colleague. "Justice Anderson. Please proceed."

"You argued that the act violated the Constitution," Anderson admonishes. "But the United States Supreme Court has upheld that enslaved persons, while human, are not parties to the Constitution. They are property, without rights or immunities."

Cornelius stands and yells, "They are not property! They are free and equal! The Constitution guarantees—"

Murray slams the gavel. "Sit down, Mr. Cole, or you will be held in contempt. California is not bound by any contract with free negroes, fugitives, or slaves. Nothing prevents her from removing any or all of them."

Cornelius drops to his seat, stunned and speechless. Carter can't help himself and grabs his hand to console him. They slump at the table.

Hannah's sobs break the silence as she stands. "You can't, you just can't..."

Chief Justice Murray bangs his gavel. He points at Hannah. "This court will remain in order. Can you contain yourself, or must we remove you?"

Hannah composes herself. "I will not be removed." She sits back, wipes her tears, and glares at the judges.

For over two hours, Murray and Anderson recite their decision, dismantling Cornelius's arguments one by one. Every sentence is steeped in prejudice. The crowd listens in silence. Even Crabb is unsure—more than he hoped for, and perhaps too harsh. The words might fuel the abolitionists.

Finally, Chief Justice Murray pauses and surveys the room.

"Therefore, the Supreme Court of California rules that the writ of habeas corpus is dismissed. Carter Perkins, Robert Perkins, and Sandy Jones are to be remanded to the custody of the Sheriff of San Francisco, and by said Sheriff delivered to Green Perkins for removal from this state. This court is adjourned."

Chief Justice Murray slams his gavel. The courtroom erupts with cheers and boos rising in a violent storm.

Sheriff's deputies move swiftly, grabbing Carter, Sandy, and Robert, forcing them to their feet. They cuff them.

Hannah cries out and runs for Carter. A deputy shoves her down.

"You can't take him!" she screams.

Carter struggles against the deputy's grip and tries to reach her.

"Forget about me!" he shouts. "You must be free!"

The deputy yanks him back, grips him by the neck, and forces him to the exit.

Green Perkins steps in front of Hannah, Hardin at his side.

"He's going back to Mississippi," Green sneers. "No more talking to him—unless you want to join him. I'm sure the Perkins can find a use for you."

Hannah's face hardens with fury.

"You're a disgrace," she hisses as she stomps away.

Moments later, Cornelius Cole steps into the street with Hannah and Doc Hill. Crabb, Green, and Hardin intercept them.

"Told you to tuck your tail and run," Crabb says, smug and defiant.

"I'm not running from anyone," Cornelius says as he braces. "We'll keep fighting."

"We fought, and you lost," Crabb sneers. "Next time, it's the streets."

"We won't fight in the streets," Cornelius shoots back. "We'll fight in court—with the law. Freedom is on our side, no matter what that court said."

Crabb laughs, low and mean. "The law's on our side. There are more of us. You'll lose in court and on the streets."

Cornelius ignores him and walks on. Hannah turns to him, her voice low.

"What else can we do?"

"I'll appeal to the United States Supreme Court," Cornelius says. "But for now, Carter, Sandy, and Robert are under Mississippi law. I'm afraid nothing can stop them from going back to Mississippi."

"I can stop them from going back," Hannah huffs as she storms off.

Cornelius yells, "I tried…"

Hannah turns and can't control her anger. "Trying isn't good enough. We must do it. We have to set everyone free." She storms off down the street.

After weeks in the dank, dark San Francisco jail, Mississippi Joe leads Carter, Sandy, and Robert onto the gangway of the SS *California*. Green and Hardin follow.

"They're all yours," Green says as he hands Mississippi Joe a leather pouch that jangles with coins. "Make sure they get to Mississippi."

"They'll be there 'fore they know what hit 'em," Mississippi Joe replies with a nod.

From the bridge above the deck, Captain Forbes watches the exchange.

After the ship casts off and is well underway, Captain Forbes makes his way to Mississippi Joe's cabin with a bottle of whiskey and two glasses. He knocks, and Mississippi Joe opens the door, already a few drinks in.

"What's this about?" he slurs.

Captain Forbes raises the bottle with a smile.

"I'd like a word. Got some good Scotch whiskey."

"Well then, come on in."

Captain Forbes sets the bottle and glasses on a small table.

"May I?" he asks, already pouring the Scotch.

"Absolutely," Mississippi Joe says with a grin.

Captain Forbes fills the glasses. "Problem is, everyone's headed west. Hard to find a crew for the trip back. I want to hire your slaves."

Mississippi Joe takes a sip, then a long swig. "They need tuh get home safe and in one piece. Workin' on a ship's dangerous."

"They're safe. Nowhere else to go, and I'll watch over them," Captain Forbes assures him, pouring another round. "I've got a storeroom full of rum and whiskey. You can drink as much as you like, if you let them work."

Mississippi Joe chuckles. "You've got a deal."

Captain Forbes holds out his hand. "I believe they're still shackled. Can I have the key?"

"You say there's a storeroom full of whiskey?"

Captain Forbes laughs and produces a key. "I'll trade you."

Captain Forbes descends into the dim stowage compartment, and a crewman trails behind. He lights a lantern, casting light on the hammocks where Carter, Sandy, and Robert lie.

"I made a deal with Mississippi Joe," Captain Forbes says. "You work for me on the way to Panama." He steps forward and begins unlocking Carter's shackles. "It's good to see you again. I read the papers. I was sure they would set you free."

"I thought so, too," Carter complains.

"We'll talk more later. Let's get you cleaned up—new quarters, new uniforms."

That afternoon, Carter, dressed in a blue-and-white sailor's uniform, mops the deck as Captain Forbes approaches him.

"Can I see you for a moment?"

"Of course, Captain."

Captain Forbes leads him to the pilot house, then leans on the rail, watching the waves.

"So, what's it gonna be?" he asks.

"What do you mean?"

"You once said Charles treated you like a brother. This isn't how brothers treat each other," Captain Forbes says. "What kind of life waits for you in Mississippi?"

Carter clenches his jaw. "We *were* like brothers. But he betrayed me. Nothing waits for me in Mississippi but working for him and his family."

Captain Forbes nods. "Then maybe it's time you set yourself free."

"I don't want to get you into trouble."

"I'm not afraid of trouble. I told you that you'd always have a place on my ship."

Carter hesitates before he answers, "We plan to escape in the jungle. I know how to reach Panama City. We'll hide, then find work when it's safe."

"It's dangerous, but it's a good plan," Captain Forbes says. "My ship will be in Panama City for a month getting refitted. If you can find your way back to the hotel, I'll help you."

"They'll be looking for us," Carter warns. "You could get caught up in it."

Captain Forbes lights his pipe. "The sea is trouble. The world is trouble. We push through anyway. If you and your family agree to work for me, I'll find you jobs on the ship and at the hotel."

Carter frowns. "I want to be honest. I don't know how long I'll stay. I need to get back to California."

Captain Forbes puffs his pipe and tells Carter, "That's risky. I doubt you're going back for gold. Only one thing makes a man take that kind of risk."

Carter laughs. "She's worth it."

Captain Forbes exhales smoke and smiles. "Let's talk more when the time comes. You look hungry. I hired a new cook—the food's good. Go on and eat."

CHAPTER 33
THE FINAL FIGHT FOR FREEDOM

Carter steps into the galley and joins the buffet line. The smell hits him—smoke, spice, and something that reminds him of Mississippi mixed with the best of California. He plucks a slice of bacon and bites into it. Spicy. He smiles. Sandy must be the new cook.

He ladles a bowl of steaming chicken soup. The scent is unmistakable.

He carries his bowl to a table, sits down, and holds it close to his nose. He takes a deep breath, then spoons a mouthful and slurps. His eyes widen. It can't be. He stands up and heads for the kitchen.

Carter opens the door slowly and peeks inside. Sandy is near the back, but Hannah is in front of the stove. He walks up behind her and kisses the back of her neck.

Hannah doesn't turn. "You can try to run and hide," she purrs, "but you're not getting away from me that easily." She turns and kisses him. They hold each other in a long embrace.

The weeks aboard the ship pass swiftly, filled with joy for Hannah and Carter. But freedom still hovers just out of reach. As they finalize their escape, the ship enters Panama City's harbor. Anticipation tightens into a thread of fear.

Captain Forbes and Hannah watch as a drunken Mississippi Joe herds Carter, Sandy, and Robert down the gangway. They are in leg irons and handcuffs. The dock teems with people.

Mississippi Joe orders them into a wagon driven by a slouching man in a uniform. They climb in and sit around sacks of goods headed east, along with several workers and guards. Mississippi Joe climbs next to the driver, and the wagon rumbles down a bustling street.

Captain Forbes and Hannah watch from the ship's deck as they leave. He leans toward Hannah. "I made sure every guard has enough whiskey for a long night. There's something extra in a few of those bottles. Carter knows which ones. They won't be waking up anytime soon."

"It's not poison, is it?" Hannah asks, alarmed.

"No, of course not. Just a little help from a doctor friend of mine. They will sleep very soundly."

That night, deep in the Panama jungle, Carter, Sandy, and Robert lay on blankets. Mississippi Joe snores like a sawmill.

One of the guards staggers over, clearly drunk. "You got more?" he slurs. "My buddies and I could use some more."

Carter reaches into a crate and pulls out two bottles. "We've got plenty," he says, handing them over.

The guard grins and wobbles off.

Hours later, the camp is silent. Joe snores. The guards are dead to the world.

Carter, Sandy, and Robert look over their bedrolls, now carefully shaped with blankets and branches to resemble sleeping bodies. They turn and scan the guards and the workers, but no one moves.

Carter reaches into a hidden pocket and pulls out a key.

"Where'd you get that?" Sandy whispers.

"From Captain Forbes. He made a copy," Carter says as he unlocks their chains.

They quietly tuck the chains into their bedrolls and slip silently into the jungle. They weave on and off the trail, dodging into the bushes with every sound.

After a few miles, they return to the trail once they are sure no one is following.

The moonlight shines brightly as they walk down the rutted trail.

"She'll be here soon," he says. "Just before dawn—we agreed on that."

They continue to walk for hours. They hear the loud echo of hoofbeats in the distance.

"We need to make sure it's her," Sandy says, and they duck into the brush to wait.

The shadow of two figures, wearing hats and driving a wagon, appears in the distance.

"That's two men," Sandy whispers. "That ain't her."

"It's got to be," Carter mutters. He cups his hands and makes a rough *kaw-kaw* sound, trying to mimic a bird.

"That doesn't sound like any bird I know," Robert complains, his voice tight. "That's two men, Carter. We need to move."

They push deeper into the undergrowth, eyes fixed on the wagon rattling toward them.

Then comes a voice, clear and familiar: a woman singing, "Everywhere I go, there's an angel there."

A man with a Scottish accent joins in, "Everywhere I go, there's an angel there."

Carter breaks from the brush. "It's Hannah and Captain Forbes!"

Carter sings along. Sandy and Robert scramble out to join him.

Captain Forbes stops the wagon, and Hannah throws off her hat, jumps down, and runs to Carter.

"You're my angel," he whispers, wrapping her in his arms.

"You're mine," Hannah says, and kisses him hard.

"We've got a long way to go," Captain Forbes advises. "They could be after you."

"They were drunk as hell," Sandy says. "Doubt they can find their boots, much less us. But we can't take chances."

"You'll need to hide for a few weeks," Captain Forbes says. "I know just the place—close to the hotel."

Carter climbs into the driver's seat and takes the reins. Hannah sits beside him. Captain Forbes climbs into the back with Sandy and Robert.

Just after dawn, back at the camp, Mississippi Joe groans and clutches his head. The men around him rustle and moan.

He shuffles to the three sleeping shapes he believes to be Carter, Sandy, and Robert. He kicks one. "Time to go!"

He kicks again and then yanks the blanket, revealing a pile of leaves, broken branches, and chains.

"Son of a bitch," Mississippi Joe spits out. "You were supposed to be watching them."

One of the guards sits up, bleary-eyed.

"Can't believe they ran. Are we gonna look for 'em?" the guard mumbles.

"The jungle'll eat 'em alive," Mississippi Joe grunts. "And if they make it to Panama City… it'd be like findin' a needle in a stack of needles."

Weeks later, in Mississippi, Charles and Emmy sit on her balcony, watching morning haze drift across the fields. A courier arrives with a letter. Charles signs for it without a word.

The color drains from his face as he reads.

"What is it?" Emmy asks, her voice trembling.

"Carter, Sandy, and Robert..." Charles begins, his voice hollow. "They escaped. In the Panama jungle."

"You wanted them to be free. Now they are."

"I wanted them to be free," he chokes. "But I wanted them safe. The jungle's no place for anyone." His shoulders sag. Tears spill down his cheeks. "I will never see them again."

Emmy wraps her arms around him.

CHAPTER 34
FREE AT LAST
FALL OF 1852

A few months later, in October 1852, Carter and Hannah stand before Captain Forbes. Carter is dressed in a crisp blue sailor's uniform, while Hannah appears radiant in a white dress. Captain Forbes, wearing a pristine white uniform adorned with gold braiding, holds Carter's family Bible. Sandy and Robert, also dressed in fine suits, stand beside Carter.

"By the power vested in me, in the presence of God and these witnesses," he booms, "it is my great privilege to pronounce you husband and wife! You may kiss the bride."

Carter and Hannah embrace in a long kiss.

"It's going to be hard to call you Carter Cole," Hannah says as she pulls back from their kiss.

"It won't be hard to call you Hannah Cole," Carter says, pulling her closer.

Captain Forbes turns to Sandy and Robert, their faces shining with emotion. "Are you two sure you don't want to work on my ship?"

"No," Sandy says. "The sea's not for me."

"Me either," Robert adds.

Sandy continues, "Robert and I—I mean, Abraham and I—plan to work at the hotel and the bar, if that's okay."

"Of course," Captain Forbes replies.

Robert turns to Sandy. "You sure you want to be named Samuel Cole?"

Sandy smiles. "I'm sure. You can call me Sam—or Sammy."

He looks at Robert. "And you? Are you sure you want to be Abraham Cole?"

"Yes. Like Abraham in the Bible," Robert answers. "But you can call me Abe."

Captain Forbes nods. "Abe and Sam. Glad to have you aboard. At least at the hotel. I'll keep your papers in my office here and on the ship. Make sure you always carry a copy."

Later, Sam—dressed in a white suit—tends the bar as Abe walks up in a dark suit with a tray of empty glasses.

"You think they're gonna be okay?" Abe asks. "Even though they're on a ship, going back and forth to California could be dangerous. Someone could see them."

Sam smiles. "We're all gonna be okay. We're all free now."

The SS *California* prepares to sail at the Panama City dock. Her smoke stacks billow, and her decks are crowded with gold seekers. Sailors shout and haul crates as the ship prepares to cast off. Captain Forbes stands at the gangway, reviewing documents with a Panamanian police officer.

"I don't remember them," Captain Forbes says coolly. "I've got hundreds of passengers every trip."

"If you see them, report it," the officer warns.

"Absolutely. You can count on it," Captain Forbes replies, handing back the papers.

Carter, in his dress uniform, approaches.

"Prepare to sail, Mr. Cole," Captain Forbes orders.

Carter salutes and hustles down the deck.

The smokestacks belch thick clouds as she steams into the Pacific.

Hours later, Captain Forbes summons Carter to the bridge. The sky burns orange with sunset, and the vast ocean stretches to the horizon. Captain Forbes stands at the wheel, the glow lighting his face.

"You wanted to see me, Captain?" Carter asks.

"I want to show you a few things. Take the wheel."

"You're going to let me steer the ship?" Carter gasps.

Captain Forbes fixes him with an unwavering gaze. "Why not? Don't you think you can?"

Carter grins. "I know I can."

Captain Forbes steps aside. Carter places his hands on the polished wood, warmth meeting his palms as he takes the helm. In that moment, he knows—this is precisely where he belongs.

Carter and Hannah spend several years working on the ship. While Hannah runs the galley, Carter works his way to becoming the first mate. The gold seekers are too busy to pay much attention to them, and no one questions their freedom, but they are very cautious when they make port in San Francisco. They never set foot on California soil again, preferring to stay safe on the ship.

Carter and Hannah decide to start a family. Captain Forbes is reluctant to lose them on his ship, but hires Carter as the hotel manager and Hannah as the restaurant manager. Her Southern recipes and welcoming spirit make the dining room a favorite.

Sandy enjoys being the concierge at the hotel when he is not helping Hannah in the kitchen.

Carter enjoys managing the hotel staff but finds himself in the kitchen helping Hannah whenever possible.

Robert visits often but spends most of his time working as a foreman, helping to build the Panama railroad through the jungle. The labor is hard, but he takes pride in it. He is paid well for his efforts, and he relishes the freedom.

Carter and Hannah live in the spacious manager's suite on the hotel's top floor. Many evenings, they sit together on their balcony overlooking the sea.

On a tranquil evening, the setting sun casts a golden hue over the ocean. Hannah gently rocks their newborn son, Cory, in her arms while softly humming a lullaby. Carter sits facing her, reading papers from a large stack on a table beside him.

He reads everything he can, mostly about California and Mississippi. He is passionate about keeping up with the news and the ongoing fight for freedom. He and Hannah often talk about returning to California and buying land to create their apple orchard when it is truly free, but the battle over slavery is getting louder. They know they are safe in Panama and will let time take its course.

He puts down a paper and smiles at Hannah as she nurses their son. He picks up a copy of a Mississippi paper. He often scans the social columns to catch up on the news of the Perkins family and their neighbors. He had read that Charles married Emmy, but there had been little mention of the Perkins family since.

He scans the paper. He breathes hard and sets the paper down. He can't control his tears.

"What is it? What's wrong?" Hannah asks.

"Charles is dead," Carter chokes out. "I always thought I'd see him again. I wanted to know..." His voice trails.

"I'm sorry," Hannah says, her voice thick with emotion. "I hoped so, too. I wish it had been different between you and Charles." She glances down at the baby in her arms. "I know he was family. But this is our home. This is our family. We're free."

Carter brushes away a tear and looks at Hannah and Cory. "As long as we are together, wherever we are is home. We are family. We will always fight to be free."

EPILOGUE

The Fight for Freedom Continues

The California Fugitive Slave Act included a one-year sunset clause when enacted in 1852. However, it was renewed for an additional three years, allowing slaveholders to retain their human property and use enslaved labor to extract California gold. California, along with other states, continued to pass laws that restricted the freedom of people of color.

True freedom did not reach California until the Emancipation Proclamation, signed on January 1, 1863, nullified the California Fugitive Slave Act and other unjust state and federal laws. Enslaved Americans were legally freed, but the chaos and bloodshed of the Civil War delayed the realization of true liberty. Laws designed to limit the rights of people of color would continue to be enacted for generations.

"I refuse to accept the view that mankind is so tragically bound to the starless midnight of racism and war that the bright daybreak of peace and brotherhood can never become a reality...I believe unarmed truth and unconditional love will have the final word."

– Dr. Martin Luther King Jr.

MAJOR CHARACTERS
FACTS AND FICTION

Carter Perkins

Carter Perkins' battle for freedom is a tragically true story, documented in court records and newspapers from the era. The racism and prejudice that plagued California during its early statehood have often been overlooked. Yet the legal proceedings and public records remain, bearing witness to this dark chapter in U.S. history.

The California Supreme Court's ruling stands as one of the most racist and discriminatory decisions ever recorded in United States law—and it should never be forgotten. Ernest Hemingway is quoted as saying, "Everyone dies twice: once when the body dies, and again when the last person speaks your name." Carter's name deserves to be remembered for millennia.

According to the 1850 census, Carter and Charles shared a close bond while living together in California alongside White miners. Although there is no definitive proof of Carter's literacy, Cornelius Cole described him as brilliant in his memoirs. It is estimated that around ten percent of the enslaved population could read and write at the time.

Records suggest that Carter, Sandy, and Robert left San Francisco after the California Supreme Court ruling and never returned to Mississippi. While no official documentation confirms their fate, rumors spread that they escaped to Panama. Cornelius Cole believed this to be true and wrote about it in his memoirs years later.

Sandy and Robert Perkins

While no records confirm that Sandy and Robert were related to Carter, all available evidence suggests they shared a close bond. Perhaps that connection is why William Perkins agreed to send them to California with Charles.

The legacy of their family lived on. Sandy's grandson, Sandy Jones II, was recorded in the 1880 census at age 46. He was just fifteen when Sandy left for California. The census indicates that he lived near the Perkins plantation and was likely working as a sharecropper. Sandy Jones II and his wife had nine children.

Charles Perkins

Charles Perkins' story is indeed true. While one can only speculate about his motives, dreams, and desires, he was like many young men who sought to prove their worth and leave a lasting impact on the world.

His father wanted his children to learn how to manage enslaved people from a young age. On his ninth birthday, Charles received Carter. On his thirteenth birthday, Charles received another gift: twelve enslaved people and a large plot of land. Among them were Sandy Jones and his wife, Patience, who are believed to have been Carter's maternal grandparents.

At seventeen, Charles left for college at Princeton University in New Jersey. His maternal grandfather, Duncan Stewart, had left him $5,000 in his will. Charles used part of that inheritance to pay for his education and intended to use the remainder to pursue his aspirations, rather than manage the family plantation.

There is little doubt he encountered conflicting beliefs about slavery during his time in the North, where abolitionist sentiment was growing. Charles became captivated by reports of gold discoveries in the

California Territory. He likely read every newspaper he could find while planning his journey west after graduating in the spring of 1849.

He returned to Mississippi and married Emmy in 1853. Their marriage was brief, lasting only two years before his untimely death in 1855. His cause of death is unknown, but most likely from a disease.

Hannah Mason

Hannah Mason is a fictional character representing the many enslaved women who fought for their freedom. Their courage deserves our profound respect.

Hannah's story draws from numerous real accounts, including that of Bridget "Biddy" Mason, who was born enslaved in Georgia. In the 1840s, she traveled to Utah during the Mormon migration and later continued to Los Angeles with her enslavers, Robert and Rebecca Smith. Although California was a "free state," Biddy remained enslaved until 1856, when she and her children were aided by free Black individuals who helped them win their freedom through the courts.

Biddy Mason worked as a doctor's assistant and midwife. Over time, she built a fortune estimated at more than $7.5 million in today's dollars, making her one of the wealthiest women in Los Angeles. She established a homestead in what would later become downtown Los Angeles.

Mason used her wealth to open a daycare center for working parents and set up a store account where families displaced by floods could obtain essential supplies. She also co-founded and financed the First African Methodist Episcopal (FAME) Church in Los Angeles, which continues to serve the community today. Affectionately known as Grandma Mason, she passed away in 1891 and is commemorated by the Biddy Mason Monument in downtown Los Angeles.

Green Perkins and Hardin Scales

Albert G. "Green" Perkins and Hardin Scales were cousins of Charles. Their actions and involvement in the case are factual. Historical records indicate that they never returned to Mississippi. Unfortunately, the details of their lives after the case have been lost. One can only speculate whether they remained in California or eventually returned to the South.

Cornelius Cole

Cornelius' story is true. He was working to bring the case to the U.S. Supreme Court, but was unable to pursue it further when Carter, Sandy, and Robert disappeared in Panama.

He helped organize the California Republican Party in 1856, serving as secretary and authoring the party's manifesto. He was elected to the U.S. House of Representatives, representing California as a Republican from 1863 to 1865.

Throughout his career, he actively opposed slavery and supported Abraham Lincoln and fellow Republicans in drafting the Emancipation Proclamation. He later served in the United States Senate from 1867 to 1873.

After a distinguished career in Washington, Cornelius practiced law in San Francisco before relocating to Southern California in 1880. He purchased one of the original Spanish and Mexican land grants—a substantial parcel that included the area now known as Hollywood. He named the land Colegrove in honor of his beloved wife, Olive Colegrove.

Cornelius lived a remarkable life and passed away in 1924 at the age of 102, leaving behind a lasting legacy.

Henry Crabb

Crabb remained active in California politics but lost a bid for the Senate in 1856. The following year, he led an armed expedition to Sonora, Mexico, in an attempt to establish a slaveholding colony. In 1857, at the age of 37, he was brutally executed by the Mexican government as a warning that colonization and slavery would not be tolerated.

California Supreme Court Chief Justice Murray

Murray served as a justice in California for several years before dying of tuberculosis in 1857 at the age of 32. Before his death, he exhibited blatant racism. In addition to the Perkins case, he authored one of the Court's most infamous decisions, which extended the legislative ban on African American testimony to include Chinese individuals. He described them as "a race of people whom nature has marked as inferior and who are incapable of progress or intellectual development beyond a certain point."

California Supreme Court Justice Anderson

Anderson left California in 1854 and returned to Tennessee. During the Civil War, he practiced law in Alabama and staunchly supported secession and the institution of slavery. He died in 1869 at the age of 74.

California Supreme Court Justice Wells

Wells practiced law and was nominated to the California Supreme Court in 1854, but he died suddenly at the age of 35 before he could begin his term.

Governor Peter Hardeman Brunett

Burnett was raised in a slave-owning family in Missouri and moved to Oregon after his business ventures left him heavily in debt. In 1843, he became the Supreme Judge of the Provisional Government of Oregon, where he pushed for the total exclusion of African Americans from the territory. He authored the infamous "Burnett's Lash Law," which authorized the flogging of any free Black person who refused to leave Oregon.

Burnett later moved to California and was elected governor nearly a year before the state was admitted to the Union. While he did not advocate for California to become a slave state, he strongly supported the exclusion of African Americans. He was also a staunch opponent of Chinese immigration and backed laws that led to the enslavement and genocide of Native Americans.

Frustrated by the legislature's refusal to support his agenda, Burnett resigned as governor. He went on to practice law and later served as president of the Pacific Bank of San Francisco. He remained active in shaping legislation until he died in 1895 at the age of 87.

The Sweet Vengeance Mine

In 1849, six free African American men established the Sweet Vengeance Mine. The original partners were Gabriel Simms, Fritz James Vosburg, Abraham Freeman Holland, Edward Duplex, James Cousins, and M. McGowan. A few years later, Moses Rodgers—a highly sought-after African American engineer and metallurgist—joined the partnership.

In 1919, historian Delilah L. Beasley wrote, "Judging from the title, it would seem to indicate that they were bent on proving to the world that colored men were capable of conducting a mining business successfully, even in the pioneer days in California." Although there was an "atmosphere of equality" among miners, the fierce competition for gold often led White miners and claim jumpers to attempt to drive out non-White prospectors.

The Sweet Vengeance miners endured repeated efforts to force them off their claim. In one incident, Vosburg was attacked by a gang of White claim jumpers. He defended himself by stabbing their leader with a long knife. *The Liberator* newspaper reported that he had acted in self-defense.

The partners successfully operated the mine until 1854. According to journals kept by Vosburg, Holland, and Simms, the Sweet Vengeance Mine was especially profitable in the spring of 1852, when they described uncovering "rich dirt."

With their earnings, the men became entrepreneurs. Gabriel Simms opened the Franklin Hotel on First Street in Marysville. Edward Duplex opened a barbershop and later made history in 1888 as the first African American mayor of Wheatland, California. Born in Connecticut, he was the grandson of Prince Duplex Sr., a veteran of the Revolutionary War. His paternal grandfather had been born a "servant for life" but was later designated a "free man of color" when he enlisted in the Continental Army.

Moses Rodgers was born into slavery in Missouri and came to California in 1849. He gained prominence as a mining engineer and built a lucrative career excavating gold. In addition to his work at Sweet Vengeance, he owned the Hornitos Mine in Mariposa County and consulted for numerous other mining companies. The Merced Express once wrote, "There is no better mining man in the State."

Moses Rodgers's home, built in 1898 on San Joaquin Street in Stockton, California, still stands today and is listed on the National Register of Historic Places. He built the house for his wife, Sarah, and their five daughters, whom he ensured received the best education available in California. One daughter, Vivian Rodgers, graduated from the University of California, Berkeley, in 1909 with a degree in Science and Letters.

Andrew Jackson

Andrew Jackson was enslaved and brought to California by his master to perform the grueling labor of gold mining. Shortly after their arrival, his master died of fever. Left to his own devices, Andrew continued to pan for gold and work to support himself, believing he was now free.

However, newspapers in the South reported that he had escaped and fled in search of freedom. Despite this, Andrew remained in California and eventually purchased his freedom from his master's widow for $1,500.

California's First Black Church

The Colored Methodist Episcopal Church was founded in Sacramento in 1850 at 715 Seventh Street and is now marked by a California Historical Landmark plaque. In 1851, it was admitted into the African Methodist Episcopal Church, becoming the first AME church on the West Coast. It remains active at 2131 Eighth Street in Sacramento as St. Andrews AME Church.

The church was founded by Daniel Blue (1796–1884), a formerly enslaved man from Kentucky who made his fortune mining gold in California. He held the church's first service in his basement, and membership grew to over one hundred. While the 1850 census reported 960 Black residents in California, the number was likely higher.

In 1855, the church hosted the first of three statewide Colored Conventions, which addressed the political and economic well-being of California's African American communities. Delegates strategized to overturn the state's discriminatory laws on testimony, voting rights, and education. Two subsequent conventions followed: one in Sacramento in 1856 and another in San Francisco in 1857.

As part of this movement, the state's first African American newspaper, *Mirror of the Times,* was established in Sacramento in 1856.

In 1864, Daniel Blue played a pivotal role in rescuing a 12-year-old Black girl named Edith from enslavement in California. He had observed that a White man named Gammon, who lived nearby, had custody of the child and was subjecting her to severe abuse—"inhumanely beaten and let go without the necessary care and clothing to make her comfortable and decent." Blue petitioned the probate court to become her legal guardian.

Gammon claimed in court that Edith was living with him voluntarily. However, because the laws that once barred Black people from testifying against White individuals had been repealed, Daniel Blue was able to present witnesses who refuted the slaveholder's false claims. Their testimony convinced the judge to remove Edith from Gammon's custody. She was declared free and lived with Blue, his wife, and their children.

Mark Hopkins

Mark Hopkins was born in New York, studied law in Michigan, and worked as a bookkeeper for his brother. When the California Gold Rush began, he organized the "New England Mining and Trading Company," a group of twenty-six men who each invested $500 to purchase goods for resale in California. He sailed around Cape Horn and arrived in San Francisco in August 1849.

Hopkins opened a store in Placerville in 1850 and launched a wholesale grocery business in Sacramento with his friend Edward H. Miller, who would later serve as secretary of the Central Pacific Railroad.

In 1855, Hopkins partnered with another Sacramento merchant, Collis P. Huntington, to form Huntington & Hopkins, one of the most prosperous mercantile houses in the state. A member of the Whig and Free Soil parties, he was a staunch abolitionist and an early organizer of the California Republican Party.

In 1861, he helped establish the Central Pacific Railroad as one of "The Big Four" (Leland Stanford, Charles Crocker, Mark Hopkins, and Collis P. Huntington). Known affectionately as "Uncle Mark," he was the eldest of the four and renowned for his thriftiness—it was said he could "squeeze 106 cents out of every dollar."

His reputation for financial prudence earned him the role of company treasurer. Historian Hubert Howe Bancroft quoted Huntington as saying, "I never thought anything finished until Hopkins looked at it." He described him as the "balance wheel of the Associates and one of the truest and best men that ever lived."

After his death at *-65, his wife spent a small fortune building a mausoleum in his honor. She carefully selected granite from locations along the transcontinental railroad that Mark had admired during its construction, including stone from the highest peak on Donner Summit. Like many California pioneers, he is buried in Sacramento's Old City Cemetery.

Jefferson Davis

President Franklin Pierce appointed Jefferson Davis Secretary of War in 1853. Davis immediately expanded the Union Army, strengthened coastal defenses, and directed three surveys for potential transcontinental railroads. Throughout his tenure, he remained a fierce advocate for slavery and Southern rights.

When Abraham Lincoln won the presidency in 1860, Davis feared the new administration would coerce the South, leading to national disaster. Although he initially opposed secession, he believed the Constitution gave states the right to withdraw from the federal union. On January 21, 1861—twelve days after Mississippi seceded—Davis delivered a moving farewell speech in the U.S. Senate, pleading eloquently for peace.

He was commissioned as a major general to lead Mississippi's military preparations. Just weeks later, the Confederate Convention in Montgomery, Alabama, unexpectedly chose Davis as the provisional president of the Confederate States of America.

His first official act was to send a peace commission to Washington, D.C., to avoid war. President Lincoln refused to meet with them and moved to resupply Fort Sumter, which blocked Charleston's harbor.

Many Southerners viewed the action as an act of aggression. "Now the issue of battle is to be forced upon us," declared the Charleston Mercury. "We will meet the invader, and the God of Battles must decide the issue between the hostile hirelings of Abolition hate and Northern tyranny."

It is said that Davis reluctantly ordered the bombardment of Fort Sumter, marking the start of the Civil War.

The conflict quickly became a war of attrition, with both sides hoping to crush the other's morale through staggering losses. Diplomacy gave way to bloodshed. Over the next four years, the war claimed the lives of over 360,000 Union soldiers and 260,000 Confederates. Civilian deaths, suffering, and the destruction of property were immeasurable.

In 1865, Davis was caught off guard by General Robert E. Lee's surrender at Appomattox, which he had not authorized. Attempting to flee to Mississippi, Davis was captured and imprisoned in a damp casemate at Fort Monroe, Virginia. He was placed in leg irons and held under guard for two years.

Released on bail in May 1867, Davis traveled to Canada to recover his health. Though charged with treason, the federal government never pursued a trial, fearing it might affirm the legality of secession under the Constitution. The case was formally dropped on December 25, 1868.

In his later years, Davis made several trips to Europe before retiring to a Gulf-side estate near Biloxi, Mississippi, which was gifted to him by a patriotic admirer. In 1880, he published *The Rise and Fall of the Confederate Government.*

Although urged to run for the U.S. Senate, he refused to request amnesty, maintaining that he had done nothing wrong by defending states' rights under the Constitution. He never regained his U.S. citizenship and remained the Confederacy's most prominent spokesman until he died in 1889.

In 1978, President Jimmy Carter posthumously restored Jefferson Davis's citizenship.

William Perkins

William Perkins purchased land in Mississippi when he was only twenty-one, just months before it became a slave state in 1817. He recognized the region's agricultural potential while serving under Andrew Jackson during the War of 1812. During the campaign, he encountered the Choctaw, a prosperous agrarian society that supported Jackson's troops through a long, rainy winter. The Choctaw also fought alongside the Americans in the decisive Battle of New Orleans.

William was the great-great-grandson of Nicholas Perkins II, who came to Virginia as an indentured servant in 1641. After serving seven years, he was granted land at the confluence of the Appomattox and James Rivers. Nicholas quickly imported four more indentured servants from England, one of whom would become his wife.

Nicholas Perkins II was one of over 300,000 Europeans brought to the colonies as indentured servants or under similar servitude. The White slave labor trade had begun in 1619 when Virginia received one hundred impoverished children under the English Poor Law, which allowed children to be bound as apprentices if their parents could not provide for them. To meet the growing demand for cheap labor, Britain resorted to kidnapping children, criminals, and prisoners of war.

That same year, African slavery was introduced to Virginia when British ships seized enslaved Africans from a Portuguese vessel bound for Mexico. Though colonial laws on slavery were unclear, these Africans were purchased as laborers. Over the next two centuries, more than 450,000 Africans were forcibly brought to the American colonies. Unlike indentured servants, their servitude was permanent, and their descendants were also enslaved.

Nicholas Perkins II's descendants amassed land and wealth in Virginia and Tennessee by relying on both African slaves and indentured servants to work their expanding tobacco and cotton plantations. Several family members fought in the American Revolution to protect their holdings and secure independence. After the war, the United States claimed British-controlled territories, including what is now the state of Mississippi.

Using his family's wealth and influence, William established a prosperous cotton plantation in Mississippi with the labor of a dozen enslaved workers. In 1818, he married Jane Stewart, a descendant of King James of England. The Perkins and Stewart families thrived in the Southern feudal system, growing their fortunes through land ownership and labor control.

The Southern elite maintained their dominance by controlling the economy and political power. While most White Southerners worked for wages or owned small plots of land, at the bottom of the social hierarchy were enslaved African Americans, deprived of freedom and rights. This system was justified by racist beliefs held by the elite and many Whites, who believed themselves superior to people of color and saw it as their God-given duty to rule over them.

The growing demand for cotton led to an insatiable need for more land, further fueling the belief in Manifest Destiny—the idea that God had ordained Christians to conquer and settle North America. This ideology was used to justify the displacement of Indigenous peoples.

In 1830, President Andrew Jackson signed the Indian Removal Act, forcibly relocating more than 70,000 Indigenous people to Oklahoma. Thousands died on the journey, known as the "Trail of Tears." The Choctaw, who had once fought alongside Jackson, were removed. William eagerly purchased their vacated lands, including the site where Spanish explorer Hernando de Soto had set foot three centuries earlier in 1541.

De Soto, the first European to explore the region, convinced the Choctaw he was a "Son of the Sun" and forced them to build barges to ferry his 600 men, horses, and Native slaves across the Mississippi River. He was convinced the West held untold riches, but his expedition ended when he died of fever in Louisiana. Of the 600 men who had started with him in Florida, only 300 found their way to Mexico.

As William's plantation expanded, he required more enslaved laborers. The U.S. had banned the importation of slaves in 1808, but the domestic slave trade within the Southern states continued to thrive, driving up prices as demand grew.

Unable to import new slaves, William focused on growing his existing slave population. Like other plantation owners, he sometimes took matters into his own hands. The author believes that he became infatuated with a young, enslaved woman named Virginia, who died while giving birth to their son, Carter. Carter was only a few months younger than William and Jane's first son, Charles.

Jane tolerated her husband's infidelity but maintained her authority over household matters. However, her patience wore thin when she suspected William of having an affair with Mary, a fair-skinned housekeeper. Jane insisted that William sell her.

In the wake of a slave rebellion in the early 1840s, which resulted in the execution of dozens of enslaved people and several White accomplices, William became increasingly concerned about the appearance of his relationships with his slaves.

He agreed to sell Mary and traded her for two young female slaves. Later, he read that Mary had been sold for $1,600—a staggering sum, likely due to her beauty. To further distance himself from his slaves, William hired an overseer and several White foremen to manage the plantation's daily operations.

William died in 1851 after a prolonged illness, most likely yellow fever. The day before his death, he gifted his eight-year-old grandson, J.J. Curry, a young, enslaved boy.

Ironically, the mosquito species responsible for yellow fever and the disease had arrived in the Americas aboard slave ships from Africa. African Americans, whose ancestors had long been exposed to such illnesses, had built some immunity. But these diseases devastated Native and European populations. Over the years, several members of the Perkins family died from mosquito-borne diseases.

Shortly after Charles Perkins died in 1855, Emmaline "Emmy" Mobrey Adams Perkins sold the land she and Charles had shared at the Perkins Plantation. She deliberately divided it into smaller parcels to make it harder for the Perkins family to manage—perhaps as an act of quiet defiance for the way she and Charles had been treated. After that, she disappeared from public record, and nothing more is known about her life.

Louisa Ann Perkins Pugh's husband, Dr. Pugh, died of yellow fever in 1855, leaving her a widow with six children, including young J.J. Pugh. She and her husband had operated a medical facility and "spa" near the Perkins plantation. After his death, Louisa Ann moved her family to Tennessee to live with the extended Pugh relatives and later relocated to Texas.

In 1857, Daniel Perkins married eighteen-year-old Caroline Campbell. The couple inherited and managed her family's plantation about twenty miles north of the Perkins estate.

In the years that followed, repeated flooding along the Mississippi River disrupted life in the region. Levee breaks in 1858 and again in 1860 sent floodwaters across the cotton fields, damaging crops and reshaping the landscape.

Nolan Perkins died in 1858 at the age of seventeen. No official records explain the circumstances of his death, though it may have been caused by illness or an accident related to the flooding.

Jane P. Perkins, William and Jane's eldest daughter, had married Stephon B. (S.B.) Curry in December of 1851, shortly after Charles returned home. S.B. and Jane Curry helped manage the plantation alongside Jane Perkins, with help from Daniel, Nolan, and James. S.B. Curry was well regarded by both the family and the community. He died in the spring of 1860.

Jane Perkins passed away in 1861 at the age of sixty-two. Her daughter Jane Curry, now a widow, took charge of the plantation. She was assisted by her fourteen-year-old brother, James, and Daniel, who divided his time between the Perkins property and the Campbell plantation.

Perkins Plantation During the Civil War

The Confederates first occupied the Perkins plantation as they fought off the invading Union forces, who marched into Mississippi after winning the Battle of Shiloh in Tennessee on April 7, 1862.

Battles between the Union and Confederacy raged across Mississippi as the Union sought control of the state—most importantly, the Mississippi River. The Confederates destroyed crops to keep them from the Union, including hundreds of bales of cotton on the Perkins plantation. Confederate soldiers allowed the Perkins slaves to remove the cotton from storage sheds before burning it to spare the buildings.

Union gunboats patrolled the river and were frequently fired upon by Confederate soldiers and sympathizers. Union forces often went ashore to fight them and were met by Confederate cavalry. Union troops raided plantations and destroyed property belonging to those suspected of aiding the enemy.

The battle and siege of Vicksburg, Mississippi, lasted for months until the Union Army's victory on July 4, 1863—the same day the Union won the Battle of Gettysburg in Pennsylvania. These twin victories sealed the South's fate, though the war would continue for two more bloody years. An estimated 26,000 Mississippians died fighting for the Confederacy, with twice as many wounded.

Daniel and James Perkins did not serve in the Confederate Army. Daniel was exempted due to an unspecified physical disability. The reasons why James did not serve are unknown. In 1864, Daniel and several known Confederate guerrilla fighters were arrested during a party he hosted at his mansion. He was detained briefly, then released.

The only known member of the Perkins family who served in the war was J.J. Pugh, son of Louisa Ann Perkins Pugh. In 1850, when J.J. was six years old, his grandfather, William Perkins, gifted him a slave named Grandville. J.J. was killed at the age of eighteen while serving as a sergeant in the Confederate Army with the Second Arkansas Cavalry.

As the Union Army soldiers advanced through the South, they freed enslaved people, including those belonging to the Perkins family. Many freedmen were recruited to join Union ranks, though it is uncertain whether any Perkins slaves fought for the Union.

During their campaign, Union soldiers seized crops and livestock and burned plantation houses and outbuildings belonging to suspected Confederate supporters. Ironically, the Perkins plantation houses, including Daniel's, were spared. After the war, Jane, Daniel, and James Perkins signed oaths of allegiance to the United States.

In 1866, Jane Perkins Curry married a former Confederate colonel named Matthew Moore. Together, they managed the Perkins plantation and struggled to adapt to the realities of the post-war South. They faced flooding, declining cotton prices, infestations of cotton worms, a lack of capital, new federal cotton taxes, property taxes, and levee taxes. They also dealt with shortages of labor, livestock, and equipment.

Slave labor had ended with the arrival of Union forces in 1863. Freedmen now had to be compensated for their work. Many formerly enslaved people moved north, and the war had decimated the young White male workforce. Some landowners paid fair wages, but others struggled and resorted to selling parcels of land to survive.

Daniel and James Perkins died in 1869, just days apart, leaving no children and marking the end of the Perkins male lineage. Though no official cause of death was recorded, it was likely due to disease or an accident.

Landless freedmen faced hardship paying for necessities such as food, clothing, shelter, and medical care. Sharecropping became a necessity for both landowners and the formerly enslaved. Planters divided their land into plots and rented them to poor Whites and freed Blacks. The system offered a degree of compromise: landowners retained their land and status while gaining low-cost labor, and sharecroppers gained limited independence.

Unfortunately, abuse of the system was widespread. Most sharecroppers were illiterate, and landowners controlled all records. Landowners often operated "stores" on the plantation, selling seeds, tools, and food at inflated prices. They also provided high-interest loans or cash advances, increasing the sharecroppers' dependence and debt.

The 1880 census lists 120 Black individuals—including a few biracial people—living on or near the Perkins plantation, referred to then as the "Moore plantation." Colonel Moore had died unexpectedly in 1878, leaving Jane a widow at age fifty-seven.

It was common for formerly enslaved people to become sharecroppers on the land where they had once been held in slavery. Many of those listed in the 1880 census had undoubtedly once belonged to the Perkins family. Among them was Sandy Jones' grandson, Sandy Jones II, aged forty-nine. The census shows him living with his wife, four children, and his mother, Matilda. His son Simon was eighteen.

In 1896, tax records indicate that Jane "Perkins" Moore owned two horses, twenty-two mules, three carriages, and a piano. County records show she held a total of 1,787 acres—746 of them cleared. She had sold some parcels of land, and the flooding of the Mississippi River had reclaimed significant portions of the plantation.

In 1907, Jane "Perkins" Moore filed a lawsuit seeking compensation for property seized by Union forces forty-four years earlier. She claimed losses totaling $23,470 for confiscated animals, grain, cotton, and foodstuffs. At the time, she was eighty-six and living in Gainesville, Texas, with her niece, Sally Pugh.

Her claim for restitution was submitted to the Southern Claims Commission, which approved it. Senate Bill 3374, dated March 2, 1907, instructed the Secretary of the Treasury to pay her $10,325—roughly half of what she had requested. The reduced amount was likely due to the claim's late filing. Jane stated she had not known about the commission's existence until recently.

Although the Senate ruled in her favor, the U.S. government appealed the claim to the Court of Claims on the grounds of "loyalty and merit." After a review and hearing on March 15, 1910, the court ruled: "The claimant, Jane P. Moore, was not loyal to the Government of the United States during the Civil War." However, it also confirmed that "military forces of the United States, by proper authority… took from the claimant in Bolivar County, Mississippi, store and supplies of the kind and character described in the petition."

Jane Perkins Moore died in 1913 at the age of ninety-three in Gainesville, Texas, having sold the Perkins plantation before her death. Louisa Ann "Perkins" Pugh's children were the only surviving blood descendants of William and Jane Perkins. They likely inherited whatever remained of Jane's estate.

On Thursday, April 21, 1927, at 8 a.m., the levee in southern Bolivar County burst. The surging waters of the Mississippi River tore through Mound Landing and Williams Bayou. The volume and force of the flood were reportedly double that of Niagara Falls. Water covered an area fifty miles wide, one hundred miles long, and up to twenty-five feet deep.

The Perkins-Moore property lay at the very center of the break. A witness described the scene to a local newspaper: "The water was leaping, it looked like, in rapids thirty feet high. And right in front was the old Moore (Perkins) plantation house, a mule barn, and two big, enormous trees. When we returned there a few hours later, everything was gone."

By late July, the floodwaters had receded enough for a survey team to conduct an investigation of the area. They discovered evidence of an ancient Native American civilization, including pottery, clay vases, and weapons. The flood had eroded four large burial mounds and stripped away five to six feet of topsoil, scattering bones over a wide area.

Unbeknownst to the survey team, among the bones were those of William, Charles, and the rest of the Perkins family, who had been buried atop one of the mounds.

William Faulkner included the Mississippi River flood of 1927 in his book *The Wild Palms: (If I Forget Thee, Jerusalem)*. "Turn out of there!" the deputy shouted. He was fully dressed—boots, slicker, and shotgun. "The levee went out at Mound's Landing an hour ago. Get up out of it!"

Faulkner's words remain prophetic: "To understand the world, you must first understand a place like Mississippi." We may never fully understand a place like Mississippi, but we must try. The great river will flow free to the sea, overcoming all obstacles. Nothing will stand in its way.

BIBLIOGRAPHY

Albin, Ray R. Wealth, Land and Slaveholding in Mississippi: A Planter Family's Life of Privilege, 1818–1913.

Barksdale, E. Laws of the State of Mississippi. Natchez, MS: State Printer, 1854.

Beasley, Delilah L. The Negro Trail Blazers of California. 1919.

Bell, James. The Evolution of the Mississippi Delta: From Exploited Labor and Mules to Mechanization and Agribusiness. Bloomington, IN: iUniverse, 2008.

Biographical and Historical Memoirs of Mississippi: Embracing an Authentic and Comprehensive Account of the Chief Events in the History of the State and a Record of the Lives of Many of the Most Worthy and Illustrious Families and Individuals. Chicago: Goodspeed Publishing Co., 1891.

Branton, Catherine, and Mice Wade, comps. Early Mississippi Records: Washington County, 1827–1880. 4th ed. Carrollton, MS: Pioneer Publishing, 1986.

Davis, Jefferson. Speeches of the Honorable Jefferson Davis. Project Gutenberg eBook, Release Date: June 5, 2002. [Updated: December 25, 2021]. Produced by Dave Maddock and Curtis Weyant.

DeLay, Peter J. History of Yuba and Sutter Counties, California: With Biographical Sketches of the Leading Men and Women of the Counties Who Have Been Identified with Their Growth and Development from the Early Days to the Present. 1865.

DeWitt, Howard A. The Fragmented Dream: Multicultural California. 1996.

Douglass, Frederick. Narrative of the Life of Frederick Douglass, an American Slave, Written by Himself. Boston: Anti-Slavery Office, 1845. Entered according to an Act of Congress, 1849.

———. My Bondage and My Freedom. New York: Penguin Books, 2003.

———. Life and Times of Frederick Douglass: His Early Life as a Slave, His Escape from Bondage, and His Complete History to the Present Time. Hartford, CT: Park Publishing Co., 1881.

Drotning, Phillip T. A Guide to Negro History in America. 1968.

Dupre, Daniel S. Transforming the Cotton Frontier: Madison County, Alabama, 1800–1840. Baton Rouge: Louisiana State University Press, 1997.

Fox, Early Lee. The American Colonization Society, 1817–1840. 3rd ed. Baltimore: Johns Hopkins Press, 1919.

Garfield, S., and F. A. Snyder. Compiled Laws of the State of California: Containing All the Acts of the Legislature of a Public and General Nature, Now in Force, Passed at the Sessions of 1850–51–52–53, to Which Are Prefixed the Declaration of Independence, the Constitutions of the United States. Benicia: S. Garfield, 1853.

Garner, James Wilford. Reconstruction in Mississippi. London: MacMillan Co., 1901.

Gillmer, Jason A. "Litigating Slavery's Reach: A Story of Race, Rights, and the Law During the California Gold Rush." Loyola of Los Angeles Law Review 56 (2023): 499. Available at:

Han, Eunsun Celeste- All Roads Lead to San Francisco: Black Californian Networks of Community and the Struggle for Equality, 1849-1877 Submitted in partial fulfillment of the requirements for the

Degree of Doctor of Philosophy in the Department of History at Brown University. 2015

Hall, W. K. Descendants of Nicholas Perkins of Virginia. Ann Arbor: Edwards Brothers, 1957.

In the Matter of CARTER PERKINS and ROBERT PERKINS. Court: Supreme Court of California

Date published: Oct 1, 1852, Citations 2 Cal. 424 (Cal. 1852)

Lapp, Rudolph M. Blacks in Gold Rush California. 1995

Libby, David J. Slavery and Frontier Mississippi, 1720-1835.

Jackson: University Press of Mississippi, 2004.

Lowry, Robert, and William H. McCardle. A History of Mississippi.. from the Discovery of the Great River by Hernando DeSoto, Including the Earliest Settlement Made by the French under Iberville, to the Death of Jefferson Davis. Jackson, Miss.: R.H. Henry & Co., 1891.

Monette, Jo. W. History of the Discovery and Settlement of the Valley of the Mississippi by the Three Great European Powers, Spain, France, and Great Britain, and the Subsequent Occupation, Settlement, and Extension of Civil Government by the United States Until the Year 1846. New York: Harper Bros., 1848.

Moore, Jo.. The Emergence of the Cotton Kingdom in the Old Southwest: Mississippi, 1770-1860. Baton Rouge: Louisiana State University Press, 1988.

Olmsted, Frederick Law. The Cotton Kingdom: A Traveler's Observations on Cotton and Slavery in the American Slave States. New York: Mason Brothers, 1861.

Peet, Stephen D. The Mound Builders: Their Works and Relics. Chicago: Office of the American Antiquarian, 1892.

Rasmussen, Louis J. San Francisco Ship Passenger Lists. Vol. 2. Baltimore: Clearfield, 2002

Robinson, Charles. Forsaking All Others: A True Story of Interracial Sex and Revenge in the 1880s South. Knoxville: University of Tennessee Press, 2010.

Scott, Robert N., ed. The War of the Rebellion: A Compilation of the Official Records of the Union and Confederate Armies. Series I, Vol. II, p. 1811. Confederate Correspondence, Etc. Washington: Government Printing Office, 1898.

Span, Christopher M. From Cotton Field to Schoolhouse: African American Education in Mississippi, 1862–1875. Chapel Hill: University of North Carolina Press, 2009.

Squier, E. G., and E. H. Davis. Ancient Monuments of the Mississippi Valley. Washington: Smithsonian Institution Press, 1998. Originally published in 1848.

Stampp, Kenneth M. The Peculiar Institution: Slavery in the Antebellum South. 1st ed. New York: Knopf, 1956.

Steele, R. J., and James P. Bull. Directory of the County of Placer for the Year 1861: Containing a History of the County, and of the Different Towns in the County; with the Names of Inhabitants and Everything Appertaining to a Complete Directory. San Francisco: Charles F. Robbins, printer, 1861.

Sydnor, Charles S. Slavery in Mississippi. Gloucester, MA: Peter Smith, 1965.

The Compendium of American Genealogy. Vol. 4. Chicago: Virkus, 1930.

Wayne, Michael. The Reshaping of Plantation Society: The Natchez District, 1860–80. Urbana: University of Illinois Press, 1990.

Journals

Albin, Ray. "The Perkins Case: The Ordeal of Three Slaves in Gold Rush California." California History 67, no. 4 (1988): 214–227.

De Dow, J. D. B. "Opinion of Judge Anderson of the Supreme Court of California." De Bow's Review 23 (1857): 100–101.

Miles, Edwin. "Mississippi Slave Insurrection Scare of 1835." Journal of Negro History 42, no. 1 (January 1957): 48–49.

Smith, Stacey L. "Remaking Slavery in a Free State: Masters and Slaves in Gold Rush California." Pacific Historical Review 80, no. 1 (2011): 28–63.

Magazines

Montgomery, G. E. "The Lost Journals of a Pioneer." Overland Monthly and Outwest Magazine, VII: 1886, 180.

Census

Fourth Census of the United States, 1820, Mississippi. Washington, D.C.: National Archives, 1958. Wilkinson County. Accessed through Heritage Quest.

Fifth Census of the United States, 1830. Washington: United States Census Office, 1830. Wilkinson County, Mississippi, accessed through Ancestry.com.

Sixth Census of the United States, 1840. Washington, D. C.: National Archives and Records Service, 1967. Madison County, Mississippi. Accessed through.

Seventh Census of the United States, 1850. Washington, D.C.: National Archives, 1958. El Dorado, Sacramento, and Yuba Counties, California; Bolivar and Madison Counties, Mississippi; and New York

County, New York. Accessed through Family Search, https://www.familysearch.org.

Seventh Census of the United States, 1850, Mississippi Agriculture. Washington, D.C.: United States Census Office, 1850.

Seventh Census of the United States, 1850, Louisiana (Slave Schedules). Washington, DC: United States Census Office, 1963. Madison Parish. Accessed through Family Search, https:/Avww.familysearch.org/.

Seventh Census of the United States, 1850, Mississippi (Slave Schedules). Washington, D.C.: National Archives and Records Service, 1963. Bolivar and Madison Counties. Accessed through Family Search,

https://www.familysearch.org/.

Seventh Census, 1850, The Agricultural and Manufacturing Census for Bolivar County, Mississippi. Washington, D.C.: United States Census Office, 1850. Microfilm Reel 175.

Eighth Census of the United States, 1860: Louisiana. Washington: National Archives and Records Service, 1967. Madison Parish. Accessed through Heritage Quest.

Eighth Census, 1860, Mississippi (Slave Schedules). Genealogy, Family Trees & Family History Records. Bolivar County. Accessed at http://t7, Ancestry.com.

Ninth Census of the United States, 1870, Louisiana. Washington, D.C.: Census Office, 1870. Madison Parish. Accessed through Heritage Quest.

Ninth Census of the United States, 1870, Mississippi. Washington, D.C.: National Archives and Records Service, 1965. Accessed through Heritage Quest.

Tenth Census of the United States 1880, Mississippi. Washington,

D.C.: Bureau of the Census, 1882. Washington and

Bolivar Counties. Accessed through Heritage Quest.

Tenth Census of the United States 1880, The Agricultural and Manufacturing Census for Bolivar County, MS. Chapel Hill: University of North Carolina Library, 1960.

Fourteenth Census of the United States, 1920, Texas. Washington, D.C.: United States Census Bureau, 1920. Cooke County. Accessed through Heritage Quest.

California State Census 1852. Genealogy, Family Trees & Family History Records. San Francisco County. Accessed through http://www.Ancestrv.com.

Diaries

Westfall, Milton S. Diary of Milton S. Westfall. 1861. Unpublished. Mississippi Department of Archives and History.

Newspapers

"Advertisement." New Orleans Picayune, June 23, 1849: 1.

"Pearl River Female Academy," Canton Herald [Mississippi], April 12, 1837: 3.

"Cotton Prospects." The Charleston Daily News [South Carolina], July 29, 1867: 1.

"Died at Memphis," New Orleans Daily Crescent, April 20, 1860: Column 4.

"Fugitive Slaves." The Pacific [San Francisco], 18 June 1852: 2.

"Fugitive Slave Case." Weekly Christian Advocate [San Francisco], August 15, 1852: 150-151.

Memphis Daily Appeal, April 28, 1857: 2.

National Era [Washington], Oct. 14, 1852: 4.

New York Tribune (New York), June 16, 1852.

"Speculation in Tickets." Panama Star and Herald, August 11, 1849

The Daily Phoenix, (Columbia, South Carolina), January 31, 1866

The Placer Herald (Auburn, CA), September 18, 1852

"The Slave Case." The Placer Times, May 27, 1850.

"Slave Case." San Francisco Herald, June 12, June 19, July 29, 1852.

Weekly Alta California (San Francisco), April 10, 1852.

Online Newspapers

Brooklyn Daily Eagle, July 22, 1927, 2. The postcard. http://fultonhistory.coro/Fulton.html, "Skulls at Mound Landing,"

The Liberator (Boston), "Slavery in California," June 22, 1849.

Sacramento Daily Union, "Fugitive Slaves," June 3, 1852.

Websites

"Passenger Manifest, Louisiana Secretary of State. soslouisiana.gov.

"Digital Library on American Slavery." University Libraries, The University of North Carolina at Greensboro (UNCG).

Bateman, Mary. "Mary E. Bateman Diary, 1856-1856." University

of North Carolina, Southern Historical Collection.

Davis, Jefferson. The Project Gutenberg eBook of Speeches of the Honorable Jefferson Davis

https://www.gutenberg.org/files/5205/5205-h/5205-h.htm

Mason vs. Smith (The Bridget "Biddy" Mason Case). BlackPast.org.

https://www.blackpast.org/african-american-history/mason-v-smith-bridget-biddy-mason-case-1856

Pioneers of Placer County." California Gen Web Placer County

https://www.cagenweb.org/placer/history.htm

University of California, Berkeley Library

https://guides.lib.berkeley.edu/history/us/newspapers - Various newspaper articles from the era.

University of California, Los Angeles, Department of Special Collections, Charles E. Young Research Library. Verdict is found in the Golden States Insurance Company Records. News clipping on the petition to free Edith Blue: "In the Matter of the Guardianship of Adda, a colored child," February 25, 1864. Sacramento Daily Union, vol 26, no 4034. Courtesy of the California Digital Newspaper Collection, Center for Bibliographic Studies and Research, University of California, Riverside.

Wilkinson County, Mississippi Court Minutes, July & August 1823. Salt Lake City: Mormon Family History Library. Microfilm roll 877088.

Wilkinson County, Mississippi Chancery Court Records. Su. 1822-1871. Salt Lake City: Mormon Family History Library, 1823. Microfilm roll 877088.

Wilkinson County, Mississippi Courthouse Land Record. Salt Lake City: Mormon Family History Library, 1824. I3ook D, Book E, microfilm roll 876533, Book G, microfilm roll 876534.

Documents

Cornelius Cole Papers, Cornelius Cole, "Essays," Department of Special Collections, University of California, Los Angeles.

In re Perkins, Case File California State Archives, Sacramento.

Naglee Family Collection, BANC MSS C-B 796, Box VII, (folder) MR552. The University of California, Bancroft Library, Berkeley, California.

William, Henry Seward Papers, (Letters from Cornelius Cole). University of Rochester, New York.